Praise for SEVEN NIGHTS TO SURRENDER

"Jeanette Grey has become a must-read voice in romance. *Seven Nights to Surrender* is lyrical, stunningly sexy, and brings swoons for *days*."

—Christina Lauren, *New York Times* bestselling author

"A must read! I couldn't put it down. Jeanette Grey's writing is *so* refreshingly honest. *Seven Nights to Surrender* is intensely emotional and sexy as hell. I need the next book ASAP!"

—Tara Sue Me, *New York Times* bestselling author

"With its sexy setting and sensual story, Jeanette Grey's *Seven Nights To Surrender* sparkles!"

—J. Kenner, *New York Times* and international bestselling author

"Sensual, sultry, and exquisite, *Seven Nights to Surrender* will sweep you away and seduce you on every page! Crackling with tension and steamy with sensuality, it's a feast for the senses you don't want to miss!"

—Katy Evans, *New York Times* bestselling author

"With her unique flair, Jeanette Grey delivers a deliciously sexy and irresistible romance that keeps you turning the pages for more. You'll savor every word so you don't miss a single sizzling moment."

—K. Bromberg, *New York Times* bestsell'

Praise for WHEN THE STARS ALIGN

"I couldn't put it down! I loved every sentence! The writing is outstanding, the setting entrancing, and the characters stole my heart. Fresh, flawed, and instantly lovable, you'll root for Jo and Adam at every turn."

—S. C. Stephens, *#1 New York Times* bestselling author

"The heat of the island has nothing on the off the charts attraction that sizzles between its feisty and fiercely unique heroine and idyllic hero. The journey to being the best you is often equal parts beautiful and tragic, and Grey sets the scene perfectly. A sassy and sexy read full of heart and adventure. This romance is like a breath of fresh air."

—Jay Crownover, *New York Times* bestselling author

"Once I started I could. not. stop. I loved every word. Refreshing characters. Unique setting. And a plot that will have you smiling all the way through.... Jeanette delivers a sexy read filled with the wonder of discovering who you are, what you want, and how to love despite your best laid plans.... Absolute brilliance!"

—Chelsea Fine, author of *Best Kind of Broken*

eight ways to
ECSTASY

ALSO BY JEANETTE GREY

Seven Nights to Surrender
When the Stars Align

eight ways to
ECSTASY

JEANETTE GREY

FOREVER

New York   Boston

Forever
Hachette Book Group
1290 Avenue of the Americas
New York, NY 10104
forever-romance.com
twitter.com/foreverromance

First Edition: April 2016

Forever is an imprint of Grand Central Publishing.
The Forever name and logo are trademarks of Hachette Book Group, Inc.

The publisher is not responsible for websites (or their content) that are not owned by the publisher.

The Hachette Speakers Bureau provides a wide range of authors for speaking events. To find out more, go to www.hachettespeakersbureau.com or call (866) 376-6591.

Library of Congress Cataloging-in-Publication Data has been applied for.

ISBN: 978-1-4555-8980-7 (paperback); ISBN 978-1-4555-8981-4 (ebook)

Printed in the United States of America

RRD-C

10 9 8 7 6 5 4 3 2 1

*To Scott, for showing me the world
but also giving me a home.*

Acknowledgments

This book wouldn't be what it is without the help of a lot of people. My thanks to:

My editor, Megha Parekh, for seeing exactly where this story needed to go.

My agent, Mandy Hubbard, who always has my back.

My critique partners: Heather McGovern, who flailed and kept me company and believed in me and these characters even when my faith was flagging; and Brighton Walsh, who's been a rock and a voice of sanity through a hell of a lot of storms.

The beautiful blogging ladies of *Bad Girlz Write*, for always raising a glass, and the amazing folks at Capital Region Romance Writers of America, for their constant guidance and support.

My college art professors, for helping me find my vision and make it come to life.

My incredible husband, family, and friends, who never questioned my messy house or my canceling plans because I needed to stay in said messy house and write.

And Sebastian. For his face.

eight ways to
ECSTASY

chapter ONE

"Then you had better make it count."

Rylan Bellamy's heart pounded as he stared up at Kate, scarcely daring to believe what he was hearing. He'd come to her prepared to beg—of course he had. She'd changed his life, made him want things he'd forgotten he could have. He'd do anything he had to for the chance to win her back.

And yet somehow, a part of him had honestly never believed that she'd say yes.

He remained there, literally on his knees for her, palms on her thighs and lungs burning as he waited for the catch. But nothing about her expression changed. This was real. She was giving him his shot.

Seven more nights together. Seven nights to prove he was the same man she'd fallen into bed with in Paris.

Damn right he was going to make them count.

Darting his gaze from her eyes to her mouth, he released his breath and licked his lips, flickering images of all the things he wanted to do to her heating his blood. Resolve made him firm up his grip. He'd prove to her exactly how good they could be together. With his flesh, with his body. The only way he was sure he could. The only way she'd made it clear she would accept.

Sliding his hand up higher on her thigh, he leaned in, and it was like the walls and miles between them shivered, ready to collapse. But instead of going for her lips and taking the kiss he'd been dying for these endless months, he skimmed his way to her jaw. With a rasping inhalation, she tipped her head to the side, inviting him in, and the first, uncertain lick of arousal in him ignited.

He could have this. After all this time, longing for her and cursing himself for his mistakes. Three months of self-imposed celibacy, and the nearness of her had him shockingly, achingly hard. He moaned as he pressed his brow to her temple, letting his nose rest just beneath her ear.

He'd done the difficult part, convincing her to let him touch her at all. But as his body vibrated, suddenly starved for contact, a whole new difficulty blindsided him.

How was he supposed to do this? To contain himself, when he wanted so much?

Forcing his eyes closed, he fought for control and prayed for patience. He shook his head, and the words that came out were too honest by half. "You don't know how badly I've wanted this."

The sparkling sound of her laughter filled the air. She smelled and tasted just the same as she ever had as he laid a soft, closed-mouth line of kisses down the column of her throat.

"I think I have some idea," she said, tilting her head farther and threading her fingers through his hair.

God, it felt good to be touched.

He slid a hand up to grasp the back of her neck, holding her where she was as he traced his lips to her ear. He bit there as softly as he could, sucking at the lobe and letting out a wet breath. "What do you want me to do to you?"

"Oh God." Her fingers tightened in his hair. "Make me—make me come."

Lightning shot down his spine and went straight to his cock. But at the same time, her bluntness made him pause.

How long had it taken him to coax the barest hint of a request from her their first time around? She'd been terrified to touch herself in front of him, had scarcely been able to admit she knew how to.

Something in his stomach squirmed. With all the steadiness he had, he fit his hand to the juncture of her thigh and hip, digging his thumb into the seam of her jeans. "Has anybody else?"

She stiffened a fraction in his arms, and a jealous flame fired off inside his chest.

Running on instinct, he dug his thumb in harder and skated his other hand to hover just above her breast. "Tell me. Has anybody else been taking care of your sweet little pussy? Giving it the attention it deserves?"

She pressed her hips into his hand and arched her back, pushing her tits out like a written invitation he was only too happy to accept. She swallowed a whimper when he molded his palm to that curve.

"Well?" he insisted, but he read his answer in her moan.

No way had another man laid a hand on her. She was too primed, too desperate. She'd been left unattended for far too long, and damn if it wasn't his new mission in life to correct that.

And her body fucking loved that he had asked.

She shook her head, and possessiveness sang through his blood. Who even cared that he had known what the answer would be? He'd been the last man to touch her—he wanted to be the last man to *ever* touch her.

He scraped his teeth against the shell of her ear as he snapped his jaw closed.

It wasn't exactly a foreign thought. You didn't cross oceans for casual; you didn't decide to change your entire life for anything less than forever. But here and now, it was too much, too soon. He'd only barely managed to talk her into giving him a chance at all.

Shaking his head, he put the thought out of his head and bent to his task again, wringing those perfect, breathy sounds from her with fingertips and lips. With words. She'd always loved it when he talked. "Let me hear you say it out loud, beautiful."

"Nobody," she panted, finally. "There's been nobody else."

Deep inside, he crowed. "And how about you? Have you been taking care of this?" He rubbed at her clit through the fabric and blew a breath across her ear. "Bet it gets so hot and achy. Needs so bad to be touched."

"Sometimes." Her other hand came to rest at his side, a warm weight against his abdomen. "When I wasn't—" She cut herself off, and he didn't like that at all.

He pulled away to look her in the eyes, and what he saw there was even worse. His gut churned. "When you weren't what?"

"When I wasn't too pissed at you to get myself off."

It stung like a slap. And yet he knew the story all too well. His body had needs, but they'd been muted these past couple of months. He'd taken care of them perfunctorily, almost mechanically. How could he blame her for admitting to much the same? Only with that twist. That edge of accusation.

It'd take more than a few orgasms for her to forgive.

For a second he feared the moment was lost, but she hadn't

let go of his side or his hair. The husk to her breath, the darkness of her eyes—they weren't gone.

Slowly, he pulled his hand from between her legs to wrap his arms around her. "I'm sorry." He murmured the apology into her neck, breathed his regrets against the heat of her skin. "I'm so sorry." With soft, chaste kisses, he worked his way over collarbones and ribs, until his mouth lay right above her heart. He turned his gaze upward and then kissed her there, too. Pitching his voice lower, he promised, "I swear I'm going to make it up to you."

Kate couldn't decide where to put her arms.

One second, Rylan had her panting, a new kind of possessiveness she'd never seen on him before driving him to whisper the filthiest things in her ear. The next she'd been saying something stupid, bringing up the rift between them again when she was supposed to be ignoring it.

That was their agreement after all. He got his chance to try to win her back, and she got sex. She got another shot at the kind of pleasure she'd thought she'd lost for good.

When it all inevitably fell apart again, she got to walk away without any doubts.

After a moment, she settled for resting her hands on his shoulders, letting him keep pressing his apologies into the tops of her breasts. Clenching her jaw, she swallowed the instinct to tell him it was all going to be okay. She couldn't promise him that. Not even close.

She'd probably been insane to promise him even his seven nights.

Restless, she shifted. The ache between her thighs hadn't

abated at all despite the awkwardness, and the heat of his breath at her chest had her ready to drag him down onto this bed with her and tell him to just get over it already. She was fine—a little more guarded and maybe still a tiny bit brokenhearted for his presence in her life. But fine. He hadn't done anything to her she shouldn't have expected, considering. The people she trusted had a habit of making her wish she hadn't. Of turning mean as soon as they'd lured her in. After the way her father and her ex had treated her, Rylan's conveniently forgetting to tell her he was the heir to a billion-dollar company was nothing, right?

She gritted her teeth and fought to push those thoughts away. She'd moved past the hurt, goddammit all. She'd been so close to moving on entirely, right until he'd shown up at her door, looking gorgeous and saying all these things she shouldn't believe. Things that'd struck her to the quick, regardless. And then he'd touched her.

And filled her with a need she'd nearly forgotten was even possible.

Stroking her thumbs against the collar of his jacket, she shifted her hips. It would be something if she were the one to throw him down and have her way with him, wouldn't it? In their past encounters, he had always been the one urging her on, challenging her to tell him what she wanted and to take her pleasure with neither shame nor reservation. That kind of sexual freedom had come more and more easily for her as they'd gone on.

But she'd been so comfortable with him then. And he was the one who was supposed to be making things up to her, after all.

Finally, after what felt like hours, he kissed up higher on her chest, withdrawing one of his arms from around her body to tug the neckline of her shirt down. Warm, damp lips met skin, his tongue darting out to taste the hollow between her collarbones, and she dug her fingers into his shoulders.

"I think you were saying something about making it up to me?"

He chuckled against her ribs and nudged her shirt even lower. "Do you have some suggestions for how you'd like me to?"

"I can probably think of a couple."

"Be sure to let me know if you do."

With that, he pulled away from her flesh, wrapping both his hands around her hips and shoving her bodily toward the center of the bed. She swallowed hard. Now that's what she was talking about.

Still on his knees, he nodded to himself, and the doubt that had seemed to cling to him these last few minutes fell away.

"For now," he said, voice deliciously firm, "I have a few ideas of my own."

Standing, he fixed her with a gaze so hot it threatened to sear straight through her. Intent lay heavy in the clear blue of his irises, the thick fall of his lashes against his cheeks. All steady, precise movements, he loosened his tie and pulled it free, folding the stripe of silk before setting it aside. His jacket came next, revealing the breadth of his shoulders. Draping it over the end of the bed, he undid his cuff links with deft flicks of his fingertips against the polished silver studs, then dropped them in a pocket and rolled up his shirtsleeves.

And it was almost too hot. Crisp, charcoal slacks and a vest to match, a sapphire-blue shirt with the collar open, and his forearms, thick and muscular. And above it all, still, that look in his eyes like he was planning to eat her alive.

If there was something lingering around his mouth that seemed more lost than domineering, it was easy to ignore, if she tried.

He settled one knee on the bed, grasping her feet and hauling them apart to make space for him to rest between them. With one ankle held in his hand, he worked the laces of her shoe as he talked. "Lie back."

He said it with an edge behind the command, one that was on a direct line to her clit. Her breath caught. "Why?"

"Because." He pried her first shoe off and sent it rolling across the floor, then started on the other one. "I'm planning to eat you out until you cry." The corner of his mouth twitched up. "If you aren't lying down for it, I'm afraid you might hurt yourself."

Jesus.

Holding his gaze, she settled herself down. Lifted her arms to rest her hands above her head.

"Good girl." He gave her calf a teasing slap as he released her leg. He nodded toward her hands. "Now keep them there."

"While you do what?"

"First"—he climbed up higher on the bed and hooked his hands in the waistband of her jeans—"I get these abominations off you." The button all but melted beneath his fingers, the teeth of the zip too loud in the quiet room.

Somehow, she kept her cool, arching a brow while her chest heaved, heat pooling in her abdomen, nipples tightening. "Abominations?"

But it wasn't just arousal making her flustered. The whole time they'd been apart, she'd second-guessed his reaction to everything. Her hair, her barely-there makeup, her taste in restaurants. Her naïveté.

Her clothes.

She lacked both the money and the time for high fashion, and half her wardrobe ended up covered in paint and charcoal anyway, so why bother? Who cared if these jeans were old, if they weren't a brand name? They were hers.

He just shook his head and clucked his tongue, peeling the denim from her hips. "They don't begin to do you justice." He dragged them lower, dipping to press his lips to the bare skin of her knees, her thighs. Warm fingertips brushed every new inch of flesh he revealed. "Then again, I'm not sure anything could."

How did he always know precisely what to say?

Oh. Right. Practice. She steeled herself and lifted up so he could pull her jeans the rest of the way off, her socks going with them. His lines had always worked on her before, but she'd never let him know that.

She was pretty sure it was why he'd decided to keep trying.

"I don't know." Her voice shivered despite her efforts to keep it steady. "You're rocking the suit thing pretty hard."

"Oh?" Warmth seeped into the question. He braced his hands to either side of her hips and lowered down, dropping kisses along the hem of her panties. "You like?"

"It does you justice," she admitted, tipping her head back and groaning aloud as he nuzzled right above the place she wanted him the most, nose brushing skin while his breath washed hot across her sex.

"I'll keep that in mind."

The first firm pressure of his mouth on her was a rolling thunderclap, a deep rumbling burst of pleasure that held the promise of so much more. Even through the cotton of her underwear—the normal everyday ones she wore when she wasn't expecting billionaire moguls to show up at her door—the intensity of the contact had her hips bucking, thighs tightening as if to close around his head. To push him off or draw him in until she was a shivering mess of satisfaction beneath him, she couldn't decide.

"Easy." His lips pursed around her clit, a gentle nibble that just wasn't fair. He fit his forearm across her belly, holding her down. "Stay still for me."

She shook her head. How could she?

And then he tongued at the fabric. Everything got wetter, the swelter between her thighs too much. She grasped at the sheets, reaching for her pillow for something to hold on to.

The first time he'd done this for her, it'd been this impossible sort of journey to her peak. No man had ever managed to make her come before, and she'd wanted so badly for him to be the one, but her mind had fought her. It'd been stop and start, the edge of oblivion a taste at the back of her throat, darting close only to fall away from her again and again, until she'd been ready to cry for it. When the pleasure had finally washed her away, she'd been left forever changed, her world tilting on its axis at this whole new realm of possibility.

Her orgasms had come easier every time since then, and that last lazy morning before everything had fallen apart, she'd found her pleasure with hardly any kind of effort at all.

But that was when she'd been on the receiving end of Rylan's attentions daily—sometimes more than daily. She'd gone *months* without that now. It should've had her tensing up, her mind and body warring again.

And yet when he slid a finger over soaked cotton, teased at her opening through the panel of her underwear, and closed his lips around her clit and sucked—

Her eyes snapped open, and she arched off the bed. How could she be— Was it even possible to— Reeling, she dug her nails into her palms and fought to keep her hands where they were, where he'd told her they should be as climax ambushed her, quick and sharp and almost violent, and she pulsed and pulsed and pulsed. Empty, and suddenly more ravenous than she had been before.

Rylan didn't quite manage to hide his shock as she struggled to lift her head. Mouth slack with surprise and lust, eyes hungry and dark, he met her gaze. And then, slowly, his expression shifted, morphing into the worst, most shameless smirk, so sexual, so overconfident, she wanted to wipe it off his face. Or maybe ride it.

"Oh, baby," he all but crooned. "You're just primed for it, aren't you? Dying for it." He traced a single finger down the still-throbbing line of her slit. "Ready to give it up with barely a touch." He pressed his lips to the fabric again. "With barely a kiss."

Rolling her eyes felt like too much work when she was shivering with aftershocks like this, but she gave it her best damn try. "Don't let it go to your head."

"Believe me." His eyebrows slanted meaningfully. "It's going to my head."

Her fingers twitched. What she really wanted to do was swat at him. Or press him down. Get him to do that to her over and over.

"It's practically a crime," he said. More soft, lingering kisses brushed over her, cruelly teasing glances of licks when she was wriggling, was writhing for the full-on embrace of his mouth. "You being so neglected like this."

And there was still that hint of a pang. She'd been all alone because of him. Too wounded to go out and find someone else because of him.

She'd known what she was missing because of him.

He slid his finger along the edge of her underwear, across the inside of her thigh, and her body gave another little tremor.

God, she was slick even all the way over there, his touch so easy as it glided across her flesh.

"I won't let it happen again." His finger slipped a little deeper beneath the cotton. "I'll eat you out every night and every day if you want me to."

She'd almost forgotten he could be like this. Shameless. Unreal.

She let her head fall back against the mattress. "You can start by"—she faltered, then closed her eyes and soldiered through it—"by eating me out right now."

He chuckled, but it wasn't mean. If anything, it sounded painfully turned on. "Look at that. Kitten's grown claws." He kissed the inside of her thigh. "But since I offered..."

Her whole body strained as he tucked his thumbs into her underwear and inch by inch dragged them down. Cool air hit heated skin. Naked from the waist down, she spread her legs. It was wanton, wasn't it? Slutty? Opening up for him, asking this of him.

Taking this, when she had no idea what they were to each other anymore. Didn't even know what she wanted them to be.

But then he ran his nose all the way from the inside of her knee to the juncture of her hip and thigh. "You don't know how much I've missed this." And he dove in.

Jesus. She'd thought the touch of his lips to her through her panties had been intense. The first hot stripe he licked along her lips was like coming home, soft and wet, this broad stroke he painted with the flat of his tongue. He fit his whole mouth to her, and she didn't even have a chance to be self-conscious.

"You taste so fucking good," he said with a moan. His tongue traced circles all around her clit, never touching it, and this was torture, was heaven. "How many times do you think I can get you to come?"

She'd managed three in one day before, but that had been with her very best vibrator and then with her hands.

But this was better. This was insane.

She was breathless, eyes clenched tight, hands curled in shaking fists. "I guess we're about to find out."

"Hell yes, we are."

And it was so visceral—so obscene. Spreading her with his thumbs, he licked inside and all around, cupped her thighs as those clever hands of his rose, pushing her legs up and apart. One clothed shoulder came to meet the underside of her knee, and she had to look.

The vision had her on the edge of coming again right then and there.

Because it was almost too much. Shirt and vest still on, basically all his clothes still on. Hell, he even had his watch affixed to his wrist. And his hair was all tousled, dark and messy, his bright eyes fixed on her, her thigh draped over his shoulder.

He finally pressed a finger inside, flicked his tongue fast and strong against her clit, right where she liked it, because of course he would remember that, of course he still knew—

Her body shattered with a whole different kind of strength this time, practically pulling her inside out. His moans against her sex were another layer to the symphony crescendoing through her, were a match for her own, and she had to bite down on his name. It wanted so badly to be let out.

In that moment, screaming and undone before him, she wanted so badly to let him in.

But no. No.

She lowered her hand to push him away, oversensitive and done, but then he raised his head from between her legs, eyes fierce, and he practically growled, "Leave them where they are."

It made her freeze in her tracks.

His eyes flashed with need. "I am so fucking far from being finished with you."

And he drove back in, thick fingers filling her, curling up and pressing just the right side of too hard to that spot inside. With warm, wet strokes of his tongue, he coaxed her straight back up to the high plateau of arousal she hadn't imagined she'd be able to climb again so quickly after coming twice already. But there she was, the twitchiness of post-climax giving over beneath the heat of his mouth, that hunger and that rush for more returning.

"Oh my God." She shook her head back and forth, dropping her hand to her forehead where she was flushed and feverish. Sweat pooled at her lower back, and her nerves were screaming at her, her throat parched.

"Give it up again, beautiful."

And she couldn't—there was no way she could. Except he'd never given her a chance to come down, and so she was still soaring, air beneath her fingertips, and she would fall someday. She had no doubt. But for now . . . for now she'd take what he was offering, and she wouldn't look back.

She arched her throat and closed her eyes, lost to it, ready to fly apart, all her barely recombined pieces tearing at their seams.

Then his thumb nudged farther back, a grazing touch between her cheeks, and her eyes flew open. "What are you—"

"Trust me."

A steadier pressure, not quite in, not taking this other way to be inside her, but close, uncomfortable in a way that was more than physical. Dirty and weird and nothing she'd ever felt before, and that alone sent another rush of wetness flowing over his tongue, even as she twisted away, because it was too much. It might hurt.

"Don't overthink it," he said against slick flesh, lips brushing her clit with every syllable. "Just let it feel good."

"But—" But what if she didn't like this?

He shook his head, silencing her with that alone, and her ass gave beneath his slow, steady pressure. She choked on a breath as the very tip of his thumb, wet with her liquid, dipped inside, and there was no question about whether or not she liked it. Illicit fullness, a raw hint of a stretch, painless in the way that it burned right through her, and she *loved* it. The fingers in her sex thrust harder, and he did something with the point of his tongue.

And this time, she just about blacked out. The first wave overwhelmed her, made her shudder and curl, and she tossed her head to the side as it crashed into her. Without her leave, her hand found his hair and dug in deep, nails rough against scalp as she held him where she wanted him, kept his mouth right there—just there—

How was it possible she could still be coming? Her third climax flowed straight into her fourth, and it hurt and it felt unreal, and how did he do this to her? Push her boundaries and convince her to try? To let herself have things she'd never imagined could be for her?

By the time she came up for air, she was shaking, and she really did tear his mouth away from her before he could try to kill her any more.

Only there was way more than one kind of death that could be had at this man's hands. He came willingly enough, let himself be dragged up the length of her body, pushing her shirt up as he went, smearing her skin with what was left of her desire on his lips. When he met her mouth, he paused, hovering for just a moment.

Dimly, it struck her that he'd used his tongue to make her come and touched her someplace no one else had ever touched her before, but they hadn't kissed. Not once. A nervous little shiver curled through her, because did that mean something? Would letting his lips meet hers, now, mean even more?

She had only the span of a breath to worry about it. His eyes dipped closed. And then he kissed her full-on, pushing her own taste into her mouth, pushing her reservations away. It was all wet musk and bitter salt, and she swallowed them down, because he'd asked her to, and how had they gone so long without this? How was this not the very first thing they'd decided to do?

"Please," he said against her lips. It was the second time he'd begged her for something tonight, and she was lying down, but her knees went weak all the same. "Please."

He surrounded her wrists with his hands and pressed them back above her head. Her heart rate skyrocketed. Because she couldn't take any more, but she would. For him, she would.

And then he reared back, and he had never looked so powerful above her.

"Please tell me I haven't fucked this up so bad you won't let me be inside you."

Chapter Two

Rylan was pushing his luck. Their first time around, it'd taken him days of tender care, of proving to Kate she didn't owe him anything. He'd waited for intensely enthusiastic consent before asking her to so much as touch him then.

A lifetime of being told she didn't deserve to be taken care of, followed by a bad one-night stand and a worse relationship had left her too shy to ask for what she wanted in the bedroom. Even before he'd known the details, he'd made it his personal mission in life to make her see that sex was for her, too, not only for the morons who wanted to get their dicks in her—and sex could be amazing, when it was done right. Patiently. Tenderly.

And now here he was, his mouth and chin and fingers wet with her, and patience was a thing of the past. He was so hard it hurt, his body singing for it. She'd come so hard that last time, with both her ass and her pussy clenching around him. He'd never so much as grazed her there before. It'd been more than enough work getting her comfortable with the attention he liked to lavish on her pussy, but it'd always been on his list of things he'd hoped she'd let him try.

Sure enough, she'd loved it. Watching and feeling and hearing her had been the hottest experience of his life, and he needed her *right the fuck now*, before his dick fell off or his brain ran out of blood.

Months. It'd been months since he'd had this, and part of him had thought he'd never get to have it again.

His skin itched and his jaw ticked as he searched her eyes. She gazed back at him, brow furrowed. His stomach dropped.

Shit, he really had pressed his luck. He should've known better than to ask for this so soon, but he was desperate, and she felt so good.

"I don't know." She curled her fingers to stroke the tips of them against his wrist. "You did screw up pretty badly." The words made his heart threaten to stop, but a subtle smile twisted her lips, one eyebrow lifting.

Wait, was she—was she *teasing* him?

He buried his face in the crook of her neck, desire threatening to overwhelm him. With the shift in position, his clothed cock brushed her thigh, and it sent lightning flooding his spine.

She dragged her foot up the back of his calf. "But not *too* badly, I suppose."

Oh thank fuck.

He wanted her naked, wanted her spread out under him. Wanted to watch her face as she came on his cock, to savor it and memorize it and then fill her up. Make her his all over again, for real this time.

He wanted to keep her.

With a groan, he lifted back up onto hands and knees. The torture of not being pressed against her, of losing that friction where he was throbbing and leaking for her, was offset by the miles of creamy skin he revealed as he shoved her shirt up. She helped him pull it over her head and took it from him, tossing it aside as his fingers found her bra strap. He fumbled with the clasp in his eagerness, but then it gave, and he tore that, too, away.

Her bare breasts felt so right in his hands. He bent to lick at them and suck at them, nipping at one and then the other. Her hips shifted restlessly beneath him, knees coming up on either side of his waist as she pushed up into his mouth, egging him on.

Only there were too many things he wanted. Her body was a feast, and he was a starving man. He'd managed to keep it together while he'd had his mouth on her, but now that his own libido had been given a bit of rein he was spiraling out of control. He slid a hand down her side, skirting all those naked curves.

Someday, he'd have to get her to draw herself for him. A nude self-portrait, and he'd put it in his study, once he found a place for them to live. A big, beautiful place close to her school and the Bellamy offices, one with gorgeous light and a spot for her easel and her paints.

Shit. He was getting ahead of himself again. The touch of her hand against his chest grounded him, reminded him where they were right here, right now. Sneaking between their bodies, she gave a tug at the topmost button of his vest.

Where they were, right here, right now, was getting undressed.

Rising up on his knees, he tore the rest of the buttons loose, sending one pinging off the wall as its stitches gave beneath his overeager hands. He got it off and threw it aside. Wrinkles be damned, anything but getting all of him pressed skin on skin to all of her could fuck the hell off for now. His shirt and watch followed, and suddenly she was sitting up, one delicate, paint-stained hand sliding over the front of his slacks, lips level with his hips, and he just about lost his mind.

He reached down to grab her wrist—too hard. She flinched and darted her gaze up to his. Forcing himself to loosen his grip, he closed his eyes and held her there, soaked in the warmth of her through the fabric.

"Sorry," he gritted out.

She wriggled her hand inside his hold, and it sent more spasms racing from his dick to his balls and all through him. "Is this all right?"

"More than." Slowly, reluctantly, he let go. His pulse thrummed, his throat tight. "I've just wanted this for so long. Wanted you for so long."

One of her brows quirked up. Her voice rose right along with it. "What a crime. You being so neglected like this."

That was a smirk, flirting with her lips. Because he'd said those words, three hard-earned climaxes of hers ago, when she'd been on a hair trigger, flushed desire-hot and desperate for him.

He smiled, an aching, raw thing that had no place here. "Don't let it go to your head."

"You know, I think I just might." Unencumbered, she tucked her fingers into his belt buckle and gave it a questioning tug.

At his nod, she worked the leather through the metal. She left it dangling, unfastened at his hips as she undid the fasteners and dragged the fabric to his thighs, taking his boxers along for the ride. His cock, screaming for her hand, her mouth, anything, sprang free, and the sudden lack of constriction had his eyes rolling back in his head. As if from outside his own body, he watched as she trailed a single fingertip from the gleaming crown all the way to the base where she finally gripped him. Angled him toward her mouth.

"Kate. Fuck, don't tease me."

But she did exactly that. Tilting her head to the side, she examined him, and there was a barely veiled wonder to her expression.

His chest expanded. "You see what you do to me?" His voice came out gruff, as rough as he felt inside.

"I thought it was only me." She caught herself as soon as the words were out of her mouth, glancing up like she'd surprised herself, admitting that.

He reached out to cup her cheek, fingertips gentling her jaw, and he wouldn't push. But she was so close, her lips perfect and pink and full. She licked them, and another hot drop of fluid beaded at his tip.

"Will you?" he asked.

And who'd have known she had it in her? She was still the same girl he'd taught to touch herself in front of him, still easy to blush when he talked about her pretty cunt, but it was like seeing her superimposed on herself. A time-lapse image, and there were changes. There was this new hint of a sex kitten to her mouth, and it filled him with pride and terrified him at the same time. It was only barely dawning on her, but she knew better now the power she had. She'd taken his lessons to heart.

She was using them against him, and fuck, he couldn't wait to see where she would go with them.

Gaze fixed on him, she leaned in. Darted her tongue out and took a soft, glancing stripe of a lick, wet and warm and centered right along his slit.

"Kate..."

With one hand, she held him, and she took him just barely inside the heaven of her mouth. He bared his throat, letting his head fall back. Then with her other hand, she skated up his abdominals, fingers threading through the coarse hairs on his chest. Her palm came to rest above his heart, where the absence of his father's ring was still a presence he could feel in his bones.

She pressed right there, while with the same breath, she hollowed her cheeks and *sucked*.

It was like being turned inside out. She was touching his heart, newly freed, and taking him in, giving him this.

He let her go on for almost a minute before the pleasure started to gather. He grabbed her by the hair and had to remind himself to be careful. As he drew her off, she let him slip from between her lips with a wet sound that made him twitch harder.

"What do you want?" he asked, breathless.

Uncertainty flashed across her eyes. "What do *you* want?"

"To fuck you. Desperately." He fought to fill his lungs. Wrapped a hand around hers at the base of his cock and gripped it tight just to contain himself. "But this isn't all about me. What. Do. You. Want."

Her mouth half-open, she stared up at him, gaze trailing from his face to his aching cock and back.

She uncurled her hand from around him.

And then, as he watched, she turned around. He nearly swallowed his tongue as her hair slipped from between his slack fingers. He tried to look at anything except her ass, round and firm and lush. Dropping herself down onto all fours, she flicked her gaze over her shoulder at him.

"How about like this?"

It had been Kate's least favorite position, back with Aaron. She'd never come with him in any case, but at least in missionary there'd been a little pressure against her clit, a little relief.

Worse, it was more or less how things had gone that one awful night. She'd consented all right, but she'd been so drunk and lonely she hadn't fully realized what was happening until he'd dragged her hips up and shoved inside.

She'd always wished she'd had a chance to reclaim it while she'd been with Rylan. If anyone could've ever made her enjoy herself like that, it would've been him. Now they had this second chance, and who knew how many times they'd end up falling into bed with each other—if they'd even make it the seven nights he'd convinced her to give him. This wasn't going to be another thing she wished she'd gotten around to trying.

Best of all, letting him have her from behind—it made it so she wouldn't have to see his face.

They'd made love a whopping total of twice in Paris. That's how long it'd taken her to get over her fears and learn to trust him with her body. It was the only thing she *didn't* regret trusting him with, in retrospect. He'd made it so, so good for her—almost too good. The first time, she'd only just realized she'd been enough of an idiot to fall in love with him. The intimacy of the act had rocked her to her bones, taking her feelings and magnifying them a hundredfold. She'd stared into his eyes as he'd pressed inside, and her heart had ached with how beautiful he was, how safe he made her feel.

Already, he was lulling her down another path to heartbreak, but she wasn't going along so easily this time. She could protect herself and her sanity. She could find a way to keep him from looking too deep.

Anyway. It wasn't as if the man was looking at her *face* right now.

She cleared her throat and worried the fabric of the sheets between her fingertips. His gaze darted from her bottom to her eyes, and he shook his head until his expression looked a little less glazed. But then his forehead scrunched up.

"Just so we're clear here." He set a hand on her hip and stroked his thumb across her skin. "You're not suggesting I fuck you in the ass right now."

Her head jerked up. He thought— She didn't— "Wait. What?"

Letting go, he raised his hands in front of himself. "Just checking." He smirked, the lines across his forehead going roguish instead of confused. "You did seem to like it an awful lot."

Her cheeks burned, and she dropped her face into the mattress. Of course. He did...*that* to her, and then she gets down on all fours in front of him. What else did she expect him to think? She turned her head to the side with a groan. "Sorry."

"No need to apologize." Warm lips pressed to her spine, and then lower, tracing the curve of her rear. His voice deepened as he kissed a line toward her hip. "I love seeing you like this."

" 'Like this' as in accidentally implying I wanted anal?"

"Oh, you do want it. I promise." He palmed her ass, and God, there was his thumb again, pressing right against the center. It felt as weird and as illicit as it had before—maybe more so, without the added stimulation of his mouth on her. "Someday, I'll have you begging for it." Rubbing more firmly, he dragged his lips up her side, kissing each and every rib. By the time the tip of his thumb teased inside, he was speaking right beside her ear. It sent a tremor down her spine as that same teasing fullness blanked her mind. "I can imagine it. Get you all naked and rub you down maybe. Eat you out for a while but keep you right on the edge until you make that little noise you do." A breathy sigh passed through her lips as he scraped his teeth across her lobe. He chuckled, dark and sexy. "That's the one. The one that means you're too turned on to really think. Then I'll open you up." He pushed a little deeper, and she closed her eyes against the hint of a burn. "Get you all wet and easy inside. Oh, Kate." He swallowed, the sound loud. "If you think you like a hint of thumb, you're going to love it when I fuck you here."

A warm, molten clench fired off inside her.

Jesus, how was this possible? Her body was showing these token signs of protest, her sex feeling tender and sore, but that throb was there, made deeper with every word he spoke. Every glancing brush of his chest against her spine, the scratch of his pants—oh, hell, he still hadn't finished taking his pants off—against her thigh. She shivered, her clit pulsing as he played with her rim, making one last circle around it before withdrawing, leaving her suddenly bereft. Empty.

And then, of all things, he had the audacity to kiss her cheek.

"But not tonight," he said. "Tonight..." He nudged his knee between her thighs, spreading them wider. Her nipples grazed the mattress as she sank. He made a show of switching hands before sinking two broad fingers deep into her sex, giving her a whole different kind of fullness. "Tonight, I want to fuck you here." He leaned in closer until the searing line of his cock pressed to her skin.

He paused for a second, and she caught herself panting for breath.

"I'll take you fast. And hard. And when I come inside you?"

"Yeah?"

"You're going to come, too. One more time for me, beautiful."

With the withdrawal of his fingers this time, she sagged, left near boneless without his touch. From behind her came the whispers of fabric, and then the sound of foil ripping. For half a second she almost considered stopping him. She'd gone back on the pill as soon as she'd gotten back to town, for all the good that had done her in her dry spell. She could tell him . . .

But no. Letting him take her bare—that was a hell of a leap from where they were now.

It was the work of a moment for him to roll the condom on, and then he was over her, on top of her. The heat of his chest pressed to her spine, his hard cock nudging at her entrance, and she was ready. Instinctively, she braced herself.

But before he took that first, long thrust, he paused, wavering. His brow pressed to her temple, and a tremor rocked the cage of his arms around her.

"I missed you so much," he whispered.

And with that, he pushed inside.

Reeling, she bit down on her lip. She'd forgotten how big he was, and the part of her that still expected pain had her fingers digging sharp into her palm. But the slide was easy, her body open and slick.

He hit something as he filled her. Something deeper than the back of her sex and harder than his thumb sneaking back around to play with her rear.

Something that remembered this, and remembered what it had meant.

That summer in Paris, they'd been so close. She'd thought they had been, and she'd loved him so much. Had given him her body and her heart, and what had he given her? Orgasms, sure. But not his story. Not himself. Yet here he was, asking for more.

His hips eased back, the retreating stroke as massive in its impact as the one with which he'd entered her. He huffed out a breath that sounded pained before thrusting home again.

"Fuck, Kate, you feel even better than I thought you would."

And he did, too, and that was the problem.

He took a few more slow, steady movements in and out, each one reaching the part of her body that welcomed him home and made her want to spread her legs for him, be easy for him. She shoved her fingers tighter into fists as her sex went warmer and slicker.

With his hips flush to hers, he stopped. "You ready?"

God, their first time around, she'd made the sex so difficult, but now it felt like the simplest part. Way simpler than the mess he'd made of her heart.

She nodded and clenched her eyes shut.

"Kate?"

"Do it." She pressed back into him, forcing him that tiny bit deeper, and how did it feel even better, when inside she was falling apart? "Fuck me."

He groaned, but instead of doing it, instead of doing as he'd promised and taking her hard, he wrapped his arms around her, hauling her up. She resisted. She was safe where she was. But he sat back on his haunches all the same, pulling her along with him until there was nowhere left to hide. Astride his lap, her weight pressing her down onto him even more, she was on display.

And he held her. Fuck, he *held her.*

"I need to feel you're with me in this, Kate."

She laughed, and it sounded high and desperate to her own ears. "Where else would I be?"

"I have no idea." He shook his head, stubble scratching her cheek as he tucked his chin against her shoulder. "You just felt really far away."

As far away as he had driven her.

She bit her lip. "I'm right here." And it hurt.

"Then stay there. Please."

He gripped her tighter and flexed his hips, and yes. This they could do.

"Stay with me," he pled again, picking up his pace.

But her throat wouldn't work. They'd said so much tonight already. She'd given him what he wanted. Couldn't she keep a piece of herself for her own?

As if sensing that he'd pushed far enough, he didn't ask her anything else as they settled into the rise and fall of bodies on bodies, flesh inside of flesh. It wasn't the hard, rough fuck he'd promised her, but the way he moved inside her—the way he moved her over him, clutching her tight and helping her ride him—was thick with intent. The pleasure she scarcely knew if she was ready for gathered low in her belly, close and yet unsatisfied.

He broke their silence with a rasp. "Touch yourself for me."

She'd fought him on this once, but it felt too easy this time to lower her hand and slip it through the slick-hot space between her legs. Her fingertips grazed his length, full and hard as it buried itself inside her, and he moaned. Then she found her clit, and the gathering heat shot sparks.

"That's right." He bit her throat. "Just like that. Feel it. Let yourself have this."

She would. Fully prepared to lose it this time, when there was nothing left to do but let it go.

As climax barreled down on her, she tossed her head back. He caught it on the wide, strong expanse of his shoulder. He spoke her name and stroked her nipple once.

"Kate—" He gulped, swallowing air. "I'm going to—"

She fell over the edge with him, exactly how he'd said she would, blackness eclipsing her vision, muscles spasming as a pleasure too vast, too deep washed over her. Within the clench-ing furl of her, he throbbed, pulsing.

And then he was grabbing her by the jaw, pulling her into a kiss it felt like she'd been waiting years for. As they shuddered through their peaks, he held her face in his hand, his gaze locked with hers.

It was too much. Too close.

She needed to protect herself, needed to hide.

Yanking her head away, she closed her eyes.

chapter THREE

For a minute, Rylan fought simply to breathe. Fuck, he had needed that. But even as his blood sang with satisfaction, worry tickled at the back of his mind, keeping him from sinking into any kind of afterglow.

The sex had been amazing, but it had been...different. She'd wanted to face away from him, and sure, it'd been hot as hell. But it hadn't been *her*. The first time they'd made love, it had been Kate and her misgivings that had prompted them to wait. He'd been patient for days in Paris, and in the end, he'd toppled right into a connection he had yet to claw his way out of—one he didn't want to, even. Being with her had been so much *better* than being with anyone else had ever been before. It made him want to throw caution to the wind, to ignore every lesson his family had ever taught him about how love was just an invitation to be discarded or used.

But maybe she wanted out.

Stroking his thumb across her cheek, he tried to will her eyes open, but it wasn't any use. She'd closed them right as their intensity had risen past the breaking point, had turned her face away. She was hiding from him, dammit all. Fire burned in his gut, a low twitch of annoyance at her for keeping him out.

And a red-hot brand of anger at himself. He had dug this hole, and he'd known he'd have to work his way out of it. She'd agreed to let him try. But all of a sudden, the gently sweeping road to forgiveness he'd imagined himself on took a steep upward climb. He swallowed hard and dropped his head, relaxing his hold as his brow came to rest against her temple.

How the hell was he going to do this?

Before he could begin to figure it out, she reached up to swipe at her eyes. His stomach sank as he pulled away enough to really see her. Dampness clung to her lashes.

"Baby..."

She shook her head. "It's fine." Patting his arm, she wriggled her way out of his embrace. He clenched his hands into fists to keep from drawing her back. "Just intense, you know?"

Of course he knew.

His body slipped from hers as she climbed off his lap, leaving him cold. With her back still turned, she retreated to the edge of the bed to grab a box of tissues. She felt miles and miles away.

Without looking at him, she handed him the box. He pulled a couple of tissues loose and dealt with the condom. The silence tore at him.

It had never been this *awkward* before.

Well, fuck it. He wasn't going to let it be awkward now.

She'd already grabbed her shirt off the floor, but before she could tug it on, he clambered onto his hands and knees to come up behind her. Dropping the bundle of tissues in the waste bin, he wrapped both arms around her, prying the fabric from her hands and tossing it across the room.

"Hey—"

"You don't need that." He kissed the spot behind her ear.

She fixed him with a look, brow arched. "It's actually kind of chilly in here."

"That's what I'm for." Him and a pile of blankets. He tried to pull her down to lie beside him, but she shook her head.

"I'll fall asleep."

His heart panged. That sounded ideal, honestly. Chilly or no, his bed had been cold for months without her there. "And what would be so bad about that?"

She looked away. "Where are you staying, anyway?"

It took him a second to catch up, but when he did, he sucked in a breath and clenched his jaw. His suitcase still stood in the corner where he'd left it, looking stupidly hopeful. Homeless.

"I hadn't figured that out yet, actually." He forced himself to relax his mouth and stroked his palms up and down her arms. Made his voice soft to conceal the disappointment gnawing at him.

It wasn't that he'd expected her to invite him to stay, precisely. But somehow, he hadn't expected her *not* to, either.

"Oh," she said.

"I was kind of busy. Had a girl I was in a rush to get to after all."

He stroked her hair back from her face. It gave him a better view, but unlike before, he couldn't seem to see in.

And then her stomach gave this long, rolling growl.

It stopped him short. "Um."

"Quiet." She huffed out a little half laugh and rubbed the heel of her hand into her eye before pointing in the vague direction of the kitchen. "I barely got to eat my terrible soup."

Ah, yes. She'd insisted that they eat ramen for supper—something that came in a packet and tasted like salt and despair.

And when he'd been tempted to hide how terrible he thought it was, she'd exploded, as if instant noodles were the root of their problems.

Really, taking that cup from her hands had been him doing her a favor. "You're welcome?"

"Hardly. It's not like I have much of anything else here to eat."

Maybe he should offer to buy her some groceries. It struck him, though—did she cook? They'd gotten this far and there were so many things about her life he didn't know. But he wanted to.

Paris had been a whirlwind of sightseeing, but both out there in the city and alone in their hotel room, they'd gotten through only the highlights.

He wanted the unabridged version now. The off-the-beaten-track insider's guide. The view of a city—the view of this girl you only got after years of exploration. He wanted to discover everything there was to know about her, piece by piece. He just needed her to give him the chance to.

For now, he hugged her tighter and pressed his lips to her cheek. "Order something then." He hesitated before adding, "My treat."

She rolled her eyes, but at least she didn't freak out. "You don't have to do that, you know."

"Of course I don't." Didn't she understand this? "I want to."

He wasn't going to hide who he was this time. He'd already promised her that. If money wasn't an issue for him, why couldn't he choose to share it with her?

"Come on," he said. "Something simple. Pizza?" Now there was an idea. He hooked his chin over her shoulder and outright pouted. "I haven't had a decent New York slice in a year."

"Now that really is a crime." Her tone was teasing, but there was an edge to it, too.

So he pulled out his secret weapon. Pressing a kiss beneath her ear, he asked quietly, too fervently, "Please?"

The warm wash of his breath across her skin made Kate shiver.

His offer was so tempting, really. She was starving, and the idea of letting him take care of her for a little while made a tired, jagged piece of her heart sigh with relief.

But ordering a pizza meant waiting for delivery, which meant more time alone with him—probably naked if his reaction to her last attempt at getting dressed was any sign. The vulnerability of it made her skin itch. She couldn't defend herself like that, and she desperately needed to this time around.

"Actually." Her voice cracked, anxiety making her breath go tight.

His arms went stiff around her.

Stomach roiling, she shifted inside his embrace, twisting until he let go. Unable to look at him, she crossed the room to where he'd thrown her top. She picked it up and pulled it on. It was long enough that she felt at least a little bit covered.

"Actually?" he prodded.

Steeling herself, she crossed her arms and turned to face him. "Actually, I have a lot of work to do."

His expression scrunched up in confusion. "But you just said you didn't have any food. It's only dinner."

Right. Just dinner. But even if she managed to survive the wait and then a meal with this man, she knew how he worked. She knew how weak she could be. Their first round had left her boneless and sated, but one look from him and she'd be ready to move straight into a second—after her recent dry spell, maybe even a third.

And then there they'd be, naked in her bed, and she'd be exhausted, and he didn't really have a place to stay, so he'd might as well crash at hers. Just for the night.

A different kind of shiver racked her frame.

It was exactly how things had gone in Paris, with them falling into each other's pockets, going on one sightseeing adventure after another until it had only felt natural to spend every waking minute together. Until she'd had to let him down to get a couple of hours to herself to draw.

Somehow, she'd managed to mistake all that time together, all those pieces of herself he'd convinced her to give away, for intimacy. His stunted, guarded replies to her most basic questions for reciprocity. It was how she'd gotten her heart broken.

She had to hold him at arm's length this time, no matter the temptation to do anything but. She'd be grateful, later, that she had.

Standing firm, she set her shoulders and lifted her chin. "Like I said, I have work to do." She gestured idly toward the stacks of canvases she'd turned toward the walls. "I have an assignment for one of my classes, and—"

"So you decided to go." His voice cut her off. The sheer wonder in his expression made her pause. "To grad school."

Oh, hell, that was right. Last he'd known, she'd still been making up her mind between an office job and an MFA.

"Yeah." She nodded, fidgeting. "Things went so well on my trip." Her heart had been left a mess, but her sketchbook had been full to the brim. "And you told me..."

It was the one good thing to come from the whole sad affair.

Rylan had looked at her drawings—really looked at them—and he'd told her she'd be a fool not to follow her dreams.

Licking her lips to wet them, she met his gaze. "When I told you I was considering it, you acted like it shouldn't even be a decision. It just..." He'd given her that extra shot of confidence she'd needed. "It meant a lot."

"I'm so glad." His eyes shone. "I spent all this time wondering, hoping you'd made the right decision."

She rolled her eyes at herself. "I'm still not sure it was the right one—"

"It was. Absolutely."

His unwavering confidence in her after all this time threatened to crack her resolve. But she had to stay strong.

"I'm glad you think so," she said, squaring her shoulders all over again. "But it's a ton of pressure and a lot of work, and I just—I don't think getting pizza with you is a good idea."

He tilted his head to the side, and for all the world, it felt like he was trying to peer clear through her. But then, instead of arguing, he rose to his feet. Her heart got stuck in her throat as his full height unfurled, muscles rippling across his chest. He found his boxers and pants and pulled them on, then crossed the remaining distance to her and ducked to look her in the eye. "Why?"

She blinked at him in disbelief. "Excuse me?"

"Why? It's not the work, so don't try to tell me that it is."

An irrational panic tore at her throat. "I don't know what you mean."

"You want me to go. I want you to tell me why." He said it like it was a completely reasonable thing to request.

And maybe that was what made her snap. Uncrossing her arms, she flung them out at her sides, stepping back, pulling away.

"Because—because you can't just," she sputtered, "just show up at someone's apartment after the way we left things. I told you when I let you in. I'm still—God, I'm still so mad at you I could—" Could what? Shake him? Deck him?

Retreating farther, she dug her nails into the meat of her palms.

"Because I don't trust you," she said. Her rib cage echoed with the words, because really, that was what this all boiled down to. "I know we had something." They'd had a connection like nothing she'd ever felt before, but finding out it hadn't flowed in both directions, not as freely as she had thought—nothing could come out of that entirely intact. They hadn't. No matter how much he seemed to want to pretend. "We had something incredible, but you don't just get it back by asking for it."

"I told you. I'll do whatever it takes to earn your trust again."

"And tonight, what it's going to take is you leaving."

His eyes widened, and a beat of silence passed as they sized each other up.

Then, all power and precision, he stalked the rest of the way toward her. She held her ground, working not to betray how inside she shook like a leaf.

He reached to curl a hand around her neck, and drew her into a soft, gentle kiss.

After a minute, he released her, and her heart leapt around inside her chest. She cleared her throat, but it did nothing for the fog he left in her head. "I just need some time," she said. And some distance, to give her any hope of keeping her feelings in check when he had the power to turn her to liquid like this. "It's a lot to take in, you know." She gestured between the two of them.

"It is." His smile went sad. "And time's exactly what I asked for from you. Time to prove myself." Seven nights to be exact. "It'd be pretty bad if I weren't willing to give you some to think this all through." He dropped his hand, leaving her skin singed. "Don't think I'm happy about it, though."

She wasn't entirely sure she was, either, honestly. But she had to hold the line this time.

Rylan finished getting dressed as she watched on, leaving only his tie undone, the fabric hanging loose around his neck. When he was put together again, he turned to her.

And something cracked behind his eyes. "It's not just the money, is it?"

"What?"

"That's not why you don't want me here. Because it doesn't really matter. I'd be happy with you in a hotel in Paris or a studio apartment in Brooklyn, or in a cave for all I care. It's just details."

It was the kind of thing only someone with money could say.

Suddenly, her lack of it felt like a brand.

"It's not the money," she managed.

"All right." He captured her lips one last time, tongue softly seeking in her mouth, body firm where it pressed to hers.

Before she could second-guess herself or let the heat he kindled under her skin catch flame, she drew away. He stopped her from going far, ducking to rest his brow against hers. "Six more nights?"

Her stomach did a little dip. It sounded like too many and too few. But maybe, depending how they went, they'd be just enough—enough to figure out who he really was. If they could even work outside a fantasy.

If she'd made a mistake, letting him in again as much as she had.

She nodded. "That's what I said."

"We'll do the next one soon. And Kate?" There was something quietly desperate to the way he said her name. To the way he clutched her close.

"Yes?"

"The next time you invite me to share your bed—" His eyes turned to liquid pools of rushing heat. "I promise. I'll make it count."

And then he was drawing away, leaving her sagging against the wall, relying on the plaster to keep her up. He grabbed his suitcase by the handle and rolled it to the door. With one look back over his shoulder, he cast the door open.

It closed behind him, and sucked all the air out of the place. Leaving her alone with her life exactly how it had been before he'd walked into it, and yet utterly changed.

Leaving her to wonder what the hell had just happened.

And what on earth she was going to do.

chapter FOUR

Rylan barely waited until they'd pulled up to the curb before he was yanking open the taxi's door and setting his feet down on the pavement. From behind the glass, the driver offered to help him with his luggage, but Rylan waved him off, clenching his jaw against the urge to snap. None of this was some random cabbie's fault.

It was all Rylan's own damn fault.

And yet there was this part of him—this small, seething part—that kept replaying the way Kate had closed him off and kicked him out. The look on her face as she'd asked him for time.

Fuck it all, he'd *begged* her for a second chance. He'd been prepared to tell her everything this time around. Whatever she'd wanted to know. But the distance he'd felt even as he'd pushed inside her had persisted, and when he'd offered her more, she practically slammed the door in his face.

Grasping the handle of his suitcase, he stepped up onto the sidewalk and took a deep breath, then let it out with a disgusted sigh.

What the hell had he been thinking, asking to be taken here? He shook his head and stiffened his spine. Not like he'd had all that many options. Kate had refused to let him stay, and the idea of an anonymous hotel room left him cold. He'd long since washed his hands of his own apartment in the city, had sold it in a fit of pique when he'd been determined never to return. All of his possessions were either back in Paris or wrapped up in boxes in some storage room at the mansion, and...and there was no chance in hell he was going there.

No, this was his best course of action.

He stalked his way past the doorman without pausing to introduce himself.

Apparently, that was a red flag in doorman land. The fellow chased in after him. "May I help you, sir?"

"Alexis Bellamy," Rylan said, not stopping.

"I wasn't told she was expecting any..."

"She's expecting me."

She probably was, even. He'd dismissed her when she'd offered to let him stay, still holding on to the hope that Kate would take him in. But she hadn't seemed entirely convinced.

The doorman followed him to the elevator, his decorum slipping as Rylan continued to stride past him. "And who should I say is visiting?"

"Her brother."

Rylan punched in the number for Lexie's floor, and the elevator doors slid closed. As it rose up into the sky, he took a long, deep breath, preparing himself.

A minute later, the chime sounded off. The doors opened to reveal his sister standing in the entry to her penthouse in a pink silk bathrobe, her phone in her hand, a smirk stretching all the way to her ear.

"I thought you were going to 'figure something out,'" she crowed.

He fought not to roll his eyes. "I managed to find my way here, didn't I?"

"You gave Laurence downstairs a heart attack, I think." She stepped aside to let him in. "He probably thought you were here to murder me."

"Let's see if we can manage not to prove him right."

He stepped inside and tasted bile in the back of his mouth. He'd been here once before, back when she'd first acquired the place. It'd been a blank slate back then; now it was anything but.

God, it was their mother's apartment in Paris all over again. All modern lines and white carpet and rose accents, Eastern influences exactly where they were supposed to be. It wasn't a home. It was a show.

Like their whole damn family. Like their whole damn life.

"Love what you've done with the place," he gritted out. "Did Mother help you?"

"She put me in touch with someone."

A designer then. "You ever think of doing your decorating yourself?"

When she didn't answer, he turned around. Her brow was furrowed, her head tilted to the side. "Why on earth would I do that?"

He faced away from her. "You know? I have absolutely no idea."

With that, he tightened his grip on the handle of his suitcase and headed for the hall.

"Last door on the left," she called from behind him.

"Got it."

And he should probably stay. Avoiding her interrogation until tomorrow would only make things worse, but he couldn't deal with it right now. Today already, he'd squared off against a boardroom full of men who would eat him alive without a second thought. He gotten on his knees for the girl who'd made him willing to face his life again, but who refused to trust him.

He'd convinced her to let him inside, only to be turned away.

He closed himself in Lexie's guest room and dropped his bag. Shoved his suitcase to the side. Twisting his hands in his hair and tugging hard, he fought to breathe.

But there wasn't any air to be found. Just a stale, ostentatious space, offered to him by the closest thing to family he had left.

He'd made such a mess of things, running away from who he was. Trying to come back to it, trying to reclaim his life... He hadn't expected it to be easy.

But nothing had prepared him for it to be this hard.

"Dammit." Kate was scurrying across the street, the pedestrian crossing sign already flashing to red, when her phone buzzed at her hip. Late, late, she was running so damn late. She hitched her bag higher on her shoulder, trying to keep an eye on where she was going as she reached into her pocket.

Oh God, what if it was Rylan? Her heart leapt into her throat.

And then she cursed herself in her mind. Just last night, she'd asked him to give her some time. If he was calling her already, she should be *pissed*. And yet here she was, her chest lighting up at just the thought that it might be him. Stupid.

Even stupider when her stomach dipped to see it was her mom instead.

Praying for strength, she flipped the phone open and brought the speaker to her ear. "Hey."

"Oh, I'm glad I caught you." Her mother paused. "Don't you have class this afternoon?"

Kate flexed her jaw. "On my way to it right now."

It was funny—her mom hadn't come right out and told her she was making a mistake choosing to go on for her MFA, but there was this tone to her voice every time she so much as mentioned it.

"Well, I don't want to keep you." That tone again. "But I wanted to let you know I booked that flight I emailed you about the other day."

Kate slipped into the art building and made for the stairs. "Oh yeah? That's great."

"I can't wait to see you."

"Me neither." And she meant it, too. Her mom hadn't been able to make it to her graduation in the spring, and they'd been trying to figure out a time for her to visit ever since. But she worked so hard. Kate's chest tightened up. Her mom had always worked hard, pulling double shifts whenever she could get them so she could support herself and Kate both. All on her own.

She'd taught Kate the value of independence, and of paying your own way. Because you could never really rely on anyone.

Her father had taught them both that.

Suddenly, she missed her mom with a fierceness that blindsided her. Things felt so topsy-turvy right now, between Rylan showing up out of nowhere and her painting mojo going MIA. Forget the occasional note of disapproval. There was something about having your mom around. Something steadying—something that reminded you of who you were.

She pulled up short at the top of the stairs, letting traffic flow around her. With her back to the wall and her phone to her ear, she blinked her eyes shut tight for one long moment.

When she opened them again, her vision was clear, even if her voice couldn't hide a hint of an edge. "Sorry, Mom, I have to go. But we'll talk soon, okay?" Her throat hitched. "Catch up for real?"

There were so many things she hadn't told her mom. Keeping the disaster that had been her fling with Rylan a secret had been plain good sense at the time, but if he was going to be back in her life, she didn't know how long she could hold her tongue. How long she could keep her fears about her creativity and her love life and her future locked up inside.

Her mom's smile came across the line. "Count on it. And I'll see you soon. Just a few short weeks."

Kate said her good-byes and hung up, then took a solid ten seconds to collect herself before she was off again.

As it turned out, she must have been making better time sprinting her way through campus than she'd realized. She snuck into the painting studio where her cohort's weekly seminar class met to find Professor Robinson still lingering at the back, talking to one of the other girls. Relieved, Kate moderated her pace. Then, from the edge of the loose cluster of students, her friend Liam gave her a lifted eyebrow and a little wave.

Oh hell. Liam.

Kate wanted to sit right down and laugh, or maybe cry. Less than twenty-four hours ago—before Rylan, before some of the best, most confusing sex of her life, before her whole world had been turned upside down—her best friend in the program had asked her out. He'd left it ambiguous, but the potential had been there, the invitation to take it as something more than friends. She'd demurred, letting him down easy. But at the same time, she'd left the door open.

Any other day, it would've been the biggest thing on her mind. And here she'd gone ahead and forgotten it completely.

Her stride went from faux casual to an absolute crawl. Liam's raised brow fell, a crinkle of concern appearing between his gray eyes, and a twist of guilty shame made her gut clench.

He was a nice guy. She'd mostly thought of him as a friend, sure, but the possibility had been there for it to grow into more. Over these last few weeks, they'd gotten to know each other as people and as artists. In coffee shops and bars and across their easels from each other, they'd *talked*.

And then she'd gone ahead and fallen right back into bed with the guy who'd never told her the first thing about himself.

She felt like something you scrape off your shoe.

Looking anywhere but at him, she dragged another stool over to the empty spot beside his.

"Hey." He nudged her with his elbow, gesturing with his head at the clock. Sure enough, they were a couple of minutes past the class's starting time. "You're cutting it a little close here."

"Yeah. Been running late all day." From the alarm she'd slept past after a fitful, awful night, to the extra trays she'd agreed to bus after she'd messed up three orders in her distraction, to the train she'd missed through sheer bad luck.

The furrows in his brow deepened. "You okay?"

Her throat squeezed. Where did she begin?

As luck would have it, she didn't have to. Professor Robinson chose that moment to pick her way to the front of the room, apologizing as she did. Liam shot Kate another meaningful look, but she shook her head. Even if she were ready to spill her guts, she couldn't do it now. Not like this.

Especially not when Robinson took her place on her stool and turned to them all. "Now, as you've probably heard, we have a special announcement today."

Kate sat up straighter in her chair. She had heard; the whole place had been buzzing about it for a week.

"More of a challenge, really." Professor Robinson opened up a folio and withdrew a stack of papers from it, unbundling them before passing them around. "Each year, we have the pleasure of announcing this opportunity to our incoming group of MFA candidates."

As she continued to explain aloud, Liam got the pile of handouts and plucked one off for each of them before passing the rest along. Kate took a copy without letting their hands brush.

As she scanned it, her heart raced.

"A fellowship," Professor Robinson explained.

A huge chunk of tuition for the remaining semesters of the program, and invitations to networking events with gallery owners and professional artists right here in the city. Kate's vision hazed. She didn't have to hear any more.

This was it. The opportunity she'd been waiting for. A kick in the pants to get her out of her creative rut. A chance to prove her mother's doubts unfounded and get a head start in really making something of herself.

She had to win this.

"I warn you." Professor Robinson adjusted her glasses. "The competition will be rigorous. Each candidate who chooses to be part of the selection process will be considered based on a portfolio of all-new works, due just before Thanksgiving break. The theme for this year's contest has been chosen by our judges, and it is"—she glanced down, reading from the paper—"'Sacred Spaces.'"

Sacred spaces. Kate's mind took off. Her whole journey into the new style she'd been exploring had begun at Sacred Heart Basilica in Montmartre. Ever since she'd returned to New York, she'd been working on cityscapes. The one on her easel right now was of a church, even. It was a literal interpretation, but she could expand from there. It was a starting point.

Hell, it was a sign.

The rest of the seminar passed in a blur. Only half paying attention to the slides Professor Robinson had selected for them to look at today, and then to the parade of works the rest of the class offered up for critique, Kate dug a notebook from her bag and got to work scribbling down ideas.

Time was just about winding down when Liam kicked her ankle, and she looked up with a start.

Though she addressed the room as a whole, Professor Robinson had her gaze fixed right on Kate. "Does anyone else have something they want to share this week?"

Kate swallowed hard. There wasn't any specific requirement to bring a piece to every critique, but this was the third one in a row Kate had failed to participate in. She shook her head and crumpled a little inside at the frown her teacher shot her way.

As they were being dismissed, Liam grabbed Kate's arm. "Seriously, what's up with you today?"

She shook free, closing her notebook and cramming it back in her bag. "Nothing."

"Bullshit. Why didn't you show that thing you've been working on? The church painting. It's right there."

Kate glanced across the studio at the canvas she'd left propped up on her easel. It was just as much of a mess as it had been the night before. "It's not ready."

"You do understand the purpose of critique, right?"

"Of course I do." They were supposed to be learning from one another. Working together to grow as artists.

"So sometimes it's okay to show a piece that's not ready. Hell, with how stuck you've been—"

"I'm not stuck." Who the hell did she think she was fooling? "I mean." She slung her bag over her shoulder and pushed her hair back from her face. "I figured it out." This new portfolio challenge had the gears spinning in a way they hadn't been before. The theme of space and evoking the power of it . . . There was potential there.

Liam's mouth tilted down. "Since last night?"

Since five minutes ago. "A lot can happen in a night."

Holding his hands up in front of himself, Liam retreated a step. "All right. Well, if you want to catch me up on it sometime . . ."

And was that another invitation? She nodded even as she was turning away. "I will. Soon."

Just as soon as she got her head on straight.

chapter FIVE

Rylan got halfway through his second cup of coffee before he had to clench his hands into fists to keep from throwing something against the wall.

He was puttering around Lexie's penthouse, reading the news, and it was just—

It was the same. He'd traveled halfway around the globe, and here he was still, killing time in an apartment that wasn't his, wishing he were lying beside the girl who'd changed his mind about so many things. Waiting, and he didn't ever know what for.

Finally, just before noon, he heard the slotting of a key into a lock, and that was something at least. As the door to the apartment swung open, he kept his gaze steady on the tablet perched on his lap. Expression serene, like he hadn't been about to tear his hair out.

Impassively, he said, "You're home early."

Heels clicked loudly across the tiled entryway before getting muffled by the carpet in the living room. Lexie plopped a white paper bag down on the coffee table in front of him and folded herself onto the other end of the couch. "Nice part about living close to the office is getting to pop home for lunch."

He snuck a glance at her as he reached forward to grab the bag. And it was strange. His sister had been a regular figure around the Bellamy headquarters for as long as he had, but before, she'd always had this little-girl-playing-dress-up air to her. That was probably a douchebag thing to say, considering how hard she'd been working to convince people to take her seriously, but it'd been true.

Whatever might have been left of that ingénue was gone. Her look now was all calculated, polished sophistication. A narrow skirt and a fitted top, black and white with a pop of purple at her belt. Her dark hair was twisted up in a severe bun at the back of her neck, but it didn't make her look matronly. No, she looked—

Shit. His baby sister looked sexy.

"Jesus, Lex. When did you grow up?"

She laughed, one short, sharp sound. "Like we were ever children."

She wasn't kidding about that. He examined her more closely this time, trying to pinpoint the change, because there had been one. In this year that he'd been gone, something had happened to her. Maybe school, maybe finishing her MBA. But he didn't think so.

Turning away, he opened the bag she'd brought him. Pastrami on rye. His mouth watered, his stomach reminding him he'd given it nothing but coffee so far today. "Katz's?"

"Where else?"

He pulled it out and took a bite, restraining a groan. "I didn't think I missed New York, you know."

"But there are some things you can't get anywhere else."

She reached into her own bag to extract a salad. "Order pizza tonight, and you'll never want to leave again."

For a flash of a second, he lost his appetite. It was exactly what he'd suggested to Kate the night before.

Something of his dismay must have shown in his expression. Lexie looked him up and down. Then delicately, she said, "So you never told me how things went last night."

"Fine."

She regarded him for another moment, then deliberately directed her attention to her salad. "Okay."

"That's it? Just 'okay'?"

She shrugged. "You were expecting something more?"

"You had plenty of questions when you came to see me in Paris."

"When I came to see you in Paris, you were a mystery wrapped in an enigma. There's not a whole lot I can't guess this time." She poked around and stabbed at a tomato. "You pulled a full-on *Good Will Hunting* and ran off to see about a girl, then came back fit to spit nails and looking for a place to stay. Now you don't want to talk about it. Doesn't take a genius to figure that one out."

A flash of pain squeezed his ribs, and he dented the bread under his fingers. "Nice to know I'm such an easy read."

"You always have been. At least to me." She shifted her position, a casual stretch that had her foot grazing his knee for just a second. "Is she in the picture at all anymore?"

"Maybe." God, he hoped so. "She asked me for some time."

"Just as well." She set her salad aside and turned to him more fully. "Because now that you're back, we have work to do."

He groaned aloud. But it wasn't just that Lexie wanted to talk shop already. It was the lunch, the requisite five minutes of conversation about personal matters. It was pure Dad, was what it was. "I got back yesterday and went straight to a board meeting."

"Which I already thanked you for." She pulled her briefcase into her lap. "And which we need to capitalize on immediately. If we want to get control back from those asshats, we've got our work cut out for us." She plucked out a file and handed it to him. "I made a list up this morning of all the major players and who are our best shots for applying some pressure. If you have any favors to call in..." She kept going, while Rylan stared at the file.

He could stand up right now. Give her back her manipulative sandwich and walk away. Or even better, slap the papers from her hands. He'd come here in good faith, intent on helping out. But the fact of the matter was he hadn't decided yet what kind of role he wanted at the company, or if he wanted one at all. The epiphany he'd had while taking off his father's ring be damned.

Yes, he wanted to fix the mess he'd made. He wanted to salvage what he could from this place his father and he had built.

But it was going to be his choice this time. Not his father's. And certainly not Lexie's.

He forced himself to take a deep breath. And then he *chose* to take the file from her outstretched hand.

Lexie positively glowed.

As she continued on, he opened the file and scanned the list she'd put together. Their father's best friend, McConnell, the one who should've gone to prison with him, was circled in red, as he should be. Public enemy number one. The rest of the board members and division heads and VPs were listed more or less as he'd imagined they would be, with Thomas, their one unequivocal ally at the top. Except—

"Where's Jordan?" he asked.

Jordan was only a decade or so older than Rylan, a Harvard-grad hotshot their father had brought in a few years ago to inject some new blood into the company—most likely to light a fire under Rylan's ass, too. A reminder that he wasn't irreplaceable if he kept dragging his heels about taking on a leadership role.

It hadn't worked. He and Jordan had hit it off immediately, and in the end, he'd been one of the select few Rylan had trusted in the whole bunch.

Lexie's eye twitched, and Rylan frowned. He'd thought the two of them had been on good terms. Right before it had all fallen apart, Lexie had recommended him to lead their European division, even. But he knew her tells.

"Lex?"

"You can add him, if you want. We don't really work together much anymore." With that she changed the topic to some other soft targets. Rylan let himself be distracted, but he made a note of it for later.

By the time both their lunches were gone, they'd agreed to a short list of people to reach out to first. Taking her portion of the names, Lexie capped her pen and closed her file.

"I think that'll be a good start," she said. She stood and smoothed out her skirt. "You bought us another ninety days, but they know we're coming now, so we have to work fast."

Rylan still didn't love the kinds of assumptions she was making about his level of involvement, but he nodded all the same. There was a familiarity to sitting around, spit-balling ideas and talking strategy with her like this. That their father wasn't a specter hanging over them made it all the better. "It's good to be working with you again, sis."

"I knew you missed me, Teddy."

He leveled her with a look.

She rolled her eyes. "Fine, fine. *Rylan.*"

"I may let you get away with it at the office, but at home..."

She leaned in and patted his cheek. "My home, my nick-names."

He really had to convince Kate to let him stay with her. Soon.

Stepping back into her heels, Lexie gathered her things and made her way toward the door. She paused to check herself in the mirror, patting down the one hair that had dared to get out of place. "I'll probably be working late, so you're on your own for the evening. If you're staying here...?"

He nodded and sighed. "For the foreseeable future."

It ached, and not because he didn't love his sister. This apart-ment just really wasn't where he wanted to be.

"You know," Lexie said, pausing with her hand on the door. "I ran into Chase at the gym this morning."

That got Rylan's attention. "Oh?"

"I hope you don't mind I told him you were back in town."

Rylan winced. "Was he pissed?"

"Find out for yourself. I told him you'd give him a call."

Great. "Roger that."

She blew him a kiss that was only 90 percent sarcasm.

Once she was gone, he picked up the detritus from their lunch and flopped down on the couch again, firing up his tablet. But the aftermath of his sister was the aftermath of a storm, and it suddenly felt too quiet, the space around him pressing in.

Different day, different continent. He'd traveled miles and hours, but some things you didn't leave behind. A hollowness that had been echoing around inside him since...since forever really, but with a new sharpness to it ever since that summer, cut into him.

He huffed out a breath and sat up to reach for his phone. He pulled up his contacts and, for the longest time, hovered with his thumb above Kate's number.

But she'd asked him for time, goddammit all. Worse, he'd only convinced her to promise him a handful of nights, and he didn't have a plan yet for them. If he wanted to make them all count, he needed to get his head on straight. He needed a strategy.

He scrubbed his hand across his face. Maybe what he really needed was a drink.

Chase was already seated at the bar by the time Rylan got there, a square-cut glass with two fingers of amber liquid set out in front of him. His coppery hair was a little longer than it had been the last time Rylan had seen him, but nothing else seemed to have changed—not the cut of his suit or the loose circle of his tie. Definitely not the smirk he wore as he chatted up the girl behind the bar.

Rylan made it almost all the way over before Chase caught sight of him in the mirror. Holding up a finger to the girl, he turned, but as he met Rylan's gaze, his smile slipped away.

Rylan braced himself. Tone was hard to read over text, and Chase's reply to Rylan's invitation had been carefully neutral, for all that it had been an acceptance.

The thing was, after his father's trial, Rylan had let absolutely everything go. His position at what was left of the company, his condo, his things. His friends. Most of them had been work buddies anyway, and his relationships with them had been strained since the indictment, when Rylan had first started closing himself and his anger away. But he'd known Chase since prep school. Chase hadn't deserved the cold shoulder or the unreturned calls.

The shit he must've gotten from everyone over at Gander and Sons when their biggest client had turned into a cautionary tale. He hadn't deserved any of it.

Rylan opened his mouth to speak, but before he could get so much as a greeting out, Chase reared back, his hand curling up into a fist.

So that was how it was going to be.

Rylan went stiff, but he didn't raise a hand to defend himself. He had this coming. His stomach dropped as Chase lunged.

Except Chase pulled his punch, and in the end all Rylan got was a soft jab to his upper arm.

Chase grinned like they were fourteen all over again. "You asshole," he said, and then he pulled Rylan into a hug.

Relief just about dripped from Rylan's pores. "Jerk." He thumped Chase's back before they both let go.

"You don't write, you don't call. And then I hear from your sister of all people that you're back in town?"

"Sorry about that." Rylan settled himself on the stool beside Chase's and gestured at his drink. The bartender nodded and got going pouring him one of his own. "In my defense, I've been back now for"—he checked his watch—"thirty-two hours?"

"Excuses."

"Anything else I can get you boys?" the bartender asked.

Chase shot her a smile as he sat back down. "Besides your number?"

"Besides that."

"Can't blame a guy for trying." Chase waved her away. "We're good."

Rylan waited until she'd moved down the bar to shake his head. "You never turn it off, do you?"

"Like you do?"

With a sad chuckle, Rylan picked up his drink. "Not sure I remember how to turn it on anymore."

Chase did a double take. "Wait. I'm sorry, I thought I was meeting Rylan Bellamy for drinks."

Rylan shrugged. He and Chase had gotten into a lot of trouble together in their day, but things changed. He had changed.

He set his glass down and managed a smile. "So what the hell have you been up to?"

As it turned out, Chase had been up to kind of a lot. Gander and Sons had been growing like crazy, even after the fallout from the Bellamy scandal. They'd stayed on as general counsel for Rylan's father's company, though Chase had mostly moved on to other accounts.

Rylan shook his head. "I'm still sorry about that. If I'd had any idea what the old man was doing..."

"No one knew."

But Rylan should have.

Rylan caught a glimpse of his own face in the mirror behind the bar, and hell. He glanced away, working to smooth out his expression, to wipe the poison from his mouth.

Chase paused for a second. Apparently sensing the need for a change of subject, he segued into an account of all the shit their social set had been getting into in the past year. Heiresses and moguls. Hushed whispers and betrayals. Rylan'd always had a vague sense of all the goings-on before, but hearing it in summary was worse than a soap opera.

"Damn." He shook his head. This was the stuff Kate feared, maybe. The detachment from reality. The waste. All of a sudden, his throat threatened to close. He coughed, then drained his drink.

Chase quirked a brow.

"You ever stop and think about how ridiculous our lives are?" Rylan asked, voice dark. When Chase didn't answer, Rylan motioned with his hand as if he could encapsulate the whole of it. "The who's-sleeping-with-who and the"—he gestured at Chase—"the suits." He didn't know what this glass of whiskey cost, but he could guess. "Even going to a place like this." One you needed an invitation and a trust fund to get access to, all dark wood paneling and crystal. "The games." Bitterness flooded his mouth.

Kate would hate it.

For a long, long moment, Chase sized him up. Then he tipped his own glass back. Setting it down, he tapped the rim.

As if she'd been waiting for the signal—because she had been, of course she had—the bartender swooped in, silent and efficient as she refilled them.

Once she'd retreated, Chase turned to Rylan again. "You always did have a shit way of looking at things."

Rylan just about choked. "Excuse me?"

"You remember how we met?"

What did that have to do with anything?

"Because I do," Chase said. "Christ, you were a little shit back then. It was our first year at Exeter, wasn't it?" At Rylan's nod, he continued on. "I was heading out of the locker room after soccer practice, minding my own business, when I stumble upon this kid. All of, what, fourteen years old? Five foot three and a hundred pounds, and beating the hell out of a punching bag, and do you remember why?"

Rylan did. Even though it was the good stuff, his next pull at his whiskey burned.

"Because your daddy got you a nice room without a room-mate, and you were *convinced* you were missing out. Like there was some lifelong connection you weren't going to make or something."

It seemed so ridiculous now. But he'd been told by the sons of his father's friends that going off to boarding school meant roommates.

It meant not being alone.

"Only you." Chase shook his head. "Any other guy would be thrilled to have a safe place to jerk off without some mouth breather snoring in the other bunk. And nothing's changed, has it?"

"Because I still get to jerk off in private?"

Chase wiped the condensation from his glass and flicked it at Rylan's face. "Poor little tiny teenage Bellamy. He has a rich daddy and has to go to a fancy school and have a room all to himself. What a burden."

Rylan grabbed a cocktail napkin from the bar and dabbed at the droplets on his cheek. "Fuck off."

"Poor grown-up, stick-up-his-ass Bellamy. His life is so terrible he has to run off to Paris for a year—"

"I said *fuck off*." It had been a mistake coming here. Reconnecting with the people from what had used to be his life. They didn't understand.

"Rylan. Dude." Chase caught his arm and gave him a shake. "Our life is *awesome*. I mean, there's shit in it, don't get me wrong. We keep a lot of therapists in business. But we can afford to."

Rylan snorted into his whiskey. "Great."

"Stop acting like it's such a tragedy, having nice stuff, or access to nice places. Just enjoy it, for fuck's sake."

And something inside Rylan snapped. Guilt had been eating at him for so long, he wasn't sure there's was anything left to gnaw. He'd fucked up with Kate, and he'd left his sister to fend for herself as she kept his damn birthright afloat. He'd let Kate's reaction to who he really was turn from guilt to shame, let her kick him out of her bed because she couldn't handle it. Couldn't handle *him*, even when he'd given his all to her.

When she'd decided the real him wasn't enough.

His glass made a cracking sound as he slammed it down too hard against the bar. "Fine." He looked to Chase. Maybe he was right. Maybe it was time to let it all go and enjoy himself, at least for a little while. Time to stop letting his own life weigh him down. "And how, precisely, would you suggest I do that?"

The corner of Chase's mouth twitched up. "I have a couple of ideas."

Chase's first idea was another, bigger glass of liquor, and after that, all of his ideas started to sound good. From the car service that took them to the other side of town to the even more exclusive club, the hundred Chase tucked into a greeter's palm and the velvet booth they slotted themselves into. The music thrummed, and there were girls. Beautiful girls, and there'd been a time, not that long ago, when they would have seemed like good ideas, too.

With a particularly busty one perched on his lap and another drink in his hand, Chase shot Rylan a raw, sloppy smile from across their booth. "See?" he shouted over the roar of the club. "Tell me this isn't awesome."

And Rylan took it all in. The girls were nice as hell to look at, even if he wasn't going to touch. Big tits and tiny skirts. The cushions were soft against his back, and the whiskey so damn smooth.

His neck didn't want to hold itself up, but it wasn't like the last time he'd gotten himself wasted. Everything felt good.

He let his head loll backward and stared up at a ceiling made up in blue velvet and stars. "It does not suck."

Chase jostled the girl and his drink both with the force of his laughter. "Finally." He kissed the girl's cheek. "My buddy admitted something doesn't suck." He pulled back, his hand drifting higher on her thigh. "I bet you do, though."

Shit, but the girl was eating it up.

Chase caught Rylan's eye. "What do you say?" He bounced his knee, and the girl bounced, too. So much bouncing. "For old time's sake."

It had been a long time since the two of them had shared a girl. It had been good, though. It'd be good.

But his gut turned over. He shook his head and his vision swam. He closed his eyes. "I don't think so, man."

Time went sideways on him then for a while, and the next thing he knew, Chase was leaning forward across the table, his entertainment for the evening gone. He pressed a bottle of water into Rylan's hand, already open, thank fuck. Rylan got it to his mouth and sucked the cool, cool liquid down. It made his stomach feel worse but his head a little better.

"Come on," Chase said.

Chase got him out the door—how? He'd had almost as much to drink as Rylan had. They didn't have to wait long for the car to collect them, and about a second after Rylan's face hit the plush leather of the backseat, he was drifting, imagining soft fingers in his hair.

Fingers that couldn't be there. A sharp stab of panic had him lifting his head.

He hadn't done anything, but she wouldn't like this. Not any of it.

He scrambled, looking around, but it was only him and

Chase. "Don't tell Kate," he managed to get out, and even that was the wrong answer, wasn't it? He was supposed to tell her everything now.

Chase laughed. "What happens in Vegas, buddy."

He set his head back down. The next time he opened his eyes, the world was a bit less blurry, and the car had stopped. Chase opened the door and coaxed Rylan along. "Pretty sure you should bunk with me tonight. Lexie'd have my head if I let you go back to her place now."

Ugh, Rylan wasn't going to argue him on that.

Chase's apartment at least was still more or less the same as Rylan remembered, open and airy, with rock album covers on the wall and the sleekest, prettiest baby grand in a corner. Flagging, Rylan dropped himself into one of the bar stools set up by the counter. He caught a glimpse of the time and groaned. "Shit, is it really that late?" Another hour and late would officially be early. Chase was hardly going to get any sleep at all.

"Yup. Coffee?"

Rylan nodded. "I'm sorry, man."

"We've done worse."

Chase didn't stop at coffee. He got some eggs and toast going, too, and by the time Rylan'd gotten all of that and a handful of Advil down, he was almost feeling human again.

"So," Chase said, leaning back in his stool. "You want to tell me what that shit show was about?"

"Not really. If you want to go try and grab a couple of hours..."

"Better just to stay up at this point." And he wasn't wrong; already, the sky was starting to lighten through the window. Then his face was in Rylan's. "Now stop avoiding the question. Talk."

But Rylan's breath was frozen. He'd been alone for what felt like so long, living in this self-imposed exile, and maybe he hadn't had to. Chase had tried to show him tonight, hadn't he? This life he hated didn't have to suck. He didn't have to be alone.

"Fuck." He dropped his head into his hands. "It's just . . . It's all so messed up."

"What's so messed up?"

"I . . ." Finally, he looked up. And the frozen piece of him cracked. "I met this girl."

After that, it all spilled out. He kept the details to himself—what Kate felt like in his hands and on his tongue, how his whole body quaked at the triumph of bringing her to a new height. But in generalities, he laid it out. Meeting this woman who'd seen through so much of his bullshit and through the emptiness he'd surrounded himself with. Who loved art and who'd made him want more.

How it had all come tumbling down as soon as she'd found out who and what he was.

"She says she wants to know who I really am, but she hates the money. She doesn't care about the company or my family or any of it."

That had been the appeal, at the beginning. It'd been such a relief to have someone like him for *him*, and not the trappings. But now the trappings were keeping them apart.

"What the fuck does she even want from me, you know?"

"Take it from me," Chase finally chimed in, clinking his mug against Rylan's. "The exact opposite of whatever the hell you seem to think she does."

"What?"

"It's how girls work. You know this."

He didn't. He was starting to think he didn't know anything.

"How many times have we picked up chicks with a round of drinks or a ride in a fancy car? They turn to butter in your hands, man. Don't you remember?"

"Those girls were different." He'd never felt like this about any of them.

Chase's mouth flattened, a grim line. His voice went eerily cold. "Girls. Are. All. The. Same."

And for a second, it was like that awful night a few years ago. The night Chase had driven all the way back to New York, hardly seeing straight, blowing off his classes, ready to blow off law school entirely, because his fiancée—his ex-fiancée had jumped into bed with someone even richer...

Rylan swallowed. "Not all of them."

A long moment passed, but then the harsh lines to Chase's face smoothed out. He let out this echo of a laugh and turned to gaze at his mug. "Enough of them." When he twisted around enough for Rylan to see him again, the deadness to his eyes was less jarring, his tone more even. "They just. They're raised on Disney princesses, you know? You joke about all the bullshit drama with heiresses, but the rest of them? They all want their prince to show up in his carriage." He glanced at Rylan with a sad, flickering smile. "They want the fantasy."

"You think?"

"I bet you. She may say she doesn't want it, but I dare you. Give her the rich guy cliché experience. If she doesn't swoon I'll...I'll..." He searched for a second, then snapped his fingers. "I'll give you a weekend with Betty. A week, even."

"Betty?" Rylan sat up straighter at that.

There was nothing—absolutely nothing—Chase was more protective of than his car. As crazy as his advice sounded, he was serious.

"Betty." Chase nodded, like that was that. "I keep trying to tell you, Ry. It's like everything else with this life. You can wallow in the parts of it that suck, or you can embrace the good parts." He gestured around at his apartment, and the contrast with Lexie's took Rylan off guard, now that he was looking for it.

Lexie had spent her money paying someone to make it look like she had taste. Chase had spent his exuberantly, with relish, on things he loved. His cars and his piano, his view of the city and his books.

He enjoyed it.

"Embrace the money," Chase said. "Show her how good it can be. And I promise you. She'll change her tune."

The cynicism behind that promise was a thickness at the back of Rylan's throat. Kate had entranced him because she was different. If Chase was right, it would mean she was really the same.

But what other choice did he have? If they were going to make this work, she had to know him in and out.

The good. The bad.

And was it really all that wrong? Wanting to show her the best parts first?

chapter SIX

Wrong, wrong, wrong, it was all *wrong*. Kate didn't actually throw her paintbrush across the room, but it was a near thing.

With a huff, she dropped the brush into a jar of turpentine and turned away.

Sacred spaces. She'd been working all week to home in on that theme, had even gone out and scouted more locations, filling up the memory card of her crappy camera with photographs of Brooklyn churches. The scene she was working from now had so much potential—gorgeous, ethereal light slanting down through leaves onto old stone. She'd had all these ideas for layering thin washes of pigment on the canvas to make the space shine. To make it look sacred. Reverent.

She blew out a sigh. Maybe the result wasn't as bad as she imagined it was.

Holding her breath, she spun back around. And tears welled up in her eyes. Damn. It was even *worse*. The proportions and the perspective were fine, but there wasn't any heart to it. Lifeless and flat, the image stared back at her, evoking no emotional reaction from her at all.

She clenched her hands into fists. Fine. She'd set it aside for now. She'd been working here in her apartment for hours now, and she wasn't thinking straight anymore. Tomorrow, she'd be able to come at it with fresh eyes.

But first. Tonight.

Crossing her arms over her chest, she leaned against the wall, letting her head drop back to rest against it. Exhaustion fell over her, and she closed her eyes.

Rylan had waited forever to call, and it had been a relief and a disappointment. Until finally, exactly three days after he'd turned her life inside out, he'd invited her to a night on the town, dinner "someplace nice" and a show. He hadn't volunteered any more details, and she'd been so close to throwing her hands up in the air and calling the whole thing off. His ridiculous, pointless plan for them to try again—to really get to know each other this time. It'd never work.

But then she'd remembered the weight of his hips pressed to hers, the warmth of his breath on her skin, his lips at her ear, the hot fullness as he'd eased inside. The way he'd looked on a hotel bed in Paris, smooth skin lit up by the dappled sun.

She'd said yes.

Two hours from now, he'd be showing up at her doorstep. And yet here she was, still in her painting clothes, hair in a ponytail. Two hours—that was how long she had to fix this.

No way he was catching her unawares this time. He'd had the upper hand at every turn, but tonight she'd be prepared. She'd let him take her out, show her "his New York," whatever that meant. She'd follow him home to his place, or maybe she'd bring him here. Then she'd ask him to put his mouth between her legs again, because the thought, the sense memory of it alone, had her clenching up inside. They'd—

They'd fuck, and it would be amazing. That part didn't scare her anymore.

And after, they would each go home. Alone. She wouldn't fall in love with him again. She had it all planned out.

What she hadn't planned for was the buzzer going off while she was still cleaning up.

She swore beneath her breath and finished rinsing out the last brush before scrambling for the intercom. If this was Rylan and he was two full hours early, she was going to strangle him.

"Delivery for Ms. Reid?"

She wasn't expecting a delivery. "Um. Okay." Usually, she'd buzz the person up, but this was weird. "I'll be right down."

It wasn't Rylan standing beyond the entryway, but it didn't take a genius to figure out he was behind it. She opened the door to find not your typical bike messenger or UPS guy, but a...a...She wasn't even sure. He wore the sort of hat chauffeurs did in movies, and a suit.

When she cracked the door open, he presented her with an armful of flowers, too many red roses to count. Perfect blooms. Gorgeous and generic, and she tried not to let that disappoint her. Rylan had brought her a single rose on their second date, had twirled it between his fingers as he'd waited for her in a sculpture garden on a Parisian afternoon, and she'd been charmed by it. This wasn't quite so charming.

Then she registered the other item in the man's grip and frowned. A garment bag?

He held it up. "Compliments of Mr. Bellamy, ma'am."

Right.

She somehow managed to take it all from him and wrestle it upstairs. She draped the bag across her bed and set the flowers down beside her palette. With uncertain fingers, she combed through the blooms until she came up with a card, printed on thick ivory stock. The good stuff. She couldn't remember if she'd ever seen Rylan's handwriting before, but the bold black strokes of ink looked like him.

A couple of options for you for this evening. Only if you like them, though.

See you soon . . . —TRB.

Her blood went to ice. Mechanically, she walked away from the flowers and toward the garment bag. Sure enough, inside were dresses. Three of them, none with price tags. She probably couldn't have borne it if they had.

She squeezed her eyes shut tight. He was trying to be nice here. He wasn't making a comment on the awful work jeans he'd peeled from her body with such disdain, or about the rest of her wardrobe. He was taking her out to see *his* New York tonight, and of course that meant dressing up. If she hadn't had anything appropriate, she would've felt just as uncomfortable as she did now, only she would've had to feel it in front of him.

Scrubbing at her eyes, she laughed. There was a cocktail dress she'd bought at a secondhand store for a gallery reception last year, buried somewhere in the back of her closet. She might even still have her prom dress in there, if she really went digging. But that was it.

He'd been right, sending her these. And it made something deep inside of her echo even more hollowly to acknowledge it.

This was him changing her. Improving her. Recognizing that she didn't have what it took, literally, to pass in his world. Her stomach churned, but she wrestled hard against the rising tide.

This wasn't her father telling her she wasn't good enough, or Aaron implying she'd never be as successful as him. This was Rylan being *nice*. She opened her eyes and sighed.

A week and a half ago, Rylan had been on another continent, had given her no sign of his intent to ever return. And yet he'd never felt farther away than he did right now.

Dread sat like a stone inside her, but what else could she do? She got herself into the shower and washed up mechanically, then blew her hair out and did her makeup with a towel wrapped around her chest.

Finally, with half an hour to go and no more excuses to delay, she faced down the dresses. Pulled them from the bag one by one and looked them over.

A little bit of the heaviness in her gut eased. There was a simple black number, and a strapless gray one. One in midnight blue that was a little showier, clear crystals sewn into the hem, but all of them were things she could at least imagine wearing. If she were a millionaire.

He'd known her taste, more or less, and he'd guessed her size. He'd misjudged who she was entirely, but at least the details he'd gotten right.

She laughed, sad and wry, then let the towel fall. She tried on each dress in turn. They were all gorgeous, all beautifully made. When she looked at herself in the mirror, wearing the blue one, she sucked in a breath.

Maybe it was the cut of it, the fitted bodice and the floaty skirt that came to just above her knees. Maybe it was the neckline, ever so slightly asymmetrical and lower than she would usually dare. She looked taller and slimmer, her chest more full.

It was a good look. Like a princess.

A princess who couldn't get the ink out from under her nails.

Decided, she turned away.

By the time the buzzer went off downstairs, she'd picked out a pair of kitten heels, a wrap, and a little clutch purse. Heart in her throat, she made her way to the entrance of her building, and...

Oh God.

At least it wasn't a limo. But the car Rylan was leaning against was one of the biggest, shiniest, blackest ones she'd ever seen, its windows tinted, and yup. That was a driver sitting behind the wheel.

Rylan stepped away from the door of the car, crossing the space toward her, and her eyes stung. He looked too good, too handsome in another, somehow even more elegant suit. The fabric faintly shone in the dying light. His hair was slicked back.

And that was the thing that made her pause.

He'd always worn his hair casually distressed, and she had loved it. Loved running her fingers through its thickness, or raking her nails across the scalp. Holding on to it for dear life, tugging hard at the roots as he showed her yet another new thing her body could do.

Her skin crackled with electricity as he closed in on her. He held out a hand, and she followed it up, past the crisp lines of his jacket to his face.

His jaw was firm, the space between his brows smooth. But his eyes...

Her heart sped, ramming hard against the cage of her ribs. Those warm blue irises contracted. Like—like he was scared. Fully in control of it, but terrified.

And then all at once, he blinked and the fear was gone, replaced by calm command. He reached his arm the rest of the way out, curling his fingers in to brush his knuckles down the side of her cheek. Sending licks of warmth blooming outward from his touch.

His fingertips grazed along her neck and came to rest at the open neckline of her dress. His throat bobbed.

"You look ravishing."

Her voice came out breathy, and her knees shook. "As good as you'd hoped?"

"Better." Something in his expression softened. Went more real. "But then again, you have a habit of blowing my wildest dreams out of the water."

He didn't lean in to claim the kiss that kind of line all but demanded. Just stood there, thumb stroking beneath her collarbone, gaze intent to the point of searing.

Then the moment broke, and he pulled away. Nodding toward the car, he held out his open palm. "Shall we?"

It wasn't as big of a leap as following him to a museum, or back to a hotel room. Or letting him inside her. She took a deep breath. And placed her hand in his.

Rylan was *not* doing this just for the chance to make Chase watch him cruise around in his Bentley. He was doing this because the money had been coming between him and Kate since day one, since the first moment he'd looked her over and seen her pride and decided not to bring it up.

Well, he was bringing it up now.

The rich guy cliché experience, Chase had called it. Rylan was set to do him proud.

Yet a sick feeling kept twisting his gut.

What if this was Versailles all over again? Something he'd

thought she might enjoy—something he'd imagined any girl should like. But she wasn't any girl.

Getting the door for her, he pushed his nerves down. She scooted across the leather seat like any good New Yorker accustomed to cabs would. Instead of going around to the other side like he would've otherwise, he folded himself in beside her, pulling the door closed and nodding at their driver.

As they coasted off, she looked around, keen gaze taking in all the details of the car's interior. Then, at last, it came to rest on him.

"So." She was sitting on the other side of the seat, practically as far away as she could get. But her body language was open, for all that her shoulders were a fraction too high. Relaxed but guarded. Ready for this to go south.

He wouldn't let it, goddammit all.

He slid a hand toward her, letting his knuckles graze the bare skin of her knee, right below the hem of the dress. "So."

She lifted a brow. "Thank you for the dress. And the flowers."

"You liked them."

Her mouth did something complicated before smoothing into an uncertain smile. "I did. You didn't have to, though."

"But I wanted to." He licked his lips. "Only the best."

"Of course."

For a long moment, they stared at each other. He wanted nothing more than to move into her space, to kiss her and feel her warmth all along his side. To hold her.

That summer, he wouldn't have resisted, but rejection still stung him. She'd left him in Paris, and she'd turned him out last week. He'd been the one to come back for her, and he still had apologies to make, but this was a grand gesture he was in the middle of.

And a deep, proud, hopeless place inside his chest wanted her to reach for him for once. She'd acquiesced and gone along with what he wanted so many times.

He wanted her to want him, too. For her to touch him because she wanted to. To make the first move.

She dropped her gaze, broke their stare. And turned toward the window.

Voice tight, she asked, "Any chance you're going to tell me what we're doing tonight?"

He pulled his hand from her leg. Settled it on his own and jostled his knee up and down. Outside the car, the city rolled by, gray streets giving way to brighter thoroughfares as they approached the bridge. "Thought I might let it be a surprise."

She hummed but didn't argue. Didn't tease.

He second-guessed himself a hundred times before they arrived at the restaurant he'd picked. It was just right for a romantic evening, all candlelight and quiet booths, excellent food. But the closer they got, the more his gut told him it was entirely wrong.

Her posture got stiffer as he led her inside. The maître d' recognized him on sight and greeted them with a smile. They were led to a cozy corner, given menus and a wine list, and left alone. Rylan swallowed hard, hating the silence. Hating everything.

Then Kate opened her menu, scanned it over once, jaw ticking, and he held his breath. But she didn't explode, or break down laughing the way he'd half expected her to. The way he'd been waiting for her to maybe this entire time. She closed the menu and set it down. Looked to him.

Her dry voice bore the tiniest hint of a tremor. "Let me guess. Your treat?"

"If you'll let me," he said, aiming for assuredness, but it came out weak.

And there was that snicker of a laugh. "Not sure I have much choice. I know what dishwashers get paid by the hour."

Of course she did. She was a waitress, right? When she wasn't working on her art.

He couldn't stand it a minute longer. He wanted her to reach for him, but here he was again, extending his arm across the table, placing his hand over hers, and the contact made him sing with relief. At the same time that something inside him went unbearably, impossibly sad.

"I want you to enjoy yourself, Kate. Have whatever you like. I want to give this to you." This experience. This night.

Her chest rose and fell. But after a second, she nodded. "All right."

She didn't stumble over her order when their server came around, didn't even argue when Rylan asked for a bottle of wine.

If only Rylan knew if that was a good sign or not.

Kate had never had a more delicious, more painfully tense meal in her life.

It was a pathetic movie trope, the unsophisticated girl who didn't even know what fork to use, but tropes were tropes for a reason. Kate worked her way in from the outside of the place setting like the etiquette teacher in some trite old film had instructed his plucky heroine to do, and she hoped for the best. Drank her wine and ate the world's most amazing, most shockingly expensive steak.

Through it all, Rylan kept looking at her, not with the apprehension he'd had in his eyes as he'd shown her to the car, but with something almost worse.

When they were done, he paid the bill without even looking at it, and led her out. Their car was already waiting. She held her breath. "Where to now?"

Rylan ushered her in, but closed the door before she could slide across to the other side. Oh. Right. Because this was a nice car. A nice dress. Only she wasn't very nice at all.

He got in on the other side and made a gesture at their driver to wait. They stayed there idling at the curb, quiet music and the muted sounds of the traffic filtering in, but the silence felt like it would strangle her all the same.

Rylan turned the full power of his gaze on her. "I have tickets for the ballet."

She tried to hide the way her eyes wanted to bug out of her skull. "The ballet?"

He'd said they'd be heading to a show, but that was the last thing she'd been expecting. The corner of his mouth twitched. "You don't want to go." It wasn't even a question.

"I didn't say that. I just—I've never *gone*." The small-town performance of *The Nutcracker* when she was eight didn't count.

"We don't have to."

And he sounded so resigned. So disappointed.

What had this whole evening looked like to him? She'd barely remembered to thank him for his extravagant gifts, been too worried about embarrassing herself at his fancy restaurant to make much more than small talk with him. And now she was turning up her nose at something he must've thought she'd like.

Her hand hovered in the air, poised to reach for him and touch the warmth of his skin. But in the end she chickened out.

Set it back down in her lap and chewed the inside of her lip. "Yes," she said, more confident than she felt. "We do."

"No." He shook his head.

So she spoke over him. "I'd like to." She forced a smile. "First time for everything, right?"

His gaze darted to hers, and there was that fire. That light that had been missing this entire night. "Yeah?"

"Sure," she said, more firm.

At least it was worth a shot.

chapter SEVEN

About five *years* later, Kate couldn't decide what was worse—the ballet, that she apparently hated the ballet, or that Rylan gave every sign of hating it, too.

It'd been pretty enough. Degas's pastel studies of dancers had come to mind with every arched back and pointed toe. She could imagine drawing those graceful forms herself, trying to capture the energy and motion, the space and the sparkle.

But to sit there in a secluded box, alone and yet surrounded by all these other men and women in outfits even more formal than hers and Rylan's, watching a story without words, listening to music she felt no connection to... They'd barely made it through the first act, or movement, or whatever it was called before Rylan was squirming. He wasn't the only one. Restlessness had had her digging her own nails into her palms to help her sit still.

There were just so many other things she could be doing. Her portfolio for the fellowship committee wasn't going to assemble itself, and her apartment needed cleaning. Hell, catching up on her sleep would've been a better use of her time. She almost did, she got so bored.

As the performance dragged on, she folded in on herself more and more, crossing her arms and then her legs, and even that seemed like such a waste. She and Rylan had never really been to a show before. She'd always figured he'd have been all over her if they had, fingertips trailing over her arm, lips whispering kisses against her ear, their feet tangling together in the space between the seats.

But he kept to his side of their armrest, face stony, jaw set. Like he knew as well as she did that this had been a mistake.

The frustration of it all, the waste, made her grit her teeth. He'd made it out like this was important to him, and now they were simmering in their own pots of separate, stubborn endurance, seeing it through.

God. What if that was how their whole second chance went? Seven nights—five more after this. If they went the same way this one had...

She couldn't bear it. They'd had a good run of it in Paris, but she'd said it herself even then. They'd been living in a fantasy, divorced from the pressures of real life, and some dreams couldn't stand up to the light. He'd shattered her dream well enough when he'd admitted to being a whole different person than he'd led her to believe, and maybe they should've let it end like that.

They hadn't, though. He'd picked up the fragments and held them up as if they could glue them back together. Sought her out and begged her for more, and she'd let herself be convinced.

But what was the point? Of any of it?

She wasn't so ill-mannered as to not applaud when the curtain finally fell. Rylan made the same motions beside her. She avoided his gaze as he ushered her out. His car was one of the first in line outside, and they got in without a word. Sat there together and apart as his driver wove through the theater traffic and off into the grid of city streets.

At her apartment building, she got out and crossed her arms, rubbing her bare skin against the evening chill. Rylan got out as well, and she opened her mouth. She'd had that whole long, awful car ride to figure out what to say, and she'd practiced it the same way she'd practiced her French. It came to about as much good.

Look, this clearly isn't working. Or, *Thank you, it was nice, but* . . .

Then she met the dark power of his stare as he rounded the back of the car, and the words evaporated on her tongue.

"I'll walk you up," he said, voice gruff, tone clipped.

It should have been a relief, to hear the same frustration from him that she felt in her heart, but it only made her stomach sink farther.

"Right." She turned toward her building. It would be better to do this in private.

So she led him inside.

The easy letdown was almost a taste on the air, a scent like dry tinder at the back of Rylan's throat.

The whole way up the stairs, Kate had dragged her heels. At the door to her apartment, she fumbled with her keys until he stepped forward and took them from her to get the lock himself. She walked inside with her shoulders tense, her fingers white where she gripped her own arms. Rylan's breath stuttered in his chest.

Since halfway through the disaster that had been the ballet, he'd been scrambling, trying to figure out a way to spin this. But he'd come up empty.

Closing the door behind them, he held out her keys. She stepped in close, and his heart pounded. At the touch of her fingertips to his, something inside of him broke.

This was it.

The jagged metal dug into his palm, probably into hers as well, but he didn't care. He caught her hand in his, twisting their fingers together. Her pulse seared into him, and he shook his head at the way her lips parted. He didn't need to hear it, whatever it was she'd been working up to telling him. He knew.

"I fucked up."

Her eyes went wide, jaw going slack.

"It— I thought—" He stopped. What had he thought? Besides all the wrong things? "I should have known."

"Rylan—"

"I thought I could give you the fantasy." A laugh bubbled up, harsh and painful in his throat. "I always knew you'd hate the money, but it's not going away, Kate. It doesn't have to be a bad thing. I thought I could show you that."

"By flaunting it around?"

"By giving you a nice night." He let her go then, and it hurt, how fast she pulled away, keys secure in her grasp. Leaving him inside her home but still on the outside, with no idea how to work her locks. "You like art, and the ballet..."

She winced. "It was a nice thought?"

A thought he'd had without any consideration for who she was.

"The ballet was a mistake."

She'd put her back to the opposite wall. Her chest rose with the force of her breath, her breasts on display in a way they never would be normally, pushed up and out by the bodice of that dress he'd sent her. The trappings he'd asked her to wear. Her voice cracked. "The thing is..." She blinked, lifting her gaze to the ceiling. "What bothered me was that you didn't like it, either." Finally, she looked at him. "Did you?"

He'd promised he would never lie to her again. "I liked sitting next to you in the dark."

"Hardly. You couldn't have been any farther away without buying another seat."

The accusation stung.

Worse, it was true.

The corner of his lips trembled, until the smile he'd tried to force became a false, flickering thing. "You didn't exactly seem to want to be touched."

It was in every line of the way she'd held herself, the rigid set to her limbs as she'd occupied that seat.

"What did you want? An engraved invitation?" She gestured at herself. "I wore the dress you wanted, went to the show you said you picked out for me. I tried."

She'd tried so hard to fit herself to the shape he'd outlined for her, the...

A light went on inside his mind. A harsh, too-bright bulb illuminating the ugly corners he hadn't wanted to see.

It was fucking Chase, telling him all women were the same, all wanted the same damn thing. It was him, latching on to that idea, because he didn't know how else to make this work.

"I put you in a box," he said, suddenly numb. Her brows furrowed, and he bit down on the inside of his cheek. But the pain didn't help.

"You..."

"I like you." Another verb sat on his tongue. Another way to look at everything he'd done, and he wasn't fooling himself about how he felt. He didn't think he had been. But the word was too big for them right now. Too much. He raked a hand through his hair, mussing it up. It'd been too perfect. Everything he'd planned for them had been. He'd just been too blind to see it until now. "I like you more than I've liked anyone before."

It'd taken him all of three days to figure that out, their first time around. He'd been so clever, picking things he'd known she'd love, tiny hole-in-the-wall restaurants and neglected wings of famous museums. And then as soon as he'd realized her value, her worth—the moment he'd grasped the uniqueness of her—

He'd started to treat her like everyone else. First Versailles, and then this. Outings designed to impress, when he'd never had to. When he could have treated her like *herself*.

He tugged even harder at his hair. "This is what I know." Letting go, he pointed to her and to the dresses lying discarded across her bed.

It was how people in his life showed they cared. A fancy new car instead of a pat on the back.

"And you're better than all of it," he said.

For the first time since he'd picked her up, her gaze softened. Her shoulders dropped. "Just—is it—is that what you want? Boring nights at shows you don't even care about? Stuffy dinners?" She plucked at the neckline of her dress. "Clothes you can't *breathe* in? For yourself? For me?" Her voice faltered. "For us?"

That she still might think there was a chance for an *us* made him bold. "No."

"Then what do you want?"

And wasn't that just the question? It'd driven him to another continent, driven him to waste an entire year, refusing to decide. Nothing had changed in that time.

And at the same time, everything had.

When he didn't answer, she pushed off the wall. "I'm not your manic pixie dream girl, Rylan. I won't solve everything for you." A shiver racked her frame. "And I won't let you turn me into yet another thing that's bound to bore you by the end."

He couldn't imagine it.

"Never."

"Then what do you *want*? Not what do you think you're supposed to want, what you think I should want. What do you want?"

The question hit him in the center of his chest.

The day Kate had left, she'd told him he needed to make some decisions about his life. She'd hated him for lying to her about who he was, but she'd called him out on lying to himself, as well. The accusation had burned like a bullet lodged in his lungs for months.

Until a week ago, nursing a hangover and staring lovelorn at her sketchbook, when he'd finally figured it out.

"So many things," he said, choking on lead. "I've made such a mess." With his father's company and with his family and with her. "I came back here to fix it all, but I don't know how."

"I told you. It's going to take time—"

He shook his head. "Not just between us." This, here, between the two of them was the most important piece, but it was far from the only one. "My father's company is a wreck. Lexie's been doing her best, but if we want to save it, then I have to step up and play a part, and I don't—I don't know if I can put myself back in that box."

His father had built this kingdom, and he had groomed him to become his heir. Rylan wanted to have hope again, to try again, but returning to New York had him stepping right back into the role and the life he'd been running away from in the first place.

But he didn't have to be that man. He didn't have to do things the way they'd always been done.

"I've been trying old solutions to old problems," he said, a light beginning to dawn. "With you and with my family, and they won't work. Things have to change. *I* have to change."

This night had been a failure of the most epic proportions. But maybe it was an opportunity, too.

"I have to start over again."

He had to start with her.

In a half dozen strides, he crossed the room. Standing before her, he fit his hands to the cool, smooth skin of her shoulders, and he cursed himself. Stupid, sending her these tiny dresses, not a one of them with proper sleeves. All night, she must have been freezing. Well, he'd warm her up all right. Her body seemed to go to liquid beneath his palms, and it filled him with a rush of power, a certainty the likes of which he hadn't felt since he'd gotten on that plane and come a supplicant to her door.

The flimsy cover of her shawl hit the floor, and a gasp left her lips as he spun her. With her back to him, he dropped his brow to the top of her head and took a moment. Soaked in the shape of her against him, the sweet, soft scent of her skin. The fact that she was still here, that he was still here. For now.

He sucked in a breath, then stooped to press his lips to the back of her neck, sweeping her hair out of the way. She trembled, and he closed his eyes.

He found the zipper that ran the length of her spine. Tooth by tooth, he pulled it down, stripping away the costume. "This." He chased the fabric from her arms, caressed her sides as the dress slid to the ground. "I want you like this."

A weak hint of a laugh passed her lips. "Naked?"

"Yes. No." Of course he wanted her bare, all that gorgeous skin laid out for him to kiss and touch and worship. But it was more than that. "I want you just the way you are." He left a trail of kisses along her shoulder and squeezed her waist. "Naked or clothed. Sexy dresses or ratty jeans." With his fingertips, he traced the edge of her hip, right above her panties. His throat went dry, his flesh stirring as she molded to his touch. "I want to take this night off of you."

"Then take it off yourself, too."

He had to squeeze his eyes shut tight. It wasn't mere arousal, wasn't only sex, though they seemed to be headed in that direction. Opening his eyes, he took his hands from her sides and brought them to his tie. He loosened it, pulled it over his head, and dropped it. The buttons on his shirt parted like water beneath his fingertips. Cuff links and jacket, belt and slacks and socks and shoes. She stayed just the way she was, her back to him, her whole body motionless but for her breath.

When he was down to his underwear, he paused. She was still in her heels, and low as they were, they changed the way they stood together, changed the height her head hit on his chest.

He sank to his knees. He'd been on them for her before, prepared to put his mouth on her or to beg her for another chance. Tonight, he slid the flats of his palms down the outsides of her thighs, curled his hands around her knees before dragging them lower. With his brow pressed to the back of her leg, he grasped her ankle. She got his hint when he fit his grip around her shoe. She lifted one foot and then the other for him.

When he rose again, it was to kiss every vertebra on his way up her spine. He stepped his bare feet to either side of hers and took her in his arms, pressing all of him to all of her. A wall in his mind collapsed, letting him really *feel* her, the curves and the edges, the smooth softness of her skin. The hard line of his cock met the small of her back, and just like that it was arousal. It was sex.

And it was so, so much more.

He turned her in his arms. Her makeup around her eyes was smudged, the edges damp, and she was so beautiful, it nearly brought him right back to his knees.

"Better?" he asked, the sound too raw.

She nodded, averting her gaze, staring at his chest instead of at his eyes, and that was wrong. He put a hand to her chin to lift it, only for her to reach up, to wrap her fingers around his own. She brought them to her lips, and it was fire, was a punch to the gut as she touched him.

He'd been so deliberate, every motion to peel away their clothes an act of sheer restraint, but all of that was gone now. With heat and a sudden need so bright it seared him to his bones, he let the hesitancy, the distance, fall away.

When he tilted her head up this time, it was to take her mouth, to possess it. She met him with a desperation he wasn't sure he understood, except that it resonated with his own.

"I'll do better," he mumbled, working to breathe past the slick glide of her tongue, the plush of her lips against his. "I promise." He cupped her neck, fit his thumb to the hollow of her jaw and held on. "But you have to let me."

He kissed her again until the stiffness in her limbs began to ease, then took a step toward her bed, guiding her along. When they reached the mattress, he shoved the other, discarded dresses to the floor. They fell in a clatter, and he didn't care. She didn't seem to, either.

At his prompting, she lay down in the center of the bed, a vision of creamy flesh and soft curves, dark hair in a cloud about her shoulders, and he could gaze at her all night, except that he was dying to touch, his hands shaking and cock screaming for it. Predatory, he settled above her with his knees caging her thighs, spine straight, arms braced. He gazed down at her. At her hands to either side of her head.

He paused. She'd put them there the last time, too, and he'd encouraged it, wanting her helpless to the pleasure his body could bring hers. But now it was different. Passive, like she had been all night, except to tell him she was mad at him.

Now, it felt wrong.

He shook his head, the words to explain too far away, too slippery. So instead of trying, he flipped them, getting himself flat on his back. Making it so he stared up at her.

Confusion marred her features, and his heart clenched. This was that skittishness he'd seen too many times before. He grabbed her by the arms before she could retreat or protest. He wanted to *shake* her.

"You have to let me do better." His throat chafed. "You have to *make* me do better."

He'd been the one to come to her, all right. Had crossed an ocean because she had shown him the holes in his own life. Because he knew he had to fill them but didn't know how to without her.

She'd agreed to give him another chance. But that was all she had done.

In another world, another life, she'd challenged him at every turn, calling him out on his bullshit and making fun of his terrible lines. He wanted *that* Kate. He wanted more limits than a refusal to let him spend the night. Than her voice, telling him she couldn't save him, that he had done everything wrong again. After. When it was already too late.

He might need to start over here, but he couldn't do it all on his own.

"You have to tell me what you want." He silenced her protests with a finger against her lips. "Don't just go along with me when I screw up." She never had before. He was finished with her acting like she had to now. He might've asked her for this chance to prove himself, but it couldn't all be for him to win or lose. "Do this *with* me. Together." His voice and his heart both cracked. "Or." Fuck. He shouldn't say this. Shouldn't even think it.

But there it was pouring out of him regardless.

"Or what's the point in us doing this at all?"

chapter EIGHT

Kate reeled.

Rylan lay beneath her, his gaze pleading, his words hanging in the air and pressing hard against her heart. Making the breath in her lungs go thick.

What's the point in us doing this at all?

An ugly laugh threatened her throat. How close had she been to asking him that herself? They'd walked in the door, and she'd had it on the tip of her tongue. She'd been so ready to lay into him for wasting both their time.

And now what? He was mad at her for *letting* him screw this up?

Ice flashed through her bones. For one lilting, awful moment, she was back in her father's home again, where everything was her fault, she'd done everything wrong, why couldn't she just do something *right* for once?

But then the ice gave way to fire. She bristled, an instinct to fight rising up in her like it never would've before this summer. Because she deserved better than to be a pawn like that. She twisted her fingers hard against the sheets, flames making their way up her face. She should climb right off him and go find some clothes. Should show him the door and tell him never to come back again, only . . .

Only there was something in his eyes, a fragility to the way he held her close. Her chest constricted, and she went still.

As if seeing his opportunity, he grasped it. Licked his lips and dug his fingers into the flesh of her arm. "Tonight was my fault. So many things in this have all been my fault." His throat bobbed. "But you went along with it."

She almost got whiplash, she snapped her head back so hard. "Excuse me?"

He squared his jaw. "You don't like the ballet, you tell me you don't like the ballet, Kate. You don't sit through it for three hours silently stewing."

"And what were you doing for those three hours?"

The weakest smile played across his lips. "Trying to figure out how I'd gotten it all so wrong."

She just— What was she supposed to do with any of this?

She flexed her arms inside his grip and winced. "You're hurting me."

His hands softened, sending blood rushing back through her limbs. With a gentle touch, he stroked where he had squeezed too tight. Then the corners of his mouth pulled to the side, his eyes going warm and sad. "See? Was that so hard?"

"It—" It wasn't the same thing. Was it?

"I saw you lying under me a second ago. You were flat on your back, with your hands above your head." Heat prickled her neck, and he shook his head. "It was sexy as hell, knowing you were going to let me do whatever I wanted. But this isn't just about what I want. Not in your bed, and not when we go out. It's not all just for you to sit back and let me plan, then reject or not."

That wasn't what she'd been doing. It hadn't.

Except—

Except maybe it had been.

He'd come crawling back to her and begged her for another chance. And she'd been nursing this deep, impossible hurt. Holding on to it. She'd resented his return, resented him assuming he had the right to interrupt her life and fit himself into it. She'd agreed to give him a chance to prove himself, but the burden had been on him. But maybe some of it was on her, too.

"This is never going to work," he said, voice quiet and soft. "Not if you aren't in it with me." His gaze met hers. "Try with me, Kate. Please."

Her anger was a stone inside her gut. She didn't know how to let it go, or how to be charitable to the man who had put it there.

The stone rocked. And maybe, just by a fraction, it shrunk.

Because Rylan wasn't wrong. There was a difference between giving him a chance and giving *them* one. Only—

"I don't know if I can."

"All I'm asking is that you try."

For what seemed like an impossibly long time, she stared down at him.

The truth was, he hadn't just asked her to trust him the once. Over and over again, inviting her to tour a museum with him and opening his mouth for the first time against her skin, he'd presented her with these opportunities, and she'd taken them. By and large they'd been amazing, but to a one, they'd been his idea.

Maybe it was time she had some ideas of her own.

Maybe it was time for her to try.

Pushing down the hurt, hard place he'd made inside of her when he'd let her down, she dropped her gaze to his mouth. They were still all but naked here, and while her arousal had waned, the vision of him lying there, opening himself up to her, had the low simmer of need in her abdomen expanding.

She put her hands on his shoulders. And then she leaned in.

He parted for her without a moment's hesitation, meeting her kiss with firm, eager lips, slipping his tongue against hers in a soft caress. She kneaded her fingers into hard muscle and stroked her thumbs across his collarbones.

"Together?" The question came out shaky against his mouth.

"Absolutely."

And it was strange, being on top of him like this. She'd tried it before with Aaron, once or twice, but she'd always been too self-conscious, too aware of the way her belly looked. Was she moving too fast? Too slow? After a while, he'd usually ended up flipping them around so he could move the way he liked.

But Rylan cradled her close, his hands moving to span her back, sweeping wide arcs over the skin there, over the lace of her bra and down toward her rear.

"Do you want?" She trailed a finger down his chest to tease beneath the waistband of his boxers.

"Soon enough." He caught her hand in his and set it flush to the smoothness of his abdominals. "When you want. You just touching me is—" He sucked in a breath as she teased a hint of nails beside his navel. "It feels amazing."

He pulled her back down into his kiss then. There was a sweetness to the way he held her, open and accepting. It gave her the freedom to enjoy this, to get a little lost in the glide of his tongue and the heat of his mouth.

The whole night long, she'd been shivering. Now all she could feel was warm.

"Perfect," he said, brushing fingertips over her spine. He folded his hand around her hip, and it softened her bones.

She shifted, edging her knees farther apart.

The first glancing touch of her body against the hard line of him had a flash of want zinging to her sex, to the points of her breasts, and he moaned aloud against her mouth.

"That feels so good." He nudged his hips up into hers but didn't try to move her. Didn't ask her to grind harder.

But she wanted to.

Could it really be that simple? She pressed her hips down with more force, lining the base of him up against her clit, and her skin flushed hot, went too tight all over.

"That's it. Doesn't that feel nice?" He slipped his fingers over the curve of her breast. Dipped inside the cup to stroke at her nipple, and she exhaled hard against his lungs.

"*Nice?*" she asked, shuddering, disbelieving. It was so much more than nice.

He *shh*ed her and delved in deeper. Without slowing the rocking of her hips, she reached to flick her bra clasp open. Her breasts spilled out, the straps sliding down her shoulders, and his hands were there, helping her shrug the thing off. When she resettled over him, her nipples grazed his chest with every motion of her body, hot licks of pleasure revving it all up higher, better.

"Baby." He groaned, tearing himself from her lips and baring his throat. His cock jumped against her clit, and oh, damn. Had she pushed him too far, just like this? She eased up, but he pulled her back down. Shook his head and opened his eyes. "Don't stop. Please."

But she did.

She could grind them and grind them, get them both off like that. An emptiness yawned inside her, though. She'd been so afraid of sex for so long. Had kept them to everything-but for ages their first time around, but he'd been so good to her, so patient. She knew when her body was ready for it now. And he had told her to tell him what she wanted...

Over the sound of his pained gasp, she lifted her hips off him entirely, tremoring at the sudden lack of pressure, the missing contact. But no. No.

She leaned over. Got her nightstand open.

The box of condoms was unopened. She tore at it, fumbling when the cardboard separated but didn't give, swore when she nicked her finger sliding it under the flap. But eventually she managed. She tore off a single square.

Then with her free hand, she cupped the long line of him through his boxers.

He bit off a curse and seized her by the wrists, stopping her stroking and closing her fingers tighter around the condom. "You still don't have to."

"I know." She swallowed down the wetness in her mouth. "But I want to." For an instant, she faltered. "Don't you?"

"Kate." His voice dropped, going gravelly and low. And there was no mistaking that tone. That fevered gleam in his eyes.

Triumph replaced doubt. She twisted free of his grip. "I'll take that as a yes, then."

She kissed him again, soaking it in when he bit at her lip, swallowed the choked, perfect groans he made as she lowered his boxers from his hips. He kicked them the rest of the way off, stifling himself against her mouth. She got her hand around the thickness of his shaft, slid her thumb across the slickness at the tip.

His fingers running up the length of her slit still took her by surprise, though.

"You sure you're ready for me? Sure you're wet enough?"

He had his hand on her. Couldn't he tell she was soaked through? "What do you think?" she asked.

He edged in under the hem of her panties, and that wasn't going to do. She let go of him in favor of getting naked.

And then she was on top of him, completely bare, legs spread wide across his thighs. The world went sideways for a moment.

Who would've ever thought she'd end up here?

His fingertips brushing slick flesh brought her back to herself. She dropped her head against his chest as he probed all around her opening, dipping just inside. Spreading her wetness around. The tease of fullness without the follow-through drove her need even higher, and she rose back up.

She tore the condom open and rolled the latex over him. Batted his hand away. "Believe me. I'm ready."

She had reason to doubt it, though, as she lowered herself onto him. God, he was huge, and she was keyed up as hell, but she hadn't let him make her come first. The stretch pulled a broken sound from her, and then there was his hand at her hip, slowing her descent.

His jaw clenched, the tendons in his neck standing out, like this was nothing but restraint for him. He eased her up a fraction, almost off him.

This time, when she sank down, it was easier, and they groaned as one. Bracing herself, she worked back and forth, taking more and more of him with each stroke, and—

And *there* it was. The fullness, the connection.

She'd been so damned afraid of letting herself connect with

him. She still was. But if she wasn't willing to meet him partway, then what hope did they have?

This time, when her hips met his, she didn't avoid his gaze. Pressing her brow to his, she let him see her.

Then ever so slowly, she started to move. Pleasure sparked outward from every point of contact, a deep mass of heat within her. Every few strokes, her clit pressed hard against the ridge of his body where they joined, and she shifted. Got her lips to the point of his jaw, to his throat, fighting to focus.

"Here." He curled a hot, broad palm around her hips, dragging her down so he was fully seated, so that perfect pressure made the heat bloom, throwing sparks. "Do what feels good to you." He kept her there, just there, helping her rock back and forth. A new depth of pleasure opened up inside her, but she couldn't chase it. Couldn't quite let go that far.

"But—"

"It *all* feels good to me." He groaned, grinding upward. Deep within, he throbbed, his fingers tightening at her hip. "I promise."

She closed her eyes. God, it couldn't really be this easy, could it?

"Does it?" he asked. "Does it feel good?"

"It feels amazing."

"Then take it." He hauled her mouth to his, sweeping her up in a kiss that was all teeth and tongues, slickness and heat. "Take everything you need."

She lost herself in the push and pull. For everything she took, he only seemed prepared to offer more, and before she knew it, the heat rose to the point she couldn't bear, his cock a perfect fullness inside her, his body this warm solidity beneath her. He palmed her breast, bit at her lip even harder. Slipped a hand in between them, and it was something sharper to grind against, a bright point of pleasure and—

"Make yourself come, baby." His muscles strained, his kiss going sloppy. "Come all around me. Let me feel it when you—"

All at once, it crested over. Her body pulsed around his, blackness like liquid exploding outward. Like completion. Like connection.

She rode it all the way to the end. Opened her eyes in a haze to find him gazing up at her as if she were the best, most incredible thing he'd ever seen. Inside, he was still so hard.

"But you—"

There was this lost part of her that half expected to get flipped over and pounded into. She'd gotten hers, which was more than she could usually say. He'd given her so much pleasure—had showed her how to take it, and for that she'd be more than willing.

He pressed a finger to her lips. "Do you think you can come again?"

Oh, hell, she didn't know. "You have to be dying..."

"Only a little." He smiled. A real smile.

She kissed it from his lips, and it tasted like desire and these echoes of love, ones she'd been denying for so long now. But there they were. With their mouths tangled, sharing air and pleasure and this chance to experience it together, she braced her arms and shifted her hips.

A half dozen long, aching strokes where she nearly lifted off him before slamming down. He panted against her lips, body straining, and a new coil of possibility unfurled within her. She took him deep and ground down, and it was almost too soon, but there was that spark, that heat.

"Fuck, yes." He teased a thumb at the top of her slit again, an offer to touch her, to help her.

She shook her head, watching the ecstasy play out across his features. Feeling it build inside her depths.

And suddenly, she got it. How he could spend so much time making her feel good, because giving this to him while also having it for herself...

It was new. It was amazing.

Finally, the shaking in his abdomen hit a fever pitch, his moans as pained as pleasured. The way he gripped her shifted from holding her to just barely hanging on.

She roared inside.

Lowering herself down, she put her lips to his ear. "Come on, gorgeous."

"Fuck, Kate. Keep going."

"Come on." Power made the second wave brush all that much closer to shore. "Let me feel you come." She swallowed hard. "Inside me."

His hands turned to iron, a rough grip. And she wasn't the only one with power here. He bucked up into her, once and twice, and on the third, his whole body seized up. With a cry of her name, he turned his face into her throat. Bit hard enough to bruise.

As he emptied into her, she got her own hand on her clit. Bore down on him until the precipice lay just beneath her feet.

She fell. Again. Into orgasm and into him, and there was further to fall. So much further. Into love and into heartbreak, and her battered heart itself was a chasm. It beat a pang within her chest, threatening to suck her down, down, down.

Before she could hit bottom, she clawed out, opened her eyes, and dug her fingers hard into the mattress. She caught herself.

She might be willing to meet him halfway. But there were still some places she wasn't ready to land.

*   *   *

They lay there afterward, tangled up and naked, the covers drawn up to their waists against the chill. Rylan rested on his back, while Kate curled up beside him, pillowing her head on his chest. She hadn't tried to escape or go get dressed again right away, so he was counting it as a win. Then again, she wasn't exactly looking at him, either. Or volunteering anything.

He flexed his jaw, fingertips stuttering against the bare skin of her shoulder. "Next time, you should pick."

"Pick?"

"Where we go. What we do."

This was their second of their seven nights, and they'd made some progress. He'd meant what he said, though. He needed her to want this, too, to have some sort of stake in what they were building. What he *hoped* they were trying to build.

Chuckling, the sound uncomfortable and thin, she drew her arm in closer to her body. "I don't exactly know a lot of fancy restaurants."

"So? Didn't we both agree that tonight was a disaster?"

"It ended pretty well."

Well, she wasn't wrong. Spent as it was, his cock gave a hint of a twitch. "True. But I don't want to repeat the same mistakes again."

Surely, there was a way to get to that end, to the two of them sharing each other's bodies with that kind of freedom. One that didn't involve pushing through so much heartache on the way.

She shrugged. "It wasn't a mistake to try to show me what life is like for you."

"But my life isn't like that." It had been a mockery.

A botched, man-made catastrophe of what he'd hoped would be a fantasy.

Her brows furrowed. "I thought that was the whole point of it. You were going to show me 'your New York.'"

"And that's what I should have done. But instead I tried to impress you. And I did it all wrong." He took a deep breath. "So I'm asking you to do it right. I want to know what your life is like. Your New York." He wasn't explaining this the way he wanted to. "What do you do for fun? What's your ideal Saturday night?"

Frowning, she shook her head. "I don't think you'd be all that impressed by it."

"Try me. Let me decide."

She didn't seem satisfied, but she didn't argue with him anymore. She glanced up, challenge written across her eyes. "If I do, then how about the one after that? Do we get to try your life again?"

Swallowing, he nodded. "If that's what you really want."

Her hand inched its way across the bed. When her knuckles stroked his palm, the tightness in his chest eased. "I think I do." A smile flirted with the corner of her lips. "After all, it can't be too much worse than tonight was."

He rolled his eyes and clasped his hand to his heart as if she'd wounded him. "Rub it in, why don't you?"

And this felt good, the flirtation and the teasing.

After a moment, though, her gaze went serious again. She rearranged herself so she was facing him more, lying on her side and braced on one elbow. "So that isn't all there is to a mogul's life? Five-star restaurants and fancy clothes?"

She said it offhandedly, but the question that lay underneath was anything but a joke.

"Honestly? My life's mostly been a combination of couch surfing at my sister's place and schmoozing with the boring old men who've been running my father's company."

He and Lexie had been running full steam ahead with their plan to shore up their position with the senior execs and the board. Rylan still needed to find his balance there, but it was good to be *doing* something again.

Of course, Kate passed that part of his statement by entirely. "Your sister's really making you sleep on her couch?"

"Fine. Less couch surfing and more staying in her guest room. Same idea." Same feeling of being without roots. Living with Lexie was like living in his parents' house, all his mother's breeziness combined with his father's guilt trips about why he wasn't at work. He sighed. "It's getting old."

"Doesn't sound that terrible."

"You've never met my sister. She's exhausting." He stretched his arms above his head. "Wonderful, but exhausting. And her décor is abominable."

Kate seemed to choose her next words carefully. "Have you given any thought to figuring out something more permanent?" Her voice rose by a fraction. "I feel bad sending you back there if you're that unhappy with it."

Oh. A scattershot pain squeezed down on his ribs. So that was her angle in this. She still didn't want him to spend the night.

"I haven't really." He shifted the covers off, uncertain how to hide his disappointment while staying so close. Rising, he grabbed his boxers off the ground.

"It might be worth starting to poke around."

"Sure." The word came out too harsh, the edge seeping in without his meaning for it to. Dismissive and rude, but how else was he supposed to react?

He wasn't a fool. He hadn't expected Kate to invite him to move in with her that first night, and he sure as hell hadn't been expecting it tonight. But he'd thought maybe, someday...

So, no, he hadn't considered more permanent accommodations. Because when he thought about permanency...

He thought about her.

"It's just..." Kate watched him as he stepped into his pants. "You said you were done running. I thought, if you were going to stay in town..." She twisted the sheets in her hands. "I'm sure your sister's apartment is nice, but it isn't yours."

He laughed. "That would be a profound understatement."

"There's something about having a place to call home. That's all."

It was like she could see into his heart. To the emptiness there.

Home. It was a concept he'd thought about so many times as he'd made his way across the Atlantic. But he hadn't found it yet. Not here, and not at his sister's penthouse.

Maybe Kate was right. Maybe he needed a space of his own.

As he collected and tugged on the rest of his clothes, Kate moved more toward the center of the bed, gathering the covers around her. Fidgeting with her nails. "You taking off already?"

"I think so." At the look of relief on her face, his heart panged. He glanced away. "It's getting late. Things to do and all." He had a ceiling to stare at, for example. A company he wasn't sure he wanted to run.

"You sure?"

Was she trying to torture him?

"Look." He grabbed his jacket, but instead of shrugging it on, he clenched it in his fist. He turned to face her. "You just all but said you didn't want me to stay here."

"I..."

She trailed off, and he wanted to throw his hands up in the air.

Then he pinched the bridge of his nose and took a deep breath. Pushed those feelings of frustration down. She'd been hurt before him, and he had hurt her even more. It only made sense that she would still be afraid to let him in.

He wasn't being fair.

Exhaling nice and slow, he dropped his hand and mustered a smile. "It's fine. But if you want me to go, I'd rather go now." Before he could press and make this even worse.

She played with her fingers, still looking down. "I'm not saying I'll never want you to stay."

"But you're not ready." Resignation made his footfalls heavy. But he returned to the bed. She leaned up and he bent forward, threading his fingers through her hair before pulling her into a kiss.

"I'm sorry," she said.

"Don't be." He hesitated before adding, "We'll get there. Eventually."

He had to believe they would.

chapter NINE

"And the grandchildren? What was it—Denise and Bobby?" Rylan let his attention drift a little, switching his phone to his other hand as one of their senior VPs started in on something about potty training that he did *not* need to know.

Three short knocks sounded on his door, and he spun his chair around. He broke into a grin when he found Jordan of all people standing there.

"Bad time?" Jordan mouthed.

Rylan shook his head and held up a finger. He'd already covered everything he needed to on this call. They were more or less just down to pleasantries now. And besides, he'd been schmoozing all morning, connecting with more of the people on his and Lexie's list of friendly execs, hearing their concerns. Turned out, the past year with McConnell at the helm had apparently given rise to a lot of concerns from a lot of people. It had Rylan itching. Seeing the company his father had built in this state chafed something deep inside.

But that could wait, for now. It'd be a nice change of pace to spend some time with someone he actually wanted to talk to.

It took a minute, but Rylan managed to exit the conversation without coming across as too much of an ass. He hung up the call and set his phone down, then rose to his feet, waving Jordan in.

"You know"—Jordan glanced around as he skirted a stack of boxes to meet Rylan at the edge of his desk—"I'd just about given up on this office ever getting used again."

"It's a work in progress." The office and his occupancy of it both.

He'd half expected someone else to have moved in while he was away, but apparently the place had sat empty all that time. He'd had to have his things brought up out of storage, but it'd still been his. If he wanted it.

After a quick man-hug, Rylan drew back and gestured at the chair across the desk from his.

"I can't stay long," Jordan warned, even as he was sitting down. "I hadn't seen you since you put the fear of God back in McConnell last week, though."

"Fear of God, huh? Is that what they're saying?"

"The way his secretary tells it, he hasn't stopped sweating since."

"Good."

"But those aren't the only rumors floating around."

"Is that so?"

"Don't pretend you don't know." Jordan leveled him with a stare. "You show up out of nowhere after a year and start chatting up every senior exec in the company."

"Hardly." He was barely halfway through.

"Enough of them. So what is it? Hostile takeover?"

"My name's on the door. I don't exactly have to take it over."

"But you're back. For real."

Rylan eyed the door. "To be honest with you? I don't know."

"If you didn't come back for the company . . ."

"I had my reasons."

At least Jordan could take a hint. "Okay, okay." He held his hands up in front of his chest. "Keep your secrets. But I noticed you haven't approached me yet to check in. You that confident about my support for the coup you may or may not be planning?"

Rylan opened his mouth to quiet him about this coup talk, but he stopped himself. A muscle in Jordan's upper lip gave the tiniest hint of a twitch, and Rylan hesitated. Jordan couldn't really be that nervous about his place here. Which meant he was nervous about something else.

When Lexie had omitted his name from the list, Rylan'd tried not to read too much into it. But now he was questioning that decision. Something was definitely up.

He reached out and grabbed his pen and gave it a twirl. "I've always had a pretty good sense of who my friends were around here." He'd long counted Jordan among them.

Jordan's expression smoothed out, relief subtle but unmistakable in the set of his brows. "Glad to hear it."

Curiosity apparently satisfied, Jordan shifted gears, and they spent a few minutes catching up. But it wasn't long before Jordan uncrossed his legs and glanced at the door. "I hate to make this so brief, but, well. You know how it is."

That Rylan did. It was part of what he'd missed his year in Paris. The energy, the pace. "Not a problem." They stood and clasped hands over the desk. "Don't be a stranger, you hear."

"I won't." Jordan pulled back. "You still have that place up on Seventy-Third?"

"Nah, got rid of it a while ago. Been staying at Lexie's since I got back."

"My sympathies. She put you in the pink room?"

Rylan paused. "You've been to Lexie's place?"

And there was that twitch again. "A couple of times." It was too casual by far. "Anyway, she said that's always where she puts houseguests she doesn't want to stay too long."

The fact of the matter was, Lex did have Rylan in a room with an awful lot of pink in it. He hadn't thought too much about it, until now.

Kate's words from the other night floated back to him.

He'd reacted too harshly to her encouragements to get his own place. It'd been a message about her not being ready for him to spend the night, sure, but it had also been about her wanting him to find a home.

His throat went rough. "Well, she won't have to worry about me being in her hair for too much longer."

"Yeah?"

"Yeah. Was just about to call my Realtor now."

Jordan took his leave, and Rylan resumed his spot behind the bare old desk his father had picked out for him. Surrounded by boxes.

Instinctively, he put his hand to his chest. But there was nothing there. No weight. No ring.

He picked up the phone and dialed.

When the buzzer rang this time, Kate was ready. She checked herself once more in the mirror. Her basic skirt and sweater and boots weren't quite as flattering as a designer dress, but they didn't suffocate her, either. She tucked a lock of hair behind her ear and nodded at her reflection.

This was her night. Her life. And despite her reservations, she was inviting Rylan into it.

Bracing herself for anything, she made her way down the stairs. She'd told him in no uncertain terms that the chauffeured town car would *not* be necessary for the evening she had planned, but after last time, who knew what he would try.

Apparently, his first move was meeting her at the door.

She'd barely made it through the vestibule before he was reaching out for the handle. The door was locked from the inside, but as soon as she gave enough of a tug for it to unlatch, he was there, pushing it wide and holding it open for her.

Sweeping her up. This wasn't any polite greeting, any restrained brush of knuckles against her cheek. All the air whooshed out of her as he pulled her right into his arms, attacking her mouth in a kiss that took her breath away, surrounding her with the warmth of his scent. Stumbling against him, she lifted a hand and put it to his chest, meeting soft wool and the firm layer of muscle underneath.

And, God, it was so familiar. If it'd been a little warmer, if the night had smelled more of cigarettes and baking bread, she could've imagined them in Paris again.

When he let her go, she was panting, cheeks warm despite the autumn chill. She staggered a step back and tried to take him in. Her throat went dry at the buttery black leather of his jacket, the cut of his jeans. The sweater that draped across his pectorals, hugging every hard angle and curve.

A part of her had thought that nothing could top the sight of him in a suit. But this was better. More real.

"You look beautiful," he said, taking the words from her mouth.

Shyness made her duck her head. "Thank you." She collected herself enough to reply, "So do you."

He cocked a brow. "Beautiful?"

What was she even saying? She mock-swatted at him. "You know what I mean."

Catching her hand, he brought it to his lips, a warm press against the back of her palm. He gazed at her over it, eyes hot and deep. "I do."

A rush of heat bloomed through her. The night she'd planned, finding dinner and hitting up a bunch of gallery openings—it all could wait. She could just take him upstairs instead. They *worked* upstairs.

It was in the rest of the world that they seemed to have so many problems.

She shook off the burn of temptation, mentally chastising herself and pulling back her hand, only for him to hold on, intertwining their fingers.

He hadn't tried to do that on their last, disastrous night out. She'd been aware of it at the time, but it was this, his tactility tonight, that threw his previous distance into sharp relief. She hadn't realized how much she'd missed it.

Clearing her throat, she squeezed his palm.

"So," she said, refocusing. "I was thinking we'd take the subway."

"No need."

He gestured toward the street. And how the hell had she missed *that*?

"Um." *That* being a sports car even she could recognize as gorgeous. Sleek and red and polished to a shine. In this neighborhood, it was screaming to be keyed up or broken into. "Is that yours?"

"For the week, it is." His tone twisted, like there was a story there, but before she could ask, he led her over to the passenger side. "So I'm taking it everywhere."

Good luck parking it, or finding it in one piece at the end of the night. But if he insisted...

She got in, sinking into the low leather seat. He closed the door for her and went around to the other side. He looked perfectly at home with one hand on the gearshift and the other on the wheel. It wasn't something she'd ever imagined doing it for her, but the confidence made her heart flutter, the image searing itself into her mind for later. Perfect composition, gorgeous contrast, the promise of motion in every line of his body.

Smirking, he turned to her, drawing her attention back to his face. "I know it's your night to pick, but do you mind if we make a quick stop first?"

She tilted her head to the side. "A stop?"

"I have something I want to show you."

They weren't on much of a schedule, so she shrugged and buckled herself in. Then he peeled off from the curb, and she had to clutch at her seat.

The man knew how to drive. That much was for sure.

He sliced the car through traffic the same way he moved through the world, all assuredness and command, expectant that the people around him would yield. His biceps flexed with every turn and every cycle through the gears, muscles cording in his thighs, a look of concentration on his face and on his brow.

And she'd never had sex in a car before. The idea of it had always struck her as cramped and uncomfortable, but as he braced his arm against the wheel and executed a sharp turn, she could suddenly picture it. All jammed together in the tiny backseat, his body pressing into hers, his hips between her thighs and that same expression on his face, intent as he drove fast and hard and sweaty and deep.

The car jerked to a stop at a light, and he turned his head, catching her by surprise. It didn't give her time to school her expression, and his gaze darkened as he took her in. He released his grip on the gearshift to settle a hot palm on her knee, trailing upward. Like he knew exactly what she was thinking, and now he was thinking it, too. Like a promise for later.

Then the light changed and they were off again.

Once they were over the bridge into Manhattan and on the highway heading uptown, he pressed a button on the dash to make a call. Through the brief exchange of words wherein he told someone he was on his way, Kate frowned. When he hung up, she raised a brow, but he shook his head, leaving her in suspense.

In the end, their destination was an unassuming brownstone in a quiet pocket on the Upper East Side. They parked in an alley, her confusion growing as they walked a tree-lined street. A woman in a smart suit and a trench coat stepped out from behind a scrolled iron gate to greet them.

"It's all ready for you, Mr. Bellamy."

Rylan thanked her and tightened his hold on Kate's hand. He led her through the gate and up the short walk toward an open door. The lights within were all ablaze.

As they passed over the threshold, she leaned in to whisper, "What are we doing here?"

"I followed your advice," he said, letting go to settle his palm at the base of her spine, ushering her in.

The brownstone was vacant inside.

Confused, but with suspicion starting to dawn, she took in the polished wood floors. Peeked through a doorway into a kitchen done up in granite and brushed chrome.

"I'm making an offer on it tomorrow."

She whipped around. "Wait. You're *buying* a house?"

"That *is* something people do when they decide they need their own place. Is it not?"

"Sure. Of course." Established people, people who had families and who knew what they'd be doing with their lives in thirty years. Hell, in three. "It just...It's kind of a big step, isn't it?"

A smile flickered across his lips. He gestured with his head toward a set of stairs.

And it was like her eyes had been opened. Now that he'd said he was planning to buy it, the little details stuck out. The polished, silent floorboards and the quality of the fixtures. Even the light switch plates were nice.

He showed her a set of bedrooms on the second floor, and then on the third...

"Okay." Kate spun around in a slow circle. It was one big room, every wall set with windows. In the morning, the sun would stream right in. "I think this is my favorite part."

"You approve?"

"It's beautiful." She walked over to the side of the building that faced the street. In the orange glow of the streetlamps, the leaves were changing colors, the whole world awash in autumn. She turned back to him. "What would you use it for?"

One corner of his lips turned down. "I have some ideas."

He stood there, unmoving. No further details seemed to be forthcoming, so she gazed away again.

"Well, it's really nice. I can see why you picked it." It wasn't quite what she would've imagined for him. Not the sleek bachelor pad or the high-rise condo. It was better. Much better than...

She smiled weakly. "Though if you change your mind, I know a guy who can get you a great deal on a studio in Brooklyn. The roaches are even free."

If anything, his eyes went sadder at her crappy attempt at a joke. "I'll keep it in mind." Then he held out his arms. "Come here."

Tilting her head to the side, she made her way over to him. Let him draw her in against his chest, her back to his front. His chin set on top of her head.

"You really like it?"

Something squirmed low in her belly. "I already said I did."

"Just wanted to make sure." He nuzzled her temple. His next inhalation stuttered. "It's important to me. That it be someplace you'll want to visit."

The squirming deepened, and she swallowed past the dryness in her throat. She'd promised him seven nights, and already they were on number three.

He wasn't talking about the other four. Of that, she was sure.

He was talking about a whole lot more.

chapter TEN

"Well, *damn* if I didn't pull the lucky table tonight."

Rylan's eyebrows already felt like they were about to hit his hairline, but all it took was a single glance up and they threatened to defect from his face altogether.

The thing was that he liked little hole-in-the-wall restaurants. He hadn't had a lot of time to seek them out in his fast-paced corporate life, but he'd cultivated an entire roster of them when he'd been at his leisure in Paris. Little places where people remembered you and asked you how you were. Anchors to make a guy feel less alone.

This place she'd picked for them tonight, though? Hole in the wall? More like a hole in the ground. They were in the bowels of the Lower East Side, at a place with dishes named after punk bands whose names he barely recognized. The tables were shoved together so tightly he was practically in the next person's lap, and the black walls displayed the kind of "art" his mother would've thrown her wineglass at. Obscene and ugly and incomprehensible by turns.

The moment they'd stepped in, he'd given the place one look and been ready to turn right back around.

Except Kate had tightened her grip on his arm and set her jaw, and he'd remembered. He was the one who'd asked her to pick, to show him her slice of life. Maybe she was trying to scare him off and maybe she really did want to eat surrounded by all this hipster bullshit. Either way, it was her call.

He still hadn't quite been ready to be served by a six-foot-tall black...*person*. With a full beard. In a dress.

"My name's George, and I'll be taking *such* good care of you tonight." The...guy?—introducing himself as George, he was probably a guy—batted his eyelashes at Rylan and smirked. "What'll you have, beautiful?"

Never let it be said that Rylan didn't keep an open mind, but this was pushing it.

Kate's hand emerged seemingly out of nowhere to settle on his wrist, and he let out a deep breath at the warm touch of soft fingers on his skin.

"Do you mind if I order for the both of us?"

It was a strange, mirrored sense of déjà vu that swept over him. Their second night, at the Ethiopian place he'd taken her to, he'd pulled this very same routine. She'd looked lost, and he'd swooped in, wanting to provide her with an experience. New tastes to try. He'd ordered for her, and when his selections had arrived, he'd fed them to her with his hands, placing bite after bite on her pretty pink tongue. By the end, he'd been fighting every instinct he had so as not to take her right there on the table. A long second passed as he stared at her, remembering it.

But at his hesitation, she faltered. Blinking, she bit her lip and moved to take her hand back. He caught it before she could.

"Be my guest," he said, voice coming out gruff. He stroked his thumb across the point of her wrist.

She took a deep breath and nodded, looking up at their server. Using her free hand, she paged through the menu and rattled off a couple of things he never would've recognized as food. Their server got her choices down, then flipped his notebook closed and tucked it into the décolletage of his dress.

"My eyes are up *here*," he said, pointing two fingers in a V at Rylan before directing them back at his own face. He grinned at Kate and then—there was no other word for it—pranced away.

Rylan blinked repeatedly, but he was never going to be able to unsee that. He turned back to Kate, who had a wincing sort of a smile straining her mouth.

"I promise," she said, "this guy I know from my program absolutely raved about this place."

In the face of her uncertainty, Rylan forced himself to relax his shoulders. "I'm reserving judgment." He was trying to at any rate.

This was her night, after all. Already he'd co-opted enough of it, insisting on driving just for the excuse to take Chase's car. He silently snickered to himself. If Chase could see the sketchy alley they'd had to park his baby in, he'd be spitting nails.

Served him right, after the shitty advice he'd given Rylan. After he'd helped Rylan nearly ruin it all.

And then the house.

God, what it had done to him to see her there. He'd toured a dozen places in the past couple of days, all of them nice but none of them *home*. The instant he'd walked into the third story of that brownstone, though, all he'd been able to think was *Kate*. It was so open and airy, and it got such beautiful light.

He'd seen it all. Her and her easel and her paints, him coming up to admire what she was working on before sweeping her into his arms. Carrying her to their bedroom.

He'd been so excited to show it to her, and she'd loved it. She had.

But she hadn't understood it. She hadn't known it was for her.

And he'd been too much of a chicken-shit to really tell her.

Mentally shaking his head at himself, he blew out a rough exhalation. He was thinking too far ahead, was the problem. Prior to this past year, that had always been his problem. Fantasies aside, he had five nights left with this girl, including this one. His only chance at securing the rest was to do what she had told him to the moment they'd agreed to this.

He had to make them count.

Refocusing, he brought his other hand to the table, cradling her palm in both of his. He ran his thumbs across the lines and creases of her knuckles; it was there, in the hidden, easy-to-overlook places, that you could catch a glimpse of who she really was.

"I miss the charcoal," he mused.

Her brow scrunched up. "Excuse me?"

"You were mostly drawing this summer." He turned her hand over in his. "There was this black dust everywhere. Smudges on your clothes and on your nose." He shrugged. "Your hands look different now."

There were colors for one thing. Deep reds and green and blues, stains of pigments that had soaked into the valleys of her fingerprints.

Frowning, she curled her fingers in on themselves. "I swear I wash them."

"It's not a complaint." Hell, it was anything but. "Just shows that you work hard at what you do."

She made a little huffing noise. "Not hard enough, apparently."

It was his turn to tilt his head in confusion. From the sounds of it, she worked all the time. She'd filled so many canvases— none of which she let him see, but still.

"I just—" She stopped, pulling her mouth to the side, and then she sighed. "Don't mind me. I've just had a couple of bad days."

"How so?"

"It isn't . . . flowing, is all." She lifted a shoulder and set it back down. "Sometimes it's like the images just come together all on their own. Other times . . ."

Ah. "Other times it's like slamming your head against a brick wall."

"Exactly."

"My brother . . ." Rylan hesitated, that old instinct not to give away too much of himself rearing up. It was suicide in the boardroom, and even in his personal life . . . His parents always found a way to twist whatever he told them.

But that instinct didn't serve him here.

"My brother," he repeated, "Evan. The artist?" At her nod, he soldiered on. "He makes sculptures, mostly. Back when we lived at home, you could always tell how things were going with whatever he was working on." A smile played across his lips. "He'd get so frustrated sometimes."

And moody as hell. But when things were going well, there was nothing better. In that awful, empty house, Evan had carried this spark of life. One Rylan had worked so hard to keep their father from snuffing out.

"Are you two close?"

Rylan's smile dimmed. "Not terribly." Not anymore.

Evan had no idea what Rylan had really been trying to do, shipping him off to a boarding school on the other side of the country instead of cutting his check to Exeter like the rest of the Bellamy men. For an instant, Rylan could see it—the way Evan had glanced back over his shoulder before he'd gotten on that plane. The anger that had been in his eyes. The betrayal.

All the times he'd come home after that, brief visits for holidays and breaks. He'd never looked at Rylan quite the same.

"That's too bad."

"It is what it is." Mostly, it was something he didn't want to think too much about right now.

Fortunately or not, he was saved from having to when their waiter appeared with a basket of vaguely green-tinged bread. Poking at the basket, Kate shrugged and took a piece. Rylan waited, watching her reaction.

Her eyes widened. "It's actually really good."

Well, color him surprised. He reached for his own piece. Then hesitated. "Are you messing with me?"

"No. Promise. I—" Her hand and her voice both trembled for a second. But she rallied, determination pushing aside the uncertainty in her eyes. She tore off a corner of the bread. "Here."

Wonder surged inside him as she took the bite and extended her arm across the table. Heat followed as her intent became clear. They'd done this before, albeit from opposite sides of the table, and the intimacy of feeding her had never ceased to excite him. It had made her cheeks flush, her breath stutter. Made her eyes go hot and dark.

He grasped her wrist, but not to stop her. Steadying her grip, he ducked his head. Kept his gaze fixed on hers as he opened his mouth.

She placed the bread on his tongue, and he closed his lips around her fingertips. He gave them a soft, wet kiss before letting go of her and pulling back.

Licking her lips, she watched his mouth as he chewed, and she hadn't been lying. Despite its hue, the bread was soft and rich and warm, and he swallowed it with relish.

"Delicious," he said, voice coming out rough. Nearly as delicious as her skin.

The restaurant around them receded until it was just the two of them—no loud neighbors or eccentric waitstaff or jarring art. Just him and her and this tiny table between them. He slid his leg forward, brushing his calf against hers, and another rush of warmth licked through his bones. The moment hung, heavy and too close. Beyond intimate.

Then she jerked her head to the side and slid her gaze away, and that was all it took. The bubble of space around them collapsed, sending the roar of the crowded room crashing back over them. She heaved in a breath that made her breasts rise, as if she hadn't managed to fill her lungs in all the time he'd held her stare. As if he'd stolen her breath away.

He was feeling a little oxygen deprived himself.

Mentally shaking his head, he refocused. What had they been talking about? Before he'd gotten lost in the taste of her skin and the depths of her eyes? In the temptation to whisk her away and find out if this place had bathrooms with locks?

Oh. Right. Art.

He cleared his throat. "So what are you working on? Something for a class?"

"It's, um." She shook her head minutely, gazing down at her hands. Tearing absently at her bread. "It's a project. A competition, actually."

"Oh?"

"Something the department offers. We have to do portfolios on a theme." She rattled off a couple of the details—the fellowship that was at stake and the idea she'd had for painting churches. Light came into her eyes as she got going, but then it dimmed. A frown marred her expression. "I thought I really had a handle on it when they first announced it. But it hasn't been going well."

"No?"

"It's like I can see what I want to make in my mind, but when it comes time to put it on the canvas..." She shrugged. "It won't come out right."

And there was a weight to her tone he didn't like. She was taking this personally.

He knew that feeling intimately. Pinning your own worth to your success.

Letting your value be determined that way.

He reached out across the table again. With all the gentleness he had, he pulled the torn-up remnants of her slice of bread from between her fingers and set the crumbs down on her plate. "You'll figure it out."

"Yeah. I know." It was dismissive, and he liked that even less.

"No, really. I'm not just saying it." The way people did. *It'll all be fine, don't worry.* "I believe it."

That finally drew her gaze back to him. A hope that hurt his heart broke into her voice. "You really mean that, don't you?"

"Absolutely." With every fiber of his being. "You work so hard and you see so much." She had drawn those places in Paris over and over and over. Notre Dame Cathedral and the view from the base of Sacred Heart.

She'd drawn him, nude, at least a dozen times. Quick hurried sketches while she worked to find her center. Until she'd found something beautiful and traced it into his very skin.

"You just have to find your connection to it," he said. "Your way in."

The space between her brows scrunched tighter as she seemed to think it over. Her gaze went to their hands. "Maybe you're right."

"Of course I'm right."

That earned him a flicker of a smile. "I wish I had your confidence."

His heart tugged in his chest. "I wish you did, too." He wished he could give her some. Stroking her palm, he ducked his head, waiting until she looked at him again. "Until you do, I'll just have to be confident for the both of us."

"I'll hold you to that." She sighed, and it was like a layer of her guard peeling down. Like she was letting him glimpse past her walls. "It's just so embarrassing, you know?"

He didn't. "How so?"

"I finally figure out who I am as an artist this summer, with—" She bit off her word, but he heard it all the same. *With you.* "I even decided to go to grad school because of it, and then I get there, and I want to make this great impression, and instead I get stuck."

Comprehension was a tickle at the back of his mind.

That first night back, when he'd gone to her apartment to convince her to give him a second chance...

She'd turned all her paintings to face the wall. Their second, disastrous night, he'd gone back to her apartment to find them hidden from him again.

He'd thought it was a lack of trust, at the time, and maybe it was. But— "Is that why you didn't want me to see?" Her gaze darted up, eyes widening. The tickle grew into a chilled certainty. He clarified all the same, "What you were working on."

She looked away. "Maybe." It sounded like a concession. "Partly."

"You know you've already made a good impression on me."

She'd stunned him with her drawings. The talent and the insight in them. The skill and the sensitivity.

He'd been bewitched by her scent and her kiss, by the heat of her body and the brilliant light of her company. By the way she'd looked at him and seemed to see something more than just the money and the name.

But it had also been the things she made. Her art was a part of her—maybe the piece that had dragged him beneath the surface of her deeps.

"I told you," she said. "It's hard for me to show people things that aren't finished."

And this was important. He squeezed her hand and took a moment to gather his thoughts. They had to come out right.

"It doesn't have to be perfect." He swallowed, throat dry. *You don't have to be perfect.* "If it's something you made, I'll love it."

I'll love you.

For a second, he couldn't breathe.

He'd fought back the thought so many times now. Every time he touched her, it rose unbidden, though, and he'd pushed it down and down. All the ideas of building a future with her and making a home for her to share. All the warmth in his heart and this *need* to be with her. It had driven him across continents and boroughs and across the threshold of this maddening restaurant.

It would drive him farther still. Because he loved her.

Not the way his parents had loved each other and used that

love like a weapon. Not the way they'd loved him, twisting it into a means to control him. Treating his own love like a weakness to be burned out of him.

But with acceptance. With faith.

With a part of him he'd thought he'd lost so long ago.

chapter ELEVEN

"So where to next, m'lady?"

It sent a little thrill up Kate's spine to have Rylan looking at her the way he was. As if he were entirely at her disposal, ready for whatever she wanted to throw at him.

And there was something more there, too, some quiet warmth lighting the soft blue of his eyes. It made her chest go all fluttery in a way she had promised herself she wouldn't give in to. She was sticking to that, goddammit all. But he wasn't making it easy.

Not with his quiet reassurances or his unwavering belief in her and her art. Not with the heat of his hand where it wrapped around hers.

The door to the restaurant swung closed behind them, the sounds from within going muffled, replaced by the rumble of engines and wind and the millions of people they shared this city with. She took a deep breath and looked away from him, gesturing down the street.

"There are a few galleries having openings tonight. I thought we could check them out? If you're interested?"

"I told you," he said, stroking his thumb across the back of her palm, "whatever you want."

He had. He'd left this entire evening up to her, and she'd thought it would be awkward. She always got nervous making choices for other people. But at least so far, he'd been true to his word, approaching everything she suggested with an open mind, even when it was a crazy restaurant in a part of town he'd probably barely set foot in before.

And he had asked her for a slice of her life, after all.

She tilted her head in the direction of the first place she had in mind. "It's just a couple of blocks. Not too far from where we parked."

"Lead on."

By the time they got to the first gallery on her list, the opening was in full swing. It was a little independent place, a converted industrial space that had been repurposed for the display of art, and the crowd was mostly people like her. Young and creative and dressed in lots of black, all eccentric, colorful hairstyles and exposed tattoos. She glanced up at Rylan as they made their way through the crush, skirting around a cluster of people who sounded like they'd been hitting the free wine pretty hard.

She faltered. While he didn't exactly stick out, he didn't quite blend, either.

"Is this okay?"

"It's fine." His eyebrow quirked up. "Definitely interesting."

Interesting was rarely a compliment. But she'd take him at face value for now. Pushing her doubts aside, she threaded her hand through his elbow and started over to one of the walls.

And it was strange, how similar and yet how different it was to their time strolling through Paris's museums. Instead of quiet, hush hallways full of old masterpieces, they were in this cavernous, modern space. And the artist, whoever he was, seemed awfully fond of soaking his canvases in images of blood.

"Imagine that in your bedroom," Rylan said, ducking in close as she stopped to consider one of the paintings.

She grimaced, because he wasn't wrong. The image was of a body bound up in wire, its heart torn out. Its chest cracked open and its shattered ribs left open to the world. The whole thing disquieted her. Horrified her. Still... "Art isn't just about being pretty."

"Didn't say it was."

"It's supposed to make you feel."

"And what does this one make you feel?"

She took a step back from the canvas and tilted her head to the side.

It certainly evoked *something* in her. Something that had made her stop to examine it more closely.

Her stomach dropped down to her toes.

Because it was too violent, too gruesome. But the image looked exactly like how it had felt to walk away from Rylan. To trust, to let someone in and believe their words. To love.

Only to find out he hadn't been who she'd thought he was at all.

"Exposed," she managed to choke out.

With that, she turned on her heel, away from that painting and on to the next. As she walked, her heart pounded hard in her chest, and that was good. That was a reassurance.

Her heart was still her own, caged safely behind her ribs.

Thanks to his mother, Rylan wasn't a complete novice when it came to the gallery scene.

This wasn't quite the corner of the gallery scene he was used to, though.

None of the other shows they'd stopped in at had been as grizzly as that first one, but they were all out there. The purpose of art might be to make you feel, but Rylan didn't particularly enjoy feeling unsettled.

He liked feeling like the world was a more beautiful place than it seemed on the surface. He liked the way *Kate*'s art made him feel.

Not the way it had certainly looked like she felt, staring at that awful painting of a broken, empty rib cage. She'd gone quiet on him again in its wake, and it made his limbs twitch with a restless anxiety, to the point where he was only too happy to move on to the next place on her list. But even there, in a brighter setting, surrounded by sculptures that didn't appear to have actively been dismembered, she remained withdrawn.

Until they arrived at their fifth—and, she had assured him, final—stop of the night, where they walked in the door and smack into a guy who took one look at Kate and lit up like a Christmas tree.

"I was wondering if you were going to show up," he said, putting down his drink. He was clearly an artsy type himself, with shaggy, dark blond hair and a streak of paint on the knee of his pants. A little shorter than Rylan was, a little leaner.

He didn't so much as spare a glance at Rylan as he held his arms out to Kate.

Something possessive sparked and flared in Rylan's chest. But he smothered it. Balling his hands into fists, he shoved them in the pockets of his jacket and tried not to glower. Kate was allowed to hug whomever she wanted. She was her own person—she could do anything she pleased. But Rylan didn't have to like it.

Fuck, but he *really* didn't have to like it when she stepped right up to the guy and slung her arms around his neck. Rylan bristled, a hot stone lodging in his throat.

At least she didn't linger. The guy made as if to keep her close, but already she was pulling back. "Sorry," she said. "We ended up hitting the place over on Rivington first."

The word *we* left her mouth, and that got blondie's attention. He looked up, away from Kate, darting his gaze around until it landed on Rylan. Withdrawing his hands from his pockets and crossing his arms, Rylan nodded.

The guy swallowed and inched backward, and that alone, that act of acknowledging Rylan's claim—it should've pacified the rumbling, angry thing in Rylan's lungs. Except it didn't. Because it was surprise that widened those eyes. Surprise and hurt.

The jealous heat that had filled Rylan flashed suddenly, painfully cold.

Kate hadn't told him. Not just about Rylan and who he was, but that she was even seeing anyone at all.

And this boy had gotten his hopes up. It was written all over his face.

Trailing off, Kate followed the guy's gaze, looking over her shoulder at Rylan and then back to her friend. "Oh. Um." She fidgeted with her sleeve. "Liam, this is Rylan. Rylan, this is my friend Liam. He's in my program."

"That's right," Liam said. He extended a hand. "It's nice to meet you."

"Likewise."

Liam's handshake was firm enough—not Wall Street firm, but most people's weren't. Rylan only clamped down harder when Liam said, "Kate didn't tell me she was bringing anyone."

"*Kate*," Kate said, "didn't know for sure if she was coming at all, if you recall correctly."

That much at least was probably true. She hadn't decided on what she wanted them to do until just the other day.

"Fair enough." Liam dropped his hand as Rylan let go.

Rylan held his gaze, made him be the one to glance away.

Of course, where else would he look next except to Kate? "The exhibit's really good. Do you want to walk around?" He gestured to the side of the room, brushing her arm with his other hand and making Rylan's blood boil. "I could get you a glass of wine? Red, right?"

And Rylan was this damn close to interjecting. He was her date. If anyone was going to get her a drink, it should be him. Being a gentleman meant leaving her alone with Liam, though, and no way he was doing that right now.

Kate nodded, and Rylan watched the guy retreat for a full two seconds before turning back to her.

"He wants you."

Kate's gaze lifted to meet his, her chin tilting up, that all-too-rare flash of stubbornness firming her lips. Determination was a good look on her. A sexy one.

"I know," she said.

And Rylan...somehow hadn't been expecting that. "You know?"

She'd seemed so unaware of her own desirableness their first time around. He'd been more than clear about his intentions, and even then, she'd needed reassurances.

She rolled her eyes. "He asked me out the same day you showed up again."

Jealousy tore at the back of his throat. "And what did you say?"

"What do you think?"

He didn't even know anymore.

Huffing out a breath, she raked her fingers through her hair. "I told him I was tired, if you must know. Because I..." Her gaze darted around for a second, her cheeks flushing. "I wasn't ready."

Pain tinged her voice, squeezing Rylan's heart.

She hadn't been ready because of him, and he kicked himself all over again for the way he'd let things unravel between them. At the same time, gratitude lit him up. What if she *had* been ready? What if he'd never come to his realization, or if he'd had it a couple of days later? If he'd knocked on her door only to find her with this *boy* . . .

All she'd given him were these seven nights to win her back, but he'd come so close to missing even that. If he'd returned to find her already involved . . . Well, he still wouldn't have given up. He would have fought for her tooth and nail. Still, he thanked the luck that had given him his chance.

And yet. His mouth went dry. If she hadn't been ready to date again, what kind of chance was he working with here? They had history, sure, but he'd admitted it to himself now: He loved this girl. Hopelessly and helplessly, and if she didn't want the more he was planning for, the future and the home he'd imagined for them to share—

He'd make her. Not by force, of course, but he'd show it to her, and she would see. They could be amazing together.

They would be.

"Kate . . ."

She shook her head. "I don't want to talk about it right now."

Would she ever?

Some of the desperation he felt must have bled into his

expression, all his training in keeping his emotions hidden deserting him in the face of this woman.

She deflated by a fraction.

"Come on," she sighed. "You might as well meet everyone else, too."

That wasn't exactly enthusiasm in her voice. But he followed along regardless.

He met a solid dozen people over the course of the next few minutes, including one of the artists on display, who was an alumnus, apparently. Rylan set to memorizing their names the way he would members of a rival board, and he did a damn good job if he said so himself. Liam returned after a fashion with Kate's drink, brushing past Rylan as he passed it to her. Acting so innocent when their fingers brushed against the plastic cup. She thanked him with a smile, and Rylan didn't punch him in his smug, intrusive face, or tuck Kate under his arm and carry her straight back to the car. Because he could practice restraint.

He wanted to, though, dammit all.

He wanted this glimpse into her life, but he wanted her to himself even more. Their first time around it had been the two of them, alone in a foreign country, surrounded by another language. Dependent on each other in a way they never could be where they lived, and he *missed* it. They'd been so insulated. So intimate.

There was so much more competing for their attention here. But he'd fight his way through it.

He'd get her to himself soon enough.

She elbowed him in the side, and he jerked his head down. "Stop it," she hissed.

"What?"

"Growling at everyone who so much as looks at me."

He hadn't outright *growled*, had he? "I have no idea what you're talking about."

"Yeah, right."

As if to test him, Liam edged closer to them at just that moment, his mouth tilting up into a conciliatory smile. "So, Ryan."

Rylan gritted his teeth. "Rylan."

"Oh. Sorry." He actually looked contrite, like maybe he hadn't misspoken it on purpose as a power play. Then again, most people outside of his family probably wouldn't. "That's unusual."

"It's his middle name, actually," Kate said, and there was a pointedness to it he chose to ignore.

"Cool."

Rylan cleared his throat. "It's a family name. My grandmother's maiden name." He looked down to find Kate regarding him with interest. He shrugged and continued. "I'm a junior, and when I left for college, I thought..." What had he thought, beyond the blinding haze of anger and resentment? Sent off to his father's college to get his father's degree so he could be shoved into the seat at his father's side, wearing his name and his suits and...His throat bobbed. "I thought I needed something of my own."

Kate's eyes were soft as she stared up at him. Softer than they had been before. "You never told me that."

He hadn't told her his given name at all, until he'd had to.

He kept his hand at his side against the instinct to reach over and stroke her cheek. "Not because I didn't want to."

With their gazes connected like that, the space between their bodies humming, it felt like a moment that could have gone on and on.

Beside them, Liam gave an uncomfortable chuckle, as if even he knew he was intruding. "So what do you do?"

Rylan didn't look away from Kate. She'd asked him that very question on an open Parisian street, and he had talked all around it. "I do some work for my father's company."

Liam said something banal about his own family, but Rylan couldn't be bothered to listen.

How different would things be now if he had only been more open with Kate at the beginning? She might not have been impressed by the wealth, but would she really have spurned him the way he'd imagined? He'd told himself at the time that the half truths were all a part of the seduction, but they'd been something else, too. They'd been a chance for him to get outside of himself. To be better than he had been, at least in this one person's eyes.

And her eyes were still the only ones that mattered to him. Her eyes and her skin and the warmth of her, the taste and the scent of her on his tongue. His gaze settled on the soft, plush pout of her mouth, the one he hadn't kissed in hours, and his skin went too tight, heat making his mind fuzz over.

Then, in the middle of his anecdote, Liam put his hand on Kate's arm. The green that had tinted Rylan's vision flashed a dangerous, violent red.

He'd been keeping his possessive instincts on the tightest of leashes, but anything under that kind of tension was destined to snap.

Ignoring the boy and ignoring his manners, ignoring everything except that bit of skin touching skin, *he* snapped.

Cutting Liam off, Rylan addressed Kate directly. "Have you seen what you wanted to see here?"

They'd barely glanced at the art. These people had stolen even that from her, and now he was taking it away from her too in his hurry, and he wanted to stop himself. But he was too far gone.

"What?" Zeroing in on his eyes, Kate crinkled her brow. And then she seemed to catch up. Her breath stuttered, her mouth stuck somewhere between indignation and arousal, and even if she was only halfway with him, he would take it.

"We have to go." He grasped her arm and hauled her bodily against him, where she belonged. Liam's hand tightened on her other wrist, and the flame inside Rylan went supernova.

"You just got here—" Liam started.

Rylan's blood rose hotter, and he reached toward him. "Listen—"

But then Kate shook free of the both of them, and Rylan's hand was ice, extended out toward her still. She turned to Liam, and Rylan's heart turned over in his chest until she gave the guy this tight-lipped, apologetic smile. "I'm sorry." She jerked her thumb at Rylan. "I think this one forgot to eat. He has a habit of getting hangry." She looked to him, gaze pointed. "Don't you?"

He was hungry all right, but not for food. Still, this was her lying for him. Covering for him. Trying to make his caveman behavior acceptable in the eyes of someone whose opinion she valued. The last few minutes washed over him, the insane way he'd been acting. She was being more patient with him than he deserved.

The jealous beast quieted by a fraction, and he nodded stiffly.

"Why don't you go grab some cheese and crackers, while I check out the exhibit." There was no room for question in her voice. "I'll meet you over there in a minute."

Rylan didn't want to let her get three steps away from him, but she radiated a need for space. He forced himself to take a deep breath. "Sure." He glanced to Liam.

He was going to walk her around the gallery. Take Rylan's place. He fit there better anyway, didn't he? Understood her art and her life, and—

She turned to Liam, too. "Sorry again. I'll see you on Monday?"

That wasn't an invitation. It was a flat-out dismissal if anything. The dark, angry well that had opened up in Rylan shrunk, if only a little.

"Sure." Liam looked as floored as Rylan felt.

Together and apart, they stood there, watching as Kate walked away.

chapter TWELVE

What the actual hell.

With measured, even steps, Kate made her way around the edge of the gallery, stopping in front of each painting for at least the count of ten. To the outward observer—maybe to the men staring holes in the back of her head—it probably looked like she was giving the pieces her full attention, appreciating them the way they deserved. When really, inside, she was a fluttery, rattled mess.

It was too bad, too. This show was easily her favorite of the night, the artist's style having at least some grounding in realism. The images were even mostly cityscapes, totally relevant to the studio work she was trying to do. They were worth examining in detail.

She was barely seeing them.

She took a step back as if to get a better view of the canvas in front of her, glancing over her shoulder to check she didn't bump into anyone. And if her gaze just happened to go to the corner of the room—to the man in black with the dark, hooded eyes and the rumpled hair and the most intense, piercing sort of glare...

Her breath catching, she whipped her head back around. She hadn't even bothered trying to spot Liam. She liked him well enough, and she sure as hell hoped they could salvage their friendship from the smoldering ruin Rylan seemed determined to make of this evening. But he wasn't her concern.

Rylan had stood exactly where she'd asked him to, next to the table of wine and hors d'oeuvre, but he hadn't looked like he was enjoying the Brie.

He'd looked like a man stalking his prey, and just that tiniest, briefest of glimpses made her pulse thunder in her ears.

Jealousy wasn't something she'd ever expected from him. The way he'd grabbed at her and all but bared his teeth at a guy who wasn't even really his competition...It was ugly. It was infuriating.

And damn her if it wasn't the hottest thing she'd ever seen.

Breathing against the burn he ignited in her just by existing—the one he'd fanned into a flame with his possessiveness—she moved on to the next painting. Maybe by the time she finished her circuit of the room, she'd have herself back under control. She didn't need to jump him or let him drag her out of there. They needed to talk about this and why it wasn't okay.

But her slow walk led her closer and closer without bringing any clarity to her thoughts. She reached the end of the exhibit a still-simmering jumble of want and indignation and *need*.

She turned and met his gaze, and the heat inside her shivered right down to her bones.

He ate up the distance between them in a dozen long strides, his eyes fiery and jaw tight. "Finished?" he asked, hot and clipped, and her throat was a desert.

She managed a jerky nod, and then before she knew it, he had his arm looped around her, ushering her toward the door.

Liam stepped forward when they were almost to the exit, concern written all over his face. She couldn't even fault him for it.
This looked bad. Looked like the sort of thing her mom had always warned her about. But her blood and skin were singing,
an exhilarated mania mixing with the arousal pulsing through
her veins. She caught Liam's eye and shook her head, trying to
tell him without speaking that she was fine. She might not be
in control of herself or this situation, but she was fully on board
and along for the ride.

Liam's mouth turned down into a frown, but he stood down.
Even when Rylan practically went out of his way to clip his
shoulder, he didn't rise to the bait. Just watched them go.

They surged through the door and out onto the street. The
cool night air washed over her, but it didn't help. Neither did
Rylan walking them another three feet, to where glass windows
gave way to brick, and then he was stopping. Shoving her up
against it.

His mouth descended on hers, the kiss hot and claiming, and
she gave in to it without hesitation. She opened for him, accepting the smooth press of his tongue and the sting of teeth
scraping over her lip. The solid muscle of his chest forced her
farther back against the wall, and she couldn't breathe, couldn't
process anything beyond the heady scent of him and the taste of
his lips.

Pulling away, she gasped for breath, but he only moved
his mouth to her jaw, sliding slick, sucking kisses along the
column of her throat. He was going to leave *marks*, and she
wanted them.

Only—

Only they were on a public street. One of her friends could
come out at any time. They might even be able to see from the

window. Hell, she was pretty sure she'd spotted one of her professors in there.

Summoning her wits, she shoved at his shoulder, and when that didn't work, only impelling him to wring a moan of need from her lungs with the heat of his kiss, she grasped his head between her hands.

"Rylan. We can't."

"Oh, we can. And we will."

She swallowed hard. Need pooled in her abdomen, her breasts tightening to twin aching points at the deep roughness in his voice. And this wasn't supposed to be happening. They were supposed to talk.

But all she managed to say, breathy and panting, was, "Not here."

Rylan couldn't even touch her.

With his hands balled into fists against the need vibrating in his bones, he walked a stiff, straight line to the alley where they'd left Chase's Bentley. It was torture, with Kate so close, taking quick half-running steps just to keep up, but if he so much as felt her skin or got a whiff of her scent, he'd be lost.

Relief trembled through him to find the alley deserted. It was a minor miracle, this time of night in this part of town, but he wouldn't question it. They got within striking distance of the car, and all the control he'd been exercising evaporated.

Grabbing for her, he pulled her in against his chest. She didn't melt into him so much as *climb* him, and he could have cried with the sweetness of it as he lifted her up. Got his hands on the curve of her ass through her skirt. Hoisting her onto the edge of the trunk, he devoured her mouth, all sharp, biting kisses, the faint taste of wine on her tongue and the rough tug of her fingers in his hair. Their hips met, and he groaned aloud at the pressure against his cock. He'd been hard inside his jeans since the moment he'd gotten her pressed against the brick outside the gallery, and at this point he was ready to explode.

Smoothing his hand down her thigh, he cupped her knee, urging it higher. He wanted her legs wrapped around him, her body open for him. She sounded as caught up in it as he was, her breath coming fast, mouth hot and kisses tinged with the same desperation searing his veins.

Fuck, he could pull himself out right now. Ruck her skirt up and shove her panties to the side and be right there, pushing in. Taking her here in the open air, where anyone could see, on the damn trunk of this fucking car.

"Rylan—"

The way she said his name had him one step closer to doing it.

But then there was the sound of laughter. Someone in the street, or hell, maybe in one of the apartments looking down over this alley, and he tore himself away. He was better than this. She deserved better.

Their gazes met as his hands froze on her skin, hers going still on the back of his neck and in his hair. His throat bobbed, arousal turning his blood to molten need.

He shifted his glance to the car behind them before connecting with hers again. He raised a brow. One beat passed and then another, every line of him tense with the strain of holding on. Of not getting himself inside her right now.

She took a shuddering inhalation. And then, in the tightest of motions, she nodded.

Oh, thank God.

Reclaiming her mouth, he picked her up again, all fumbling motions as he got them around to the side of the car. He'd never been so grateful in his life for keyless entry as he was when he wrenched the back door open with one hand. He all but threw her down onto the leather seat. Chase's whole car was going to smell like sex by the time they were done, like the sweetness of her pussy and the tang of their shared sweat, and he couldn't wait.

Tumbling in after her, it struck him—was this what it was like to be a normal teenager? Making out in a borrowed car and hoping no one walked by? The desperate rush, like there was nothing in the entire world more important than getting your hand up under a girl's skirt? This *need*?

His head thunked hard on the roof of the car as he twisted to pull the door shut behind them, and he swore aloud. She squeaked, barely managing to draw her foot back in time before it closed. Double-checking that the doors were locked, he turned, and Jesus.

It was so cramped in here. He had one knee on the seat between the splay of her thighs, the other leg braced against the floor, his whole spine bent so he could fit, and she was scrunched up even worse. But it didn't matter.

She was gorgeous. And for now at least, she was his.

In a rush, he fell back over her. Her spread thighs welcomed him in, and he shoved at her skirt, forcing it up and out of the way as he fit himself to her. A jolting shock pulsed through him at the hot pressure. He ground down against her, his cock rubbing hard into that soft, wet center of her through their clothes. Swallowing her moan, he bucked and pushed, cupped her tit with his free hand. But it wasn't enough. He needed skin, needed inside. He needed too much.

He stopped, breath ragged, scarcely seeing straight as he reared up.

It was only habit at this point. She seemed to be right on the same page with him, ready to jump off this cliff and fall into the steamy crush of their bodies all twisted up together in this tiny space, but she'd started out so timid with him. He'd had to take such gentle care.

There wasn't any gentleness left in his hands.

"Are you ready for this?" he asked, and every word was a low rumble. Thunder and lightning, and she was the rain. Was the only relief.

"Ready?" Her eyes were glazed over. Even in the dim light, her mouth looked red and swollen, her lips bitten, and he wanted to scrape each one even harder with his teeth.

He took his hand off her breast and clamped it against the back of the seat, the leather giving beneath the strength of his grip. "This isn't going to be sweet, or slow, or soft." He sucked in a ragged breath. "It can be. If you need it to be." He'd promised he'd always take his time with her.

"But that's not how you want it."

"I want to fuck you so hard, Kate." He wanted it rough and fast, just the pounding of his body into hers until all this weight, all this greed in his hands and his limbs and his cock gave way. Until there was nothing but her in his blood and on his tongue.

A long, aching moment passed between them. Then, fingers trembling, she wrapped her hand around the back of his neck. Drew him down until they were sharing air. Against his lips, she breathed, "Then fuck me hard."

His lungs emptied forcefully, like the oxygen itself had been punched out of him. He tangled his tongue with hers in a kiss that was all teeth and wet muscle and need. Desperate, he dragged his lips to the point of her jaw and sucked. All down her throat, too hard, pausing only long enough to insist, "Tell me you're sure."

"I'm—oh God—I'm sure."

He tugged the collar of her shirt aside and bit and laved at her skin, waiting until she cried out before moving on. Blood would be blooming to the surface, deep marks of possession so all the world would know. She was taken. She was his. Only his.

The thin, tender skin of her inner thigh molded to the grip of his palm. He reached the hot space between her legs and had to claim her mouth again just to keep the hissing shock of pleasure that drove from her lungs. His cock throbbed at the wet clench of her as he slipped his fingers past her underwear.

"Jesus, you are ready, aren't you?" He could plunge in right now, take what was his, come inside her, fill her up and press harder and harder until she was dying for it.

He spread her slickness around just to be sure, dipping his fingers just inside before circling them around her clit. The first glancing brush there had her knee kicking up, legs spasming as her head fell back.

"That's right, baby," he said.

She gave a low grunt as she reached for his belt. "Thought you were going to fuck me."

"Oh, believe me, I am."

It didn't matter how much he was aching to take her right then and there. He'd never hurt her, would never make her regret him the way she'd regretted the others. Shifting his thumb to that hot little nub above her slit, he plunged a couple of fingers inside. They slid in and out with slick, perfect sounds, and God, he wanted his mouth on her, even if only for a few seconds.

But in this damn car, he'd have to fold himself in half. Probably have to hang out the damn window. There was no way.

Tugging his fingers free, he went for the next best thing. He sat up on his knees, ducking so as not to hit his head. Caught her gaze before slipping his fingers between his lips.

The hot taste of her went straight to his cock, and he closed his eyes.

Only to have them fly right back open at the feeling of her fingertips at the waistband of his jeans.

"Fuck," he hissed, "Kate."

Lips between her teeth, she got his belt undone. Fumbled with the buttons at his fly, but they gave, and then she was reaching in.

The first touch of her hand on bare skin was a shock of pleasure, sliding up his balls and into his damn spine. God, she felt good—not just that she was touching him, but the way she curled her fingers around his base as she pulled him out. The way she stroked, drawing liquid from his tip and sliding it around. His eyes about rolled back in his head.

Gone was the passivity of their past two nights. She was here and with him, present in a way that made him tremble.

Enough hesitating. Enough waiting.

He gave his fingers one last suck before withdrawing them. He got his wallet out and plucked the condom from its pocket. Tore the packet open with his teeth. She moved her hand out of the way as he placed the circle of latex over his tip, but then she was there, skin brushing his as she helped him roll it along his length, and he had to squeeze down hard around the base to try to get himself under control.

"Lie back," he said, the gravelly darkness of his voice surprising even him.

Pulse roaring, he followed her to the seat, rearranging her legs, lifting one knee and pressing it hard to her chest. Getting her open and ready for him.

And shit, he had no leverage in this position, but he didn't care. Tugging her underwear aside, he dragged the tip of his cock up and down the slick gash of her cunt, little nudges to just barely press himself inside before shifting up to circle her clit, over and over until his head spun. He nipped at her lips, kissed his way across her cheek and to her ear where he scraped his teeth across the lobe, and it wasn't enough. Nothing would ever be enough.

Not until she was his.

The fire from back at the gallery filled him, sending filthy thoughts, needy words bubbling up into his lungs.

Groaning against her ear, he slid himself harder against her, so close to but not quite giving them what they both needed. "Tell me you want it," he ground out.

She whined, angling her neck to the side in sheer invitation. "I already—"

He shook his head. "You told me you were ready for it. Tell me you want it. You want my cock, want to get fucked, want *me*—"

He bit off the word. Because that was what he needed. What he'd always needed. Someone to want him. Not his money or his power or what he could do for them. Just him.

Just like she had.

Once, back in a different life, she had.

"Tell me," he insisted, and it was a command and a plea.

"Rylan." Her voice walked an edge of desperation that made his skin go shivery and tight. Wrapping a leg around his hips, she reached down and into his waistband to clutch at his hip and yank. God but that would've done it for him, if he weren't so intent on getting her to ask.

He gritted his teeth, held firm at the cusp of her entrance. He was so hard it hurt, but no way he was giving in. She had to be aching, too, had to be so close to begging him for it. "Aren't you empty, baby? Say the word. Just say it—"

"Rylan," she repeated, and this time she threaded her fingers through his hair. The sharp pull made his eyes burn, but he rose up. Braced a hand against the window above her head, and she was gazing at him with these hazy, lust-drunk eyes. There was clarity behind the desperation, though. Like she saw right through him. Like she knew.

"Rylan. I want you."

Something in his chest clicked into place.

He drove inside in one long stroke, buried himself in wet heat, and he could have cried. Shuddering, he moaned her name and fell back over her. Their lips met in a not-quite kiss as he fought past the shock of being surrounded by her, consumed in her warmth and her words. The hand at his hip gripped him harder, and he rocked forward, clenching his jaw against the pressure already gathering, the need to pour himself into her.

And he should wait, slow down. Make it last. But this energy vibrated through him, reaching a fever pitch. He snapped.

"Hold on," he managed to grit out.

Scrambling for purchase, he drew his hips back. After a bare second's pause, he drove forward, and his vision whited out, it was so good. He'd scarcely bottomed out before drawing away again, faster this time, and he couldn't stop.

His rhythm was punishing, so much rougher than he ever would've dared with her had he been in his right mind. He'd make it good for her regardless, only this fucking car... There wasn't any room to get a hand on her, to even ask her to touch herself, but he'd try, goddammit all. He shifted, working to get an arm free.

But his foot slipped, jamming into the door, changing his angle, and a low, whimpering sound made its way out of her, her fingers digging into his skin, and *fuck yeah*, he loved it when she used her nails.

Except. Shit.

He buried his face in her hair but didn't slow, panting hard. "Too much?"

It was beyond too much, and it would never be enough. Here he was. Pounding into her, taking her like an animal, using her, because he needed to lose himself in her body. Because *he* needed, not because she did—

Fuck, he had to stop.

But she shook her head and arched up into him, meeting his strokes, and it was a burst of lightning in his brain.

"It's good," she insisted.

The thunder of her pleasure deafened his senses.

"Yeah?" Oh God, he was in so deep. Speeding his thrusts, he drove into her again and again, but he needed her voice. Needed to know she was still with him. "You like it hard?"

Her nails dug in. "Yeah."

"Tell me. Tell me you like it when I fuck you."

"I—" Her voice cut off, this throaty sound escaping. Shooting straight to his balls. "I love it."

I love you.

He bit down on his tongue hard enough he feared it would bleed. All his life, he'd seen how love could be used, how easy it was to discard, but it was welling up in him with such force now. Threatening to drown him.

And all he wanted to do was give it to her. For her to take it.

"Tell me you're mine," he choked out, and this wasn't the time. She wasn't his. She'd barely agreed to see him, still seemed reluctant more often than not. She'd been so *angry* at him—

"I'm yours. Rylan—"

And that was it. Climax took him by surprise, surging through him and turning him inside out. With the first gasping pulse of it, he opened his mouth to warn her, but she was pulling him into a kiss that tasted like heaven and her, and he lost himself to it. Shuddered inside her hands, inside her body. He emptied himself until there was nothing left, his legs and arms and lungs all giving out on him.

When he came back to himself, he was splayed out on top of her, his mouth open and damp against her throat, her fingers petting stiffly at his hair. Groaning, he worked to get an arm under him to take some of his weight. He had to be crushing her, and worse, he'd come before she had and then practically blacked out. Pathetic. But he'd do his best to rectify it.

He withdrew from her with a low grunt, only to have his knee lock up on him as he fought to rise. The awkward angles of his limbs and the crick in his spine he hadn't cared about as he'd been careening toward orgasm suddenly made themselves painfully clear. He spit out a low curse and she laughed.

"Car sex always sounded like such a good idea," she said, voice tight.

"Especially in a car as sexy as this."

"Not as good in practice, though, is it?"

Not *good*? Any better and he might have broken a hip.

"I don't know about that."

He'd prove it to her in a minute. Just as soon as he got his breath back.

With effort, he lifted himself off her, all but collapsing to the floor in a heap. He tied off the condom and dropped it into a handkerchief before setting it aside. He licked his lips, more focused now. Ready to do better. But by the time he twisted back around, it was to find her struggling to sit up, tugging her skirt back into place. Like she thought they were done.

Well, fuck that.

A growl rose to the back of his throat. "What do you think you're doing?"

She looked up at him, eyes wide, hands freezing at the hem of her skirt. "Um..."

The male center of pride in him quaked. "Did you or did you not just tell me you were mine?"

"I—"

"I take care of what's mine."

With a fresh burst of energy, he took her by the wrists and shoved her hands out of the way. Flipped her skirt back up.

Fuck, but her panties were soaked.

Ignoring the way she squirmed, he got her sitting up, arranged her in the middle of the seat, and spread her legs wide. Hooked his hands under her knees and hauled her forward so her ass sat at the edge of the seat.

"Jesus," she said as he dove in.

He sucked at the wet panel of her underwear, scraping his teeth over her clit through the fabric. It was even more awkward of a position than he'd imagined earlier when he'd wanted to get his mouth on her, but he didn't care. Slinging a trembling thigh over his shoulder, he tugged her panties to the side, exposing all that sweet, ripe flesh.

Her breath stuttered as he slicked a thumb down the length of her slit. "Oh God."

"Hold on to that thought," he murmured, spreading her open and leaning in.

The taste of the condom mingled with her sweetness, but he worked past it, pursing his lips around her clit. It was his own fault anyway—too impatient to do this for her before he got inside.

But there were benefits to her having already gotten fucked. She was so close to the brink, legs trembling around his head as he dove in, kissing her wet and sloppy, pressing his tongue inside before laving hot stripes over her clit. And she was open for him, too, taking three fingers easy. He fucked her with them as punishingly fast and hard as he had with his cock, and she cried out his name.

He glanced up her body, and his cock, spent and done, gave a painful, wrecking throb. God, she was gorgeous. All pretenses at restraint and decorum gone. No protests on her lips, because he had taught her how to accept this. How to give herself over to it.

With one hand, she helped hold herself open for him, while with the other she yanked at her hair. Her head was thrown back, sweat painting the exposed tops of her breasts, and he could do this for her forever. He would, so long as she would just...

"Give it up," he said. "Give it to me."

Her pleasure and her body and her fucking *life*.

When it finally crested over, she screamed, and he hoped the whole world heard it, that everyone for blocks around knew he was ruining her, bringing her to heights no other man ever had or ever would. Chasing the pulsing clench of her pussy around his fingers, he licked and licked, until she reached down. Put a hand on his head.

With one last kiss to her clit, he slipped his fingers free. He pressed his brow against the inside of her thigh and closed his eyes.

The space around him spun.

He'd had sex so many times before, and in far more comfortable locations. But it had never been like this—not with full awareness of how he felt and of what he stood to lose. It made something hot curl up inside his lungs, pressing too hard. Like it was aching to break out.

When all he wanted to do was stay here. In this safe, defined place. With her.

Kate still hadn't quite gotten her balance back by the time they pulled up outside her building. Rylan shifted the car out of gear and turned to her. His blue eyes glinted in the dim light coming in from the streetlamps, and his throat bobbed.

"So," he said.

She dropped her gaze, staring down at her hands as if they could hold the answer.

By a lot of standards, it had been a good night. She'd gotten to see a lot of art and do a little bit of networking. She'd tried a new restaurant.

She'd had incredible, strange, intense sex in the backseat of a car she was never going to stop having extremely inappropriate thoughts about. And it had been...different. Rylan's touch on her skin had held a whole new kind of power as he took what he wanted from her, be it her body or her words. And then, when he'd been done, he'd come back to her. Made sure she got as much from it as he had—maybe more.

Maybe less.

The possessiveness in his hands and in his eyes had shaken her to her core.

His. He'd begged her to tell him she was his, and in that moment, surrounded by him, speared by him, her flesh melting beneath the heat of his stare, she'd felt like she was. She'd given him the affirmation he'd seemed to need so badly. It was only after, while she was coming down, his face hidden against her thigh and their breathing loud in that tiny, silent space, that it had all come crashing down around her.

She was her own. She had to be. She'd let him have her so completely back in Paris, and it had only brought her heartbreak. When she'd agreed to let him try to win her trust again, she'd promised herself she'd keep some part of herself. She'd sworn she'd guard her heart.

But he wanted it all. And that was a problem, on so many levels.

Starting with the shit show that had been his behavior around her friends.

She'd held her tongue about it all on their silent ride home. But they had to talk about it. There were so many things that couldn't go unsaid this time around.

Picking at her nail, she took a deep breath. "So. Do you want to tell me what all of that was about?"

He huffed out a dry echo of a laugh. "Which part?"

"Liam is just a friend." She had to emphasize that point. She was under no illusions that Rylan's jealousy hadn't been at the heart of the way he'd acted tonight. "Yes, he's interested, and under other circumstances, maybe I could've been, too. But for now at least, that's all there is to it."

"For now."

She shrugged. "Things change. I'm not going to promise I'm

never going to consider him if this"—she gestured between the two of them—"doesn't work out."

"I want it to work out."

"I know." A part of her did, too. A bigger part still couldn't trust it, though. Couldn't trust his assurances. Couldn't trust herself.

She'd thought he was different the last time around, and just look where that had gotten them.

She met his gaze for the first time since he'd parked the car. "I'm not going to stop being friends with him."

"I wouldn't have asked you to." The bitterness to his tone said he wanted to.

"Really?"

He lifted his hand and pinched the bridge of his nose. "I know I acted like a caveman tonight—"

"Yeah, you did." And it hadn't just been that. "You were rude to him and you were... *insane* around me." Hadn't her mother warned her about precisely that kind of crap? Jealousy seemed flattering and sexy at the time, but when it cut you off from your friends... When it served to leave you isolated and dependent... "Don't get me wrong, it was hot. But it wasn't okay."

"I know. I'm sorry."

The sincerity in his apology made her pause.

She'd been bracing herself. This was the kind of fight she'd heard her parents hash out over and over. Any time her mother tried to raise a concern, her father would escalate, throwing it back in her face, turning it around as if she'd been the one to do something wrong. *She* made him act the way she did—if she were only better, he wouldn't have to get like this...

As the silence stretched out, Rylan reached across the gap between their seats, taking her hand. The warmth of it, the soft kneading of his thumb against her palm, helped ground her.

"It won't happen again," he promised.

She wanted to believe him, but she couldn't just accept his assurances like that. She had to be clear.

"Back in Paris," she said, "it was so easy. It was just the two of us. No work, no classes, no..." She gestured in a broad circle at him, as if to encapsulate all the things he'd been hiding back then. "...companies. Or families. Or friends."

"It was amazing." He flashed her a soft, nostalgic smile.

"It wasn't real." Deep in her chest, something cracked. Because it hadn't been. The whirlwind romance, the foreign locale, the abandon with which they had approached it all. "It was a fantasy."

A fairy tale.

In the real world, you didn't marry your prince. You threw out your remaining shoe and got back to sweeping your chimney.

Voice gravelly, eyes dark, he asked, "Can't it be both?" She raised an eyebrow at him, and he squeezed her palm, dragging her hand in closer so it rested in the space between their seats. "It may have been a fantasy, but for me. The things I felt. The things I feel. They were real."

Her heart did something complicated in her chest.

What she'd felt had seemed real enough at the time. But now, she didn't know. She'd loved the version of him she'd been allowed to see. Even that hadn't quite been reality.

"Whatever we feel..." She steeled herself. "Whatever we want to happen here. It has to happen around the rest of our lives. I—" Her words got all twisted up on her tongue, but she had to say this. She couldn't let herself be her mother. She couldn't be the old version of herself. Worrying the inside of her

lip with her teeth, she blew out a rough breath. "I can't be getting dragged out of art openings just because my—" And she
got tripped up again. *My boyfriend.* Was that even who he was
to her now? "Because the guy in my life doesn't like the way
other men look at me. All the other people in my program were
watching. They were *worried* about me." God, it was going to be
such a mess explaining that on Monday.

"I'll do better," he swore, swooping in, rescuing her from the
mess she was making of what she needed to say. "It just...took
me by surprise." The corner of his mouth twisted, somewhere
between a wry smile and a frown. "I knew you had a life. Friends.
A career. I didn't realize how it would make me feel to see it,
though."

"How's that?" Jealous, obviously.

But instead, he answered, "Proud. And terrified."

She let that sit on her chest for a moment. "I like the proud
part."

"Well, that part never goes away." With that, he brought her
hand up to his lips and pressed a soft kiss there.

Swallowing, she curled her fingers around his. "We'll see
what we can do about the terrified part."

"I'd like that."

He let her go, and she returned her hand to her lap to unzip
her bag and pulled her keys out. By all rights, this was the point
in the evening when she invited him in, and she wanted to. For
the first time since their reunion, the idea of sleeping tangled up
beside him, of letting him get that close, didn't scare her.

But she wasn't quite sure if she could do it, either.

Apparently, his thoughts had gone to the same place. "Would
it be cliché to ask if I could come up and see your etchings?"

Her art was one thing she definitely wasn't ready for him to see, despite the confidence he'd expressed in her before. And that alone told her it wasn't time yet to ask him to stay. "No etchings, sadly."

"A cup of coffee."

Her heart was heavy as she said, "Not tonight."

"Ah." He set his hand back on the gearshift and glanced away.

She wasn't going to apologize for not being ready. "Maybe next time."

"All right," he said, still not quite smiling.

"Rylan..."

He turned to her again, looking over at her side of the car.

And she'd just said no to him. So if she wanted more...She didn't have to wait for him to start everything.

Screwing up her confidence, she undid her seat belt, then leaned over across the space between them. The slight rasp of stubble on his cheek bit into her palm as she cupped his face. Their lips met, and he let her direct the kiss. Let her keep it soft and sweet.

Exactly the way she wanted it, after everything else.

She pulled away after a long minute. "Good night."

His lips curled up, small but real this time. "Good night."

He waited until she'd made it into the entryway of her building before he pulled away. At the last second, she very nearly called him back. But in the end, she let him go. It was easier that way. Safer.

It was a reminder that she was really still her own.

chapter THIRTEEN

You busy on Friday?

Kate scrunched her face up at her phone, neatly dodging another pedestrian on the sidewalk. She was coming off a six-hour shift and heading straight to campus to see if she couldn't get some work done.

And because she needed to rip the Band-Aid off.

The temptation to paint in the comfort of her own apartment had been especially hard to ignore today. But she hadn't seen Liam or any of the other people from her program since Friday night at the gallery opening, and if she didn't face them soon, how was she ever supposed to be able to?

In the back of her mind, she kept picturing the look Liam had given her as Rylan had ushered her out. The worry that had furrowed his brow. She was still trying to figure out how the hell she was going to explain the whole thing to him.

Keeping half an eye on where she was going, she hit the button to reply.

No...Why?

It was a minor miracle, actually. She never had class on Friday, and somehow or other she'd managed to end up with the entire long weekend off from work. It meant the rest of her week was going to be hell, but it might almost be worth it. She'd really be able to dig into this portfolio project, maybe. Get some space in her head at last.

Or she could while it away with Rylan. She mentally rolled her eyes at herself. The man seemed to have a sixth sense about the time she'd budgeted to spend with her sketchbooks and canvases. It was a tension that had plagued them since their first days together in Paris, and it showed no sign of going away any time soon.

Yet another thing they were going to have to figure out if he wanted to try to make a go of it. Be a couple, here in the real world, navigating all the people and things and commitments their lives were filled with.

She was really starting to believe he did.

His reply came through a few seconds later.

Move in day at the new place. Wondered if you wanted to come lift some boxes with me.

Her brows rose about an inch. Did he expect her to believe he'd be doing the move himself?

She'd scarcely thought it before her phone pinged again.

Well, watch some movers lift some boxes.

At least she appreciated the honesty.

Will there be beer and pizza? she asked. Even if he'd hired guys to do the hard work, that was a tradition that transcended social class. Right?

Consider it done.

It wasn't exactly what she'd had in mind for her weekend, but it might be sort of fun. She'd never gotten to see the actual place where he lived in Paris, and he hadn't invited her over while he'd been staying at his sister's apartment.

She couldn't decide if that bothered her or not.

Another text came through as she was crossing the street toward the art building.

Some of my friends will be there, too. Thought you might want to meet them.

She considered that for a second. Your sister?

Y, if she can manage to take a day away from the office.

Her heart beat a little harder. He was really inviting her into his life here. For the very first time, he was asking her to peer behind the curtain. The whole point of this second chance had been for him to prove to her that he was the man she'd fallen for back in Paris—before she'd known the reality of his life. So far, she hadn't gotten to see much beyond what he wanted her to see. Maybe this was her chance.

Before she could second-guess herself, she messaged back, It's a date.

Their fourth date, in fact. Officially halfway through the seven he had begged of her. And it felt like they'd barely cracked the surface.

Putting her phone away, she headed in and up the stairs. As she crossed the threshold of the painting studio, she shed her jacket and pulled her bag over her head.

And then came to a screeching halt to find Liam right on the other side of the door.

He looked the same as ever, sandy hair disheveled and tight jeans paint-streaked, but the *way* he looked at her was different. Not quite accusing but...

Disappointed.

Something turned over in her chest. She had plenty of experience with that particular look, thank you very much.

"Hey." He paused with his own jacket halfway on. "I was just about to go do a coffee run." He gave her a pointed look. "You want to come with?"

Dammit, she'd just gotten here. Taking a deep breath, she reminded herself: *Band-Aid.* "Sure."

She got her own stuff tugged back on as she turned around. It was a short walk right across the street, and yet it felt like it took about a year. The whole way over, he held his tongue—possibly literally, based on the pinched expression on his face. When they finally had their drinks in hand, he nodded toward an open table in the corner.

He settled into the seat across from her and turned his cup around between his palms. Bracing herself, she sat there, ready to defend Rylan. He wasn't usually so possessive or so antisocial. He was usually charming and insightful and—

"I didn't know you had a boyfriend."

Oh. Or they could start with that.

She shrugged, fiddling with the cardboard sleeve around her cup. "It's new. Sort of." She frowned. How much did she really want to get into this? "We had a—a fling, over the summer. We ran into each other a couple of weeks ago and decided to see if there was anything more to it."

He paused for a second, and then his voice dropped. "You could have told me."

She'd felt like shit every time she hadn't. "I wasn't sure how much there was to tell." She hadn't really thought it would last even this long.

"Anything would've been nice. Here I was, thinking..." He trailed off. There was a bitter, wry slant to his mouth.

They hadn't exactly spoken about Liam's interest in her out loud, but there it was, on the table between them now. They'd might as well get it all out.

"I thought so, too. Maybe." She took a deep breath. She'd resisted putting a label on what was going on between her and Rylan, or apparently even acknowledging it at all. But she couldn't lead Liam on. Even if she had seen some potential between them, Rylan had walked back into her life and reclaimed this piece of her heart she hadn't even realized was waiting for him. The piece he'd crushed, but which had started to beat again the second she'd seen his face. She was working to guard herself harder this time, but there were some things she couldn't deny. "But I'm with Rylan."

If it fell apart again tomorrow, it still wouldn't leave any room for anyone else. Not for a long time. Maybe not ever.

They sat there in silence for a minute.

Finally, he sighed. "He seems...intense."

With a half laugh, she agreed, "You have no idea." It was hard to believe their original affair had been as brief as it was. She'd fallen in with him so quickly, had been swept under by his looks and his charm and the way he touched her. The things he taught her body it could do.

But for all of that intensity, he'd never acted quite the way he had the other night.

She chose her words carefully. *He's not usually like that* had abuse victim written all over it, and she didn't want to paint this in the wrong light. "For what it's worth, he didn't really know about you, either."

"I may have gotten that," he said, desert-dry. "Guy has a jealous streak a mile wide, huh?"

"Apparently." She took a sip of her coffee. Rylan's possessiveness had taken her by surprise, opening her eyes. He'd always been so in control of himself before. Seeing him wild like that...It'd been sexy. And concerning. "I told him after that I wasn't going to stop being friends with you."

"Well, thank goodness for small favors." And there was that same wryness again.

Her stomach squirmed. She was being presumptuous, wasn't she? Looking up to meet his gaze, she forced a smile. "If you still want to be, that is."

He regarded her evenly for a beat, and the uneasiness in her gut went harder. But then one corner of his mouth twitched up. It wasn't as natural as it might have been a few days ago, but when he reached out and mock-punched her on the arm, it felt like pure relief. "Come on. Like I'd ever get through seminar if I didn't have you to joke around with."

She exhaled out all the breath in her lungs. Okay. She could work with this.

"True story," she said, voice quiet.

She didn't have all that many people in her life right now. Knowing she had a friend, a guy even, who would stick by her without conditions. Without the promise of sex.

It just meant a lot to her, somehow.

chapter FOURTEEN

There were a lot of things Rylan had kissed good-bye the day he'd walked out of a courtroom and onto a plane, on a one-way trip to Paris with no intention to return. As the smoking ruins of his father's dreams for him had disappeared beyond the horizon, he'd made his peace with it. He'd miss his sister and Chase and maybe, at least to a certain extent, his work. But the rest of it could rot.

Nothing more so than this place.

The churning in his gut hit a whole new peak as he came in view of the big, wrought-iron gate that surrounded the property. The ivy had always been thick, but it was overgrown to the point where he could scarcely see inside at all now, and that was good. That was right. No one should be able to look at what was left of his family.

At the empty, lonely house where he had once been a boy. But where he had never, ever been allowed to be a child.

He swallowed hard as he approached the entrance. Balancing the coffees he was holding in one hand, he got his key ring out.

Flipped through it until he hit the old brass one that for some reason he'd never taken off.

The door to the gate was as smooth and silent as ever as it swung open. For all that the gardening had apparently been let go, the caretakers responsible for the mansion's upkeep continued to do their job. He should probably be grateful for that.

He gazed inside at the brick and stone monstrosity his father had built as a monument to his own damn ego, and his entire chest went tight.

He froze, there on the boundary.

And he should go in. The movers would be here soon. *Kate* would be here even sooner. There were a million things to do.

In the end, he made it as far as a low stone bench in the center of the courtyard. He sat down hard, gazing out across the barren grass, and then up.

Instinctively, his gaze went to the southeast corner, second floor. His father's study. How many times had he stared up at that as he came home? Peering in to see if it was still alight.

Hoping that it would be as a boy. That his father would still be up, and maybe he'd want to talk. To give Rylan just an ounce of his attention.

Praying it wouldn't, those few awful months he'd lived here as an adult. That he wouldn't have to hear another fucking word about how he was wasting his life at these parties. He needed to work harder, be more, do more. Forget he already put in eighty-hour weeks. The future of the company was depending on him, for fuck's sake.

He put the coffees down on the bench and braced his elbows on his knees.

The future of the company still depended on him—probably even more than it had back then.

But that was a line of thought for another day. For now, he was here. At his father's home. To take what was his.

And to build something new from the salvage.

Movement at the edge of his vision had him jerking his head upward. Fuck, he was so tense. As the gentle ringing sound of knuckles rapping on iron echoed across the courtyard, he uncurled his fingers from his fists, the white crescents his nails had left in his palms bleeding back to rosy flesh.

The gate he'd left ajar swung wider, and a second later, Kate poked her head in through the gap.

A little more of the stiffness in Rylan's spine faded away. He didn't even have to force a smile.

"Hey," he said, sitting up straighter.

"Hey yourself." Kate slipped inside and eased the gate back into place.

His grin grew as he took her in. She looked ready to work, for all that he'd assured her he had people coming to do the heavy lifting. Her long, dark hair was tied back in a simple braid, and he envisioned untying it later, combing his fingers through the loose locks. He licked his lips, looking forward to taking off her jeans.

Sliding those little purple Converse from her feet.

But first, he had to get them to that point. Not for the first time, he second-guessed his decision to ask her to meet him here. If anything would scare her off, it would be his father's mansion. It typified all the things he'd originally imagined she'd abhor. Huge and hollow and useless. A waste.

Like he had been, when she'd met him. She'd accepted him then all the same.

He had to give her credit—she did a pretty good job of pretending not to notice her surroundings as she made her way over to him. Her stride remained casual, her shoulders loose. But her gaze kept wandering, her brows gradually creeping toward her hairline. He could almost see the questions bubbling up to her lips.

He patted the space beside him as she neared, beckoning her to sit.

She did, pointing at the coffees to the other side of him. "Is one of those for me?"

"It might be." He picked hers up and held it out to her, but as she went to take it from him, he grabbed it back. "It isn't free, though."

"Oh, no?"

"Nope." He presented his cheek for a kiss in payment.

Rolling her eyes, she sighed, but she leaned in easily enough. Her lips lingered against his skin, and he reached up to clasp the side of her neck, holding her in place as he turned.

Her mouth opened beneath his, and he hummed into the kiss, darting out his tongue to taste the soft pout of her lower lip. She smelled shower-fresh, sweet and warm, and her hair had the tiniest bit of dampness to it as he slid his palm higher, cradling the back of her head.

She pulled away a long second later, blinking slowly at him, her eyes a little glazed. She came back to herself quickly enough. "That was an expensive cup of coffee."

Chuckling, he handed it over and watched as she brought it to her lips. The gentle pink curve of them eased upward.

Her gaze darted over to him. "You remember."

Of course he did. Two more sugars than he thought was a good idea and enough cream to turn it a pale, milky tan.

He remembered everything that gave her pleasure. Everything he could do to make her smile.

He couldn't help the wistfulness that crept into his voice. "I've been hoping I'd be able to fetch it for you some morning."

After he stayed over or after she did. Leaving her naked in bed, maybe still sleeping while he went off to the bakery down the street, or even just to the kitchen. Returning to her, mug in hand, and peeling back the sheet. Waking her up with the press of his lips all down the line of her spine...

Her smile faded. "If you ever want to meet for breakfast..."

"Not what I meant." He wasn't in any mood to pussyfoot around.

"I know."

They sat there in silence for a few moments, sipping their coffees, before she cleared her throat and looked around. "Are your other friends here already?"

He shook his head. "They're meeting us at the house. This..." He faltered for a moment. How precisely was he supposed to explain? "This is just you and me."

Her gaze slipped past him, finally alighting on the elephant in the room. "Is this your family's home?"

"It was."

It had only been his father's at the end. Rylan and Lexie had moved out years ago. Evan usually spent his breaks at Lexie's if he chose to spend them on this coast at all. Their mother was still off to destinations unknown.

And anyway. It had been so long since it had felt like a home.

"Wow." She worked her jaw back and forth a couple of times, and there was that discomfort he'd sensed in her as she'd made her way up the walk.

"It's just a house," he said, an unwelcome note of pleading working its way into his voice.

"Right."

His stomach dropped. But he refused to apologize, either for who he was or for inviting her here. Part of this whole trial period was getting to know each other better, and like it or not, this place was a part of his history. A part of him. He'd wanted her to see it.

And selfishly, he hadn't wanted to face it on his own.

Rising, he grasped his coffee in one hand and held the other out to her. "Come on." He kept his tone firm. "I have something I want to show you."

She narrowed her eyes at him in consideration, but before his heart could stutter too badly, she slipped her palm into his and let him help her to her feet.

He wrapped his arm around her shoulders as they made their way to the big bronze doors. He took a deep breath before he let them in.

The wall of memory and silence that met him at the threshold tore the air from his lungs regardless.

"Are you okay?" Kate asked, looking up at him.

"Fine." He gave his eyes a moment to adjust to the dimness. His ribs squeezed like a vise in his chest. "It's just been a while."

Since his father's sentencing, at the very least. He peered past the foyer, into dusty rooms, at the furniture and lighting fixtures all draped with big white cloths. Someone must have come and closed the place up after he had gone. As he led them forward, their footsteps echoed off the marble, the whole place feeling empty and cavernous.

And haunted. He shivered at the memory of his father's voice calling from the top of the stairs. The faded peals of his brother and sister's laughter. Their mother, home for once, and scurrying past in her heels.

Overwhelmed, he fought to block it out. Giving her his best, most reassuring smile, he headed for the grand staircase in the center of the room. Up and up, spiraling higher, and with every step, he breathed a little better. Felt a little less like his history was pressing in. They were past the worst of it, the parts of the house for entertaining and impressing guests. Past his parents' rooms on the fourth floor.

At the fifth, he finally relaxed. This was where he and his siblings had lived. All in little suites, with an apartment for the nanny, too. The whole way up, Kate had kept craning her neck, trying to slow him down or to glimpse around corners, and here, at least, he didn't mind.

He turned, taking both their coffees and setting them down on an empty shelf. Walking backward down the hall, he loosely clasped her hands in his.

"Those rooms were my sister's," he said as they passed the open door. The pink walls.

"Lexie, right?"

He nodded, then tilted his head toward the left. "And those were my brother, Evan's."

"The artist."

"You have a good memory."

She slowed her gait, veering as if to peek in. "Are any of his sculptures still here?"

Rylan's heart gave a little pang. "I doubt it. He never kept much of it around the house."

And with good reason. After Evan had left for school, Rylan had crated up what little he could find and shipped it to him. So he wouldn't lose it. Not the way that Rylan had . . .

He forced the corner of his mouth up as he pulled her on. Back into the final set of rooms. "And these"—he spread his arm wide—"were mine."

"Oh." She dropped her hands as he released them, letting them fall by her sides.

He didn't miss the disappointment to her tone. He couldn't blame her for it, either.

Taking a slow turn, he tried to see the place through her eyes. The tasteful, bare blue walls and the beige carpet. Ivory linen curtains with a pinstripe to match the paint. He was half-surprised they hadn't even found drop cloths to go with the color scheme.

He wandered over to the bed, covered in another flat white sheet, and flopped himself onto it, lying back to stare at the ceiling. It was a familiar view.

"So what do you think?" he asked.

"I thought it would be more..." She trailed off. He could finish the sentence well enough himself.

She'd thought it would be more interesting. More revealing. More *anything*, except what it was.

A blank slate.

For a long moment, he chewed on the inside of his cheek.

When he spoke, the words were low. The hurt a still long-simmering thing. "They sent me off to boarding school, you know."

"Oh?" And there was the interest he'd been waiting for.

"Yup. Exeter. Just like my old man. I was gone nine months of the year. Studying." Making connections. Getting a head start on the life his father had arranged for him to lead. He closed his eyes, and the back of his throat burned. "I came home for winter break that first year, and everything..." All his pictures. What little he still had left of his toys. "It was all gone."

They'd said they had turned it into a man's room. They'd turned it into *anyone's* room.

"How old were you?"

"Fourteen."

Old enough to be thinking about his future. About who he wanted to be. As if that had ever mattered.

"So what, they just boxed it all up?"

"I don't even know." His father said they'd gotten rid of it. For all he knew, it could be up in the attic somewhere. He doubted it, though.

The bed dipped as she sat down beside him, and he opened his eyes. She was so lovely. Especially when she looked at him like that.

Not like a poor little rich boy who'd been told to grow up too soon.

But like she understood.

Placing her hand on his chest, she frowned. "That's awful."

"It could be worse."

Her gaze rose to settle on his face. "Still sucks, though."

His mouth cracked into a smile, and he was suddenly so damn glad he'd brought her here. For the first time all day, with her, here, staring at him and touching him, he could breathe.

He clasped a hand over hers. Let the rest of it drain from his mind. Let his expression go soft. "Doesn't seem all that bad right now."

Still holding on to her, he lifted his other arm to curl around her neck and tug her down. He tasted her mouth and slid his palm toward her shoulder. Down her side to cup her hip and sneak his thumb beneath her shirt to touch her flesh.

She came along so much more easily than she had in the past. At his nudge, she swung a leg over him, straddling his waist. Bracing her hands to either side of his head and parting her lips as he swept forward with his tongue. He cupped the bare skin of her side, pushing her top up and out of the way, and it would be so easy to lose himself like this. To forget where they were or what he still had to do.

"Kate," he murmured, pressing up, body awakening. She eased down, and the center of her brushed where he was already half-hard. A low groan forced its way out of his lungs, and he flipped them, getting her on his back for him, there on that bed he'd always hated, in this house that hadn't felt like home in so long. Her cheeks were flushed, lips bitten, and he danced his fingertips toward her breast—

When the doorbell sounded from downstairs.

"Fuck." He dropped his face into the mattress beside her head. "That'll be the movers."

"Maybe if we ignore them, they'll go away?"

"Maybe." Lifting himself off her, he let out a frustrated sigh. "But then I'd just have to hire them again for another day."

And he could work with that. A whole day with nothing to do, and with Kate here beneath him . . . It was beyond tempting.

He rolled to the side, breathing to the count of three before sitting up straight.

No way was he bunking down in his sister's spare room for another night. He was making himself the home he'd come to New York to reclaim. Kate was going to help him make it, along with his sister and his friends.

He gazed back at her, at the smooth skin of her stomach, the rosy hue working its way up her neck. The soft, warm brown of her eyes.

Smoothing her shirt back into place, he leaned in for one last kiss.

Tonight, he'd have her in his own bed. In his own home.

Even he could be patient enough to wait for that.

*   *   *

Rylan Bellamy was the worst kind of tease there ever was. Kate's pulse was racing from the heat of his kiss and the weight of his body, and her arousal wasn't the only thing he'd piqued.

There was also the small matter of her curiosity.

Setting herself to rights the best she could, she followed him back down the stairs to the foyer of his . . . his *mansion*. The place where he'd grown up. God, and she'd thought the brownstone he'd decided to buy was excessive. Here was this place that was bigger than her entire apartment building, and it had all been for one family. Back when it had even been occupied at all.

Apparently they didn't have any more time to poke around as they descended than they had on the ascent, and sure, there were people waiting for them downstairs. But who invited their girlfriend to a place like this without at least giving her the tour? At every flight of stairs, she gazed longingly down the empty corridors. What lay behind those doors? What had this place been like back in its prime?

What had Rylan been like? A child surrounded by this kind of extravagance.

A teenager coming home after months at school to find all of his possessions cleared away.

Her heart clenched hard at the thought. She couldn't even imagine it. She'd scarcely been home in years, but she still had a room in her mother's tiny apartment. Her ancient teddy bears and books might be sharing space with an elliptical machine these days, but they were there. She would always be welcome back.

Then again . . .

She shivered as she hit the third floor landing and kept on climbing down.

Her father's house had never felt like a home. She'd had her own room and her own things, but there'd been a perilousness to it all. When her dad got angry, everything was fair game. Figurines smashed and pages torn. The door that hadn't had a lock.

Maybe some things transcended how nice of a house you got to live in. Maybe some people had to leave to find anything that was truly their own.

Rylan had outpaced her by a wider and wider margin as they'd made their way toward the first floor. She turned the landing for the final flight expecting him to already be at the door, but instead, he'd pulled up short. He waited for her at the base of the stairs, one hand on the banister while he extended the other one toward her. She slowed, coming to a halt on the next-to-last step. It put them on more even ground with her above him like this, and she met his smile with her own, letting him pull her down into a soft, sweet kiss. The angle was all different like this, and she fell into it. Fell into him.

He pulled away after a long minute, his hand lingering on the back of her neck to steady her. She blinked her eyes open to look at him.

And there was a flicker of something in his gaze. Something naked and open to him that made her tremble.

"Thank you," he said, voice low. "For doing this with me."

It resonated deep in the shaking part inside of her.

Like he wasn't thanking just anyone, like he hadn't simply wanted to not have to do it alone. Like he'd needed *her*.

Her throat went tight with the closeness of their bodies. The whisper of his breath across her lips. "Any time."

And a piece of her really meant it.

He let her go after that, retreating to the door just as the chime rang out a final time.

In the end, the crew he'd hired was made up of six big men in white uniforms. Rylan shook hands with them all in turn and nodded his head toward her, introducing her to them as well. Then he led them down a different corridor, past a series of rooms each bigger and grander than the last. The furniture was draped just as it had been upstairs, but a dining table large enough for a state dinner was hard to miss. A chandelier in what must have been a ballroom that could have been in *The Phantom of the Opera*.

It's just a house, he'd told her when she'd questioned him outside. Considering the casualness with which he swept through it, to him it really had been.

The corridor took a sharp turn after the ballroom. At the end of the next hall, Rylan reached out and opened a door. "This is the loading dock." He explained to one of the men where to pull the truck around, then turned.

When Kate realized what she was looking at, she gawked. "There was an elevator here the whole time?"

Rylan smirked. "Says the girl in the three-story walk-up. I thought you liked taking the stairs."

Without even thinking, she reached out and play-smacked his arm, only to have him catch her wrist. Entwining their hands, he dragged her into the elevator with him, standing way too close to her, considering the movers crowded in around them, all pointedly averting their eyes. Giving them room.

"Don't worry." Rylan leaned in close. "They've seen much worse."

It didn't really make her feel better.

The elevator dumped them out in the biggest, most cav-

ernous attic she'd ever imagined, much less been in. The place
was filled to the brim with boxes and crates. Statues and furniture. Paintings even, probably worth fortunes. It was practically
a Room of Requirement, for goodness' sake.

"What is all this stuff?" she whispered.

He apparently felt no compunction to keep his voice down.
"Fuck if I know."

He took them over to a corner of the space, where a stack of
crates sat all by itself. He gestured at it expansively. "This is it."

While the men set to work, Rylan took Kate over to a spot
a little ways down the row. He picked out a box and blew the
dust from its top before sitting down and inviting her to join
him. Together, they looked on as the guys figured out their dol-
lies and started getting things loaded up.

She shook her head. "Well, this is the easiest move I've ever
'helped' with."

Rylan smiled. "I can get you a cart if you'd like to pitch in."

"Nah." She nudged him with her hip. "Really, though, you
have no idea what any of this stuff is?"

He pointed at the section he'd set the movers on. "I know that
that is the previous contents of my condo."

"And the rest of it?"

"Family detritus," he said with a shrug. "Most of it's always
been here. The rest..." He trailed off, looking over his shoulder
toward the center of the room. "Some of it's probably my
mother's. I'm sure there's stuff of mine and Lexie's and Evan's,
too. Just never seemed worth going through."

A heaviness weighed down his words, making it sound like it
was less about the things themselves and more about the memories.

And she could understand that, at least. If she'd had to go

to her father's house—if she'd had to sort through the mine-field he'd left of her head, much less an attic the size of a literal field...She didn't know if she could do it, either.

That said... "The curiosity would be killing me, if this were mine."

For just a second, the strangest smile passed over his face. But it was there and gone in an instant, and then he was putting his hand over hers. "You're welcome to poke around anytime you want."

She swallowed past the sudden lump in the back of her throat. It was access, and to way more than just a home.

Leaning her head against his shoulder, she squeezed his hand. "I'd like that."

chapter FIFTEEN

The movers were about a quarter of the way through unloading the truck by the time the rest of Rylan's people started showing up. He was in the front room, directing traffic, when the sound of a particularly familiar purring engine caught his ear. He glanced up from a crate of old business school textbooks to see the bright red of Chase's Bentley pulling in to double-park outside his new house. Grinning despite himself, he rose to his feet and instructed that the box be taken to his study, then called over his shoulder, "Kate?"

She'd set herself to unpacking his kitchen, finding places for all the pots and pans and gadgets he barely knew how to use. She emerged around the corner into the front room with the pitcher portion of a blender still in her hands. He gestured with his head toward the big picture window looking out onto the street. "Company's here."

"Oh." Her shoulders stiffened as she followed his gaze. "Right." She disappeared again, returning seconds later without the pitcher, hands smoothing back the stray strands of hair that had escaped from her braid.

The corner of his mouth twitched up at the nervousness in her limbs, the way she gnawed at her lip and made these little, vague efforts at sorting out her appearance. "They're going to love you."

How could they not? If they saw even a fraction of what he did...

Well. Then he'd be fighting them off with a stick, so hopefully it wouldn't come to that.

Rylan directed Chase down an alleyway so he could park Betty in the tiny garage out back. Now he had a place to put them, Rylan would have to get one of his cars out of storage, too. One of the sporty ones, since apparently Kate had a thing for that.

He couldn't keep the smile off his face, remembering how they'd desecrated Chase's backseat. Or the way Chase had narrowed his eyes at him when he'd returned the thing.

With his arm wrapped securely around Kate's waist, they waited on the front steps for everyone to make their way around. Along with Chase, there were a couple of their other buddies from prep school, who he'd been more or less expecting. Rylan tilted his head in surprise, though, to see Sophie bringing up the rear.

"Well, look who's back in town," he said with a grin.

Sophie rolled her eyes at him. "I could say the same."

She'd been a childhood friend of Chase's, and after prep school, she'd by default become one of Rylan's as well. Before Rylan had taken off, she'd been gone for a year at least, saving babies in Nepal or filming a documentary on abuse in China. Or maybe nursing abandoned bonobos in Brazil, for all he knew. He never could keep her projects straight.

"It's good to see you." He let go of Kate just long enough to give Soph a quick hug before stepping back and taking Kate's hand. "This is Kate."

"Oh, is it now?" Chase, the asshole, cocked a brow, and Rylan instantly regretted ever telling him anything, ever.

Shooting him a look that said *behave*, he introduced each of them. They all stood around for a long minute sizing each other up.

Before it could get too awkward, though, Chase swept his arm out toward the brownstone. "So this is your new place."

"Yeah." With a mover making his way up the walk, another box balanced in his arms, Rylan beckoned everyone inside, to get them out of the way if nothing else. "You want the tour?"

"Absolutely."

The house already looked less empty, even with just a handful of boxes strewn about the place. He showed them the first couple of floors, pointing out the rooms he'd chosen to serve as the master bedroom and his office.

"Who're you getting to do the place?" Chase asked, poking his nose in one of the closets.

Rylan shrugged. "Might see what I can do with it myself."

Chase spun around, forehead furrowed. "You?"

"Well." And he hadn't asked about this, but he pulled Kate in against his side. "I'm hoping I might be able to get some help picking things out."

It was Kate's turn to act surprised. "Me?"

"I like what you did with your place."

She looked away, casting uncertain glances at his friends and at the bare walls all around them. "I don't think you want your place filled up with flea market stuff."

Well, no. The idea kind of made his skin itch, actually. But that wasn't the important part.

"I want it to look...homey."

He wanted it to feel like a home. To both of them.

It was funny—Rylan hadn't told Kate much about his sister. He hadn't even shown her a picture. All he'd really said was that she was an overachiever and a workaholic and a force of nature.

And Kate recognized her for exactly who she was the second she blew through the door.

"Teddy!" she called, not even bothering to knock. She had a tiny pink purse hanging off her arm and a phone in her hand, her dark hair falling in graceful waves around her shoulders. While none of Rylan's friends had come dressed for a hard day of work the way Kate had, this woman put them all to shame in a flowing top and perfectly tailored jeans, topped with heeled boots that looked straight off the runway.

But what Kate got stuck on was her face. She had Rylan's eyes and Rylan's nose, and this set to her shoulders. Kate had only seen it on Rylan a handful of times, when he was putting particular effort into projecting authority—say scaring off a male friend of hers he saw as a threat. While this woman... Well, this woman looked like she walked around like that all the time.

Behind her was a man with a chauffeur's cap juggling three pizza boxes, two white paper bags, and a case of beer.

Lexie stopped in the middle of the front room, causing the man behind her to come up short.

Kate, who'd been going through a box of books, leapt to help. "Here," she said, reaching to take the beer. "That all can go in the kitchen."

Lexie whirled around, gaze landing immediately on Kate. It lingered there, making its slow way up and down, until Kate's stomach squirmed. At least she knew what her frog had felt like back in high school biology class now.

But she refused to be daunted. "Hi." She would've held out a hand, but the case of beer was heavy enough gripped with two. "I'm—"

"The girl." One corner of Lexie's mouth curled up. "Oh, this should be fun."

Kate's mouth dropped open, but the thing about it was that she sounded like she meant it. Possibly in a brother-torturing way, but with sincerity all the same.

Lexie tilted her head back and to the side, calling again, "Oh, Teddy..."

Rylan came hurtling down the stairs a bare second later, eyes narrowed, but his attempt at a scowl was all for show. "Uh-uh, Lex. My house, my nicknames."

"Your *house* indeed." Lexie swept her arm around as if to encompass the entire place. "What, the old condo was too cramped for you? Feeling domestic in your old age?"

She shot a glance at Kate that made her cheeks heat, but Rylan ignored it.

"Hilarious." He made as if to ruffle Lexie's perfect hair, only to be batted away. Letting himself be shooed, he swooped in on Kate, taking the beer from her with one hand. "I see you've met Kate?"

"We were just having the pleasure." Lexie pointed at herself. "Lexie. The prettiest sibling."

"Oh, I don't know about that," said Chase, appearing from around the corner. "Your brother is pretty." He took the boxes of pizza from the poor, apparently long-suffering driver. "Did you get anchovies?"

"Half of one, just for you."

"You're a doll." He kissed Lexie on the cheek as he passed her. "Come on. Kate and Soph already got his kitchen put together."

More or less. They'd spent the better part of the afternoon at it. It'd been...nice. Surreal, but nice.

It got even more surreal as they all piled in around the big dining room table. One of the bags Lexie had arrived with contained paper plates and napkins, as well as a couple of plastic boxes filled with salads, which Lexie and Sophie both dug into while the boys set into the pizzas as if they'd never have another meal.

After dishing a little of each onto her own plate, Kate took the empty seat to Rylan's left, and he slipped a hand onto her knee, looking at her with a question on his brow. She nodded to tell him she was fine. Picking up her fork, she settled in to watch the show.

In so many ways, it was exactly like any other moving day she'd participated in with her friends back in undergrad. The pizza and the beer, especially, were much, much better than she was used to, the setting nicer by leagues. But it was a bunch of people who were comfortable around one another, taking a break from unpacking boxes to share a meal.

There were all the little things she'd learned to notice since hooking up with Rylan, though. No matter what they were doing today, the guys wore expensive watches and sweaters and jeans that were just a little too nice. Sophie was more casually dressed than Lexie, but with her long, silky blond hair and ivory skin, she looked like some sort of wood nymph come to life.

Kate sat back, content to observe for a while as conversation seemed to circle with a sort of inevitability toward work. Talk of money and mergers and clients and boards that left Kate dizzy.

Through it all, Rylan kept a hand on her, touching idly at her knee or letting his arm drape across the back of her chair. It was grounding, made her feel less like she could just float away and disappear altogether from the cozy company of these beautiful people in this beautiful home. Into the woodwork.

Into the voice in the back of her head that kept insisting she didn't belong here at all.

Sophie was the one to speak up, though. To turn to Kate during a pause in conversation. "Sorry, these guys tend to get carried away."

"It's not a problem," Kate said.

"It kind of is," Chase said from across the table. "Half of how this lug"—he pointed at Rylan—"got us to show up and do all this manual labor was the chance to meet his new girl."

Just like that, all the eyes on the place were on Kate. She shifted in her chair and put her slice of pizza down. "Oh. Um."

"Yeah," Lexie chimed in. "It's not every day we get to meet a new lady in Rylan's life."

"Guys." A note of warning colored Rylan's tone.

Chase waved him off. "*Shh.* Let her talk." He focused in on her. "Tell us all about yourself."

The sensation of being pinned down to a dissection tray reasserted itself with force, in the way Chase was regarding her particularly. He'd been shooting her these sorts of glances all afternoon, curious and suspicious in turn. Like maybe he knew more about her and Rylan than he was letting on. Like maybe he didn't approve.

And that was fine. Just because Kate hadn't felt comfortable confiding in anyone about her love life right now didn't mean

Rylan shouldn't be able to. She was glad he had someone in his corner.

But it didn't exactly set her nerves at ease.

Shrugging, she took a sip of her beer. "There's not a whole lot to tell." Forcing herself to keep her gaze even, she gave them the CliffsNotes version of her life. Midwestern mom and out-of-the-picture dad. Degree in painting and her current work on her MFA.

They listened on with varying levels of interest, and if she had the vague impression of being a sociological experiment, at least that was an upgrade from an amphibian with its guts on display.

Winding down, she tilted her head to the side. "So. You know. Basically just your ordinary girl."

Rylan's hand on her knee tightened.

She looked up, meeting his eyes, and the fire that lit them ignited a low, warm glow inside of her. Too fervently, too quietly for that space, he said, "You are anything but ordinary."

Just like that, it was as if the rest of the room receded, fading off into the background until it was only the two of them and the swimming way he made her feel, telling her these things. Making her want so badly to believe them, until bit by bit, no matter how many times she'd told herself she wouldn't, she found herself beginning to.

The sound of a throat clearing had her shaking it off. She turned toward the table and directed her gaze down at her plate. Her whole face went warm.

But she was done being the demurring flower. She took another drink, then set the bottle down. "Well, part of him getting me to show up was the promise of meeting all of you. So, why don't you tell me..." She bit down on her smile, then pointed at Rylan. "...about him?"

Beside her Rylan groaned, and noises of excitement went up around the table. Rylan lifted his hand from her leg to wrap it warmly around the back of her neck, giving a quick squeeze there that was all affection and approval.

"You're going to wish you never asked," Chase said, before launching into a story about some of their more youthful pursuits. Kate grinned the whole while, through that story and into the next. It was all new information, and she listened avidly.

Yet for all that these were tales she hadn't heard before, she recognized the main character. Rylan as a young, rich man with something to prove, getting himself into trouble with his best friend. It wasn't completely easy to hear about the part girls played in some of their exploits, but Rylan had never pretended not to have had his share of conquests. Considering the way Kate had met him, it wasn't even the tiniest bit out of character, and if Chase gave her an appraising gaze through some of the more colorful bits, she met him full-on.

The others added commentary and detail for the episodes they'd been present for. Rylan sat back, looking like he wanted to be annoyed but couldn't quite bring himself to be.

Then Chase trailed off, and Lexie, mostly quiet until then, spoke up. Rylan shifted, stiffening slightly with his hand against Kate's nape.

"One summer, I dolled him up in our mother's dresses."

A chorus of whoops went up around the table, and a smile flickered at the edges of Lexie's lips. But if anything, Rylan only went more still.

"Wait, wait," Chase interrupted, "how old were you?"

"I was six, so Teddy would've been, what, nine?"

"And are there pictures?"

"Sadly no." Her smile faded by a fraction. "We were in London for a few months and we didn't have any friends, because God forbid Mommy and Daddy take ten seconds to arrange a playdate for us." Her tone went darker, and the hoots and hollers died down. "Teddy and Evan always wanted to play boy stuff, and they outnumbered me, so they won. Then Evan managed to get shunted off into some kiddie art program, and it was just me and Teddy, and I decided fifty percent of the time, we were going to do what *I* wanted to do."

"Bossy little thing," Rylan said, all fondness, but a tension lingered to him.

"You should have seen this guy." Her eyes shone as she gazed across the table at him. "He put up with so much. Mother's evening dresses and heels and tea parties with stuffed animals."

That got Rylan some more ribbing, but he took it in stride. "What can I say? I can't resist it when you pout."

She plumped out her lips, demonstrating her best doe eyes, and Kate had to admit. It was effective.

Then Lexie wiped the expression away. "You're unnaturally good at resisting it now."

"Decades of experience," Rylan said. "I hadn't built up my immunity back then."

"It was a good couple of weeks." For a second, Lexie faltered, a flicker of something unhappy crossing her eyes. "Until Dad found out."

Rylan's hand flexed hard against Kate's back. She looked over at him to find his gaze hard.

"He came home early one day, and—" Lexie cut herself off, her mouth curving down, and around them, the table went silent. A beat passed and then another before the line of her lips evened out. Then she picked up her beer and shrugged, as if it had been nothing. As if there was no more story to tell. "And that was the end of that."

When Rylan spoke again, it was with a bitter edge to his voice. An old, lingering hurt. "He always did have his ideas about how his heir should behave."

And Kate's chest squeezed in, because she'd heard this pain in him before, but rarely so explicitly. She'd never seen it so close to the surface.

She sucked in a deep breath and held it. Because a part of her—a growing part—wanted to follow it down, far off into the depths. Deep enough inside his ocean she could drown.

Rylan checked all the other floors of the house first. Kate wasn't in the kitchen or tidying up one of the bathrooms, or even dealing with the linens in the guest room. He was 98 percent sure she hadn't managed to sneak off without his noticing. Which left only one last place to look.

He climbed the stairs as quietly as he could. Just shy of the top, he came to a halt.

There was music playing. Something quiet and sweet, lots of airy guitar, and a female vocalist. And overlaying it, ever so faintly, was another voice.

Heart in his throat, he took the last couple of steps. Then he stood there, mesmerized.

The third floor—that big, open space he'd fallen in love with the same way he'd fallen in love with this beautiful, open girl...it was all lit up. Kate had apparently found some Christmas lights he didn't even remember owning and strung them around the edges of the room, casting it in a soft, warm glow. She sat in the very center of the space, going through the box of old vinyl albums he'd saved when his mother had been planning to throw them out. Resting on the floor beside her was an ancient record player, jerry-rigged to a couple of speakers, and all at once, he recognized the song.

His vision overlapped with memory, and he reached for the center of his chest without thinking, for the ring that didn't live there anymore.

He must've been...what? Five years old? He'd snuck out of bed long after he'd been supposed to be asleep, and crept down the stairs to find Mom and Dad in fancy clothes. Home after some sort of a party, this record playing in the background as they held each other close. Not fighting for once. Not ignoring each other. But dancing. Laughing.

He could've stayed and watched for hours.

The image before his eyes faded, and he blinked until the here and now came back into focus. Kate's lips moved as she sang along, almost but not quite under her breath, and his chest swelled to the point where he thought it might burst. She looked at home here. Right where she belonged.

Clearing his throat, he stepped forward. "I wondered if I might find you here."

She started, jerking her head up. As he crossed the space toward her, he took in the rest of the things strewn around her, the half-emptied boxes. There were more albums, of course, some pictures. Plunking down on the floor beside her, he frowned, then picked up a black leather bag.

"It's a camera," she explained. "An old-school one."

Really, really old-school. He unzipped the bag to find exactly what she'd described. "It was my father's, I think." Another sentimental castoff Rylan had rescued for reasons he hadn't been able to explain at the time.

"It's nice." She said it with a certain wistfulness to her voice.

He closed the bag back up and held it out to her. "You can have it, if you want."

"I couldn't."

"You could. If you think you'd use it. I might even have some film somewhere."

"But it was your father's..."

"So were a lot of things." He'd kept it because he remembered the days when his father would take pictures of them. When he'd seemed so interested in what his children did and not just in what purpose they might serve. He pressed it into her hands. "Take it. I want you to."

She accepted it this time. "Thank you."

He paused for a second, reaching into his pocket. Second-guessing. But the segue seemed natural enough. "I have something else for you, too."

"Oh?"

He squeezed his hand around the metal, then drew it out and passed it over.

Forehead scrunching up, she let him place it in her palm. "What...?"

"A key." Obviously. "For the house."

He could actually see her getting ready to pass it right back. "I couldn't—"

He wrapped his hand around hers, closing her fingers around the key. "You can."

"But..." She didn't seem to have much of an argument. Probably something about how it was too soon, and was he really sure?

His voice threatened to stick in his throat. Pushing past it, he nudged her hand toward her lap. "I trust you," he said.

Just like someday, somehow, he hoped that she would trust him, too.

With apparent reluctance, she tucked it in her pocket, and something in his chest loosened. "I promise I won't abuse it."

"As long as you don't throw a party here without inviting me, abuse it as much as you want." At the joke, she rolled her eyes, but it wasn't all just teasing. "I mean it." The words came out too serious by half. "Come over whenever you want."

He had nothing to hide. Not anymore. Not from her.

The track on the record changed, and they sat there for few beats, listening. The same vision from before rose up in his mind. And maybe it was a day full of too many memories. Maybe it was seeing her in this space, blending seamlessly with his friends. The high of her accepting his invitation to make this place her home.

Before he knew what he was doing, he rose to his feet and held out his hand.

She looked at it, head cocked to the side.

"Dance with me," he said.

"Really?"

His throat went tight. "Really."

She might've just been humoring him, but she let him pull her up and into his arms. Maybe he should show off a little—show her some of the steps he'd learned as a teen. But she shuffled in close, and in the end, he just rested his head against hers, holding her and basking in her warmth.

They did a slow couple of circles in place as the music played on. With every turn, she relaxed a little more, the exhaustion from a hard day's work starting to show on her face.

Putting her ear to his chest, she asked, "Did everyone else take off?"

"A little while ago." Leaving just the two of them.

They danced in silence through the end of the song. The arm of the record player picked up with an audible set of clicks, and she sighed. "It's late."

"Very." A full day of hauling and unpacking and still so much more to do. But he didn't have any more in him. By the way she was sagging into him, he doubted she did, either. "Do you want me to call you a car?"

At that, she pulled away, and it was glass cracking, the soft, perfect space in which they'd spun threatening to collapse. To shatter. "Probably should."

Swallowing against the tightness in his chest, he reached for her, cupping her shoulders so gently in his hands. His voice came out deep and rough. "Or you could stay here. In my bed." *In my home.* "With me."

Something inside him trembled, he wanted it so much.

She shook her head. "I'm so tired."

"No expectations."

Lifting her head, she settled her gaze on him. Looked him right in the eyes, and he tried to make everything about him soft.

He wanted her, of course. He'd never had her in a place that felt like his, and there was nothing in the world he wanted so much as to take her apart, to leave her boneless with pleasure and to pour his own need out into her.

But it would be enough. More than enough. Just to hold her. Just to sleep.

Her breath blew out, and with it, all the resistance in her shoulders. "All right."

His heart felt too big to fit behind his ribs.

Leaning in, he placed a single, soft kiss to her lips. Then he took her by the hand and led her down the stairs.

chapter SIXTEEN

Kate blinked her eyes open to an unfamiliar room. Pale light poured in through the bare windows, and she was way too comfortable, the bed too soft, the sheets smooth beneath her skin. Stretching, she rolled over onto her back and stared up at a distant ceiling.

This was Rylan's room.

The bed was empty beside her, but it didn't matter. Her ribs squeezed in hard, taking her breath away. She'd sworn she wasn't going to do this again. But she'd been so exhausted last night, and it had been late. And Rylan had been looking at her with this naked hope in his eyes, his outstretched palm extended toward her. He hadn't even tried to get her naked, had simply pulled off her shoes and helped her skim off her jeans. Had watched, hands off, as she'd unclasped her bra and pulled it through her sleeve. He'd stripped down to his boxers and turned the covers down, and she'd had no will left to refuse.

She'd fallen asleep tangled up in him, her spine to his chest, the warm strength of his arms curled around her, and it had been perfect.

Maybe too perfect. All her resolutions to guard her heart, and here she was, tumbling headlong down the same path she'd wiped out on once before.

Except it was different this time. Wasn't it? He'd invited her into his home and introduced her to his family and friends. If he was still lying about who he was, it would be obvious, right?

If he only wanted her for sex, he would've asked for it last night.

Yet there were still these silences. These unspoken pockets of his life that made her doubt.

Before she could second-guess herself any further, quietly creaking footfalls seeped in from the hallway, and she propped herself up on her elbows in time for the door to crack open. And there was Rylan. Blue eyes bright and smile soft as he peered in-side.

Her stomach dipped. Because just seeing him had her heart melting, her whole being lighting up. All her doubts slowly melting away.

Pushing the door wider, he stepped inside. He was dressed as casually as she'd ever seen him in a black T-shirt and jeans, his messy hair less intentionally fussed with than usual. In one hand, he held a cardboard carrier with two takeaway coffees, while a couple of mismatched bags dangled from the other. "You're up."

She scrubbed at her eyes and swung what was left of her braid over her shoulder. "Barely."

"Well, let's see what we can do about that."

The bed dipped beneath his weight as he came to sit beside her. His movements were all careful, his voice quiet. "Here." He handed her one of the coffees. "Just how you like it."

Propping herself with a pillow, she sat the rest of the way up and took the cup from his hand. She sipped at it and nodded. "Perfect."

"Good. There are some pastries, too. And"—he pointed to one of the bags he'd come in with—"would you believe I found a place in this city that still sells film?"

"How long have you been up?"

He shrugged. "A while. Never been much good at getting back to sleep. Those didn't help." He gestured toward the windows. "I was thinking we might do some shopping today, if you're up for it. Need some curtains if nothing else."

A hundred movie montages of happy couples laughing their way through Ikeas floated through her mind. Probably not quite the shopping experience he was suggesting, but still. It sounded fun. Easy.

And there was that sensation again of careening down a path. Of falling forward into something deeper than she fully trusted, and it felt *good*. The last thing she wanted was to slam on the brakes.

But a part of her needed to tap on them. To test and make sure they were at least still there.

She faltered, fiddling with the sleeve around her coffee cup. "You know if I spend the whole day with you, it still counts as two."

Four out of their seven nights were already gone, and it looked like they were starting on their fifth. More than halfway through, and it made something clench in her chest.

He shook his head at her, grin wry. "You're onto me. Keeping me honest."

"Somebody has to."

Placing his hand on her knee through the sheet, he leaned in closer, skimming the point of his nose along her jaw. Grazing his lips against her cheek. "What can I say? I'll do whatever I have to. To get more time with you."

Her breath stuttered, the warm amber scent of him surrounding her, making it hard to think.

But she managed to all the same. Because that was what he'd said when she'd found him out. From the very first day, he'd hidden who he was from her because he wanted her to sleep with him, to spend time with him.

A memory of bile rose up in her throat.

She didn't need him to do that now.

With a hand on his chest, she pushed him away. Not far. Scarcely a few inches—only far enough to see his face. Looking him right in the eye, she said, "Just ask."

For a long moment, his gaze searched hers, throat bobbing. But then he gave this slightest hint of a nod. Closed his palm over hers and brought them both to his lips. "Please. Spend the day with me. I'm not ready to let go of you yet."

All the thoughts she'd had of getting to the studio evaporated, burned away by the heat in his eyes. Her voice cracked as she said, "Okay."

And the force of his smile split his face. He dropped their hands and swooped in, kissing her full on the mouth.

He pulled away just as she was letting herself get lost in it, the heat she'd been too exhausted for the night before rising up in her blood. It stayed there, lingering at a low simmer as he climbed his way over to sit beside her and opened up a pastry bag.

Between sips of coffee and idle discussions about what he should do with the house, he fed her bits of the half dozen different pastries he'd brought, placing each sweet, flaky bite on her tongue. When she returned the favor, he nibbled at her fingertips. Grasped her wrist to suck a sticky bit of icing from her thumb.

And he looked so beautiful like that. Perfectly casual and relaxed in his bed. Eyes dancing. Grip warm.

So beautiful she wanted to capture it.

She didn't have her sketchbook or her charcoal. But then it struck her—she had something else. Maybe even something better.

Letting out a shaky breath, she pulled her thumb out of his mouth and stroked it wetly across his lip. "Stay right there."

She barely took the time to wipe her hands off on a napkin before reaching for the camera bag she'd brought up with her the night before. The thing was clunky and ancient and solid, and she loved it. Adored the mechanical clicks it made as she opened it up. She dug through the rolls of film Rylan had brought back with him, selecting a black-and-white one she could develop at the darkroom she had access to at school.

"What are you doing?"

"What do you think?" It had been so long since she'd done this, but her hands remembered how to load the canister. She fiddled with the settings for a minute, then brought the viewfinder up to her eye.

She fit him into the frame, this close-up shot of his eyes and his smile.

"Do you know what I miss about this kind of photography?"

"What's that?"

"The mystery." Her vision flashed black as she pressed the shutter, capturing this image of him. This moment.

"Oh?"

"Digital's nice. You know how the picture turned out right away." She rose to her knees and backed away, fitting more of him into the shot. "But with film, there's this anticipation. You have to wait."

The corner of his mouth twitched up, and she took the photo of him, just like that.

"Not a fan of immediate gratification?" His voice dipped lower, going sultry and dirty, and she felt it in her breasts. In the tender, warming space between her thighs.

"It has its place." She kept snapping shots, framing each one with care, moving around the bed to get him from these different angles.

Slowly, she lowered the camera from her eye.

He was closer than she'd realized, hidden behind the lens the way she'd been. His chest rose and fell with every breath, and there was an openness to his posture. As well as a tension. Like how he'd posed for her the last time.

He'd let her in, back then. In this way, at least, he'd let her see him fully exposed, and yet, both then and now, this aura of uneasiness radiated from him. He didn't give this part of himself to people very often.

But he was giving it to her.

In some vague attempt to ease the dryness of her throat, she swallowed. Licked her lips and summoned her courage.

And then she asked him, "Take off your shirt?"

Rylan rarely hesitated when a gorgeous woman asked him to undress—it generally tended to go well for him. He reached one hand behind his head and grasped the back of his collar, all set to tug the fabric over and off.

But he hesitated. Kate sat on her knees a scant couple of feet away from him on his bed, her long, bare legs going on for miles, the soft swells of her breasts pressed against the cotton of her top. It hadn't been that long ago that he had been dying for her to ask just about anything of him. For her to be in this with him, meeting him halfway. Well, she was asking now. She'd started this.

She'd asked him to reveal himself, to her and to the camera, and already, he felt nearly as naked as he had in that room where they'd shared so much of themselves. Back a handful of months and an entire ocean away.

He worried the collar of his shirt between his fingers and his thumb, a restless, nervous energy making his pulse race. His dick was firming up inside his jeans, and he'd normally be all the way to hard with how close she was, how gorgeous she looked against his sheets. But the crackling of static in the air between them, her request for him to strip. It wasn't only sexual. It was more. Better.

More terrifying, and maybe that was why he was stalling.

"You're not going to put these on the internet, are you?" he asked.

She shook her. "They're just for us."

Us. That one simple word had him nodding to himself. The world disappeared behind black cloth for a fraction of a second as he finally gave in and pulled his shirt off. The click of the shutter fired away while he was still partway through the motion. He balled the fabric up in his hand and braced his arms behind him on the bed. Stared straight into the lens through which she watched him.

She took another couple of pictures before the restlessness of being observed like this got to him. It felt too one-sided. Which gave him the idea...

Sitting up straighter, he reached out toward her. She snapped a photo of him with his arm extended, then lowered the camera. Tilted her head at him.

"Let me take a few."

The idea seemed to surprise her. She shook her head. "I must look—"

"Beautiful. Come on." He wrapped his hands around hers where they gripped the metal body of the thing. "Show me how it works."

Their bodies pressed together as he came to sit beside her. She walked him through how to focus, delicate fingers dancing over the controls. Once he had it, she surrendered, letting him take the camera from her hands. Reluctance was written all over her, and the first picture he took was of her with her lip between her teeth.

She laughed despairingly and covered her face. "I wasn't ready."

"But I was." He snapped the next one with her peering out from between her fingers, and it all but stopped his heart inside his chest.

This was precisely how he wanted her. Real and genuine and imperfect and his.

"Stay right there." He got up and walked around to the other side of her. With careful motions, he slipped the elastic from the end of her braid and set it aside. He combed out her hair with his fingers, the dark strands slipping like water through his hands, falling into waves exactly how he'd thought they would. When he was done, he stepped back, waiting for just a moment until her impatience got the better of her. Until she turned to look over her shoulder.

He caught her just like that, and he wished he could check the image right then and there. Make sure it had come out the way he'd pictured it, but she'd just said it herself. Film was about waiting. It was about a finite, fleeting moment, here and gone in a flash, and you didn't know until it was all over if you'd captured it at all. If you got to keep it.

His chest squeezed in. Fuck, but he hoped he did.

Sitting down beside her again, he lowered the camera from his eye and reached over to tug at the sleeve of her shirt. "It's only fair," he said to her pout.

And she didn't fight him on it. She stripped the fabric up and over her head, unveiling the creamy flesh of her abdomen. The bottoms of her breasts and then the rosy circles of her nipples, tight points peaking harder as they were exposed to the morning air.

"Well?" Her chin tilted up, challenge shining at him from within those deep brown eyes. She didn't cover herself, and his breath sharpened, his own flesh responding. His brave girl. His brave, beautiful girl.

He took one last picture of her, and then he set the camera aside.

"Well," he repeated. Restraint was a trembling thing inside his limbs, but he was running out of it and fast.

He'd just wanted this for so long. Not only the promise of sex that lay in the faintly crackling space between their bodies—though fuck knew he'd take that, too. But what he longed for was something deeper. The shy, intimate way she'd looked at him through a camera lens. The slowing of her breath as she fell asleep inside his arms.

The heaviness to her eyes as she stared at him right now.

And suddenly, the inches of space separating them were too much.

Reaching out, he put a hand to the bare flesh of her thigh, and the distance between them broke.

Restraint was never something he'd had a lot of anyway.

His pulse thundered hot inside his veins as he rose to his knees. Within the span of a breath, he was upon her, pulling her against him. Her breasts pressed warm and full against his skin, and he groaned aloud as their mouths finally met. It was sex and it was intimacy, and it was everything.

It was the photograph he'd taken of her naked smile, the one he didn't know yet if he'd get to keep. But damn him if he wasn't going to try.

Encircling her in his arms, he kissed her deep and wet, losing himself in it. In this moment.

In her.

It all changed so fast.

One moment Rylan had been gazing at Kate with this quiet sort of adoration, and the next he was kissing her within an inch of her life. Her head spun, dizzy, as the scent of him surrounded her, the weight of him. She grasped at his shoulder and his hip, just for something to hold on to. But it wasn't enough.

Her breath caught as she let him bear her down into the mattress. The softness of it welcomed her, the cool slide of the sheets a contrast to the heat of his skin and the slick press of his mouth.

"Fuck." He scraped his teeth across her lip and worked his way toward the point of her jaw. "You don't know."

She tipped her head to the side in invitation. "Don't know..."

"How bad I've wanted you. Here." His words set off a pang inside her chest at the same time that the wet kisses he laid against her throat sparked a low, warm roll of arousal, heavy in her breasts and pulsing thickly in her sex. "In my bed. First thing in the morning. Wanted to sleep beside you. Wake you up with my mouth on you."

Biting down, he fit a hand to the underside of her thigh and pushed it wide. She moved with him, making space for him between her legs, and he fit himself down into it. The rough fabric of his jeans rasped against her bare skin, and she arched up into the pressure, until the hard line of him pressed right where she needed it. Moaning at the spike of pleasure, she threaded her fingers through his hair, dragging his mouth back to hers to muffle the sounds he choked out of her with the grinding of his hips.

And yet there was more to it than the heat of his body or the electricity zipping through her at every glancing brush of skin on skin. There was an intensity to him, warmer than the possessive way he'd taken her in the car behind the gallery. Fuller than the shallow way she'd laid back and allowed him to have her upon his return. It was his words and his touch, combining and echoing, and it reminded her—

She scraped her nails down the length of his spine.

God, it was like their first time. Right after she'd drawn him, when she'd still been shaking from the realization of how deeply and how fast she'd fallen. Every kiss and every touch had been bright with possibility, yet shadowed by the looming specter of the fact that they had always been doomed, and there was just that sharpness to them now. That knife's edge they skated upon.

How many times had she gone back to that moment in her mind? Even in the depths of her fury, she'd held fast to that one golden afternoon. Imperfectly remembered, all flashes of need and the rush of finally giving in. Surrendering and receiving everything from him in return.

She wanted to remember it better this time.

"Wait." The word came out breathless, her chest heaving beneath the hot touch of his hands, throat thick and lips stung.

Freezing, he groaned aloud. He lifted up to stare at her, and the concern on his brow alone made her heart swell. Unable to explain, she fumbled blindly at her side until her hand connected with the cool metal of the camera. She curled her fingers around the strap, tugging it closer.

His gaze followed her movement, and his breath caught. When he looked at her again, it was with his eyes going molten and dark, Adam's apple bobbing hard.

"Kate. Fuck." He hung his head for a long moment before seeming to get himself back under control. "Always knew you had a little bit of a voyeur in you. Remember that first night you let me make you come?"

Deep in her sex, she pulsed. "As if I could forget."

"You told me about your roommates fucking in the bunk across the room from you. Your cheeks went all pretty and pink."

The same kind of warmth bloomed over her face right now. Shot down her spine and into the space between her legs.

His voice deepened, liquid sex rolling through his every breath as he skated his fingertips up her thighs. "You like to watch, pretty girl?"

"I like to watch you."

His thumbs brushed the edges of her panties, and her whole abdomen flexed. For half a breath, she squeezed her eyes shut tight. She could just give in to this. Let him touch her and make her come.

Forcing her eyes open, she fought for focus.

Somehow, she got her hand around the body of the camera, bringing it up toward her eye. But before she lost the view of him to that of the lens, she worked her jaw. Summoned her courage. How many times had he told her to ask for what she wanted? Proved to her that it was her right, in bed and in every other part of her life? She darted out her tongue to wet her lips, then skated her gaze down his body.

Her voice scarcely shook at all as she said, "Take off the rest of your clothes."

The space between them seemed to vibrate as his chest rose and fell. He sat up straighter, rising onto his knees between her spread thighs, muscles tensing.

And then he brought his hand to his throat.

God but the man was lethal. Fire raced through her, her mouth going dry as he dragged his fingertips over his collarbones. His smooth skin gleamed in the morning light, golden and perfect. He traced the edges of his pectorals, flicked a thumb against his own nipple, and let out a huff of air, and wasn't that just an idea for later? To touch him there and see if it made him pant the way it made her.

Then his hand drifted lower. The points of her breasts went tight, her sex slick and hot.

Exhaling hard, she brought the viewfinder to her eye, and it put him both closer and farther away. Made it easier to breathe at the same time that his teasing coiled the tension inside her to the point where she felt like she might break.

She snapped the shutter with his hand flat against the dips and ridges of his abdominals. Again as he swept over to touch the crest of his naked hip above the waistband of his jeans.

And then he tucked into the denim. Made as if to stroke the hot flesh underneath, and she couldn't stop the whine of need that escaped from her throat.

"You want me to touch myself?" Gravel roughened his tone. "I'm so hard for you, Kate."

No. Yes. She wanted that, and for him to be on top of her already, pushing her open and pressing inside. Wanted his mouth and his hands and his cock, and how was she possibly supposed to decide?

Well, there was one place to start. "Show me."

In slow, dragging movements, he withdrew his hand. He circled the button on his jeans for an infinite moment, swirling a single fingertip around the metal, and it took her too long to recognize the motion. She jerked her knee up, brushing her foot along his calf as her center throbbed. It was the way he liked to slip his finger along her clit, the way he got her warm and ready and wet for him.

And then he was popping the button free, pulling the teeth of his zipper down one by one. Heat bloomed in a fresh rush when he spread his fingers, palming the long line of himself through the fabric, and he made a low groan as the heel of his hand rubbed over the tip.

"Show me," she said again.

And it was a heady ache when he did. He hooked his thumbs under his waistband at his hips, pushing the denim down maddening inch by inch, taking his boxers with it. Revealing coarse, dark hair and endless skin, and she clicked the shutter. Advanced the frame.

Then the base of him came into view. With a shudder, he reached in and pulled himself out. His cock was thick and flushed, glistening at the head as he curled his palm around himself and took a slow stroke forward, forcing a noise of pure need from his lungs.

"See how hard you make me? How much I love it when you tell me what you want?"

She fumbled with the camera in her haste to set it aside, but he was there, taking it from her. Bracing himself with one arm, he collapsed back over her, capturing her mouth, and how had she gone without this for so long? Survived for even a second without kissing him? It was cool water to the inferno between her thighs, and a conflagration to her flame, stoking her higher even as he eased the need within her, helped her keep it banked and contained.

Beside their heads, the shutter clicked, registering only dully in the back of her mind as she scraped her teeth over his tongue, met his lips again and again. She wanted to touch all the places he'd had his hands, wanted the hot length of him against her skin. Moaning, she skated her palms across his chest toward the center of his hips. When she brushed the wet tip of him, it punched the breath from him, but then he was there, pushing her hand aside.

Sliding down her body with the hot glide of his mouth.

He took a picture with his tongue on her breast and another sucking a kiss beside her navel. She choked on his name when he dipped lower, running his nose along her slit through her underwear. Scrambling, she rushed to get the fabric off, to get him closer to her bare, slick flesh, but again, he caught her hand. Pulled it to his mouth and sucked her fingers between his lips. Then he was pushing her own hot hand into her panties, glancing up at her with eyes gone black with lust.

"Show *me.*" It was almost a growl, the way he said the words.

And who was she? She barely recognized the scared, repressed, naïve girl he'd had to coax into touching herself in front of him at all as she slipped her fingers through her wetness, probing just inside before gliding back up to circle around her clit. The shutter fired off again, and Jesus, she'd have to develop these in the middle of the night, would have to barricade herself inside the darkroom, because no one was ever seeing this.

No one else could ever see her. Not like this. Not the way he did.

The camera hit the mattress with a bounce. She pushed up into his touch as he set his palms to her thighs. Eased the panel of her underwear out of the way only to dart in with his tongue, grasping at her wrist to keep her right there. A whole new kind of heat shivered through her as he licked around her fingertips, dipping into her opening and then kissing higher to suck hard at her clit.

Her eyes slammed shut as she shattered, clenching hard around nothing, and God, those were tears beading at the corners of her eyes. "Inside," she pleaded, "I need—"

He filled her just as the second wave of it hit, fingers pressing exactly where she needed them, tongue hot and wet as it lapped at her clit, coaxing her through the tremors. Through the searing flashes of darkness washing over her and pulling her down.

She came back to herself what felt like decades later, groaning and letting her leg fall to the side. He kissed a line across her sex to the point of her hip, then tilted his head up, a sultry softness to his shining lips as he stared at her. Still hazy from the pleasure, she slipped her fingers from her body and brought them to his face. Pressed them into his mouth where he scraped her knuckles with his teeth.

Without a word, he let her hand fall away. He stalked his way up her body like a man possessed. On all fours over her, jeans still clinging from his hips, he pinned her with his gaze.

"Those pictures." He swallowed, throat working, muscles straining. "I want to see them. All of them."

She managed a bare nod. The heat in his eyes had her body

thrumming again even as the aftershocks from her previous climax echoed through her.

Something cracked in his expression. "They're going to be beautiful." He lifted a hand and pressed it to her cheek. "You're so beautiful."

And her stomach dipped. He kept telling her that. She'd never doubted that he believed it, but it butted up against all the things she'd always been told about herself. The messages that had been thrown at her over and over again, to the point where they'd sunk in.

For the first time, his words sunk deeper. She *felt* beautiful. Like he made her beautiful, just by looking at her.

She reached for him. Curling her hand around the nape of his neck, she pulled him down. He tasted like sex and like her, and she could drown in his scent, in the warm way he hovered over her. Falling to his forearms, he pressed his chest against hers, and she couldn't get enough.

She'd been trying so hard to hold him at a distance. But he'd invited her into his home. Had taken her to the place where he'd grown up and introduced her to his family. Had asked her to help him *make* his home. And now he was here. Sharing a camera and a kiss she felt down to her toes, making art with their bodies and with film, and distance was stupid. Distance was a waste. Every inch of space she'd kept between them all this time collapsed.

Every muscle in her body went soft. As if he could sense the change, he moaned into the kiss. Cupped her breast and lowered his hips, letting the hot line of his cock graze her skin.

"I want you," she breathed against his lips.

She wanted this. She wanted it to work.

Time went strange for a minute, melting the way her resistance had. The rest of their clothes seemed to fall away, pushed from their skin by eager hands. She almost told him to go ahead and press in bare, but before she would get the words out, he rolled on protection and she parted her legs.

"Like this?" he asked, dragging his tip over the ridge of her clit.

The familiarity of it made her dizzy. "Exactly like this."

Like their first time. Face to face and skin to skin.

He held her gaze and entwined their hands.

The first hot slide of him into her body turned her inside out. It was all fullness and the pressure of his hips, the shaky warmth of his breath against her lips. He kissed her wet and deep as he drew back, and she curled her legs around him as if she could keep him there. Inside her. In this room where it was only her and him and this sun-filled space. Forever.

For the longest time, he moved inside her. The low roll of arousal in her abdomen flowed into every thrust, and she kept her eyes open. He did, too, until it was this complete circuit between them.

The feeling built and built until finally he faltered. His lashes fluttered, a choked moan and a stuttering of his hips betraying him. "You feel so good." He ground his hips into her harder. "Can you— I want you to—"

"Yeah." She let her head tip back, focusing on the drag of his hips against her clit, the sweet ache every time he pressed flush against her.

"God, Kate, I need to feel it, want to hear you—"

His hands squeezed harder over hers, bearing her down, and she tilted her hips. Stared up into perfect, beautiful blue eyes.

And they were full of awe. Full of love.

Her whole body seized. Blackness rushed over her, and then

his mouth was on hers, his breath pushing into her lungs as she pulsed and pulsed. Without a hand on her, without a tongue or a toy, and the deepness of it felt like it would pull her under. Like she'd never break the surface again.

He moaned her name, slamming in hard. When he came, it was with his body buried so she didn't know where he ended and she began, and that was fine. That was perfect. She didn't *want* to know.

She wanted to stay right here, in this golden, glowing morning, when it was just him and her.

When she could ignore the voice in the back of her mind insisting it could never last.

chapter SEVENTEEN

Okay. There were a few things Kate could get used to about staying at Rylan's place. The water pressure was definitely one of them.

Steam filled the air, making it sultry and thick, the hot spray washing over her skin, and she never, ever wanted to leave this room. This expansive, gorgeous marble-tiled shower.

This perfect little moment where everything seemed okay.

Her fingers were starting to prune, though.

Sighing, she leaned back against the other thing she could seriously get used to around here. Rylan hummed, the broad, naked expanse of his chest meeting her spine, thick arms curling around her. He kissed the spot beneath her ear, and she practically melted.

"Finished?" he asked.

"Do I have to be?"

"Never." With a hand at her cheek, he turned her into him and into a deep, slow kiss.

They were long past clean. Phantom traces of his hands slid-

ing lather across her skin made her warmer than the spray—
nearly as warm as his lips.

Finally, even she started to run out of excuses to dawdle,
though. With reluctance, she broke the kiss and reached for the
shower's controls.

Apparently the wrong one. There were so many dials and
nozzles, and the one she touched turned the smooth flow of
water into a stuttering, pounding jet. Laughing, Rylan took
over, turning a different handle all the way to the right and stopping the water altogether.

She scowled at the knob. "That was going to be my next guess."

"Never doubted it."

He slicked his hair back from his face, and she got lost for
a minute, just staring at the droplets of water slipping over his
body, the shifting of muscles in his shoulders and arms.

She zoned back in as he stepped out and passed her a fluffy
white towel.

"Thanks." She took it and swabbed at her face and neck.

Rylan made quick work of drying off while she stood there in
a haze, barely remembering to move the fabric over her skin as
she stared. He smirked to catch her gawking. Hanging up his
towel, he leaned in for another quick kiss. "I'm going to go get
dressed."

Pity. But for now, it was probably for the best.

Nodding, she let him go, watching the round globes of his
rear as he walked to the door and through.

The quality of the air in the room shifted once she was alone.
She held herself up a little less straight, toweling off faster without the distraction. Wrapping the terry around her chest, she
padded forward across the room, combing her fingers through
the wet strands of her hair.

With a washcloth she cleared off a section of the mirror above the sink. Her gaze caught on her own dark eyes in the reflection, and for a long moment, she stood there, staring at pink cheeks. At the tops of her breasts and the patch of red Rylan's mouth had left on her neck.

And it was strange. Lying beneath Rylan, allowing him to snap image after image of her running her own fingers through the slickness between her legs, she'd been struck with this lilting vertigo. As if watching herself from above, barely able to recognize the girl she'd been when Rylan first found her. She'd been so terrified then, and the sheer wantonness of putting herself on display like she had this morning...It was something she never would've been able to do before. Rylan hadn't even had to coax her into it—she had been the one to start the whole game of taking photos of each other like that. He'd given her the confidence to do it, though. And she couldn't argue with the results.

Leaning against the counter, she studied herself more closely. She didn't *look* different. But she felt it.

"Kate?"

She stepped back, peering through the half-open doorway into Rylan's room. "Yeah?"

"Your phone's ringing."

She scrunched up her face at herself in the mirror. "Coming."

By the time she made it out there, her phone had gone silent again, and she almost forgot about it entirely. Rylan had tugged on a fresh pair of boxers, but other than that, he was still gloriously nude, dark hair messy and damp.

"I am just never going to get over that," she mused, bringing a finger to her mouth.

"Hmm?"

"How good you look." How good he made her feel.

His lips curled up into a soft, beautiful smile. "I don't think I ever will, either."

She shook it off with reluctance, making her way to the bedside table where she'd left her phone. "Hope you don't mind me borrowing one of your shirts again."

"Hope you don't mind me ruthlessly trying to take it right off you again."

"I'd be disappointed if you didn't."

She picked up her phone and flipped it open, then frowned. There were three voicemails in addition to a couple of texts. She glanced at the clock, and her frown only deepened. Even with their morning activities, it was pretty early for a Saturday.

Then she pressed the button to look at the messages, and all the blood rushed out of her face.

"Oh, shit."

Rylan was up in an instant, sitting straight. "What?"

"Oh *shit*."

The messages were all from her mother. She checked the date and went a little dizzy.

How could she have forgotten?

She swore a half dozen more times, paralyzed there in the corner of the room as the world around her spun.

Strong hands settled on her shoulders, and she couldn't help it. She flinched. Hard. Every neuron in her body braced, ready to look up into an angry face, and she could already hear it. *So stupid, what were you thinking, never pay attention—*

She jerked away without even thinking, but the hands refused to yield, and she went stiff, turned her head away before the yelling started.

But then, Rylan was there. His face dipped down so there was nothing else in her vision, and his eyes were wide, the lines on his brow all concern. Not anger. Not yet.

"Kate." There was an urgency to his tone, like this might not be the first time he'd tried to get her attention. "Talk to me."

And maybe it was the steady calm of his voice that finally snapped her out of it.

"My mother's here." She shook her head at the question forming on his lips. Paged through the increasingly frantic series of texts her mother had left. "Not *here*, but here. In the city." Her head spun harder. "At my apartment."

Crap. It was just like her father had always said. She was so careless, so scatterbrained, and between work and school and her terrible portfolio and Rylan—she'd been running around like a crazy person these last few days.

A hysterical bark of laughter forced its way past her throat. She'd gone to work at the diner that Monday and looked at the schedule and been so damn relieved to see these four days off in a row. Found time, she'd thought. A chance to get some painting done, or apparently to hole up with a guy she barely knew and that her mother was going to *hate*...

Except Kate had been the one to request those days. Her mother had sent her the dates for her trip, and Kate had put them on the calendar for work, had even taken off the day before so she'd have time to clean her apartment. Oh hell, her apartment was going to be a mess.

Scrubbing a hand over her face she sat down hard on the edge of the bed. She needed to call her mother back. She needed to get dressed. She needed to get over there, and it was going to take forever, the trains ran so infrequently on weekend mornings.

Just as her planning was threatening to spill over into outright panic, Rylan reappeared in front of her. He was on his knees, half-dressed now in an undershirt and jeans. With careful, gentle hands, he eased the phone from her grip.

"Is there someone who has a key who can let your mother in?"

Kate nodded dumbly. "Mrs. Stephens in 3A."

"All right." Rylan flipped open her phone, grimacing as he started to type.

"What are you doing?"

"Texting her back and telling her you're on your way and to try Mrs. Stephens's place."

"I need to call her—"

"You need to get dressed." He snapped the phone shut and set it down on the table, then pointed to a spot on the bed beside her.

And there, neatly piled, were her jeans from the night before and one of his dress shirts. A thin pair of what looked like athletic socks.

"There's nothing I can do about underwear, I'm afraid."

She heard her own voice reply, "That's all right."

He leaned in to press a single quick kiss to her lips. "We have this under control."

With that, he rose to his feet. She was still in a daze as she watched him pull out his own phone and call for a car, ambling back toward his closet as he did.

And it struck her—*they* didn't have this under control. *He* did.

She'd managed to pull on her jeans and last night's bra by the time he returned. He'd finished dressing himself in a soft-looking gray sweater and a black pair of shoes, and it wasn't fair. Here she had to do the walk of shame back to her mother of all people, and he got to look like...well, *this*.

The question was out of her mouth before she could stop it. "Why are you doing this?"

He came up short, furrowing his brow. "Doing what?"

"Helping me."

For a fraction of a second, his eyes flashed dark, the point of his jaw flexing, and her breath hitched. Here they came. The recriminations. *I have to do everything for you, don't I—*

But then his expression cleared. He came over to sit beside her on the mattress. Tucked a tangled strand of her hair behind her ear. "Why did you come help me move into this house yesterday?"

What did that have to do with it? "Because you asked me to."

With an arm around her shoulder, he tugged her into his side, pressing his lips against her temple. "And if I hadn't asked, you would have offered."

She shrugged. Probably.

"Because that's what people who care about each other do." His voice and his grip both tightened as he said it. Like he was hearing it for the first time coming out of his own mouth. Like it was a revelation to him, too. "They help each other when they need it. Whether or not the other person asks them to."

He held her there for a long moment. Then, letting out a huff of breath, he withdrew his arm and picked up the shirt he'd brought her, shaking it out.

With him looking at her like that, gaze expectant, confidence radiating from every inch of him, the panic that had all but incapacitated her finally eased. He didn't blame her or berate her for her mistake. Instead, he stepped in. He handled it.

All she had to do was trust him. And let him.

The car arrived while Kate was still upstairs. Rylan stood in the front room, watching through the window. As soon as it pulled up, he turned to call for her over his shoulder.

She emerged down the stairs a minute later, and he had to give her credit. She cleaned up well. Her head was held high, her hair neat. But there wasn't any hiding what was going on. She looked like exactly what she was—a woman coming home after a night spent with a man. If it wasn't her lack of makeup, it was the mark he'd left on her throat. The too-large, stolen shirt. Seeing his clothes on her was still sexy as hell, but it was sexy for a reason. His shirt on her frame screamed of possession, of his having had her less than an hour before.

"What?" she asked, pausing on the next-to-last step.

He blinked away the thoughts of how he'd laid her out in his bed, of the slow, soft love they'd made. Of how she'd looked at him as she'd clenched up around him and come.

He shook his head, stepping forward to get the door. She had her purse slung over her shoulder, as well as the camera bag, and he got distracted all over again remembering the pictures they had taken, but he forced those thoughts aside.

He hadn't met very many girls' parents. He'd rarely dated anyone for long enough. But he'd been dealing with people older than he was all his life, people with influence and power, and he was good at it. From board members to society types, he knew how to turn on the charm. He could do it with Kate's mother, too.

But when they reached the car and he extended his hand to get the door, Kate turned to him. "Thank you," she said, and it wasn't a simple acknowledgment of what he'd done to help. "I'll give you a call—"

He interrupted her. "I'm coming with you."

Her mouth dropped open. "But—" She snapped her jaw closed. "You don't have to. My mom, she's..." She trailed off, and Rylan frowned. She'd always spoken of her mother fondly. "She can be a little much."

"I'm good with mothers."

"Still." She avoided his gaze, looking at anything but him.

And then it hit him.

Her mother didn't know about them, either. There were a hundred other explanations, but this was the only one she wouldn't want to say out loud. Especially after she kept them a secret from her friends, too. He swallowed hard against the low punch to the gut. He understood her reasons, but being her dirty secret like this—it *hurt*.

That was the only justification he had for gritting his teeth. For saying the first, most cutting, most effective thing to come to mind.

"Would you really rather show up looking like that"—he pointed to his shirt, to the bruise on her throat—"alone?"

His father would've been so proud.

God, he was an asshole. She flinched, and she'd been supposed to. There was no other reaction any rational person could have. He cursed himself in his head. Opened his mouth to apologize.

She threw the car door open herself before he could. He stepped back, prepared for it to slam in his face, and he'd have deserved it. Except then she did like she always did and slid across the seat. He hovered there at the curb for a wavering moment. Then, from within, she asked, "Are you coming or not?"

When she put it that way . . .

He got in and closed the door behind him. The driver caught his eye in the rearview mirror and rattled off the address Rylan had given over the phone. Rylan nodded tightly, then waved for him to put the partition up.

As the car rolled forward, he turned to Kate. "I'm sorry, that was—"

"The truth."

He hesitated. "But it wasn't kind."

"Sometimes, the truth isn't."

"I just thought..." Because there had been kindness behind the bluntness. "You seemed so upset back there." She'd freaked him out, was what she'd done, and he had vaulted into problem-solving mode in response, making assumptions. Moving too fast. "I didn't know if she would judge..."

"Oh, believe me, she will." But there was an edge to how she said it. Some silent double meaning behind the words.

His heart rose into his throat. It was protectiveness, and it was love, and his ridiculous upbringing had only equipped him with so many ways to show that to a person. So many he would even consider showing to her, that was. "I only want to make things easier for you."

Her shoulders softened as she finally met his gaze. He'd been creeping his hand across the seat, wanting to reach for hers but not quite certain if he should. Her own fingers twitched. With a sigh, she closed them over his, and it was as if the air had been let out of him. He hadn't fucked this up beyond repair.

"I know," she said.

But there was still something she wasn't telling him.

chapter EIGHTEEN

Kate made it all the way to the patch of hallway outside her door before she had to stop. Turning to Rylan, she put a hand on his wrist.

He gazed down at her, one eyebrow quirked.

Glancing away, she took a deep breath. "Are you sure you want to do this?"

God, it was such a cop out. The real question was whether or not *Kate* wanted to do this. Her mom wasn't some awful shrew or anything. She'd be nice to Rylan to his face.

It was the after part that filled Kate with dread. When her mother picked every single thing he'd said or done to pieces. Looking for Kate's father in his tiniest turn of phrase. The fact that Kate had hidden his very existence from her for this long wasn't going to help matters. Then again, if she had told her mother anything, then they would really be doomed.

Kate might be overly sensitive to white lies and half truths. She might not be the best at trusting.

But she had absolutely *nothing* on her mom.

With a warm, broad hand, Rylan tilted her head up so she

was looking at him again. "I do." He worked his jaw, tightness growing around his eyes. "But if you want me to go..."

He trailed off. He didn't want to leave her, but he'd hold his nose through it if she asked him to.

And if she wanted him with her, standing strong and steady by her side, then in a heartbeat, he'd be there.

Her sudden certainty about that fact hit her like a blow. It settled into her, warming her very bones. Making her decision for her, really.

Shaking her head, she placed her hand over his and twisted to kiss his palm. "Come on, then."

Time to face the music. Together.

She started apologizing before she'd even fully made it through the door.

"Mom, I am so, so sorry—" She cut off.

Her mother was sitting in the chair at her desk, her luggage beside her. And in her lap was Kate's sketchbook. Not just any sketchbook, either, though a stack of them were piled up at her elbow. The sketchbook from Paris. The one full of pictures of Rylan.

Kate's breath left her in a rush. "Oh."

Her mother looked up at her. She'd cut her hair again at some point since the last time Kate had seen her. It was a bob now, and redder than usual. She had new glasses, too.

And a new slant to her brow, a different, sly twist to her smile. "You never told me they hired such pretty models for your figure study classes, honey. If you had, I might've signed up for—"

Kate watched it all happen, like a car wreck in slow motion going on right in front of her. Nothing she could do to stop it. No chance of getting out of the way. Her mother's gaze shifted to the side as Rylan followed Kate in, closing the door behind him. Eyes widening, she looked back down at the drawing in her lap and then to Rylan again.

Rylan, who'd put on this smile Kate had never seen on him before. It wasn't the one he used to seduce young women with, and it wasn't the real one she'd come to recognize and treasure in the time since she'd let herself be seduced.

It was one that reminded her of the other life he'd only barely told her about. The one full of boardrooms and negotiations and a father who always wanted more from him.

Then it all seemed to catch up with him, too.

And it was just like that accident on an icy road. Kate's first instinct was to swerve, to let the panic creeping over her win, to run. But sometimes, you had to steer into the skid.

She was a grown woman after all. She had adult relationships, and she'd had sex. She'd seen a naked man, and dammit all, she'd drawn more than one of them in her life. Never with the kind of intimacy and adoration that bled off the page her mother happened to have open, of course, but that should only make it easier to own up to.

It really, really didn't, though.

Still, she took a deep breath. "Mom." Nothing for it. "This is Rylan. Rylan, this is my mom."

At least that seemed to break a little of the tension. Without closing it, her mother set the book aside and stood. She was dressed pretty conservatively, for her, in a black turtleneck and a flowing red skirt, a round wooden pendant hanging from a cord around her neck. Somehow, her outfits still took Kate by surprise—the color and the personality in them. Back when her father had been around, there hadn't been much of either to go around. It was good to see. Even now.

"Rylan," her mother said, glancing meaningfully at Kate. One of her brows seemed permanently glued to her hairline. Fat chance of it coming back down anytime soon.

Rylan recovered quickly, that smooth, slick smile of his going brighter. He crossed the rest of the distance over to her mother and extended his hand. "It's an honor."

"Oh, I wouldn't go that far." Kate's mom took his hand. Her gaze went to Kate even as she continued addressing him. "I'd like to say I've heard a lot about you, but I certainly have *seen* a lot of you."

So apparently they weren't going to be talking around it. If it was possible, Kate's face heated even more, but she held her ground. "I wasn't the one to tell you to go nosing around in my sketchbooks."

Her mother rolled her eyes as she retracted her hand. "I had to find something to do while I was waiting for you."

Ouch. "I'm sorry, I just..."

"We lost track of time," Rylan supplied. He returned to her side, putting a hand at the base of her spine, warmth and support seeping into her from that single point of contact. "Kate was helping me move into my new place, you see."

"Oh, is that what she was doing?"

Among other things, Kate was tempted to retort, but she kept it in. She tried to put some warning in her tone as she said, "Mom..."

"Oh, come here already." She held out her arms.

And that was an offer Kate couldn't resist.

As she fell into the hug, she remembered that day after Rylan had returned, when she and her mother had been talking about this visit, and the longing that had nearly choked her. Her mother could be prickly, and she could be mistrustful, but she was still *Kate*'s. No matter how much shit she was going to get over this whole Rylan thing, Kate was suddenly intensely, terribly glad she was here.

"It's good to see you." Out of nowhere, her eyes prickled.

Her mother squeezed her tighter. "You, too."

They let go after a long minute. And then there they were, the three of them in her tiny, messy apartment, with no couch, no kitchen table, no real place for three people to sit.

And nothing to say, either, apparently.

Rylan let another few seconds pass before he cleared his throat. "Have you eaten yet?"

"Not since breakfast back in Cleveland."

As if on cue, Kate's stomach growled. They'd only made it partway through their pastries before they'd gotten . . . *distracted* that morning.

Rylan wrapped an arm around her shoulder. Rubbing her arm, he suggested, "Brunch?"

Clearly, the man was a genius.

As it turned out, brunch turned into brunch and a walk in Prospect Park, which turned into a walk and this little indie movie that hadn't made it to the art theater near Kate's mom yet, which turned into a movie and dinner, and with every new addition, Kate felt like she'd been given a reprieve. But the thing about reprieves was that eventually you ran out.

After dinner, Rylan opened his mouth as if to suggest yet another possibility, only for Kate's mom to hold her hands up in surrender.

"I was up at four to catch my plane, you guys." She shook her head. "I'm beat."

Rylan nodded tightly, glancing to Kate and sticking his hands in his pockets. "Of course."

They'd been running around like this all day, and his politeness hadn't slipped once. He'd been charming and outgoing, and while he hadn't precisely volunteered the specifics of his situation, he'd been honest to a fault every time her mother had asked him about himself. He'd been this perfect, model boyfriend, honestly. It had impressed Kate at the same time that it had left her completely turned around.

Even though it didn't make a lot of sense for Rylan to ride back with them, Kate wasn't entirely surprised when the car pulled up outside the restaurant and he got right in. At her building, he followed them out onto the sidewalk, making some signal to the driver. "I'll just walk you up," he said, nodding toward the door.

As Kate let her mother into her apartment, Rylan lingered in the hallway, giving her a meaningful look. Waving her mother inside, Kate said, "I'll be right in."

The door closed behind her mom, leaving Kate and Rylan on the other side. Rylan heaved out a breath, and Kate hadn't even realized how stiff his shoulders had gotten until he relaxed them.

A sudden, intense gratitude swept over her. He'd performed so beautifully today that it hadn't even been recognizable as performance, but the effort behind it all made itself apparent, now that he'd given up the act.

She let herself sag, too, putting her back to the door and slumping into it. Shaking her head, she glanced up at Rylan through her lashes. "That probably wasn't what you were expecting when you asked to spend the day together."

"No, not exactly." He mirrored her position, coming to stand beside her. He nudged her with his elbow. "I didn't mind it, though. It was better than the ballet, right?"

"Much." At the mention of their second night together in New York, she recalled their conversation from this morning, when he'd originally asked her to go shopping with him for furniture. "We don't have to count this one if you don't want to."

She'd promised him seven nights, and this would've been their fifth. It didn't seem fair, considering how it played out.

His smile dimmed by a fraction. "I don't know. You told me if we spent the day together, it counted." When she started to argue, he pushed off the wall, shifting to stand in front of her. He took both her hands in his. "I want every second with you I can get. But I'm not going to quibble with you to get more of them. You gave me a certain amount of time to earn your trust, and if I can't..."

He trailed off, and her heart clenched hard. Was that what he'd been doing today? Just being nice to her mother to win her over? It wasn't a very charitable thought, but she'd been manipulated enough in her life.

Before she could get herself too worked up, something in his eyes went soft. He tilted his head toward the apartment behind them. "She reminds me a lot of you, you know?"

"My mom?"

"Yeah. You've got her eyes." He let go of one of her hands to brush his knuckles down the side of her face. "Her spark."

The tightness in her chest eased with the warmth of his touch against her cheek. The warmth in his voice that said this hadn't been mere obligation or putting in time.

Dropping her gaze, she focused on a point beneath the hollow of his throat. "I got that a lot growing up. People always said how alike we were."

Her father said it all the time. They had the same faults, the same weaknesses.

They'd made so many of the same mistakes.

A fingertip under her chin tilted her head up. Soft blue eyes stared into hers. "You're both beautiful."

She laughed, tipping forward to rest her brow against his chest. "Please tell me you aren't hitting on my mother through me."

"I'm hitting on *you*, silly girl." With that, he wrapped his arms around her, hugging her close. There was something about the way he held her that made her feel so cared for. So safe.

If it weren't for her mother waiting for her, she might've stayed right there all night, but after a while, she couldn't drag her heels any longer. She pulled away. "I'll call you after she leaves?"

"Or earlier, if you need me. Or if you just want me. For anything, you hear?"

She nodded. Somehow, she actually believed he meant it.

Leaning down, he drew her into one last embrace, a soft kiss that didn't build but that still warmed her from the inside. Then he smiled, parting from her lips. "Good night."

"Good night," she echoed. It was almost a physical ache, how much she longed to spend it in his arms. She'd gotten a taste of what that felt like again, and having to go without was going to be even harder now.

She watched him all the way to the end of the hallway, returning the little wave he gave her before he headed down the stairs. As soon as he was out of sight, she thunked her head back against the door. She inhaled nice and deep and held it to the count of three.

Then she opened the door and walked in.

Kate's mom was sitting in the same chair Kate had found her

in that morning, her arms crossed over her chest. A heavy silence shrouded the apartment as Kate made her way to the kitchen and poured them each a glass of water. She handed her mother's over without comment and retreated to sit on the bed.

"All right," she said, steeling herself. "Let me have it."

Her mother pursed her lips. "I'm not sure what you're expecting me to say."

Kate swallowed a laugh.

After her father had left, it had been like this weight had lifted off them both. They'd been untethered, floating around in space, and it had been amazing. If anything, her mom had been too permissive, encouraging her art and her social life and whatever made her happy.

With one exception. Never, not once, had Kate so much as introduced her to a boy without getting a rundown of his faults. She'd spent all of an hour with Aaron in the whole year they dated, and it had given her ammunition for months. Kate huffed out a breath. Of course, that could've had something to do with his having been her father personified, only she'd been too swept up at the time to realize it.

She was swept up now, too. All the cool calm she'd meant to maintain when it came to Rylan, all the walls she'd constructed around her heart after he'd revealed himself to her—they were crumbling. Maybe her mom would see what she hadn't. Maybe she could help her avoid another round of heartache.

Kate set her glass aside and wrung her hands. "I expect you to tell me what you think."

For a long moment, her mother stared at her, sizing her up. "I think you're a grown woman who can make her own decisions."

This time, Kate laughed aloud. She'd been out on her own for a while now, but she always felt about two wrong steps away from bankruptcy or disaster. Right now, she felt so close to the edge that it wouldn't even take one.

Her mom's voice softened. "You're clearly very taken with him."

"He's been really good to me." When he was being honest with her anyway.

"He's certainly handsome enough, and money doesn't seem to be an issue for him."

Understatement of the century.

"Just..." Her mother trailed off.

"What?"

Her mom's expression faltered, something pained emerging behind her smile. Something old. "Just...be careful. Men like that, men who seem too good to be true..." She met Kate's gaze. "They usually are. They have a wife or another life or *something* they're not telling you."

And Kate heard all the things her mother didn't say.

Kate's father had seemed too good to be true at one point, too. How many times had her mom told her that? He'd been sweet and charming, and she'd *known*...She'd known there was no reason for a guy like that to fall for a girl like her. It'd taken him years to show his ugly side, and even then, it'd been tiny things. Little preferences and offhanded compliments that slowly evolved over time until they were demands and insults, until by the end, Kate and her mom had both felt like captives in their own damn home. Unable to question, always tiptoeing around. Too terrified to leave, because they were too stupid, too flighty, how would they ever manage alone...

Kate dug her nails into the meat of her hand. Clenched them there until it *hurt*, until it felt like it would bleed.

"He's not Dad," she said, the words torn from her mouth.

How many times had Rylan told her she was incredible? That he admired the work she did and the way she saw the world, that she deserved the very best...

But her mom just kept gazing at her, and her eyes went sad. "Not yet he's not."

She got up then, while Kate's mouth was still hanging open. Kate watched in dumb silence as she opened up her suitcase and pulled out her things to get ready for bed. The door to the bathroom closed behind her with an echoing ring.

But still Kate sat there. Her mother was wrong. She had to be.

chapter NINETEEN

"So what about you?"

Kate sat across from her mother, picking at the last of her lunch. They'd spent the morning shopping in Williamsburg and had stopped in at one of Kate's favorite little cafés for a bite.

Her mother frowned. "What about me?"

"We spent the whole day yesterday with my boyfriend." It still felt so strange to call Rylan that. So unreal. "Just wondering if there's anyone special in your life."

Her mother never mentioned anyone she was seeing when they talked on the phone, and in general, Kate didn't press. But in person it was different.

Her mother made a face and set her fork down. "I really don't have any interest in dating. You know that."

"Things change." Kate hadn't thought it strange that her mother didn't date while Kate was still in school, though she'd wished sometimes that she would. Those first couple of years after her father had left had been a breath of fresh air, the two of them just stretching their wings after so long in a cage, and that freedom alone had been enough for both of them. Things had been good after that, too, but there'd been a growing loneliness to her mother, one even the new passel of girlfriends she'd made since the divorce couldn't quite seem to touch. Once Kate was out of the house, she'd figured her mom would branch out more. But it had been four years now, and nothing.

Kate's mother shook her head. "I don't know if this will."

"Is it—" Kate caught herself before she could blurt out the question on her tongue. It was relevant, though, wasn't it? How long had she held herself back because... "Is it Dad?"

She laughed. "Your father hasn't had a say in my life in a decade."

Except he had, hadn't he? His voice still lingered in the back of Kate's mind. Still held sway over her and her decisions to an extent she never would have expected.

Not until Rylan had come along. Not until he'd listened to the whole sad story of her life and her father and the failed relationships that had followed in his wake. He'd heard it all and held her as she cried and told her she deserved so much better than she'd gotten. He'd made her start to believe that.

"I don't know." Kate dropped her gaze to what was left of her sandwich. "I mean, he messed with my head pretty bad." And here she had to tread carefully, because this wasn't about blame. "He must have messed with yours even worse."

Her mom sighed. "I don't really want to talk about this, Kate."

"Well, maybe you should. If not with me then with someone."

"Kate."

And Kate knew that tone. She was overstepping.

Finally, her mother's hand extended across the table to close over hers. "I promise you. I am happy with my life. I don't need a man to make it complete."

Kate had never doubted that. Once after Aaron, and then again after the mess with Rylan that summer, Kate herself had resolved to never let a man get close to her again. Both times, she'd done it out of pain, and out of fear.

She turned over her palm and squeezed her mother's fingers, lifting her gaze to look her in the eye. "Okay. Just...I worry about you, you know?"

She worried about her mother in that apartment all alone, making decisions around the parts of her life her father had burned to the ground.

"I know. But I'm telling you: Don't. I'm fine."

But her words were brittle. They didn't set Kate any more at ease.

They finished up what little was left of their lunches in relative silence and gathered up their things. As they stepped back out onto the sidewalk, her mother looked at her expectantly.

"Where to next?"

Neither of them had bought much, but Kate was mostly shopped out. Peering both ways down the street, she considered.

"Actually." She hesitated, patting the side of her bag. The weight stashed in the bottom of it had been an itch at the back of her mind all morning. It seemed selfish, though, using part of their limited time together to run an errand of her own. She chewed at her lip. Ugh, why was she so afraid to ask for things? It wasn't as if her mom had proposed any ideas for what she wanted to do. "If you don't mind too much, I was hoping to maybe take a quick detour?"

"Oh?"

"Yeah." She nodded toward the left and started walking. "There's this project I'm working on for school. A series of paintings. I need some more reference photos for it."

Her mother fell into step beside her. "Sounds like fun to me. What's the series about?"

"Churches, mostly."

"Churches." Her mother raised a brow.

"I know, I know." They'd never been terribly religious. "I didn't pick the theme."

Except that she sort of had. The "Sacred Spaces" assignment might've been handed down from on high, but it was broad enough. Open to lots of interpretations. She'd been the one to decide to pursue it so literally. There was no one to blame for how poorly the project was going besides herself.

Her mom shrugged. "Lead on."

It was a few short blocks to the big old cathedral she'd had in mind. It stood on the corner, gorgeous, gritty red brick standing out against the yellowing leaves and the bright blue autumn sky.

As they approached, she handed her mom the one shopping bag she'd been carrying and dug out her camera. Her heart did a little stutter as she fiddled with the settings. Foolish, probably, bringing Rylan's ancient film camera instead of her tiny digital one. But it had felt so right in her hands the previous morning as she'd used the lens to frame his body. As she'd mapped out the dips and ridges of his abdominals, the strong lines of his shoulders and jaw.

Maybe, just maybe, the soulfulness of film would help her capture what she'd been missing in this whole project. Maybe it'd help her crack the thing wide open.

She hunched down on the sidewalk to shoot up the height of the building, playing with the perspective and the depth of field. As she walked the length of the place, her mother stood to the side, letting her work.

When she was done, she snapped the lens cap back on.

Her mom stepped in closer. Her voice was quiet as she asked, "Did he give that to you?"

Kate froze.

For a second, her throat didn't want to work. "Excuse me?"

"It's a nice camera. A really nice one." And a softness had crept into her tone. "I used to do some photography, you know. Artsy stuff. Before you were born."

Her mother's creativity had never been a secret. If anything, it had been a weapon. Her father's words echoed hotly through the years. *She gets this shit from you, Carol.*

Kate nodded, her chest going tight.

"That right there?" She tapped a finger against the top of the camera. "That's the one I always dreamed of saving up enough for."

Oh.

Her mother dropped her hand and her gaze. When she spoke again, it came as if from a long way away. "Back before we got married. Back before he convinced me to drop out of school. When things were still good..." She blew out a breath. "Your father gave me one of them, too."

It wasn't as if Rylan had really expected Kate to need him while her mother was in town. He'd made the offer, though, and so he kept his phone a little closer to him than he might have otherwise. All it got him were a couple of pictures—one of a dress she was trying on that he wholeheartedly approved of, followed later that night by a selfie of her pouting while lying on what looked like an air mattress on her floor.

It'd made his heart pang. Made his own perfectly comfortable bed feel entirely too large.

By the time he headed in to the office on Monday, he still hadn't heard anything of substance from her. With her mom scheduled to fly out soon, though, he had hope.

In the meantime, he had plenty to do to keep him occupied. Reports to catch up on and phone calls to make.

Terrible strategies to figure out how best to shoot down.

He was just digging into the latest bullshit new business plan McConnell had been circulating around when Lexie swept into his office without so much as a by-your-leave.

"So apparently in addition to being a douchebag, McConnell's forgotten how to count." She flopped down into one of the chairs opposite his desk with a dramatic sigh.

Unruffled, Rylan kept his gaze on his computer screen. "Hello, sister dearest, how are you? I'm well."

"Save it, Teddy."

That got him to look up. He shot her a glare, and she rolled her eyes. She knew what she was doing.

Glancing back over her shoulder toward the door, she crooked one finger in a beckoning motion. A guy Rylan hadn't noticed unpeeled himself from the doorframe and made his way to join Lexie in the chair beside her.

Rylan furrowed his brow. How had he *not* noticed that guy? He was big, nearly as tall as Rylan himself, but it was more than that. He had a quiet presence that about near filled the room.

As soon as he let himself be seen in it.

Lexie followed the guy with her gaze, and as he sat, she smirked at him, and oh hell. His sister hadn't had a sexual harassment case filed against her yet, but Rylan had a whole new headache coming on. Their luck on that front might be about to run out.

The guy was just her type, was the thing—as least based on

the kinds of boys she'd used to sneak into the house. Short-cropped, ashy-brown hair, and under the lines of his suit, he was clearly built.

And yet he was different, too. Had a certain kind of rugged-ness that didn't look like it came from a health club or a gym. One that didn't quite mesh with the high-rise office in Manhattan, either.

"Rylan?" She emphasized his name. "Have you met Dane?"

"Can't say I've had the pleasure."

Dane nodded. "Sir."

"I pulled him out of the temp pool to help us with our whole corporate takeover thing."

Rylan leveled her with his best *you've got to be kidding me* stare. "Really, Lex? You want to be that bald-faced about it?"

"There's no reason for her not to be, sir." Dane shifted, pulling a piece of paper from the folio he'd been holding and sliding it across Rylan's desk. He had a rough, low voice, and he spoke in unhurried tones. "Nobody else is at this point."

Rylan kept his gaze on him for a long moment before picking up the memo. As he read, his eyebrows crept higher and higher.

"See what we mean?" Lex sat back in her chair.

"Yeah." He glanced up from the page. "Where did you get this?"

"Dane found a copy lying around."

Rylan darted his gaze to the side. He had to give the guy credit—Dane didn't so much as flinch at the obvious lie. Rylan shot his sister a pointed look. "We are going to have a talk later about adding corporate espionage to the corporate takeover thing."

Lexie waved a hand dismissively. "Focus."

Heaving a sigh, Rylan did just that.

He read the private memo McConnell had sent out one last time before setting it down. "Well, he's not being subtle."

Ninety days. That was the time period Rylan had proposed to the board, and that was what they had voted to accept. Ninety days until Rylan had to make a decision about where he wanted to go with the company next. Until his final chance to stop the interim board from becoming permanent.

"This meeting McConnell's calling for," he said. "It's in two weeks."

"He must think he has the support to keep you out."

Dane cleared his throat. "Actually." He pulled out a tablet and opened up a calendar. "He must think the golf trip he offered to half of your supporters will be too tempting for them to bother to show up."

Rylan's blood flashed hot. He curled his hands into fists. "He thinks he can buy them that cheap?"

"Believe me, sir. It's not cheap."

The pressure mounting behind Rylan's temple grew. This was bullshit, was what it was.

Those ninety days—he hadn't realized how much he'd been counting on them.

To get his head on straight. To figure out his life.

To summon up the strength to face his father's legacy.

"Well," he said, gritting his teeth. "It looks like our timetable is moving up."

After all of this was over, the first thing Kate was going to do was buy a calendar.

With everything else going on, apparently her mother's visit wasn't the only thing she'd forgotten. She put her mom in a cab to the airport just after breakfast with about three seconds to spare before she was on an inbound train heading for campus.

Her program was fairly hands-off, all told. There was a long list of credit requirements, of course, but the only really mandatory things she had to keep up with were her weekly seminars with the rest of her cohort.

And her monthly meetings with her adviser.

She was fully out of breath by the time she knocked on Professor Robinson's office door. Professor Robinson was sitting on the floor in the middle of the room, gorgeous black-and-white monotype prints spread out on the carpet around her. She looked up, and a thin smile spread across her face.

"Ah, Ms. Reid. Right on time."

A miracle, basically.

Kate nodded, nerves making her hands fidget at her side. While she saw Professor Robinson in class regularly, this was only their second one-on-one. Who knew what she should expect.

Professor Robinson regarded the prints in front of her again, then with a few graceful movements stacked them into a couple of piles and rose. For a few minutes, they made small talk about Kate's classes and how she was settling in, but her professor didn't make any move to sit, or invite Kate to do likewise. Finally, Professor Robinson gestured toward the door. "Well. Shall we see what you're working on?"

Oh, hell. This was the part Kate had been dreading.

She was always shy about showing off her works in progress, and with how blocked she'd been since the semester had begun, her shyness had begun to approach a phobia. She hadn't presented anything at critique in weeks, and the disappointment on her teachers' faces had been growing and growing. But there was no more putting it off now.

Like a woman on her way to the gallows, Kate led her professor to the painting studio. As she stood in front of the cubby where she stowed her canvases, her skin flashed hot and cold, all the voices she spent so much of her time trying to ignore ganging up on her at once. *You don't belong here, you're no good at this, God why are you such a disaster...*

She pulled out what little she had to show for herself, one terrible mess after another, and she lined them up against the wall. There were only a handful of people working in the studio, but she felt every single one of them, felt their gazes on her like searing brands, until she thought she'd burn up from the inside.

She was going to get laughed at. Her professor would take one look at this train wreck and...and...rescind her admission. Kick her out on the street, and Kate had worked so hard to be here. She'd *tried*.

But it wasn't enough.

"None of them are finished," she hedged. Her hands were damp and clammy, her lungs tight.

Professor Robinson waved off her concerns, walking the row of paintings with her hand at her mouth, a serious set to her eyes. Swallowing past the crawling anxiety that had her about ready to go out of her skin, Kate waited. Bit at the inside of her cheek to keep quiet and let the woman think.

Finally, after what felt like hours, Professor Robinson tilted her head toward Kate, gaze still on the canvases laid out before her. "Walk me through what you're thinking here."

"Well." And Kate could do this. The whole point of going to school was to collaborate with people who knew what they were doing. To let them help her. "They're for the Sacred Spaces project."

"Mm-hmm."

Concern colored that hum, and Kate's stomach did another flip inside her abdomen. "And they're..." Her frustration was bleeding over. She said this so often to herself in her head, but admitting it out loud was another thing altogether. It was inviting criticism, it was opening herself up to the censure that made her feel flayed open and like this little girl who was never enough, who kept messing up. She wrung her hands. Then finally spat out, "I hate them."

Professor Robinson's head jerked around at that. For this fraction of a second, the cool, detached calm she radiated shivered, the corner of her mouth twitching. "Oh."

"I just." And thank God she'd had the presence of mind to come at least a little bit prepared. She dug into her bag, fishing out her sketchbooks. "See." The book on top was the one she'd finished in Montmartre, and she flipped it open to the final pages. "I took this trip to Paris this summer. A graduation present to myself."

A last-ditch, floundering, desperate attempt to rediscover her muse and prove to herself that she had what it took.

She held out the drawing she'd done there, looking out over the city, the one she'd been so proud of at the time. "It's from the top of Sacred Heart, and I did these other ones of Notre Dame."

"I see." Professor Robinson reached out and took the book, freeing up Kate's hands to fumble with her other set of sketches.

"When you announced the theme for our portfolios, I immediately thought of these." She'd thought of sitting on the steps of these grand old cathedrals and how her art had seemed to come to life.

"I understand why."

"Yeah?" For the first time since that summer—since she'd

placed these same images in Rylan's hands and waited with bated breath for him to render his opinion—she felt this spark of hope.

Professor Robinson swept her hand across the page. "There's a gorgeous *space* to this."

"That's exactly what I was going for."

"While with these..."

The hope Kate had harbored sputtered, going sour in her throat. Professor Robinson cast her gaze back at the canvases, and Kate's stomach sank.

"It's not there," Kate said.

"Not yet."

And that was something, wasn't it? Her professor thought there was potential at least. That she had a chance.

Then she turned to Kate. "I'll admit. I've been concerned."

"Me, too."

"I was one of the ones to review your application, you know." Actually, Kate hadn't. "Oh?"

"I saw a lot of possibilities. I was hoping that this program might help you develop your voice. Your vision."

That was exactly what Kate had been hoping for, too. She nodded enthusiastically.

"But," Professor Robinson said, gesturing at the paintings again, "these are just as scattered as your previous work. They're not up to the levels we were expecting."

Of course they weren't. Kate was going to be sick.

"The studies from Paris, though. They're making me feel better about things." She passed Kate's sketchbook back over to her. "So what do you think will get you on track again?"

"I don't know." Kate chewed at the inside of her lip. "I've never been this blocked before."

"There's a lot of pressure in a program like this. You're working outside of school, too?"

"Just a little waitressing job."

"That's a lot."

She wasn't wrong. What Kate would give to be back in Paris again, to have a whole week with no agenda, no obligations. That freedom had been part of what had empowered her, she was sure.

That and the beauty of the city. The chance to wander around museums, to surround herself with art and architecture.

Her breath caught. There had been one other factor, too.

Rylan. Taking her to all these amazing places and getting her to talk about what she did and who she was. Touching her so softly in the quiet of their rooms. Whispering in her ear that she was amazing.

Professor Robinson had kept talking as Kate retreated to the safety of that summer in her mind, and Kate heard herself replying back, agreeing that she needed to focus more, that maybe she should try working in different mediums.

"And it might be a matter of connection, too," Professor Robinson said.

Kate's attention came flaring back. "Connection?"

"There's a sense of investment in the drawings from Paris that I'm not seeing in these. Think carefully about your subject matter. Why are you choosing these places? What about them speaks to you?"

It dawned on her, a sharp thud to the skull that left her reeling.

"Nothing," she said.

Her paintings were hollow because she didn't care about them. They were *sacred*, sure, but not to her.

The ringing in her ears wasn't a concussion, but it might as well have been.

All the work she'd done for this portfolio...it was garbage. She'd known it was in bad shape, but she'd thought she'd be able to rework the canvases. Tweak them and bring them to life once they were dry.

But there wasn't anything to rework. Nothing to tweak.

She needed to go back to the drawing board completely.

"I know these are due soon," Professor Robinson said, and Kate's gut twisted harder. "You've got your work cut out for you."

Kate nodded dumbly and closed her sketchbooks.

Professor Robinson gave her a gentle smile. "I'm excited to see what you come up with."

Excited was one word for it.

Kate would've chosen *filled with crippling dread*.

Her professor excused herself back to her office not long after, leaving Kate to gather up her things with a numbness slowly spreading its way through her limbs. The smart move would be to double down and get straight to work. Pressure loomed over her head like a blade about to fall, and she could use that to help her kick her own ass into gear. This wasn't just about winning the fellowship anymore—it was about proving herself to everyone in the program. To her adviser. To herself.

She stowed the last of her paintings in her cubby again and worried the hem of her skirt. She looked up, across the studio, at the empty easel in her corner of the room.

She knew what would be the smart thing to do.

But more time painting more churches she couldn't care less about...

That wasn't what had fueled her art-soaked afternoons in

Paris. Hell, even *art* hadn't been what had powered half of those.

She knew what had.

Turning her back on her easel, she stormed her way out of the studio. And pulled out her phone.

chapter TWENTY

Rylan was this fucking close to just letting the call go to voicemail. He was hunched over another pile of McConnell's paperwork that Lexie and Dane had managed to get their hands on, and the penned-in, clawing feeling that had haunted him for the last decade had his lungs going tight, his legs jittery with the fight-or-flight reflex he'd been so good at ignoring at one point in his life. Right up until he'd finally let it win out and flown, all right.

Yet here he was again. Stuck, with no good options left. If he wanted to keep the company out of that asshole's hands, he had to step up and take over. He had to become exactly the man he'd been groomed from birth to be. He'd spent so damn long railing silently, fruitlessly against his fate. Fuck life and fuck him if he was going to walk right back into it and slam himself into that cage.

He'd thought he'd have more time.

From the breast pocket of his suit, his phone gave another buzz, and he hauled it out. If it was Lexie again, he was going to tell her to go to hell for real this time.

Except it wasn't.

Kate's beautiful, smiling eyes stared back at him from the screen. And he felt like he could breathe again.

He hit the button to answer the call and brought the speaker to his ear. "Hey, gorgeous."

"Hey."

He sat up straighter in his chair. It was just one word, but the tightness to her voice carried over the line. "What's wrong?"

And then she laughed. "Nothing. Everything." He could almost hear her shaking her head. "I just...Listen, are you busy today?"

She had no idea. But he was already shuffling the papers in front of him and putting his computer to sleep. "I can be in Brooklyn in half an hour."

"No, no, I'm actually just leaving campus."

He paused with his hand on his mouse. Was it something with school, then? His brain had gone instantly to things going south with her mom, but apparently he was two steps behind. "Tell me where to be and when."

"Are you at your house?"

"No, I'm out." He stood up straight. "Kate, you're worrying me here."

The quality of the sound around her changed, filling with distant echoes of traffic and wind. She must've stepped outside. "I'm fine. I'm...well, I don't know what I am, but I just— This is going to sound crazy."

Compared to the other things he'd heard today? "Talk to me."

"Can you meet me at the Met?"

Okay, that made him pause. "The Met?"

Emergency summons landed you at hospitals and police stations. But a museum?

Her voice pitched higher. "Can you?"

"I'm leaving right now."

It was the work of a minute to finish closing up shop, sweeping the pile of paperwork into a drawer and turning off his monitor. He paused long enough to trade his suit jacket for a leather one, and then he was off, out of this glass box in the sky and down on the ground, feeling the earth beneath his feet.

He wasn't a completely irresponsible asshole, though. While he was in transit, he fired off messages to Lexie and to his admin, letting them know he'd be out of the office for the rest of the day for personal reasons. That earned him a barrage of replies from his sister, but he cut them off with a simple Thanks, Dad.

It was a dick move, but it was effective, making his phone go silent.

Christ, his father would've laid into him for pulling a stunt like this. But dear old Dad wasn't here right now.

That fact alone made the air a little sweeter, oxygen and space flooding his lungs. He laughed out loud, and who cared who heard? Half an hour ago he'd been facing a life sentence, one he himself had handed down, and the freedom of setting it all aside for an afternoon... It wasn't the angry flight of last year. He wasn't running away from the past and off into an abyss of a future. Off into free fall. He was running toward something.

Someone.

As quickly as he'd left, Kate still managed to beat him there. He spotted her at the top of the steps, and a whole new rush gave him wings. He took the stairs two at a time, darting around a couple of old ladies until he was within feet of her. Only then did he slow.

She looked terrible.

Scratch that, she looked amazing, in a short black skirt and tights and low-heeled boots that made her legs look even longer, but that wasn't the point. Her hair was in her face, the ends of it astray, and there was a brittleness to every line of her. Like you could shatter her with a teaspoon if you knew the right place to strike. Her eyes were red.

"What happened?"

She shook her head, and his heart clenched hard inside his chest, his throat going tight. A sheen gathered at the corner of her eyes.

He crossed the remaining steps to her in an instant. She melted into his arms, and he gathered her up close, burying his face in her hair.

"It's okay, baby, it's all right." He held her tighter as a shiver racked through her. For a long moment they stood there, letting traffic go around them. With a stuttering breath, she made to pull away, but he caught her before she could go too far. "Tell me everything."

But she shook her head, a fierceness setting into her gaze and the line of her mouth. "Can we just—can we not?"

His brow crinkled. "Kate—"

"I know." A hot sort of a desperation crept into her tone. "I know, but I—I want to forget about it."

Jesus, what the hell had happened to her? He clenched his jaw. "If someone did something—"

"No, that's not—everything's fine. It's just been a really"—her lip crumpled—"a really terrible day."

Well, that much he could understand. It had been a hell of a morning for him, too, and it wasn't as if he wanted to talk about that. She'd called him, and he had come, and seeing her, being away from it all...It was a balm for his soul. It was relief and freedom and things he hadn't even known he could have.

He rubbed soothing circles into her skin. "Okay."

"Things are just so messed up right now, and I want—I want to get away from it all." Her eyes went suddenly, unbearably soft. "And the first thing I thought of was..." She trailed off, gesturing helplessly at the museum behind her.

A cleansing fire swept through his lungs.

She'd wanted to escape, just like he had. And the first idea to come to mind had been their time together in Paris.

The first person she'd thought of had been him.

"Please," she said, and it shocked the breath from him, the fervency in that word. "Can we forget the rest of the world? Can we pretend?"

Can we pretend it's just the two of us again?

She'd scarcely suggested it, and he was drunk on the concept. No classes and no companies, no sisters and no art school friends. No phantom fathers breathing down their necks. The messy parts of their lives could just go away for an afternoon. Maybe forever.

All he needed was this.

"Yes." His agreement spilled from his lips, and he was leaning in. She tasted like the freedom he'd been so desperate for, but which he'd been unable to name. She tasted like *escape*.

"Yes, yes." He pulled away from the kiss to touch his brow to hers. "Of course we can."

The smile that swept across her face floored him, so beautiful he had to meet it with his own. Grinning against her mouth, he curled his arms around her waist, lifting her up and spinning them.

And she felt so good against him, all those soft, lush curves. The euphoria of slipping out and meeting her like this was tempered, the air between them shifting. Static hummed between their bodies, and he swallowed past the tightness in his throat.

It had only been a couple of days, but it felt like forever since he'd touched her.

He could wait a little longer.

"Come on," he said as he set her down, her body skimming his as he released her, making him only want to hold on tighter. But he held out his hand, and she slipped her soft, warm one into it. He pointed to the museum's front door. "Let's go get lost."

In art. In their memories from that summer.

In each other.

It was like a montage out of a movie. Rylan took her hand and led her past the admission line, and she didn't even give him a hard time about whatever it was he did to get them in without waiting. Once they were in the museum proper, he led her straight to the European wing, and with every gallery they wandered through, a little more of the tension that had been dogging her slipped away.

This was what she'd needed. The rest of her life would come crashing back around her soon enough. She had a portfolio to completely rethink and a boyfriend she still wasn't on entirely certain ground with and a lonely, suspicious mother and a mountain of debt.

But here, with Rylan, surrounded by Postimpressionists, all of that was easy to forget.

It was like being in Paris all over again. At the Louvre or the Musée d'Orsay.

God, why didn't she do this more often? Connecting with your muse wasn't just about taking weeks off at a time to fly across the globe. It was little moments of inspiration, quiet afternoons away from the pressures of real life.

All those hours she'd spent painting churches because they were supposed to be sacred. Maybe she should've set up her easel right here. Painted these echoing rooms and brilliant canvases, sketched in the profiles of museumgoers filling their souls with images from decades and centuries and millennia ago.

Rylan rubbed his knuckles against her upper arm as they ambled past a grouping of Cézannes. He was so warm against her. So solid. And it still took her breath away, how he could make her body light up with these tiny touches. Another little coil of anxiety bled away from her spine, replaced by a heat humming right below her skin.

Forget churches and forget museums. Maybe she should've been painting *him*.

And then it struck her. Maybe she should have.

"Hold that thought."

She slipped out from under his arm, shaking her head at the questioning look he shot her. She'd been carrying his camera around with her pretty much since the instant he'd given it to her. Half the rolls of film he'd bought were done, but she had a fresh one already loaded.

He caught her gaze as she fished the camera out. She shot the first image of him just like that, staring levelly at her through the lens. She moved the camera away from her eye and waved a hand at him. "Act normal?"

He gave her a questioning look, but in the end he did as she asked. Turned half away from her and made another circuit of the gallery, pausing in front of each painting. She burned a dozen frames like that. Rylan and art, and art and Rylan, and they were both so beautiful. The two of them together . . .

No wonder she'd fallen into his bed. This had been his first move on her, after all. He'd taken her to a museum and guided her through room after room full of masterpieces.

And then he'd taken her back to *his* room. He'd shown her the masterpiece that was his body, and he'd taught her what it could do. How hers could feel when it was pressed to his.

Another blooming tingle of awareness flooded her skin, making her breasts go heavy. They'd had sex a handful of times since he'd been back. Two days ago, he'd laid her out and they'd passed this very camera between them, taking their time and snapping images of passion and flesh, and it had been fun. Revelatory, even.

But when was the last time he'd really taken her out of her own head with it? Since he'd shown her something new?

chapter TWENTY-ONE

The instant they made it through the door of his house, Kate was on him. Her bag hit the floor, and then her hands were on his shoulders, her mouth on his. He groaned into the kiss, the low simmering hum of desire that'd been heating his blood since he'd first set hands on her on the steps of the museum rising to a boil. He walked her backward, and she pulled him along until he wasn't sure who was leading who. Her back connected with the closing door, and he shoved a fist up into it, slamming it the rest of the way shut.

Thank God this hadn't just been him.

She played her cards close to her chest when she wanted something, but he hadn't imagined the heat in her eyes. How could he have? Everything they did was a callback to another moment. Running through galleries together like they had the first time they'd met, when the flush of desire between them had been uncomplicated and naked and new.

Letting her look at him with those artist's eyes. The way she had as she'd drawn him stretched out and bare on a hotel bed.

The way she had through a camera lens as he'd stripped off his clothes and taken slow, torturous strokes over his own needy flesh.

Before he'd thrown her down and pressed inside and taken pictures of that, too.

He kissed his way across her jaw and to her throat, tugging her collar out of the way to suck a bruise into the hollow where her shoulder met her neck—right where the old one had started to fade. "God, Kate."

Lightning ran up his spine as she traced her foot along the back of his leg. She tilted her head to the side and dug a hand into the meat above his hip, inviting him in.

And fuck but he had needed this. She might be having a shitty day, and she might escape from it by looking at pictures in a museum, but this was how he washed it all away. Even back before he'd known what sex could mean, he'd racked up the notches on his bedpost as a way to get out of his head. He'd run and he'd lifted and he'd fucked the anxiety and the anger out of his blood. The boredom and the purposelessness, once he'd gotten to Paris.

He lost himself in his body. Like this.

Running a hand up under her jacket, sliding from her hip to her chest, he circled the warm curve of her breast. "What do you want, baby?"

He'd give her anything. Do anything to make her feel good and to earn him his chance to be with her like this.

"I want—" She cut herself off, gasping for breath as he cupped her fully. As he scraped his teeth along the shell of her ear. Her hand found its way into his hair, and *yes*, fuck yes, he loved it when she tugged like that. "It's been so good—"

"Damn right it has."

But she shook her head, even as she kept pushing into the wet kisses he laid and sucked into her skin. "The museum."

"Just the museum?" He ground into her hip, pressing that hardness into her and having to bite down against the sound of need the contact pulled from his lungs.

She clutched him tighter. "The museum, everything. Like being in Paris again."

It was. So much like it.

The scratch of her nails against his scalp had him pulling back, looking at her with eyes that felt wild, nearly as wild as hers looked as she stared up at him. Her soft, red mouth parted, her breath coming hard.

"Pretend we're in Paris again," she said, and it was like his whole body lit up.

Their time together that summer had been a rushing whirlwind, preserved in flashes in his memory. She'd been so innocent and so terrified, but he'd coaxed out the sexiest, bravest creature with patient hands and soft kisses. With his *mouth*.

He dragged his tongue across his lips, going harder in his jeans. "Happily."

He dropped to his knees right there in the entryway. With a firm grasp at her ankle, he tugged her legs apart. Fuck autumn and fuck tights and fuck boots. He nipped his way up the fabric from her knee to well under the hem of her skirt.

She groaned as he mouthed to the top of her thighs. With clenched fists, she helped him ruck the fabric higher. The sound of her pleasure meshed with a choked, high peal of a laugh. "That's not what I meant."

"It's not?" He remembered doing a lot of this back then. It had been one of so few things that hadn't scared her off, and God but it had worked like a charm. Even that first night, when she'd been so tense, so afraid of her own pleasure and so doubtful about his promises that he could bring it to her...this was what had gotten her there. Soft, wet kisses against her cunt and the wet flicker of his tongue over her clit. He slid a hand up ahead of himself and rubbed a thumb over her. Even through the layers, she was damp and warm.

"It's not the *only* thing I meant."

A hot punch of arousal rocked through him as he turned his head. Laid his cheek against her thigh and gazed up at her while he primed her with low strokes of his thumb. Her face was red, the flush creeping down her neck and past the marks he'd left there, toward her breasts. And he knew this blush. Knew the embarrassment and the hard work it always took her to push past her inhibitions, and...

And the desire. She *wanted* something.

Oh, this was going to be good.

He barely recognized his own voice, gravelly with need as he asked, "So what else do you want?"

She seemed to have to dig deep as she flexed her hands and her jaw. But she found it, gaze connecting with his. "Whatever you want to give me." Her throat shivered. "Something I haven't had before."

Moaning aloud, he buried his face against her leg. "Oh, baby."

His cock was a dense ache as a thousand possibilities roared through his mind, his skin too tight and his flesh throbbing. He could get his mouth on her and feed himself to her, fuck her throat while he fucked her pussy with his tongue. Could turn her around and pound her right into this wall, or get her to ride him, find a way to help her do it with abandon. Watch her tits or—or reverse cowgirl and watch her ass and—

Oh hell. He knew what he had to do.

It killed him to pull away, blood pounding in his cock and through his veins, every inch of him crying out to have her right then and right there and *right the fuck now.*

Well. Not every inch.

In a movement that was so much smoother than he felt, he rose to his feet. The shiver of bare air between them hummed, shooting sparks. With all the restraint he had left in him, he grazed the backs of his knuckles down the side of her face. From her temple to her chin and down. All the way to the center of her chest.

Then he lifted his gaze to meet the dark heat in her eyes. Low and deep, he said, "Bedroom. Now."

Kate just about flew up the stairs. Her lungs were full, her nerves alight, thrills running from her breasts to the hot pit of need in the center of her abdomen and back again. Thundering footfalls on the bare wood behind her shot her heart into even higher gear, giving her a fresh burst of speed, and she laughed aloud. She wanted to be caught, but that wasn't the point. Being chased was a rush of adrenaline zooming through her tingling skin, was *amazing*—

But it was nothing to his overtaking her. She bit down on a scream as strong arms wrapped around her waist. He hauled her bodily over his shoulder, and she kicked her legs at empty air, feeling alive, feeling like everything that had been weighing her down was floating off of her at once.

The whole mattress bounced beneath her as she made impact with it. He threw her down and then rose up to stand above her. A predatory gleam lit his eyes, making the liquid pieces inside her go hotter. Wetter.

As she watched, he pushed his leather jacket from his shoulders, letting it fall with a clatter to the floor. All precise, efficient movements, he set to work on his cuff links and the buttons of his shirt, his only acknowledgment to her a curt, gruff "Strip."

She didn't need to be told twice.

Her clothes melted like water beneath her fingertips. None of the hesitance that had once plagued her remained as she pulled off her own jacket and her top and her bra. Naked to his waist already, he caught her ankle in his hand, tugging at her boots, and she shoved the whole jumble of her skirt and tights and underwear down her legs as one, only for him to tear them away. And then he was hooking his hands under her knees to haul her to the edge of the bed.

Her breath caught, her lungs seizing when he lowered himself down to sit on his haunches on the floor, hot hands on her thighs, spreading them apart. Nostrils flaring, gaze intent and searing as it focused singularly on hers.

And then he leaned in.

With her legs over his shoulders, the room around her spun. He'd been bald-faced in his intimation of doing this for her in the entryway of his home, but even the knowledge of what was to come, even the experience of having survived the impossible heat of his tongue before couldn't have prepared her for the wet kisses he peppered all around her sex.

"Rylan—"

"*Shh.*"

The first hot stripe he licked up the center of her had her back arching, her hands scrambling, twisting in the bedsheets above her head. But he pulled away, eyes flashing.

"Give me your hands."

She did just that, only to have him rest them securely in his hair, and, oh God. His mouth bent right back to its task, a hard sucking glance right over her clit as two fingers pushed inside. She hung on for dear life, but every time she feared she was grabbing too hard, yanking too savagely at the tangled strands, he groaned, the sound unmistakable as anything but pleasure.

So she gave in to her own. Jesus, it was shameless, the way she pushed up into the motions of his tongue, bucking to try to get his fingers deeper.

Only to go shatteringly still when he slipped his other hand lower.

It wasn't the first time he'd touched her there. She quivered, throat going tight at the soft pressure at her ass, and she remembered this. Remembered the fullness and the explosive way he'd made her come.

But it still felt so naked. So vulnerable.

He parted his lips from her flesh for just an instant. "Let me. Let me in, gorgeous. I promise, it's gonna feel so good."

And who was she to question? She'd been the one to beg him to show her something new. Pulse roaring in her ears, she dropped her legs to rest them lower on his biceps, spreading her thighs wider for him. Slipped her hand from his hair to the warm, solid muscle of his shoulder.

It was a dual assault as he lowered his mouth to her again. The pressure against her other opening wasn't a gentle nudge this time. His fingertip was slick with her liquid, pushing inside with an inevitability, and there was that burn, that sharp spike she'd anticipated, but at her wince he sucked her clit between his lips and hit that perfect spot inside her sex.

Her body yielded to it, the intensity and the stretch soaring past discomfort and into something hot and deep.

"Oh God," she mumbled.

"That's right. Give it to me."

He pressed and pressed, warm strokes into both her openings at once, and she was light. Was light and sensation and fullness—

Until she was devastatingly, achingly empty.

"No—" Her eyes flew open, and when had she even closed them?

His hands landed to either side of her head, the lean lines of his chest and arms gleaming as he held himself over her.

"This is what is going to happen," he said, and something turned molten in her spine. His voice rumbled hot in his throat and resonated through all the wanting places in her body. "You're going to keep this"—he shifted his weight, taking her hand and setting it to the swelter between her legs—"ready for me."

She slipped a fingertip through her folds, whining at the easy, slick glide. "And what are you going to do?"

His eyes darkened. "I'm going to go find our toys."

Brushing the base of her clit, she bit the inside of her cheek.

"You remember them?" he asked.

God, did she ever. A long, cool piece of glass with a little swell that pressed just right once he helped her push it inside. A nice deep rumbly vibe that he'd coaxed her through stroking along her clit, and he'd been there behind her the entire time, eating up her moans and whispering filth into her ear. Naked and hard and rubbing off against her spine because her pleasure had turned him on that much, because he wanted her so badly—

He dipped down to place his lips beside her ear. "And you know what then?"

The warm wash of his breath, the wet sounds of his words sent tremors humming through her skin. "What?"

"I'm going to fill you up. Watch that pretty glass slide into this soft pink pussy." His hand dipped down between her legs, one of his fingers sliding in alongside hers, making her spine arch and twist. "Give you that vibrator."

"Yeah?"

"And you're going to get yourself off with it, aren't you? Gonna get yourself so worked up?"

More worked up than she was already?

"And I'm gonna be right there." He scraped the line of her throat with his teeth, perfect and sharp. Then his hand slid lower. "I'm gonna be right here."

"Oh God."

His fingertip circled her ass again, and she shook down to her bones. "Remember I told you you'd be begging me to fuck you here someday?"

He had. That first night he was back.

Nose against her jaw, he groaned. "You're gonna beg me, Kate. You're gonna need it so bad, and it's going to be *amazing*. You'll be so tight—"

Her whole body hit a peak that wasn't orgasm—was instead this impossible breaking tidal wave of want crashing over her. She surged up into him, grabbing at his neck and hauling him down. Their lips met, tongues thrashing and teeth clicking, all messy and wet.

Then, gasping and breathy, she pushed him away.

Power poured through her limbs, electricity humming just underneath her skin. "You'd better get on with it then."

And for a second, this fleeting instant, the hot spark in his eyes softened.

"You are the sexiest thing I have ever seen," he said.

And then he was off her.

She did just as he'd asked her to as he stalked across the room, pulling open drawers and running the sink in the en suite. Closing her eyes, she slipped her fingers through her wetness. Spread it around in slow, teasing circles and kept herself warm.

As if anything about her could even remember being cold right now. He'd brought her to the heights of ecstasy before, but it had never been like this. It was arousal like free fall, like floating, like she could hold here on this bank of air and never, ever come down.

The toys made a dull impact as he tossed them down on the bed beside her head. They were followed by the little foil square of a condom and—another hot pulse throbbed through her when she recognized the clear liquid in the bottle. He was going to press that into her, open her up where she was unyielding, where she'd never taken a man before. Make her wet and easy for his cock, and she was going to let him.

With a hand on her hip, he flipped her over and pushed her higher on the bed. Warm broad palms settled on the backs of her thighs, spreading them farther, making space for him to settle between.

"Lift up."

She got her arms under herself, levering onto her knees. He slipped a pillow under her hips, and then there were soft lips and damp kisses on the curve of her rear, gentle fingers sliding along the lips of her sex.

"Beautiful," he said, a low rumble she felt in the hot pit of need he'd created within her.

The glass was cool and smooth against her body. He ran it up and down her slit, over her clit and then back to hover at her opening. She pushed into it, wanting it in, wanting him to sooth this empty ache, make her full, make her real.

He *tsk*ed her, grip going to steel against her hip. Pulsing around nothing, she choked on her own breath. Her shaking arms gave up on her, and she fell forward, face mashing into the sheets.

"Rylan..."

God, this was torture. The floating became plummeting, became the ground flying up to meet her, and she needed—she *needed*—

"Ask me for it."

"Please." Her breath shuddered, and her eyes flooded.

And then it was perfect, was right, her body held aloft as the toy pressed inside. She soared on every twisting ridge of the glass as he eased it in, her sex pulsing, hot flesh parting, and she was full, full.

"God, yes," she groaned.

Sliding it home, he traced a rough thumb around the edge of the glass. Flicked his finger across her clit, and she sobbed.

His whole face pressed against the small of her back, a noise that was pure sex sending more hot rushes pulsing through her veins.

"You have no idea," he said, and it was almost a growl.

With a kiss to her hip, he lifted up. And then he was draping himself over her. Denim scraped against her rear, the hard ridge of his belt and then the longer line of his cock as the bare skin of his chest brushed her spine.

The harsh buzz of the vibrator rent the air, and her body clenched down hard, making the glass press against an electric place inside her. He slipped the shivering head of the vibe to her clit, and it was too much, too soon. She shot a hand down, grasping the handle, shifting his grip until she could get it angled better.

All the air left her lungs in a rush, punched out of her by the hot spike of pleasure flooding through her sex.

"That's right. Doesn't that feel good?"

She moaned, rocking her face into the mattress, pushing her hips up into his. "Feels amazing."

"Don't stop." Pulling his hand away, he left her to the work of driving herself higher. His palm skirted its way up her side, over her shoulder to her neck. Tugging at her hair, he turned her head, and then his mouth was on hers, the kiss deep and wet and *dirty*, and she wanted more.

"Don't you stop."

"Never," he said, and there was a sharpness to it. A vehemence and a biting edge of teeth.

Her whole body flashed cold when he lifted himself off her. She looked back to find him settled on his knees, his chest heaving, abdominals tense. His gaze was full of fire as he picked up the bottle.

She swallowed hard, throat rasping. Lube was something new to her repertoire, but she couldn't hold back the fresh shiver of arousal at the gleam of his fingers as he drizzled them slick. Rolled the liquid around.

His eyes bore into hers as he trailed a soft, wet touch down from the base of her spine, lower and lower. She blinked her lids closed, bracing herself.

The pressure against her ass was so gentle, though. He had to be shaking with the restraint, and she was trembling herself. But the breach was easy, painless.

Melting into the bed, she gave herself over to it. The sparkling buzz against her clit and the hard fullness in her sex, and Rylan, always Rylan, working her open, deeper. A second and then a third finger pushed in until the fullness crescendoed.

She dug her face into the mattress, rocking back and forth. She needed escape and more and to get away and for him to *take* her already.

"I can't." It came out a whine, a high sound that couldn't have come from her except that her throat was raw from it. "I can't."

"You can. Baby, hold on, you're so close. Just relax and let me and—"

Inside her, something melted. And then the slide was easier, the fullness all pleasure.

"Oh Kate, that's beautiful, that's perfect."

But it wasn't.

"Please." Real, actual tears bubbled up at the corner of her eyes. She felt wet and vulnerable and open and like she would fly apart. She needed to be pinned down. Held to this earth. To be made his. *"Please."*

He swore aloud. His fingers pulled free, and time went taffy-slow. A crystalline moment of empty waiting. Some long, far way off in the distance, clothing rustled. Foil tore, and then there was his low grunt. Slick sounds.

The searing line of him pressed to the cheek of her ass, and she was liquid, was all need and heat and pleading cries, babbling for his touch. His cock.

A hot hand landed at her hip. Voice gravel, he asked, "Are you ready?"

And her heart thundered.

How much of her life had she spent fearing pain? Sex had hurt her once, and it had made her shy away from it for ages.

Because she'd let a man touch her without patience. Because she hadn't been able to tell him what she needed.

She knew how to say that now.

People had told her this would *hurt*, but she was with Rylan. There was no fear. No pain.

She opened her eyes, and her vision swam. "Yes."

"You trust me?"

His breath caught on the word, and it was a hook under her rips, prying her open.

She'd sworn she'd never trust anyone—*especially* him—again.

But how could she not? How could she go on, accepting this from him—touch and heat and a kind of tenderness she'd never known, even when he was asking her to do this?

How could she have ever, ever imagined she could stop herself?

The world went still.

And she heard the word fall from her own numb lips. *"Yes."*

She'd known that he was bigger than his fingers, but it still took her breath away when he pressed the head of his cock against her opening.

"You can do it, baby. Easy, easy, just let it happen."

He pushed and pushed, and she squeezed her eyes shut tight. Focused on the waves of warmth from the buzzing at her clit, the soft clench of her sex where he'd filled her there, too, and the way her body fought her mind. Tried to keep him out, refused to yield.

Then all at once, the head slipped in, and she arched her back. Her cry pierced the air, but it didn't hurt.

"It's okay, it's okay, fuck, tell me it's good, Kate, tell me—"

She choked on her own breath. "It's good."

It was amazing.

He fell back over her again, as if the strength in his arms wasn't enough to hold him up. It drove her down, too, until she was flush with the mattress, sweaty skin driven hard into cool sheets. Prone and helpless and with her bottom in the air, hips propped up by the pillow. The motion only forced him deeper. She sobbed his name into the bed as he opened her around his cock, made space inside her for himself and claimed it—conquered it and filled it.

"Rylan." She tilted her head to the side, reached out with the hand that wasn't still on the toy. She pulled him forward and panted hard as he drove that extra inch deeper. All his hot flesh blanketed hers. She was surrounded and held and . . . and *fucked*.

And she was kissed. His tongue swept through her lips as he rocked his body into hers, forcing breathy gasps and whines and all these sounds she usually kept to herself from her lungs, and she was at his mercy. There was nothing to hold back and no way to contain the *brilliance* flaring up and down her spine.

The blinding, impossible release.

"You're beautiful, you're amazing." Rylan was babbling against her mouth, maybe as overcome as she was. "So tight around me, can you come? Wanna feel you—"

She choked on another scream as she flicked the vibrator up higher, and they both groaned aloud.

He kissed her cheek and her temple and the corner of her lips, and his hand at her hip felt hard enough to bruise, and she *wanted* that. She'd be feeling this for days as it was, and every mark he left was another point of heat. Another thing to *keep*.

Because she could keep him. She could have this. All she had to do was—

"Kate, I—"

He pulled back once and pushed in hard, and it was an explosion, all the fullness and the heat balled into something too big and too much, and it consumed her, dragged her under, every cell another point of flame radiating into nothingness. Climax claimed her in shattering pulses, and it was oblivion and love and giving of herself and receiving, and he was right there with her, breathing her name against her ear. Stuttering in his thrusts until he slammed in deep. Until he poured himself into her.

All she'd had to do was let him in.

And she was golden. Complete.

chapter TWENTY-TWO

"Okay." Kate flopped backward onto the carpet, starfishing. "I have got to play hooky more often."

She twisted her neck to look over at Rylan, and it made something in his heart glow warm. She was here, in his home, comfortable and happy and relaxed, and in that moment, it felt like everything he'd ever wanted in the world.

She blinked at him, the soft haze to her expression shifting. He'd been staring at her, lovesick, for too long.

Clearing his throat, he reached over to the bowl of grapes between them and plucked one out.

It had taken them a while, but eventually, they'd put themselves together enough to get their clothes back on and stumble down the stairs. His whole body still thrumming with satisfaction, his mind blanked by how completely she'd let herself go, he'd been stymied by what to offer her next. But he shouldn't have worried. She'd hit his kitchen, and from whatever had been included in his grocery delivery, she'd managed to assemble a veritable feast. A picnic, there amid the boxes and the drop cloth—covered furnishings still jumbled together in his living room. Spread out on the floor in front of the flickering flames in his fireplace.

Perfection.

Dropping onto his side, propped up on one elbow, he reached over to hold the grape above her lips. With a smile in her eyes, she opened her mouth and let him place it on her tongue. His body was done for the night, but it still managed to stir as he traced the bottom curve of her lip.

"Vacation does seem to suit you," he agreed.

She sighed, and a little of the exhaustion he'd seen in her back on the steps of the museum cast a shadow across her cheeks. She hadn't been ready to discuss it then, and he hadn't blamed her. She wasn't volunteering anything now, either, but whatever it was that had happened was simmering close to the surface.

Swallowing, he shifted to brush his fingertips along the edge of her face. "Do you want to talk about what made you need one so badly?"

She shrugged and looked away. "Just stuff with school."

"Oh?"

It had taken some adjustment, and he still had to fight the instinct to jump in, but he'd grown more accustomed to the silences in her conversation over the past few weeks. He had a better sense of when he needed to let her wait.

Finally, gaze still on the fire, she said, "You remember that portfolio project I was telling you about?"

"The one that was frustrating you so much?"

"That's the one. I had a meeting with my adviser about it this morning. It... didn't go so great."

A hot well of protectiveness opened up inside him. "How so?"

"She basically agreed with me that the stuff I've been doing for it isn't good enough." God, the hollow way she said those last few words made him ache.

"I'm sure that's not how she put it." How would she dare? With Kate's insecurities, with how hard she worked. How could anyone dream of saying that to her?

She gave a dry, sad little laugh. "She might as well have. I believe 'not up to the levels we were expecting' was the exact phrase."

Rylan would kill her. He'd find the professor or teacher or whatever and he'd make her regret ever even thinking something like that.

But Kate waved away the fury that had to be written across his face. "She's right. The paintings, they're just . . . they're awful. I'm honestly relieved someone was willing to tell me the truth about them."

And he felt that one between his ribs. The truth. He'd been nothing but truthful to her the whole time since he'd returned.

Besides. His throat went tight. It wasn't as if she'd let him see any of the things she'd been working on. She'd taken pains, every time he went to her apartment, to keep them hidden from his sight.

"I've seen your work." In the past, he had. "There's no way—"

But Kate shook her head. "She's seen the drawings I did in Paris, too, and she loved them. It's the new stuff. The work I've done since I've been back. I'm just *stuck*."

"Is there anything I can do?" Maybe she needed a better place to work. He still hadn't figured out how to tell her the top floor of the house was hers, but she could have it now. She could have anything money could buy if it would help.

"Honestly?" She turned her head to the side to look at him again. "You've already done it. Today, getting away from it all, getting out of my head." She flashed a weak smile. "I needed that."

"Then I'm glad I could give it to you."

Letting out a long, low sigh, she started to haul herself up. "That said, I should probably get going."

"You don't have to." *Stay*, he wanted to say. *Stay forever.*

"I wish." Sitting up straight, she combed her fingers through her hair. "I think—this whole time with this project. I've been half assing it, you know? Not really committing. I think it's because I was so wishy-washy about it. The subjects I picked." She folded her hands together in her lap. "I have to buckle down. Focus."

She could have been talking about his life. The world shivered in front of him.

Ever since he'd come back from Paris, he'd been walking a line. Asking for more time from the board, doing the bare minimum he had to to keep their options open. He'd been floating along the surface of his involvement with the company, with his family. Refusing to commit.

Except now the board was threatening to force his hand.

"After all," she said, her voice coming as if from a long, long way away. "You can't play hooky forever."

When the world resolved itself again, it had a different shape.

Sitting up, he reached out. Put his hand on her wrist and held her there. "But what if you could."

The idea formed out of nowhere, complete and perfect and crystal in his head. He'd been walking a line, and today, with his sister hounding him, he'd resigned himself to a certain side of it. But nothing was making him fall that way. He could do whatever he wanted to, could make whatever choice he decided was right.

He could fall to the other side. It hadn't worked the last time he'd tried it, but this time it could. This time he could do it better.

Her smile, fake as it had been, faded away. "Excuse me?"

"What if you could play hooky forever? What if *we* could?" His thoughts snowballed, taking on mass and speed. He tightened his grip on her arm, shifting onto his knees. "You're getting all this bullshit at school, and this shit with my father's company—"

"Wait, what?"

There was too much to catch her up on. "It doesn't matter. I just— They're trying to force me to step up and be CEO, and I thought I had to let them, but what if I don't?" His pulse raced, and it was like he could breathe again. "We could go. Get on a plane tonight and leave it all behind. I'll take you anywhere in the world you want to see. Florence is gorgeous this time of year, or Kyoto. Have you ever been to Japan? It's beautiful. Or we can go back to Paris and you can paint whatever you want."

He'd come to New York to try to reclaim his home, but home didn't have to be a place. Not a house or a city. It could be a person.

He reached for her face, capturing it between his palms. "Kate, just say the word and—"

"No."

"—and we'll go and—"

That wasn't the word he'd been waiting to hear.

Stopping dead in his tracks, he refocused, seeing the room around him again instead of all the corners of the world. All the places they could fly to.

He saw her. And she was pale. Shaking.

She pulled away from his grip, and it was like a slap. In one terrible, lurching movement, she threw herself to her feet, and he reached out for her, but his hand connected with nothing. With empty air.

And all the dreams he'd just begun to construct around himself came shattering, crashing to the ground.

All Kate could hear was her mother's voice, echoing around in her head.

. . . before your father convinced me to drop out of school.

Because that was what Rylan was suggesting here. He wanted her to give up everything she'd worked so hard for, and what? Become his mistress? Randomly tour around the world with him while he turned his back on everything and everyone?

She squeezed her eyes shut tight, because that was a whole other layer of cognitive dissonance.

They wanted him to become CEO.

It was news to her, and he just threw it out there so casually. Didn't bother to explain it. Didn't even pay any attention to the fact that he'd been hiding this entire part of his life.

He'd come back here to save his father's company, sure, but when had it become about him taking over? What was he doing day to day?

Who *was* he?

Men like that, men who seem too good to be true. . . They have a wife or another life or something they're not telling you.

And Kate had tried to tell her mother Rylan was different.

Oh God, it was Paris all over again. Except it was even *worse.* It was him forgetting to mention all these things about himself, and maybe he wasn't doing it with the intent to fool her, but he was doing it *now*. After they'd already fallen apart once because he'd been holding back.

After she'd let him into her life again, pushed aside her own doubts and decided to trust him. Even though she'd known better.

It had all been too good to be true.

Now here she was, with Rylan on his knees in front of her again, but it didn't soften her heart. It made her heart sick.

"Are you serious?" she asked.

He was gazing up at her as if he had no idea why she was upset. "Deadly."

Her stomach gave a lurching twist. "You want me to drop out of school."

Brow furrowing, he recoiled. "That's not what I said."

"But you want me to give up everything and go prance around the world with you? What part of that doesn't involve me dropping out?"

"I mean—only if you want to."

"Why would you think I want to?" Had he only been humoring her? Listening to her talk about her program, following her around to galleries. Telling her he loved her art.

"You just said it wasn't going well—"

"But that doesn't mean I want to stop."

She'd been working herself to the bone this semester. No way in hell was she giving up now. But Rylan—giving up was basically his thing, wasn't it? His whole time in Paris, he'd been running away from his responsibilities. His first instinct when she hit a stumbling block was that she should run away, too, and didn't that just tell her everything?

His jaw flexed. "Well, then fine. Don't. But if it's not helping you, you have options."

"Like being dependent on you?"

"Like letting me take care of you and show you beautiful things."

A hysterical laugh ate like acid through her throat.

She'd been around for the part of her parents' marriage when her father had made both her mother and her believe they needed him because they honestly couldn't survive without him. Because they weren't good enough. She'd survived the part of her and Aaron's relationship when he'd started the long process of tearing her down.

But those weren't the only ways to trap someone. Apparently, her father had begun by building her mother up. Buying her things, encouraging her photography.

Only to change. Later, when he wanted her to be someone different.

"Did you know that my dad bought my mother a camera? Back before they got married."

The hard set to his mouth softened, going confused again. "What does that have to do with—"

She shook her head. Her eyes stung, her whole face going hot with humiliation and a rage that went right to her bones. "And here I told her you weren't anything like him."

She might as well have slapped him. Fire lit his expression, and then he was climbing to his feet. Towering over her, and she took an unconscious step back.

"Because I'm not," he spat. "How can you even— Where is this coming from?"

This had been coming all along. Since the moment she'd met him. Since the second she'd let him in.

Bile churned in the back of her throat. Since she'd been an idiot and let him in *again*.

Her back hit the wall, and her skin crawled. She was stuck. There wasn't enough space in this room, wasn't enough air in her lungs. And he kept creeping closer.

Rising up to her full height, she lifted her chin. "What do you mean they want to make you CEO?"

His eyes just about bugged out of his skull. "Are you *trying* to give me whiplash?"

And there was the dismissiveness she'd been waiting for. The frustration.

"I'm trying to figure out who the hell you are and what you want from me."

Hurt bled across his features for all of a second before he schooled his expression. "We're back to this?"

"Did we ever stop being about this? You tell me nothing about your life, and you promised this time." That might be what gutted her the most. He'd promised to do better, and she'd let herself believe him.

"I tell you about my life all the time! You were the one who showed up today and said you wanted to forget about the outside world. Was I supposed to tell you about my day before or after that?"

She scoffed. "Like this all happened today?"

"It all came to a head today, yes. I thought I had another couple of months, and then I find out today I only have weeks."

"But you still knew it was coming. Yet you never managed to bring it up in conversation once—"

"I tried!" He actually threw his hands up in the air at that. "Do you know how many times I've tried to tell you about what I've been doing with my days? But every goddamn time, you change the subject." His voice rasped, grating and awful. "You say you want to know about me, yet when it comes down to it, you don't want to know anything that fucks with your precious little poor girl starving artist worldview."

Her breath caught in her lungs. "That's not fair."

A raw, angry huff of a laugh escaped his throat. "That's rich after all this...this *bullshit*."

This time, she felt like the one who'd been punched. She reeled, tightening her hands into fists. Her vision swam, and shit, crap, she hated this. This was why she'd sworn she was never going to do this again.

"I wanted to get to know you," she said, and it hurt. "I wanted to know who you were. I asked you time and again about your life, your family. At your father's house the other day, you had a million chances to show me anything at all about your life, and—"

"I took you to my father's house." Every word dripped poison. "Do you know the last time I did that? The last time *I* went there, even?"

"That's not the point."

"That's exactly the point." His nostrils flared, his eyes burning. "I make overture after overture, but it's never the one you want. It's never enough."

And she heard the dull, rasping echo of the words he didn't say. *I'm never enough.*

Well, she could relate to that, at least.

But she held her head high, even though her insides were churning. "You're right. It's not enough." Her voice shook. "Because I deserve better. You know who told me that?"

The darkness in his eyes said he sure as hell did.

And she remembered it so vividly. The two of them, naked in that bed together in Paris, and she'd clung to him, crying with abandon as he told her she deserved the whole world.

But he wasn't willing to give it to her.

She turned away from him, pushing off the wall. She was half blinded by tears all over again, but they were angry tears. Hot tears.

And achingly, impossibly sad ones, too.

He was right. They'd ended up right back here again, and if that wasn't a sign, what was?

This wasn't going to work. *They* were never, ever going to work.

She shoved past him trying to get to the door, bracing herself in case he tried to stop her. And he did, but it wasn't with a hand or a grab. It was with a word.

"You know, I always thought to myself how brave you are, Kate."

She froze a half dozen feet from the door. She'd felt brave. Every time he'd pushed her to overcome another one of her hang-ups. Every time she'd dared to let him in a little further.

"But you're a coward."

Her ribs squeezed hard, choking her.

And he wasn't done. "You got hurt, okay? I get that. Your dad was a monster and your exes were assholes, but I'm not any of them. I'm the guy—" He sucked in a breath, and it rattled and it ached. "I'm the guy who loves you."

She couldn't breathe. She closed her eyes and put her hand to her mouth, trying to swallow the pained sound forcing its way past her throat.

He loved her. And she loved him.

She'd imagined she had. Back when she thought she knew who he was.

"And I'm trying for you, Kate. But you're so damn scared of getting hurt again, of letting anybody even have a chance of getting in your head, that you'd rather end up alone."

It was a hot knife tearing through her abdomen.

That weekend, with her mom, Kate had practically accused her of the exact same thing. Of wrapping herself up in all this pain and fear and refusing to let herself feel anything.

Her father had always said they were so much alike.

But this wasn't that. This wasn't fear. This was Rylan disappointing her again. Exactly like she'd known he always would.

"You're wrong," she said, the words shredding her throat.

"Bullshit. After what we did today, after what we've been doing all this time." They'd been so close that afternoon. So connected. "And then you come up with this crap. You're just trying to push me away."

She whipped around. "And so what if I am?" Maybe she was the problem. Maybe she always had been. Maybe *they* had been. "God." She tore her fingers through her hair, and her scalp tugged. Her hands trembled. "We were a fantasy."

Those were the only times they had ever worked. In a cloud of a dream as they floated through Paris, and today, skipping their way through a museum, all because she didn't want to face the honest criticism of her work, and he didn't want to face . . . whatever the hell was happening to him. That he refused all over again to explain to her.

In the real world, they fell apart. They got into fights and caused scenes in galleries.

They were reduced to this. Two strangers who'd come together for this brief moment of time, and maybe they'd made each other feel good. Maybe he'd shown her things no one ever had—things no one ever would again.

But they didn't *work*.

She looked up at him through wet, stinging eyes, her chest collapsing. Just like this dream. "That was all we ever were. A fantasy."

He took a step back, and it felt like a mile.

He'd been so persistent. In her head, there had always been this part of her that had thought he'd follow. That he'd fight.

"Maybe for you," he gritted out. "But for me, it was real." He gazed at her with haunted, hollow eyes. "And if you don't believe that, then maybe you should go."

What. The. Fuck.

Rylan shook his head. This was a dream. This was a *nightmare*. It had to be. They were still spread out on the carpet, full on love and sex and grapes and bread and cheese, and he'd fallen asleep. Even better, they were still naked and entwined on his bed, drowsing in the post-sex haze. It was the only explanation. All he had to do was wake up, and everything would go back to normal.

An hour ago—hell, fifteen minutes ago—he'd been the happiest he'd ever been in his entire fucking life. And now it was all crumbling.

Kate stood in front of him, his words echoing on the air. Her whole body was one long line of outrage, and his was, too, his jaw aching with the restraint it took to not step forward and *shake* her. He dug his nails even harder into the flesh of his palm, and it hurt, it bit, sharp pressure on tender flesh narrowing his focus and honing his senses.

But he didn't wake up. This wasn't a dream. This was real.

And all at once, he wanted to pull his ultimatum back. She should *go*? The last thing he wanted was for her to leave, for this to have the chance to fester.

And if he spent one more second staring at that accusing look on her face, he was going to snap.

How dare she? Everything had been going so well. They'd been the closest they'd ever been, intimate and open with each other, and she was going to trot out this bullshit?

He wasn't her father. He wasn't *hiding* things from her.

Fifteen minutes ago, he would have given her anything in the world to make her happy. To make her stay.

But he wasn't going to put up with this again.

He took an unconscious step forward, he wasn't even sure what for.

It broke the spell.

Her defiant, furious expression shattered, tears that had been so close to spilling over this entire time finally falling, and it made the very heart of him ache. But before he could so much as begin to react, she turned on her heel.

She didn't say a single thing as she ran. Just scooped up her bag from where she'd dropped it by the door, and kept on going. Out of his house and out into the night, and the whole house shook with the slamming of the door. Like his heart. Like his *life*.

And then there was silence. Emptiness.

For a long moment, all he could do was stand there, fighting against the crushing pressure in his chest, struggling just to get a full breath. Every muscle was hard.

Right until the trembling set in.

Oh, hell. Fucking fucked-up *fucking*—

His legs gave out on him first. He stumbled backward, scarcely managing to control his fall. A rocking thud jolted through his body as his ass made contact with the floor. Burying his head in his hands, he fought back the urge to *scream*.

How dare she. He'd given her everything he had, he'd come crawling to her on his knees and offered her his money and his time and himself—the one thing he'd never really given to anyone before, and she'd tossed it all right back in his face. Christ. This was why he never did this. He'd avoided ever letting anyone see past the trappings, and the one time he did—

The trembling became a shaking became a wracking shudder, destroying everything in its wake.

He couldn't *breathe*.

The déjà vu of it all had him tearing his fingers through his hair, pulling hard at the roots until his scalp lit up with the pain.

Love was a trap. That was the one lesson he'd learned growing up the way he had. People saw it in you and they used it and they threw it away. His parents had done it with each other, and they'd done it with him, time and time and time again. It was his mother packing up her things and leaving in the middle of the night.

It was his father convincing him he had to fit himself into this box, do this, work like that, become this spitting image of him, and for what?

His father had left him, too. His father had burned the crops and salted the earth. On his way out the door, he'd destroyed the only thing he'd ever created, leaving Rylan to pick up the pieces. The shattered remains of something he'd never asked for in the first place, and which he'd given his entire life to.

Now Kate was gone, and all Rylan had left were these fragments of the world he'd tried to build around her. This hollow, echoing mockery of a home, and still these responsibilities...

The ones he'd been half assing. Refusing to commit to.

The ones he'd been so ready to run away from, if only Kate had said the word.

He laughed out loud, the sound raw and biting at the back of his throat. Maybe that was exactly what he should do now. Leave tonight, get on a plane and never come back. God, Lexie would kill him, but what did he care? His sister was so distant anyway, and she'd survived the same bullshit excuse for a childhood he had. She'd get over it.

He squeezed his eyes shut tight, clasping his hands at the back of his neck as lightning seared him to his bones.

She'd survive his doing exactly what their mother had and what their father had and what he himself had done a year and a half ago...

As he became what he had promised he never would. Faithless. Cruel. Unworthy of anyone's trust.

No wonder Kate had been repulsed.

And yet, if he stayed... His heart sank in his chest, heavy as a stone.

He opened his eyes to look around him, and the whole place shivered.

How the hell had he ended up here?

What was he going to *do*?

He dropped his hand from his neck to rest against the center of his chest. His fingers twisted in the fabric of his shirt, clutching at nothing, trying to grasp at something that wasn't there...

His father's ring.

Fuck. Sitting up straighter, he tore his hand away, but it was too late. The empty space above his ribs burned.

How many years had he worn that ring around his neck? It had been this symbol of the hope he had for better times, but it had all been hope for other people. It had turned into a noose, keeping him from making any choices, from pursuing any kind of happiness for himself. The night before he'd come back to New York, come back to the work and the life and the people he'd left behind, come back for *Kate*, he'd taken it off.

That one small act had felt like freedom. In the first real breath of air he'd had in years, he'd boarded a plane to face all of his mistakes.

And yet he hadn't, really. There were some he'd left alone.

Some he still hadn't been able to really talk about. Not even to Kate.

Her accusations burned into his lungs.

The world around him still spun as he rose to his feet.

He knew what he had to do.

chapter TWENTY-THREE

It didn't matter that Rylan got in to the office an hour earlier than he usually did. Lexie was there, looking fresh as a daisy where she sat behind her desk. And across from her, entirely too big for her tiny office chairs and too rugged for his suit, was her new "assistant." Dane.

Inconvenient, but whatever.

Rylan knocked on her door with three sharp, harsh raps.

She didn't even look up from her screen. "Good, you're here. We've got work to—"

"Get your stuff. We're going upstate."

That made her pause. Her head tilted to the side, the tick in her jaw the only sign he'd caught her by surprise. "Upstate?"

"Upstate," he confirmed.

Bracing himself for a fight, he crossed his arms over his chest. Dane's gaze darted between the two of them, and there was something in his posture that went tense. Rylan ignored him, keeping his attention on his sister. Keeping his shoulders back and his chin high.

Just go along with it, he prayed. He didn't have the energy to argue with her about this.

He'd slept like shit, mind circling over every damn thing Kate had accused him of. Reliving the moment when she'd run out his door. Maybe he should've chased after her, or at least called her after she got home. Maybe he should've kicked her out sooner.

So much of what she'd said had been total bull, but some of it had hit its mark.

Kind of like the things she'd flung at him on her way out the door in Paris. When she'd told him he needed to figure out what he wanted.

He dug his fingers into the meat of his biceps, acid burning the back of his throat.

That's what he'd thought he'd been doing this whole time since he'd returned. Really, he'd been skirting around it, doing every possible thing he could *not* to.

Well. Not anymore.

He'd face his future, all right. But first he had to face his past.

He just really, really didn't want to have to do it alone.

Lexie's considering stare softened out of nowhere, and Rylan squared his jaw. Fought to school his expression. She saw through it anyway.

"Well it's about damn time," she said.

Every muscle in Rylan's body sagged in relief. "You'll come?"

"I half considered dragging you there myself, but there was never a free minute." She was up and out of her chair and stuffing files and her laptop into her bag. "I should've figured McConnell making his move would flip the switch."

Rylan didn't exactly love being that predictable, but at the moment he'd take it.

He focused on Dane, who'd stood as well. "Sorry to interrupt," Rylan said, beginning to make Lexie's excuses for her. "You can reach her on her cell, or—"

"Or from right across the car, since you're coming with us."

Rylan's brows reached for his hairline as he turned back to Lex. "Excuse me?"

Looking at him like he was crazy, Lexie shook her head. "It's like a two-hour drive. We have work to do."

He should've known this was all going too smoothly. No point pushing his luck. Turning around, he led them down to the garage, where a car was waiting.

In the end, he was almost grateful Lexie was so insistent on making the trip a working one. With the morning rush under way, it took forever to get out of the city, and if he'd had nothing to occupy himself he'd have gone out of his skin—or out of his mind. Talking shop was a good distraction, and Dane was a buffer that kept either of them from having to put words to what they were actually thinking.

The guy was a steadying influence, too. Big in presence and sparse of words, nodding when Lex told him to do something, asking questions where it made sense to and derailing her a couple of times when she was starting to get too worked up.

If that involved Dane putting a hand on her knee or her arm once or twice, Rylan could look the other way. Lex was a big girl, and she could navigate that particular minefield on her own.

When the car finally slowed and pulled off the highway, it almost came as a surprise. Rylan jerked his head up. His throat went dry as the sign came into view. Without a word, he and Lexie started packing up the work they'd spread around the seat. Dane's brow furrowed.

If Rylan were a better man, he'd tell the guy what he was in for. Instead, he shifted in his seat. Directed his gaze out the window and set his jaw.

As it was, he'd barely had a sense of what he was in for himself.

A man thought he had an idea of what a prison looked like from articles and movies and TV. Iron bars and gray cinder-block walls. Dead-eyed, agitated, nervous guards. But the reality of it hit even harder. Everything moved like molasses, and if Rylan found the searches and the waiting and the silence dehumanizing, the concept of being on the other side of it all made him cold in his very bones.

Christ, how did a person bear the reality of fifteen *years* of this? An endless swath of idle time, lost time.

A lost life.

And Rylan had thrown his own away so casually.

Finally, they were directed to an empty table in a windowless room. Rylan took his chair with numbness spreading through his limbs. He'd expected Dane to wait in the car with the driver, but he'd followed them without a word, only shaking his head when Rylan had opened his mouth to offer him an out. Between them, Lexie sat up primly, hands folded in her lap, a blank expression on her face. Because of course. Of course this wasn't her first time visiting.

Deep inside his chest, Rylan's heart panged. All the shit their father had put her through. Denying her the life she wanted every chance he got, refusing to support her at each turn, letting the company she'd sacrificed so much for go to vultures rather than giving her a shot at the reins. And yet she'd done right by him. She hadn't abandoned him.

And it was strange. Rylan's father had always been this looming presence hanging over him, dictating his actions and stealing his choices from him. He'd been larger than life—even at the trial, even in handcuffs, he'd taken up all the space in the room.

So Rylan had never, ever seen him look so small.

His father's height hadn't changed, of course. But something in his posture had. There was a stoop to his shoulders that hadn't been there before. Wide swaths of gray in his dark hair and a weariness behind his eyes. A khaki shirt and khaki pants made him look paler, and he'd lost weight—not enough to be worrying, but enough that his cheekbones stood out a little more starkly.

Rylan's throat went tight, a dizzy vertigo making the world around him lurch.

This was the man he'd been so intimidated by. The one he'd allowed to set the terms for his entire life, and why? Memories of yelling and disappointment crowded into his mind, a deafening hum of static that surged and then all at once went to nothing.

He was just a man. Not a lion or a god. But a mortal, normal, human man.

And then his father looked up.

The transformation had Rylan sitting up straight in his chair, his breath quickening and his muscles going tense. Gone were the bowed shoulders and the dead eyes. His father's gaze connected with his, and his jaw went hard.

There was the tyrant Rylan had come here expecting. There was the part of himself that wanted to curl up and be small.

He buried the instinct. He had enough training to manage that much, at least.

Never let them see how you're afraid.

Rylan kept his composure as his father was led across the room. His father's hands were released, and he gave a nod to the guard before slipping into his place across from them. For a long moment, silence held.

His father leaned back in his chair. "So. You finally decided to grace me with your presence."

It was an opening salvo, blame and greeting all rolled into one, and Rylan ignored them both. "You're looking well."

"Please. I taught you to lie better than that."

Yes. He had.

Leaning forward, Lexie cleared her throat. "I told you Teddy was taking care of some things in Europe, Daddy."

"Taking care of his own selfish ego, maybe."

He wasn't even wrong. Rylan's jaw clicked as he gritted his teeth. "I should've come earlier."

"Damn right you should've." For the first time, he flitted his gaze to Lexie. "Did you at least bring—"

"Of course." She pushed a brown paper sack across the table.

Rylan's brow furrowed. The guards had taken a long time to clear Lexie, but he hadn't realized it was because she came bearing gifts. Their father reached into the bag and hauled out a sweater, along with a handful of paperback books and snacks. Once he'd finished his inspection, he turned back to Rylan.

And that was what pulled him out of himself. Fuck, but it was their childhood all over again. Diligent, persistent Lexie going the extra mile and receiving nothing in return while Rylan got all the focus. He glanced over at her to find her face flushing, her arms crossed over her chest as if that could shield her from the never-ending parade of bullshit.

He curled his hand into a fist beneath the table and glared. "You could thank her."

"Do you want me to thank you, too? For showing up?"

"I want you to show your *daughter* a little gratitude."

Lexie shook her head. "Rylan, it's fine."

"Cut to the chase," Rylan's father said. "This clearly isn't a social call." He darted his gaze to the side, acknowledging Dane for the first time. "You brought, what, a lawyer? An attack dog? Haven't I given you enough?"

"Sir," Dane said, "I'm—"

Lexie cut him off. "Don't worry about him."

Their father scoffed. "Fine, I'll just ignore—"

And Rylan's patience was done. His temples throbbed, a dull ache building behind his eyes.

The words exploded out. "Why did you do it?"

Everything went very quiet. His father recoiled, a brief instant of unguarded surprise overtaking his features as he whipped around to stare at Rylan.

"Now? You want to ask me that now?"

There were so many reasons it was now. Kate's accusations and McConnell's machinations and all this pressure Lexie kept putting on him.

But in the end, it was Rylan. Rylan needed to know.

He needed to know they weren't the same.

"Better late than never," he gritted out.

For a long moment, his father regarded him in silence, and Rylan was this close to flinching. To wavering and taking the question back, or just getting up. Storming out, leaving without getting the answers he'd come here for, washing his hands of that smug expression the way he had once before. When the sentence had come down and the world he'd known, with his father at the helm, had crashed, thundering, to the ground.

But he'd said he was done running. He had a life to live, with

Kate or without her, as the head of this family or in another lost, self-imposed exile. He only had to figure out how.

The silence faded and cracked as his father tilted his head back. The whole room erupted with the force of his father's laugh, and something in Rylan's chest went cold.

"For you, you ungrateful bastard. I did it for all of you." He waved his hands expansively, as if to encompass Rylan and Lexie, and who knew, maybe even Dane. Maybe even Evan and their mother, on the other side of the country or the world. "And this is the thanks I get, fifteen years in a fucking cell without a visit, without a letter."

Rylan dug his nails into his palm until it threatened to bleed. "We never asked you to—"

"You don't wait for the people who depend on you to *ask*." His father's nose wrinkled with distaste and scorn. "None of you know what's good for you."

"And what would've been good for us was more money?" The one thing they'd always had. Not affection or approval, God no.

"*Enough* money." As Rylan and Lexie exchanged glances, their father shook his head at them. "The place was going up in flames. We never should've gone public. The board is full of idiots."

"So you stole from it."

"It was mine in the first place!" His nostrils flared, his whole face going dangerously red. "I built it. I made it from nothing and then they try to act like I'm the one committing a crime."

"Because you did." Rylan's throat was raw. What the hell was this? This indignation, this self-righteousness.

Rylan's father straightened his back, managing to loom even sitting down. Even sitting at that damn table and being on the wrong side of it. "I made a decision on how to use *my* company's resources. And it was to reallocate them so you—so *we* could start over. That place was going up in flames, and we were going to come out of it standing strong. We'd rebuild."

All the breath punched out of Rylan's chest.

That's what he'd meant by *enough* money. Enough to take it all and let the ashes burn.

Rylan's whole life, his father had been grooming him to take his place at the helm of Bellamy International. He'd picked his prep school and his college and his major, and when that had all been done, he'd trained him in the rest of the business himself. Rylan had been made to know that company inside and out; he'd given up all his choices, all his time, for it. He'd done what had been asked of him *for that company*.

It was worse than he had imagined.

Because all the while, his father hadn't just been sabotaging it from the inside. He'd been plotting how to do it again.

His father scoffed. "Don't look so damn surprised. Why do you think I did it?"

He'd never known. Never really asked, and maybe he should have.

His field of vision narrowed, everything going fuzzy around the edges.

Oh, hell.

Rylan had been so intent on *not* becoming his father. But was he any different at all?

Not communicating. Not telling anyone what he was up to, and seeing a problem—seeing something not going his way, and forget *fixing* it, for fuck's sake.

Abandoning it.

Like his father had abandoned his children. Had driven his

wife away with his faithlessness and his work, laughing as he set everything he'd ever worked for alight and watched it burn.

Rylan knocked his chair over in his haste to throw himself out of it.

He'd let Kate walk away from him. He'd been ready to watch the company that bore his name slip through his hands.

There was no way his father could know what was happening in his head, but the man laughed at him all the same. "Don't be so horrified. I did it for you, and I've made my peace with the fact that it was all a damn waste. I sink all those years into you, and you want nothing to do with me, with your legacy. All my children. Wastes of my time."

Then Lexie was standing, too, Dane following suit, and it was like there was some instinct in the man that had him putting his body between Lexie's and their father's. Only Lexie was having none of that.

"You blind, selfish old man," she spat. She stepped around Dane, fists clenched at her sides, shoulders up.

Their father waved his hand. "You're the worst of them. You think I didn't know you wanted the company for yourself? You were all prepared to push me out and stab your brother in the back."

Her face got redder. "I would never."

"'Just give me a seat at the table, Daddy,'" he simpered, a mockery of an impression. He pointed at Rylan. "And you always humoring her."

Apparently the gloves were off. More than a year since it had all gone down—a silent, simmering year—and now all at once it was boiling over.

"Because she deserved one," Rylan said.

"No one takes her seriously. Even if she weren't a woman."

Their father shook his head. "You prance around in your little outfits and bark at everyone, you sleep with the staff."

All the color drained out of Lexie's cheeks at once. She opened her mouth, but no sound came out.

So Dane was the one to speak. "I assure you—"

"Oh, not you. Though if you are, good for you." Their father pointed to Lexie. "I finally had some hope for you, but you couldn't even get a ring out of Jordan."

And Rylan's vision clouded over for a totally different reason. *"Jordan?"* The name had barely made it past his lips before the pieces clicked into place. Jordan knowing about her apartment, Lexie's failure to include him on her list. The look on her face when Rylan had brought him up. But— "He's fifteen years older than you."

Lexie's hands shook, and she didn't even look at him. All her focus was on their father. Her throat bobbed, but then she found her voice. Quiet and razor-sharp, she said, "I didn't get a ring out of him because he only wanted me to get to you."

So it was true.

Rylan was going to kill that piece of shit.

Still trembling, Lexie turned on her heel. It wasn't the dramatic exit she might've hoped for as she waited for the guards to let her out. Swabbing at her eyes, she ran for it the second the doors opened. Dane gave them each one look before following after. And then it was just Rylan and his dad, and he couldn't make his feet work. His throat was knives.

"You just gonna stand there?" His father was still in his seat, as calm as could be, an imperiousness to his eyes that Rylan wanted to wipe right off his face with his fist.

He stopped himself, just barely. This wasn't the place. This wasn't the time.

Fighting for composure, he drew himself up to his full height. Put on the same bullshit posture his father wore. The one he himself had taught him to affect.

"No. I'm going to walk out of here, because I'm a free man." Licks of fire filled his chest. "I'm going to go pick up the pieces of my sister and all the other messes you left behind."

He was going to do what he'd been refusing to for so long. What he always should've done.

"I'm going to lead this family," he said, and the flames in his lungs curled and spread, fueling him. "I'm going to do what you never have."

What only Rylan could.

chapter TWENTY-FOUR

Lexie couldn't breathe.

She pushed through the last of the three hundred fucking doors to emerge out into too-bright light, a brilliant blue autumn sky stretching out in front of her, but then it was narrowing, her peripheral vision graying out as static filled her ears.

She kept walking, though. That much she knew how to do. Her heels might be killing her, her Spanx strangling her, and her eyes were stinging from more than just the wind, but she'd made it through worse.

She wanted to toss her head back and *laugh*.

How many times had she visited her father since the trial? A dozen at least, and maybe their meetings hadn't been perfect, but they'd been polite.

She shook her hands at her sides and blinked hard at the sun.

What the hell had she been thinking, bringing Rylan here? She couldn't even pretend he'd twisted her arm. He'd made the faintest hint of a suggestion, and she'd been all over it. Eager to show off how much their father appreciated her now. To be the one who brought the prodigal son home at last.

To maybe, finally, be recognized as the one who had stayed.

She was never going to learn, was she?

God, but her father hadn't been pulling his punches today. He'd set eyes on Rylan, and he'd been lashing out from practically the first word. She'd just gotten caught in the cross fire, was all. He hadn't meant any of it. Hadn't meant to leave her one throbbing bruise.

She bit down on the inside of her cheek until she tasted blood.

Except it was all stuff he'd said to her before, if not so bluntly. He'd never thought she was cut out for corporate America. She definitely wasn't good enough to take the reins of the company with *her name on the door*. She was frivolous and ridiculous and—

But he'd never called her a slut before.

Stopping right there on the pavement, still what felt like miles away from the car, she squeezed her eyes shut tight.

Jordan. How the hell had he known about Jordan? Had *everybody* known?

The laugh she'd choked back before bubbled out of her this time, unstoppable and raw. Christ, she was such a cliché.

The ingénue. The little girl with her pocketful of daddy issues being seduced by the older man who told her she was special.

And who'd left her as her world splintered into pieces.

"Ms. Bellamy?"

The static in her ears flared and faded as a voice from behind her shouted through the roar.

Right.

Because her father hadn't only had to bring up how much of a disappointment and a joke and a whore she was. He'd had to do it in front of Dane.

She started walking again, fast clicks of her heels against the asphalt, and then behind her, the steadier, deeper thud of a man's even gait, and everything in her told her to run.

Nothing had even happened between them yet. When she'd needed someone to help her out around the office, she'd gone to the temp pool. His had been one of a handful of files she'd pulled, his credentials no better or worse than any of the others. She hadn't expected much.

And then this *man* had walked into her office, his shoulders as wide as the door, his manner quiet and his blue-gray eyes so deep she'd thought they'd see to the very heart of her. He'd been crisply efficient and preternaturally calm, and the first time he'd reached into the space between them—the space she kept around herself like it could protect her somehow—the warmth had seared her to her bones. Just a touch of a hand on hers or at the bend in her arm and all the cold places inside her threatened to go to water.

Right now, her skin was crackling, fire racing through her nerves. If he got too close she'd burn him. She burned through people. It was what she did.

If he touched her, she wouldn't melt. She'd shatter.

"Ms. Bellamy. Wait up."

"Go away," she managed to force out.

A hand grabbed her wrist, broad and warm, and she yanked it back. But that grip refused to let go.

She shook her head, still walking, still pulling away, but then somehow Dane was in front of her, and she stopped short, breath catching.

All these little reassuring brushes, but he'd never been this close before. The woodsy scent of him surrounded her, the solid expanse of his chest all she could see.

"Ms. Bellamy." His throat bobbed. "Lexie."

He'd never said her name like *that*.

And she always had a rejoinder, a snarky reply, something to say to deflect. But her tongue had turned to stone.

He'd just witnessed her worst nightmare, had seen her completely humiliated.

He was her employee.

And right now, all she wanted was comfort. It was all she'd ever wanted but had so rarely allowed herself to accept. Hysteria made her lungs seize up.

Look what had happened the last time she'd let someone get close.

Trembling, she tried again to pull away. She had to be radiating hurt and mortification and this need for someone, please, someone, to take care of her. But if he tried to put his arms around her, if he tried—

Then his hand settled warm on her shoulder. The rough pad of his thumb stroked her collarbone.

"Tell me what you need."

And it wasn't suffocating. It didn't make her feel small or coddled. Instead of sending her to pieces, it helped glue just a couple of her fraying edges back together.

It gave her strength.

She looked away.

Strength enough to say, "I need you to leave me alone."

chapter TWENTY-FIVE

Kate was dragging her heels.

It'd been nearly a week since she'd walked out of Rylan's house, and every day she hadn't heard from him had brought this overwhelming relief. And this aching sting of disappointment.

He was closed off and he was irresponsible, and she was better off never having anything to do with him. Once was a fluke, but when a person did the same things over and over again, they started to form a pattern.

In Paris, he'd been running away from his family and his responsibilities. Sure, he'd acted reformed enough when he'd returned. But he'd suggested running away again so easily and with such fervor in his eyes. He'd meant it. He'd have done it if she'd so much as hinted at being willing to go along.

A man whose first instinct was to take off wasn't a good bet. He wasn't willing to work hard, or to dig in when the chips were down, and how long would it have been before things had gotten tough between the two of them? How long before he would've wanted to escape her, too?

Her career and her life—they were about persistence. Making

art was an exercise in patience and in sitting back down at that easel day after day after day. If she'd given up the first time things had gotten rough...

Well, she wouldn't have made it as far as she had. Not even close.

And his silences. The things Rylan refused to tell her about his life and his past and who he *was*. The first time he'd held his tongue, back in Paris, she'd called it betrayal. Now she just called it sad. What kind of man kept the woman he purported to love in the dark like that?

What kind of life would they have had with him lying to her? Not talking to her.

What kind of life was she going to have without him?

Her heart rose higher and higher into her throat as she turned the corner onto his block.

By the time she had heard from him, she'd very nearly resigned herself to them being well and truly over. He was so fond of running away from his problems—for all she knew, he could've given up on her completely. He could've meant it when he'd told her to go.

She should've known better.

Then finally he'd called her. His voice had come across the line in calm, neutral tones, and she'd been all set to hang up on him. Until he'd reminded her that she'd promised him one more night. One more chance to prove himself to her, and there'd been this part of her...

He hadn't been the only one to flee when the going got tough.

Twice now, she'd turned her back on him. One hint of a betrayal and she was heading for the door. Hell, maybe she'd always had one foot out it.

Maybe it was just like Rylan had said.

She was a coward. She was scared. She was going to end up alone.

Just like her mother had, after she'd finally broken free. Too damn hurt after that one betrayal to ever give anyone a chance at loving her again.

The first time around, she'd stayed far too long, but now she wouldn't let anybody in.

There were a lot of different kinds of mistakes in love. This was a fine, fine line Kate was walking between trusting too easily and refusing to trust at all. Falling to either side was perilous.

She took a deep breath and placed one foot in front of the other.

Halfway down the block, Rylan's house loomed. Temptation gnawed at her to slow her pace even further, but with a sigh, she kept going. He'd say what he had to say, and she'd hear him out. She just had to keep her head on straight. Maybe there was some insane parallel universe where he'd come up with precisely what she needed to hear, but they'd already tried this twice, and she couldn't keep doing this to herself. No matter how gorgeous he was or how he made her feel. No matter how much the pieces of himself he'd allowed her to glimpse had drawn her in.

She let herself into his gate, then climbed the steps of his porch. She knocked twice before reaching for the key she still couldn't quite believe he'd given her. Locking up behind herself, she stepped into his foyer and called his name.

His voice floated down to her. "Upstairs."

She dug the edges of the key into the meat of her thumb. He'd taken advantage of how much she wanted him the last time he'd begged for forgiveness, and she didn't entirely regret giving in to it. That wasn't going to work today, though. No matter how much her body craved his, sex wasn't going to fix things between them. Not this time.

With her chest tight and her shoulders square, she made her way up the stairs. But just as she was about to poke her head into his bedroom, her whole body steeled against whatever he might be up to, he called out again.

"Upstairs upstairs."

Oh.

The giant, open third floor with all its windows was her favorite part of his house, and apparently he knew that. The space was laid out much the same way it had been the last time she had been there, the stereo set up by the far wall and the fairy lights still draped across the tops of the windows. And had it really only been a week since she'd helped move him in? Since they'd put on that old record and danced across this floor, her body safe in his arms? Everything feeling right and easy between them for once?

Then she zeroed in on him. He stood in the very center of the room, looking too good for words, his dark hair tousled and his eyes a bright, earnest blue. He was dressed casually, much the way he would've been in Paris, and she screamed at her heart not to read too much into that. Not to hope.

Surrounding him were boxes.

She furrowed her brow, pausing midstep a dozen feet away from him. There had been plenty of boxes strewn out across this space while she'd been helping him unpack, but not this many.

Not as old of ones.

Her gaze darted from one to the other, to the labels made out in black marker in a feminine hand. *Teddy, age 5. Albums 1995–2000. Teddy's room.*

Her chest tightened as she finally looked to Rylan. "What is all of this?"

His throat bobbed. "It's everything I have. And if you want it, it's yours."

It was a complicated concept, honesty.

Navigating the world of businessmen and hedge fund managers, led by a man who'd been hiding his embezzlements behind manipulated numbers and an authoritative frown, Rylan might've gotten a skewed view of it. He'd knowingly chosen not to practice it with Kate their first time around, and he'd paid the price in her trust.

This time, he'd been nothing but truthful with her, but he'd done it the only way he knew how. Passively. He hadn't lied and he hadn't tried to hide.

But honesty was like love, and it was like kindness. It was like any other thing that really mattered in this world. It wasn't enough just to not do its opposite. He'd been angry at Kate for accusing him of continuing to be less than open with her, but the fact of the matter was that she'd been right.

To really, truly tell the truth was an active endeavor. You had to consciously decide to do it, and you had to do it with intent.

And so here he was.

The distance between them yawned, the space strewn with all the pieces of his life he'd managed to gather over the preceding week. With his chest tight and his blood cold, he'd returned to his parents' mansion, to that cavernous attic. All the boxes he'd overlooked the last time, the ones Kate had been so intrigued by, were still there.

And so he'd dug into them. Sifted through his life and his

past, and then he'd taken what he'd found and he'd brought it here. So it would be a part of his present. A part of his home.

Kate's gaze danced over the faces of the boxes, and he fought the instinct to fidget or to close up. She tilted her head to the side. "Is that—?"

She was pointing at the one labeled *Teddy's room*.

He'd told her this story, about how he'd been shipped off to prep school, only to return and find all the ephemera of his childhood swept away. Stolen.

But apparently not lost.

He nodded. She took one step forward before stopping herself. "Can I?"

"Of course."

They met at the stack of boxes. His heart rose into his throat as their fingertips brushed against the cardboard, and her gaze shot up to his.

"Let me." He slid his thumb under the flap, prying the box open.

And then he began the process of shining a light into all the darkened, dusty corners of his life. Of sharing it.

Of loving Kate the way she'd asked to be loved.

She kept a certain distance as he unpacked model airplanes and books. An ancient computer gaming system. When he dug out a single blue stuffed rabbit, she put her hand to her mouth, and her laugh was a sparkling sound that lit the recesses of his heart.

"Who is this?" she asked, reaching for it.

God, he hadn't thought about this in years. "Fitzwilliam." That had been this ratty, ridiculous toy bunny's name. His eyes stung. "Mother had gotten Lexie into *Pride and Prejudice*." And so together they'd named this thing after Mr. Darcy himself— but his secret name. His first name.

"Did you sleep with him every night?" There was this soft, teasing note to Kate's voice, but he refused to be abashed.

"I did." The rabbit had sat beside his pillow night after night, long past the point when any boy should be afraid of monsters.

Long before the time he'd come to see that monsters were real, and that one of them wore his father's face.

Warm brown eyes lifted to gaze into his, and her thumbs rubbed at the worn blue fur. After a moment that seemed to hang forever on the air, she looked back down at the stuffed animal in her grasp, and the edge of her lips rose. "Well, he obviously can't go back in a box."

"Where would you put him?"

She set him on top of one of the stacks. "Somewhere he gets to see the sun." Her mouth twitched. "Maybe we'll have to find him an Elizabeth."

Which part was better? Her making a happy ending for his childhood companion, or her talking as if they'd do it together?

Once that box was empty, they moved on to the next one, sinking to sit together on the floor as they pored through it. His voice felt as dusty as the items they uncovered, the stories gray in his mind from age, but he offered them up without prompting. Showed her baby photos and middle school trophies. Even his terrible attempts at kindergarten art had been preserved here.

"Did you even know your parents kept this stuff?"

He shook his head. "I had no idea." His whole life long, he'd been left to believe these memories had been discarded. So he'd filed them away, too, because they hurt too much to look at.

"Are these Lexie and Evan?"

He peered over her shoulder to get a better look, and his chest brushed the warm curve of her spine. The picture in her hands had been special enough at some point that it had merited a frame. In it, he was maybe nine, his siblings younger.

He nodded. In the photo, they were all smiling, but they weren't good smiles. They were the ones his father had trained them in.

His own grin faded as he took the frame from her. "Dad wanted us to know how to deal with the media from an early age." It had been good training, too. They'd been photographed with him coming in and out of the company's headquarters more than once, and in all the pictures they'd had these same dead eyes.

Digging back into the box, he came up with a loose photo. "This is a better one, though." He remembered his mother shaking her head at them as she snapped the shutter. "I think she took it with the same camera I gave you."

She studied it for a long moment. They were jumping around a hotel room, allowed to blow off steam for once. Their father must have been at work.

Reaching out, she ghosted a fingertip along the curve of his boyish face. "You look happy."

"Every now and then we were."

He added the photo to the pile, looking up only to find her gazing at a different one. "And these are your parents?"

The picture had clearly been misfiled. It predated him at least by a couple of years. The lines around his father's mouth weren't so carved in, and his mother's eyes were bright and smiling. How many times had he seen her like that? Engaged and present that way?

"That's them," he confirmed.

Her fingers traced the edge of the picture. "They were beautiful."

All at once, he was back in a museum with her. Their very first day together, and Kate had been so pretty and so soft, her gaze sad but also hopeful somehow.

He'd taken her to see a painting that had always made him think about his parents—about how, before the acrimony, before the distance, they must've been happy.

"Yeah. They were."

Around them, the sun started to set, but they pressed on. Kate's attention showed no sign of flagging.

She didn't really touch him, though. He was opening himself for her, but there was this space separating them. A deliberate one.

Finally, his throat hoarse and his heart sore, the dust and the memories making his lungs tight, he closed the last of the albums from the box. The sound of plastic pages clapping together echoed in the room.

"There are probably more," he said. There were, he'd seen them. "But..."

But he was worn out, the work of opening himself up like this having taken its toll. It was a muscle he wasn't accustomed to using. He'd learn to strengthen it, though—he'd practice and he'd get better. If only she would let him.

And that was the question, wasn't it?

For what felt like forever, silence hung over them, pressing in, and he wanted to break it. But what more was there for him to say?

Finally, she turned to him, her gaze fixed someplace just south of his eyes. "This is a lot to take in."

"And it's only the beginning." He set the album aside and placed his palms face up on his knees. An invitation. "You're welcome to come up here any time. I'll take you through it, or you can look for yourself." He swallowed against the tightness in his lungs. "I'm an open book. I'm trying to be."

But he still had more he had to say.

He'd given her his past, but his present...Did she have any idea the role he saw her playing in it?

"Rylan..."

"Do you know why I bought this house?"

Her brow crinkling, she darted her gaze up, meeting his at last. "You—"

And this wasn't just opening the book of his life for her. This was making a hole in it and asking her to fill it. If she said no...

The emptiness wouldn't be going away any time soon.

But if he didn't ask, it would still be there. Unexposed yet just as hollow. His life had always felt hollow before he met her. The part of it that ached was that now he knew.

"It was this. This room." He swept his arm out across the space. His voice broke as he said, "I saw you in it."

She drew in a sharp breath that resounded across the walls.

"It was always going to be yours. Your studio, or whatever you wanted to do with it." The idle daydreams he'd had about her here. Covered in paint and lost to that fog of creation that swept over her.

Him coming up here and finding her and stripping her bare. Dancing his fingertips over the streaks of pigment on her skin and pressing himself inside her in all that gorgeous morning light.

"I saw you everywhere. In the kitchen and in the shower and in the bed. Your easel in this attic and your clothes hanging up in *our* closet. I was looking for a home." He bit off the end of the word, because this was exposing even more. Too much, but that was how this was supposed to feel.

Being honest with her meant telling her everything, and this was it. The most important piece.

Extending his hands, he wrapped them around hers. Pulled them close and rubbed his thumbs across the backs of her palms. If only he could press the things he felt into her skin with his touch.

But he needed to do it with his voice.

"I was looking for a home, and I found it. With you. I want to make a home with you. I want to share it with you. Every detail of it." Past, present, and future. His ribs squeezed in, and it was hard to breathe, but he could do this. "For the rest of my life, Kate."

And he didn't have a ring. It had seemed too much to presume, but if he had, he'd have offered it to her right then and there. He'd have given it to her along with everything else.

His words hung heavy on the air, his heart pounding. Blinking, she stared at their hands.

Her voice tremored. "That's a *lot*, Rylan."

"I know." Fuck, he hoped it wasn't too much.

"I..."

And he waited and waited, but nothing else seemed to come out.

Then she gave this one hiccuping laugh. "I thought we were going to break up today. For real."

His heart stuttered, the center of his chest threatening to collapse. "Do you want to break up?"

"I half figured we already had. We keep coming back to these same things."

"But we come back to them better every time." They did. Slowly but steadily, they'd been finding their way. He lifted one set of their joined hands, swinging it as if to encompass the en-

tire room. "What I've shown you today, it's just the beginning."
They were just at the beginning.

"And what about what you said the other night?"

Fuck. What was she even talking about? So many things had
come out of him as they'd fought. He'd been angry, and rightfully
so, but that hadn't given him any excuse to lash out. To hurt her.

Her lip wobbled, and she took her hands back from his, leaving his palms cold. The pain behind his ribs cut deeper.

"This was—" She pointed at the rabbit and the albums and
the boxes. "This was amazing. But what if it's me?"

What?

She shook her head. "What if I just can't trust *anyone*?" Mashing her lips together, she pointed shining eyes up toward the sky.
"I was so afraid of turning out just like my mother, you know?
Ending up with someone who tried to control me or told me I
wasn't good enough. But what if it's just the opposite?"

"Kate—"

"She's old and alone now, and she might always be. It hit me
when she was here last week. She let this thing that hurt her scar
her, and maybe—" She looked back at him, and her smile was
horrible and aching. "Maybe that's what happened to me. Maybe
I just *can't*."

She had to be kidding him. She had the biggest, most gener-
ous heart. She'd shown it to him so many times.

"I don't believe that. Not for a second." He reached out for
her, but she didn't just pull away. She stood, and oh hell—if she
ran away from him again. If she didn't give him a chance, after
he'd laid himself out for her like this...

"But you said it yourself. You keep doing this thing where
you won't let me in, and maybe you're getting better at that.
But I keep doing this, too."

"What?"

"Finding reasons not to trust you."

And he had said that. In anger, he'd thrown it at her, and apparently he'd hit his mark.

"Kate..." What could he say? What could he do?

Except give her the final piece. The one he should've started with.

He rose to his feet. And his heart cracked open all over again, but he forced out the words. The ones he'd all but thrown at her in his outrage the last time she'd been here.

"Kate. I love you."

Like he'd never loved anyone before. Like he hadn't even known he could love.

The corner of her mouth wavered. "But what if that's not enough?"

And that was it. Collapse. All the air was crushed out of him, and the hand he'd extended toward her fell with the weight of the stones crashing in on him. Filling his ribs, and maybe he'd never, ever breathe again.

Wrapping her arms around herself, she took a single step backward, but it might have been a hundred. "Thank you. For showing me all of this."

It had always been hers.

"I'm not saying no."

"It sounds like you are." He couldn't even stop the edge that bit into his tone.

Voice creeping higher, she gazed at him with overflowing eyes. "Can I just have some time? Please?"

Time. Fuck. That was what he'd asked her for when he'd first returned. Well, this was the seventh of their nights.

And just like that, he regretted every single one. What if he had given this to her that very first night? If he'd been open with her the way she'd wanted him to?

Would it even have mattered?

With a hollow echoing inside him, he met her backward step with one of his own. "Take all the time you need."

But he didn't have much hope.

"Will—will you be all right?"

No. Not ever again.

Did it count as a lie to shrug? "I'll muddle through." Then he took a deep breath. Because there were still things he was supposed to tell her, for all that it felt he had nothing left. "I'll keep busy, anyway."

She tilted her head to the side in question.

"I'm slated to take over my father's company next week."

"Oh." It came out in the barest gasp of a breath. "But I thought you didn't want to."

He hadn't. For the longest time, it'd been the last thing in the world he'd wanted to do.

But that had been a different him. A different world.

"It's time," he said, squaring his shoulders. "To face my responsibilities. To fix my father's mistakes." To do things *right*— to do what his father had never managed to do. "It's time I live the life I was meant to lead."

Not because he'd been forced to, but because he chose to.

"That's—" she started, but he cut her off.

"And I want to live that life with you." It took everything he had to back another step away. "But in the end, that choice is up to you."

chapter TWENTY-SIX

Time. It was one of those things Kate could never seem to get enough of. There weren't enough hours in the day, weren't enough weeks left in the semester, weren't enough days until her portfolio was due.

There wasn't any of it left with Rylan. She didn't owe him another second.

But she did owe him an answer.

Fingers and toes half-numb, she fumbled with the key to the art department's darkroom, nearly dropping it twice before she managed to get the lock to turn. She chuckled darkly at herself, throat raw and eyes dry. Lord knew how she'd even managed to get here. The train ride over from Rylan's house to campus was a blur; she'd been completely zoned out. Thinking.

She'd asked for time to *think*, and Rylan had told her take as much of it as she needed. After all the time they'd already spent. Seven nights, and he'd had to guilt-trip her into giving him the last one, and then he'd had to use it to—

Hell. He'd used it to bare his soul. All those days and nights they'd spent together, she'd wanted nothing more than for him to let her into his world, to prove that he could really give himself to her. That she could trust him.

And then tonight...

He'd spread out his entire life for her, answering questions she hadn't even known to ask with photographs and ancient toys and *stories*. He'd told her about his plans. His responsibilities. He'd talked and talked, all these words he'd never said to her before—three words she still couldn't believe he'd chosen to say.

He'd talked until her head had spun. Until the only person in the room she couldn't trust was herself.

Letting her bag fall to the counter, she braced her arms against its edge. Squeezed her eyes shut tight against the urge to cry.

He'd done so much for her. Taken command when she was a wreck about having forgotten her mother's visit. Helped her escape, after, when she'd so desperately needed to. He'd touched her...

God. The way that man had touched her. From their very first night, he'd shown her all these things about what her body could do and be and feel, and he kept doing it. Sex with him wasn't a pain or a chore. It was a revelation.

She wanted to trust him. He'd done exactly what he'd said he'd do—he'd earned it.

But she didn't know how. After all this time trying to protect herself, how did she let this person in? This person she...loved.

She bit down hard on her lip and sucked in a deep, ragged breath. She'd loved him for so long now she'd almost forgotten what it was like not to. Even when she'd tried so hard to deny it. She'd never really stopped.

And yet that hadn't kept her from snapping at him the other

night. Her reasons that had been all-consuming then—they seemed so feeble now.

Releasing her lip from her teeth, she bit back a broken echo of a laugh, and it burned her lungs. The fact that she loved him was probably *why* she had snapped at him. It was just like he had said—she was so damn hurt, so scared. She'd take any excuse to run.

She'd keep running. Unless she could find a way—a reason not to.

She lifted her head and loosened her grip on the counter, blood rushing back into her hands and making them sting. Swiping the back of her wrist across her eyes, she took a deep breath.

Time. Rylan had given her time.

And she had work to do.

Her portfolio was due so soon, and by all rights she should be in the studio right now, figuring out a plan and starting the entire project over again. But even she could only fool herself so much. She was a wreck, and anything she tried to paint right now would be an angry, emotional mess. But there were other things she could do. She'd been meaning to develop all the rolls of film she'd shot for a while now anyway. Maybe there'd be something, somewhere, in one of the hundred-odd frames that she could use.

Relying on muscle memory, she got to work. It had been so long since she had done this, but it all came back to her. Unspooling the film and loading it into canisters. Mixing up the chemicals. The scent of the developer grounded her almost as much as the physicality of it all, and her hands got a little surer. The shakiness Rylan had left her with beginning to bleed away.

By the time the negatives were ready, it was the middle of

the night, and a part of her was ready to collapse, but she was so close now. She flushed, remembering what kinds of pictures were hidden somewhere in those frames. This facility didn't get much use, but it was probably for the best that she was doing this now, when no one was going to walk in.

In the end, she just about overloaded the developer bath making all her contact prints and proofs. She didn't let herself watch the images slowly emerging from beneath the grain of the paper, forcing herself to wait. When they were finally done, she drained them off and dumped the wet sheets into a spare tray and took them out into the main room. Into the light.

Her heart fell as she started to pin them up. Each photo of a church or a "sacred space" was as lifeless as the last. God. She'd fucked things up with Rylan and she was fucking things up with school and her career and—

And then she her fingers fumbled on the first image she'd taken of Rylan at the museum. He wasn't even looking at her. But the lines of his face in profile, the slope of his shoulders and the strength in his stance, relaxed as it was, his focus on a painting...

She raced to see the next and the next. He was just... *beautiful*. In black-and-white, he was a study in contrasts, dark hair and clear eyes, the gleam of the black leather of his jacket and the pinpoints of stubble on his cheek and jaw. He was a work of art in his own right, and he was surrounded by even more of it.

But the pictures she'd taken of him hadn't just been in galleries.

Her whole chest seized at the first flash of skin, and in a breath she was back there. In his bedroom in the soft morning light, asking him to bare himself for her, framing each new piece of himself he revealed. The camera loved the swells of muscle, the dips and hollows of abdominals and collarbones, and she loved... She *loved*...

And then there was a picture of her.

And it wasn't that she was particularly averse to seeing herself in photographs in general. But this was different, and not just because you could see her breasts. The images weren't as refined or as well-focused as the ones of him, an amateur's hand clear in the composition. But all the skill she'd acquired in a lifetime hadn't been enough to make her photographs of cathedrals come to life, while these *glowed*.

They'd traded the camera back and forth for a while there, and there were images of her and images of him.

Images of *them*. Blurry and overexposed and barely recognizable. Lips pressed to lips, a soft chin and a roughly chiseled jaw and a flash of tongue.

Images of her sex. Splayed open and strange, a broad hand against a pale thigh, and she should be embarrassed. Once upon a time, she'd have been mortified. But with him, she hadn't been. Even now, she couldn't bring herself to call forth an ounce of shame.

With him, she'd been free to be herself, to be naked in every possible way.

And she'd pushed it away. She'd shut down on him and for what? To protect herself? Her throat went raw.

God, what had she done?

She sifted through the rest of the pictures until she found a close-up of his face. He was looking right at her through the lens, eyes warm, this faintest hint of a smile coloring those soft, full lips, and it just about cracked her open.

She pinned the last of the photos up with shaking hands, then staggered back. Collapsed down into the chair in the corner and dropped her face into her palms, but there was no burning those images away—the ones of him and the ones of them. They were beautiful. They were...

They were...

She lifted her gaze, and the world went stunningly, startlingly clear.

They were sacred.

chapter TWENTY-SEVEN

"You ready for this?"

Rylan caught his sister's gaze in the mirror on the back of his office door. She was as well composed as she ever was, not a hair out of place, but he recognized the strain around her eyes.

He turned back to his reflection and recognized it in his own.

It had been a long week since he'd offered Kate his past and his whole goddamn life, and he had yet to hear a word from her. It was a cold stone sitting low in his gut, weighing him down with every step, but he hadn't let that keep him from moving forward.

Kate was the one who'd put paid to his fantasies of leaving it all behind. He was here. And he had work to do.

Straightening his tie, he gave a single sharp nod. "Ready as I'll ever be."

It was just the two of them today, with Lexie's temp off taking care of something else, and that was for the best. It'd been the Bellamy children against the world for the longest time. He chuckled to himself beneath his breath. If only Evan were here, the picture would really be complete.

Rylan shook off that particular line of thought. Evan was pursuing his dreams on the other side of the country. Lexie was realizing hers here.

And Rylan...

Rylan was embracing the person he'd always been meant to be. The one he wanted to be.

For one last, long moment, he studied his reflection.

How many times had he looked at his own face and seen his father's stubborn cruelty and his mother's selfish faithlessness?

Today, he was choosing to see other things. Beneath the stubbornness lay strength. Beneath the urge to run away was the will to stay.

They may have dictated this life to him, but he alone could make it his own.

Turning away from the mirror, he squared his shoulders and lifted his chin. "We have the votes?"

"We should."

They'd been scrambling the last couple of weeks, working around McConnell's machinations and shedding light on his plans. It had taken some work and more than a few promises of favors, but they had the support they needed.

He had the resolve.

"Let's do this."

The focus his father had instilled in him took over, crowding out everything else around him. Adrenaline surged through his veins, and people parted for them as they made their way down the hall. The doors to the executive elevator swept open in front of them.

And all the energy and the power simmering in his bones suddenly boiled over.

"Hey." Jordan stepped off the elevator and strode toward him. "Headed to the big meeting—?"

Before he'd even decided to do it, Rylan's fist was connecting with his face.

"What the—"

Behind him Lexie shrieked, but Rylan didn't hear it. Jordan came up clutching his jaw, a hell of a bruise already starting to bloom, and Rylan's knuckles stung, but the red tide over his vision didn't fade or recede. He curled a hand in the fabric of Jordan's shirt and got up in his face.

His voice came out dangerous and low. "You touch my sister again, and I will end you."

"Rylan!"

He released Jordan and shoved him back, not breaking stride as he stepped into the elevator. Lexie rounded on him as the doors closed behind them.

"What the hell," she sputtered.

He pinned her with his gaze. "You do whatever you want, with whoever you want. But someone hurts you and they have to take it up with me."

He hadn't been kidding when he'd told his father his intentions. He was taking care of this family now. This company and all the people he was responsible for.

With a nod, he turned to the elevator operator who'd been studiously not looking at them this entire time.

"Ninety-fifth floor, Marcus."

"Yes, sir."

As they started to rise, Lexie stared at him. "You've really changed in the past year, haven't you?"

Rylan's heart panged.

He'd thought his father's crimes had been what had changed him. That the sting of betrayal had been what had given him the strength to leave it all behind.

But really, he'd always had one foot out the door. Resenting the choices he'd never gotten to make, he'd always been ready to run.

Whether or not Kate could ever love him—could ever trust him—what had really changed him had been wanting to be worthy of her.

He let out a long breath. "I'm certainly trying to."

"I wasn't sure if I should bring chicken soup or whiskey, so I brought both." Liam flashed Kate a hopeful half smile as he stood in her doorway, two brown paper packages clasped in his hands.

Kate chuckled and stepped aside to let him in. "Coffee would've been more appropriate, actually."

"I don't know. Somebody doesn't show up to class for over a week and they're usually either dying of the plague or on a bender." He stopped dead in his tracks about three feet in the door, and Kate's heart rose up into her throat. "Though I guess there's more than one kind of bender."

Her pale imitation of a laugh rose up into something higher. Definitely more unhinged.

"Truer words."

A *bender* wasn't a terrible way to describe her past week. Except instead of being drunk on booze she'd been high on paint and color. Lost to the sweeping arcs of brushstrokes over collarbones and shoulder blades. The dabs of cerulean in brilliant blue eyes.

"Jesus, Kate." Liam turned to her. "Did you seriously do all of these this week?"

She scrubbed a hand over her eyes. "This isn't even all of it."

There were drawings, too. Studies she'd done to prepare for taking a brush to canvas. Lines and planes sprawling out across paper as she'd fought to solve the puzzle of a single face and how it went together. How to *put* it together once she'd taken it apart.

"Did you sleep?"

"Occasionally." Not enough. Not even close.

She hadn't been able to, was the thing. Deep into the night she'd been loading her palette up, startling awake from dreams about the shape of hips and the play of light across lips and hair.

Until the wee hours of this morning, when she'd put down her brushes and stepped away from the most ambitious piece of the series, and something in her chest had finally, finally relaxed.

Her gaze went to the canvas. To Rylan's face in close-up, blown to ten times life-size. The presence of it taking up the entire room.

She'd found space in his eyes and his ribs and the cleft of his chin. She'd found space in her *heart*.

A space he'd made.

She'd found her muse again, and of course it had been him.

This summer, he'd been in every drawing—even the ones he hadn't served as a model for. He'd been in her thoughts and her breath, and how could she not have seen it before?

How could she have walked away from him?

She shivered, wrapping her arms around herself. How could she have let this thing between them sit in silence for so long? Now that she knew—now that she'd figured it all out—

Would he let her back in?

Unclenching her hands, she took a deep breath. Liam had set

the soup and the whiskey both down, venturing farther into the room, leaning down to get a look at one of the paintings.

And she paused.

She'd been gripped by this strange conviction, this certainty all week. But now, a pang of doubt fired off behind her ribs.

"So what do you think?"

He jerked his head around to stare at her over his shoulder, brows raised, a twist of disbelief to his mouth. "What do I think?"

"It's a valid question."

He straightened up and turned the rest of the way around.

And it was strange, because it wasn't as if he'd been all that tactile with her before. Little flirty touches here and there, maybe. Sometimes standing a bit too close.

But here, today, he kept a careful distance. He stood as far away as he could yet still reach out to briefly squeeze her arm.

"Kate, they're *incredible*."

She just about sagged with the relief. Taking a couple of steps back, she let her spine hit the wall behind her so it could bear her weight.

Turning to the room full of paintings again, Liam asked, "How are you going to spin it?"

"For the artist's statement?" The piece of paper she had to assemble to explain her vision for the series.

"I assume this is your portfolio?"

It was. Her sacred spaces were the hollows of Rylan's body. They were the lines around his mouth and eyes.

"Honestly? I don't know. I don't care."

They could flunk her for all she gave a damn. She shook her head at herself and fiddled with her nail. That wasn't right. She hoped they'd pass her and that they'd give her the fellowship she'd been so focused on.

But if they didn't, she'd survive. It wasn't her teachers' judgment she was worried about.

Her degree and her work—they weren't the most important things in her life.

Liam shot her a knowing look. "You'll figure it out."

"Somehow or other."

"So." He ran a fingertip along the edge of one of the canvases, probably testing to see if the paint was still wet. Chances were it was. "We loading these up or what?"

"You brought your truck?" Not that it was the only reason she'd asked him to come by. She'd wanted an outside opinion, had needed a sanity check from somebody who wasn't in her head.

But a buddy with a pickup in this city was basically every art student's best friend.

"Sure did."

A sudden surge of gratitude washed over her. "Thank you, Liam."

His brow quirked up.

"For just..." How did she even put this into words? "For coming. For your truck and your feedback and—"

For being a good friend, even after everything.

As if he heard the parts she couldn't seem to voice, he took a step toward her, and suddenly their whole, admittedly brief, history seemed to hover over them.

The tentative invitations and the night in the gallery and Rylan's possessiveness.

Then the warmth in his gaze shifted, the curve to his smile faltering. "You really love him, huh?"

Something inside her cracked. "Yeah," she managed to choke out, her vision blurring over. "I really do."

More than she had back when she'd barely known him, and even then she'd been in so deep.

And now it was time to go deeper still. To take a breath and take a plunge, and if he'd let her . . . if he still wanted her . . .

To let the water close over her head.

To trust him like the air inside her lungs.

chapter TWENTY-EIGHT

It was finished.

Theodore Rylan Bellamy III was officially chief executive officer of Bellamy International. By this time tomorrow, the ink would be drying on the appointment of Alexis Claire Bellamy to head of North American and European operations. The family legacy was saved, his destiny fulfilled. It was his greatest triumph—everything his father had ever wanted for him. If perhaps not quite how he might have imagined him coming by it.

And yet, as Rylan made his way up his front steps, a hollowness settled over his shoulders. Lexie and the others were still toasting their victory, but drinks and too-loud music weren't the kind of celebration he had in mind.

He'd known well enough that it might come to this. But somehow he'd never really processed that he might be enjoying his success alone.

He let himself into the house, and the walls echoed.

Every day he hadn't heard from Kate, his hopes had diminished just that little bit more. What had he been thinking, telling her to take as much time as she needed? He should've asked her for something, anything. A date to call and at least check in or—

A dark laugh bubbled at the back of his throat.

He'd asked her for *everything*. For the rest of her life, if she'd have him.

A week of silence was one kind of answer, he supposed.

Taking off his overcoat, he flexed his jaw. There were three things he wanted right now, and two of them—a hot shower and a good night's sleep—were things he could have, so he'd focus on them. He opened up the closet in the hall—

—And froze.

Because there, beside the black and gray and navy of his usual outerwear, was a flash of vivid green. A little jacket that hadn't been there this morning, and his heart skipped a beat. It could be Lexie's, except she was still at the club.

Except there was a streak of charcoal on the cuff.

"Kate?" It came out barely a croak.

How did he even have the hope to put that name into the air? He was hallucinating, or maybe he was asleep, passed out on a velvet couch in a booming room. But he didn't typically dream about coats. Fingering the sleeve, he leaned back, glancing up the stairs and fighting the pounding of his heart.

Louder, he called, "Kate?"

And a voice floated down to him. "Rylan?"

His rib cage threatened to melt. He dropped his own coat to the ground, didn't even bother to close the closet door. In a handful of strides he was at the base of the stairs—her voice had come from the second floor, right?

Then it sounded out again. "Rylan, is that you?"

No. It was coming from the third.

He surged, his muscles and lungs coming alive for the first

time in what felt like ages. Taking the steps two and three at a time, he thundered upward.

And there, halfway down the final flight, stood Kate.

Everything in him screamed to cross the distance, to catch her up in his arms and kiss her breathless. He'd scarcely touched her skin in weeks, and he wanted to drown in it. He wanted her under him and over him, naked and glorious and *his*.

But the tightness to her posture stopped him short. Still three steps away, he paused, stretching his arms out to the sides, grasping the banisters for something to hold on to. Forcing himself to slow down, he raked his gaze up and down the length of her. The soft drape of a gray sweater over her curves. Black jeans that hugged her legs, and the little purple shoes he'd met her in a lifetime ago. The dark fall of all that gorgeous hair, and her face—

His heart constricted as he met her eyes. She looked like how he'd felt a handful of minutes ago. Exhausted and heavy and—*shit*. This might not be the reunion he'd been yearning for.

But if it wasn't—if she had come to him to break his heart, would she have done it *here* of all places? On the doorstep to this room he'd always imagined was for her? Where he'd told her he loved her?

Would she have come to him at all?

Then she shifted, crossing her arms over her chest, biting down on the plush pout of her bottom lip. A little crinkle appearing in the space between her eyes. And a glimmer of memory tickled in the back of Rylan's mind. Recognition.

He'd seen this look on her before. The fatigue and weight and sheer nervousness.

Just like that, he was naked in a hotel room in Paris. She'd just drawn him all spread out and achingly vulnerable on their bed, and she was staring up at him with so much feeling in her eyes, offering to let him look at what she'd made ...

All the words evaporated from his head. All except one.

"Kate ..."

"I'm sorry," she said, and God, what was she apologizing for? "I hope you don't mind I let myself in."

"Never." It came out too fervent by half, but he could scarcely breathe for the depth of love and need rising beneath his skin.

Her voice trembled. "I have something to show you."

He would've followed her anywhere. It was nothing to take those half dozen steps, to trail after her into the space he'd tried to give her in his home.

He got as far as the threshold before his feet refused to move.

"Jesus." His throat blocked up before he could say any more.

There had to be a dozen paintings propped against all the boxes and the walls. They were gorgeous, glowing with color and rich with shadows. She'd lit the room with the little fairy lights she'd strung up around the windows and with the soft heat of candles. All that warm, flickering light bounced off the planes of the canvases, making them shine with ...

With love.

This space he'd given her ...

She'd filled it with *him*.

Fractions and pieces of him, extreme close-ups of musculature and portraits of his face in profile. Vignettes that showed only the arch of a spine or the crest of a hip, but he saw himself in every one.

He saw the man he'd always wanted to be—the one he'd been trying so hard these last few weeks to become. The very best version of himself. The one she trusted.

He turned to her, and the points of brightness in the room

were the glow of her soft, brown eyes. Were the fledgling hints of her smile.

Were a spark going off in his chest—in his *soul*.

And he was alight.

Why on earth had Kate been so afraid of this?

Opening herself up to Rylan, giving him these pieces of herself, these glimpses into the most carefully hidden places in her heart—it was always worth it. He'd treated each and every one of them with respect and care.

She'd offered him her body, and in return he'd taken her to heights she'd never known. She'd told him about her father and her former lovers and her dreams, and without fail he'd met her with tender hands and a warmth that chased away the chill.

And her art.

It was a lilting vertigo, an impossible rush as she watched him take in this impromptu gallery she'd created for him.

Her art was one of the very first things she'd let him see. He'd paged through her sketchbook with open eyes, with concentration and consideration.

Only once had he ever failed to grasp what she was showing him.

That first time, after she'd drawn him. When he'd stared at her sketches without the barest hint of comprehension, completely missing the feeling she'd bled onto the page. Too caught up in his own conception of himself, perhaps, he'd somehow let his gaze skate past how much she'd loved him, even then. Even when she'd scarcely begun to get to the bottom of him.

Before he'd let her.

This time, he didn't miss a thing.

Those sharp, bright eyes went softer with each canvas he surveyed, some of the stiff set to his shoulders, the reserve within him, bleeding away.

Until he came to face her again, and the last of the defenses he'd erected were demolished. Blown clean away, until there was nothing left to his expression but naked hope.

And the anxious terror that had lived within her breast the whole way over here, the entire time she had waited here in the silence for him, surrounded by her own visions of his eyes and mouth and flesh... it faded away, too.

And yet she couldn't bring herself to bridge the space. She was barely holding herself together, her disparate pieces bound with spit and glue. If he touched her, she'd fly apart, and she was so close to being ready for that. But not quite.

"It's funny." She raked a shivering hand through her hair. "This whole time, ever since Paris, I haven't been able to get anything right."

All her canvases and all her drawings had been pale imitations of the quick sketches she'd put together that summer. Her hands had wrapped around charcoals and brushes, and only ash had shaken out.

Tucking her hair behind her ear, she grasped the back of her neck and dug her fingers in hard. "I was supposed to be painting 'sacred spaces,' and it was all just empty."

He took a step toward her, and she took an unconscious step back. Stopping, he held out a hand, but she shook her head.

She had to get through this.

"I was trying so damn hard to find meaning in these things that were *supposed* to be meaningful, you know?"

She'd been listening to everybody except herself. Her professors with their naysaying and her mother with her fear. The voices of her father and Aaron in her head telling her she'd never be good enough, and even if she was, a ghost of her former self was in there, too, whispering at every dip in the road that it wasn't worth it. Trusting someone only led to heartache, and Rylan's own sins of omission had reinforced those mantras in her ears.

"You were right." Her voice kept threatening to break, the torrent of tears behind her eyes to overflow. "I was so damn scared. You *terrify* me."

"I don't—"

But she cut him off. "The things I feel for you..."

All she'd ever wanted was the kind of love you read about, the beautiful kind, but the only sort she'd ever seen had been ugly and wrong. It was what people used to control you or drag you down. To make you think you were less than you were.

Rylan's had never been like that. He'd held her while she cried, had told her she deserved the world, and had made her believe it. He'd looked at her with so much awe and touched her as if her body were the heaven he'd been waiting for. As if she were the one saving him.

"So I kept finding excuses *not* to trust you." She'd hooked into the very first sign that he wasn't what he'd said he was. That she could disregard the things she hadn't been ready to hear or feel. "I pretended you were the one who wouldn't let me in."

When really, it had been her. She'd been the one with a foot out the door. The one ready to run.

Her eyes burned, a single hot tear spilling from the corner, but she didn't wipe it away. She let it fall. She let herself feel.

"And then you brought me here." She gestured around the room. The life he'd dug up still surrounded them, spilling out of box after box, and he'd opened them all for her. Finally, she met his gaze. "You showed me all these things, and then I developed those pictures."

Black-and-white photographs, bare glimpses into this intimacy they'd built without her even realizing. Still frames of a life in motion. And they'd been *beautiful*.

Not controlling, but freeing. Instead of filling her with dread and self-doubt, they'd filled her with light.

Her throat caught, her cheeks soaked now, but she had to get this out. "I stopped looking everywhere else in the world, and I started painting you."

And the art had flowed from her fingertips.

The days had floated away, lost to the high of creation. Shades of gray had bloomed into vivid color as she'd filled her palette and emptied it again and again. The only time she'd left her apartment had been when she'd run out of canvases, and so she'd had to make new ones, and then she'd covered them, too.

In the sharpness of his jaw, she'd found the tender places inside her bones. In the shadows between his ribs, she'd found his heart. She'd found her own.

"You weren't keeping me out," she managed to choke out, and for all that the words tore at her throat, they healed a wound inside of her she hadn't even known had still been bleeding. Flinging a hand to the side, she pointed at the canvases. "You were letting me in."

"Every way I knew how," he said, and his eyes were as glassy as hers felt. An echo of a laugh tumbled out, beautiful and broken. "I learned some new ones. For you, I—I would've done anything."

She finally stopped fighting the pull between them, and it was like magnets as her feet carried her forward.

"Love doesn't have to be a weakness. It doesn't make you less than you are."

It gave people the power to hurt you. But if you trusted the right person...If you let the right person in...

It could make you better than you were.

With Rylan, it could make her strong.

He took an echoing step toward her, and the depths to his gaze could've taken her to her knees. "Not everyone will throw your love away," he said.

Like his father had. Like she had when she'd run.

She bit down on the inside of her lip. Worked her jaw. "I don't want to push you away again."

"Then don't."

And then he was on her, pulling her into the strongest, most giving arms she'd ever known.

"I trust you." She spoke the words into his neck, and he forced the air from her lungs, crushing her to his chest.

"I'll never give you a reason not to again."

"And I won't go looking for them."

Because that was love, wasn't it? It was lowering your guard. It was giving a man your heart and resting in the knowledge he would keep it safe.

She pulled back just enough to look him in the eyes, and his face was so beautiful, for all that it was blurred. Her ribs cracked open, but she let them. She refused to be afraid.

"I love you."

His hands came up to cup her cheeks, thumbs soft and warm beneath her eyes. "And I love you."

And her entire chest had split, every tender spot in her exposed, but she was whole.

She was better than she had ever, ever been.

She had the bare span of a breath for a smile to spread across her lips before he was on her, darting in. His mouth met hers as he picked her up, hauling her against him. Grasping at his shoulders, she opened to the wet heat of his kiss, and he spun her in a shuffling circle, never letting her feet touch ground, and it was perfect, was like floating. She let him carry her and hold her up.

Then she folded her legs around his hips, and suddenly the bright spark in her heart shifted. It didn't dim and it didn't fade.

It *smoldered*, rippling with heat.

With a low groan, he gripped her tighter, hands drifting lower.

"Kate—"

"Yes, yes," she said, answering the question in his eyes, and then he was shifting her, dropping her by inches. A soft sound fell out of her throat as her hips met his.

"We should talk." He bit out the words, but it was with a flexing of his thighs, the hard line of him grinding into her and making the whole center of her flash searingly, impossibly hot.

God, but had it only been a week? She'd gone that long without sex before—she'd gone months without him and with no hope of ever seeing him again. But even then, it hadn't felt like this.

Maybe it was all the barriers coming down. Maybe it was him holding her again, as if there were no fears and nothing to forgive. Him staring at her with that dark intentness to his gaze.

"We should," she agreed, dipping down to kiss him again, all hungry teeth and lips and tongue. She wanted to devour him.

"I meant it," he managed, panting between kisses. "I'll give you anything. My whole life."

"I'll take it." And she'd give him every damn thing in return.

Her body and her heart and her trust.

He scraped his teeth across her tongue. "No holding back."

"No running away."

With a moan, he fell into this kiss, and for a second she'd thought they'd both fall as he staggered. They were in the center of this room, nothing to keep them up, surrounded by his past and by her future, her visions of him and of them. The things she had made out of love and need.

"We're not going to make it downstairs, are we?" he asked against her breath.

She shook her head and clutched him closer.

And how did he control their descent? One second they were standing there, his solidity and strength supporting them, and the next she was on her back, no impact and no pain. Hovering over her, he rose up onto his knees, and her throat went dry. He skated a hot hand down the center of her chest.

"Whatever you want," he said. "Anything."

"You." She closed her palm over his, and its heat burned all the way through to her heart. "I just want you."

She wanted to finally let go. To take what he was offering and to not be afraid. Not of anything.

Desire was a living, breathing thing inside her veins, making her blood hot and her breasts taut, the space between her thighs going liquid and warm. And it would be so easy to lie there, letting him move over her and in her, accepting the pleasure he always brought to her body.

But this was about more than that. This was about loving actively, trusting with intention.

Making love and making the first move. Not waiting for him to reach for her.

Not just taking, but giving.

Swallowing hard, she closed her eyes. Just for an instant, she visualized, and the images sprawling out across her vision were in the most brilliant, sparkling hues.

Looking up at him again, she pushed his hand away.

Then with her heart in her throat, she urged him over onto his back. She climbed on top of him. She gazed into bright blue eyes gone simmering and dark.

And she was unafraid.

Chapter Twenty-Nine

And here Rylan had thought he'd have to celebrate his victory alone.

Fuck, it was almost too good to be true. He'd embraced his destiny and his future, and the future he'd been dreaming of—the one he'd thought he'd let slip from his grasp—had been waiting for him here all along.

Kate hadn't spent this past week ignoring him or trying to figure out how best to let him down easy. She'd spent it immersed in him. He'd seen how she got when she was lost in her art. The laser-like focus and the passion with which she attacked a subject and made something beautiful of an empty page.

She'd made a work of art out of him, there on her canvases and here in his life.

And yet none of it held a candle to the vision she made as she settled over his hips. She *glowed*, confident and resplendent above him. Gone was the timid girl he'd had to coax through every touch, who didn't know how to accept the least kind of pleasure. She'd been replaced by this goddess, and for the first time, he was pretty sure she knew precisely how magnificent she was. How gorgeous she was in his eyes.

Bracing her hands against her shoulders, she shook out her hair. There was a hot flush to her cheeks and seeping down, over her throat and across her chest. Her pretty nipples had to be all tight and needy, red and waiting for his mouth, and he was going to suck them until they were sore. His cock, already achingly hard for her, gave another kick as she shifted her weight, sliding over him, and he jerked his hands from his sides to grasp her hips. Tilting his head back, he guided her through another slow stroke, had them practically fucking through their clothes, and shit, fuck, it was too good.

He groaned, imagining it *without* the clothes. "You like that, baby? Want to ride me?"

Panting, she leaned down to kiss him. The heat of her mouth was another layer of need settling into his skin as he licked past her lips. Scraped across that slick flesh with his teeth.

"You can drive," he offered. "Take what you want from me. Fuck me nice and slow or ride me hard. Get it so deep. Is that what you want?"

He slid his palms over the wide splay of her thighs as she groaned, rocking over him, and that shouldn't feel so good.

"Or..." He swallowed hard, his eyes about near rolling back in his head. "You wanna ride my face? Get my tongue all over you—"

It drove a sharp gasp from her, and she ground down to the point where it almost hurt.

"Yeah?" he asked, because he knew her tells. She'd flushed even brighter, and her eyes were dark, her hands biting against his shoulders. Damn but he could get into that. Arousal was a punch straight down to his gut, making his balls go tight and his tongue loose. "Doesn't that sound good? My chin all slick with you? Get on your knees over me, ride my mouth until I can't breathe. Till all I can smell and taste and think is your pretty pussy—"

"God, Rylan." She tore away from his kiss, something in her expression gone wild. "Do girls really—"

"Only girl who matters here is you." She was the only girl who would ever matter to him again. Growling, he tucked a finger in the waistband of her jeans. "And if you aren't on my mouth in the next five seconds..."

And there was a part of him that half expected her to demur, for that same shy girl to reemerge in the wake of his dare. His throat went dry as her hands dropped to join his. Together, they popped the button of her jeans and undid the zip. She rose off him to push both the denim and the lace beneath away, to slip those purple sneakers from her feet, and God, he was flat on his back on the floor, still dressed in a suit. As she dragged off her sweater and bra, too, he sat partway up, just enough to shrug out of his jacket. He tossed his tie and his cuff links to the side, and then her hands were there, slipping button after button through its hole, warm fingertips dancing across his skin and brushing over his heart. Stripped to the waist, he grabbed her by the hips, manhandling her up. His cock was a throbbing weight inside his slacks, but he couldn't wait any longer, needed her taste on his tongue, her thighs to either side of his face. Needed this.

She was straddling his chest when nervousness seemed to take one last stab at her. "Are you sure?"

Had he ever been so sure of anything in his life?

"Gimme," he insisted, hauling her the rest of the way up.

It threw her off balance, but she recovered well enough, planting one knee and then the other to the side of his head.

He cupped her thighs and licked his lips. Soft fingertips buried themselves in his hair, and she gazed down at him. There was a shakiness to her, but just when he thought she'd balk, she lowered herself down.

Fuck. The very scent of her made him dizzy, and there had been this part of him that had thought he'd never have this again. Never be able to put his mouth on her or make her come, never hold her. Even in his wildest dreams where she'd returned to him, he couldn't have imagined her *here.*

"So goddamn sweet," he mumbled into her cunt, licking up. The first hot stripe he laved over her choked a cut-off moan from her throat, and she swayed over him. He reached up with one hand, interlacing it with hers, giving her something to hold on to, and she squeezed his palm tight.

"Rylan—" She rocked against his mouth, and it was better than he'd imagined it would be, letting her take her pleasure from him.

Sucking at her clit, he grasped her thigh and gripped her hand. The fingers in her hair dug in harder, practically steering him, and had she ever been this free with him before? So unselfconscious about how good he could make her feel?

"That's right. That's beautiful." He snuck out fragments of words each time she raised herself off him, giving him handfuls of seconds to breathe before slotting herself onto his mouth again.

God, he loved her. He loved the way she sounded when he skated his teeth along her outer lips and how the flush crept down her chest with every wet stroke he took across her clit. How the soft, slick sounds of him eating her out made her embarrassed and aroused. The spill of her liquid across his tongue and the rasping way she said his name.

She shifted, pressing him against her clit at just this slightly different angle, and her whole body seized. "Oh God—"

And he was going to burst, was going to go off like a damn rocket without so much as a hand on his cock, she felt so good and tasted so lush. He skated his hand off her thigh and got up in all that sweetness, slipped two fingers inside and crooked them—

And she *screamed*. Tearing at his scalp, she went rigid over him, pulsing around his fingers and over his tongue, and he couldn't breathe and didn't care.

She came and came and came. When she lifted up, he gulped in a ragged gasp. Released her hand to grab at her thigh, trying to pull her back down to him, because he hadn't had enough.

He would never, ever get enough.

But she shook her head, and her eyes were black with desire, her lips bitten and red, and she collapsed onto all fours before climbing her way down his body. His fingers slipped free of her, and he let them trail along her, gliding wetly over soft skin to her breast where he slicked them around her nipple.

Then her mouth was on his, licking her taste from his lips, and he was so hard beneath her it ached.

"That," he choked out, "was so. Fucking. Hot."

She'd let him do that for her. She'd let *herself*.

Gazing down at him with wonder, she slipped her hand down to rest against his heart. "You are never going to stop showing me new things, are you?"

He'd probably run out eventually. They were going to make love on every surface of this house, in every position he'd ever imagined and maybe some that hadn't been invented yet. For the rest of his life.

And it would never, ever get old.

Not with this woman. This amazing person who challenged him, who saw in him things he'd never seen in himself. Who made him *better*.

"We'll discover them," he promised her. "Together."

The corners of her mouth lifted up into this smile that lit her face and his life, beatific in its brilliance. "That sounds amazing."

She bent to kiss him again, lips so warm and soft against his.

Then she raised herself up, and her grin shifted, going sultry, her eyelids drifting lower. "You know what else sounds amazing right now?"

Groaning, he gripped her side and licked his lips. She dipped her hips into his, a teasing brush that made his skin feel too tight, his whole body on edge with the barest hint of a touch.

"I can think of a couple of things," he said, spinning with the possibilities.

And her eyes gleamed. "So can I."

Back before Rylan, Kate's understanding of sex had been very, very confused.

To make a man feel good meant giving up a part of herself. It was uncomfortable, and sometimes it hurt, and the parts of it that people talked about—the parts that drove them to crave it . . . they had never seemed to be for her.

Then Rylan had walked into her life, and he'd shown her that they *were*. She could have the intimacy and the closeness, the surrender. Her body could shatter over and over beneath his hands or her own. Around his cock or against his tongue. He'd brought her to ecstasy relentlessly, with patience and passion.

Before him, she'd known she had to give of herself. But she'd never understood what she had to gain.

Hovering over him, the hot ache of her sex dragging over where he was so hard for her, a long line of need beneath the fabric of his clothes, it was like she'd won the entire world.

God, the things he'd asked her to do. Illicit pleasure danced up and down her spine at the sense memory of sliding herself against his mouth, of taking her satisfaction that way, and he had loved it.

He loved her.

Something deep inside her clenched, a hungry pang that wasn't just about the sex, for all that that was mixed up in there, too. He was staring at her with anticipation written on every line of him, and she wanted to drown in him. To live with him, filling up all her empty places.

She wanted to draw his face in the morning and learn how to cook with him and trade stories over dinner about their work and she wanted to *fuck* him. She wanted everything.

Pulling in a ragged breath, she skated her hand down his chest. The warm skin and firm muscle glided beneath her palm until she met the leather of his belt. She drew the end of it through the buckle. Found the little extra clasp hidden in the waistband of his pants. When she lifted her hips, he helped her push the fabric down.

And it was like seeing him naked for the very first time. He was splayed out beneath her, so much strength in all his limbs, but for her he made them pliant. He made his grip soft.

Heat bloomed anew within her as she circled the thick flesh of his cock with her fist, and he arched into it, throat bared. Releasing him, she settled herself over him. She dragged the slickness of her sex over that hot length, pulsing deep within. When her clit slipped over the head, he was so close. She could just tip her hips. Just take him in.

"I have—" His Adam's apple bobbed, his voice stuttering as he reached back toward his pants.

Things went very quiet in her head. Because she could. She could.

She heard her own voice as if from a long way away. "When was the last time you got tested?"

Eyes going wide, he gripped her thigh, and beneath her, his cock throbbed. "Before I left Paris. There's been no one. But—"

"It's safe," she said. She'd never been safer.

She was on the pill and she was clean and she was with this man. This man who gave her wings but kept her rooted to the earth.

"Fuck, Kate." His fingers dug in hard, restraint and desire carved into his skin. "Be sure."

"I'm so sure." She wanted this. To be so close to him, no barriers and nothing between them. And— "I trust you."

She didn't breathe as she slid that extra inch forward. As she pressed back, the slick tip of him settling against her opening.

And then he was pushing inside.

The noise it punched out of him zipped through her breasts and on a screaming line to her clit, a pulse of lightning deep within.

"Oh Jesus, Kate." His hands clenching at her hips were meant to still her, but she took him the rest of the way in.

God, she was so full, and he was naked and bare inside her, beneath her. She reared up over him. Power tingled through her every nerve and cell.

And she was home. Complete.

With a strangled groan, he tugged her down to him. Their mouths met in a tangle of lips and tongues, and she'd never seen him or felt him so undone. "You feel—you don't know—"

Except she did. "It's the same. For me, it's..." *Everything.*

In slow motions, she rocked over him, and every one seemed to wind him higher. The tendons in his neck stood out against his skin, his abdomen tensed, his breath rasping harsh inside his lungs. His hand at her hip inched inward until his thumb pressed into her clit, and she sped her strokes, a hot ball gathering deep within.

"Baby," he said, "please."

And she was so close—as close as he was maybe. She needed just a word. Just a breath.

His cock throbbed inside her, and she stared down into those warm blue eyes. At this face that had first pulled her in and this heart that had taught her to stay. To be brave.

As the feeling gathered, she gasped for air, but there wasn't room for it. Wasn't room for anything left in her chest except—

"Love," she choked out. "I love you."

His mouth fell open, thumb digging in harder. "I love you."

And her body snapped. Hot waves of relief and release washed over her, her vision spinning, but at the center of it all was Rylan. Rylan calling her name and pulling her close, filling her, and everything went wet and warm as they crashed over the edge. Together. As one.

chapter THIRTY

"I think your bunny is staring at us."

Rylan lifted his head and craned his neck to the side. Sure enough, the stuffed rabbit they'd unearthed the other day was still sitting on top of one of the boxes on the other side of the room, his little plastic eyes pointed straight at them.

He chuckled, dropping back down. "Poor guy's going to be scandalized."

They were still spread out naked on the floor, the wadded-up ball of his suit jacket tucked under his head as a pillow. Kate was curled against him, one hand on his heart and her head resting on his shoulder. It was going to get uncomfortable before too long, and they would have to move, but at the moment the whole place could go up in flames and he'd be unperturbed.

He was home.

With his heart glowing almost too brightly to bear, he shifted to press a rough kiss against her hair, squeezing her tight against his side. For a long moment, they rested there just like that, quiet and content.

Then she smoothed her hand down his chest, repositioning herself so she could look up at him. "Did you mean it?"

Categorically, yes. But... "Did I mean what?"

He'd said a lot to her, both today and the last time they'd met, and he'd meant every word of it.

Her gaze flicked between his face and the room around them, like she was realizing there was a lot to choose from, too. After a moment she settled on, "About this room, first of all."

"That it's yours?" He nodded. "Absolutely. I can have someone come by while I'm at the office tomorrow and move all those boxes out. You can bring your easel or whatever else you want."

He hoped she would.

"I'd like that," she said, and the warmth behind his ribs redoubled. It didn't burn him, though.

It filled him, taking all his hollow spaces and bringing him to life.

Another beat passed before she asked, "The office, huh?"

Right. Because they hadn't talked about this, really. "Yup. You're looking at the new CEO of Bellamy International."

It didn't hurt him to say that anymore. But something in him tensed all the same.

Kate just hummed, though, tracing little circles against his skin. "You're okay with that?"

"I am." For so long, he'd run from it, but the running part of his life was over now.

"It never seemed like something you wanted..."

"It wasn't, back when I met you." He'd been so angry then, unable to think of anything beyond his father's fuck-ups and the box he thought he'd been forced into, the one that had been suffocating him for years.

But only because he himself had closed the lid. Because he hadn't made any choices of his own.

Well, he was choosing now. He'd decided on this life and this girl, and all of it felt right, straight down to his bones.

Combing his fingers through her hair, he took a deep breath, making her head rise and fall with the settling of his lungs. "But I had a lot of time to think about things. I..." And he hadn't told her this, either. "I went to see my father, after you walked out."

"You did?"

"It was a disaster." His father's bitterness and his lashing out had taken both him and Lexie and rocked them hard. "But it was good, too."

Kate made an encouraging noise, flattening her palm out against his ribs.

"I'm my father's son," he said, and it didn't weigh him down anymore. "I don't have to pay for his mistakes, but I can learn from them." He met her gaze. "I can run his company and make it my own. I can take care of my family..."

And that word hit him square in the gut.

He'd fought so hard his entire life to protect Evan and Lexie and to help them get what they wanted from their lives, but it had been about protecting them *from* his family.

But they *were* his family now.

Kate was his family now.

"I can do things right," he said, throat hoarse, voice numb.

All that time he'd spent romanticizing his parents' early years, hoping that maybe, at some point, they'd been in love. That before the bickering and the acrimony they'd been happy.

And yet the bitter distance they'd fallen into had kept him from ever letting himself have that with anyone.

He was happy now. He was in love. He could hold on to that. He would.

And it was as if Kate was right there inside his thoughts, reading his damn mind. Because her breath sounded as shaky as his own.

"And did you mean..." She swallowed, an audible gulp against the stillness of the air. "About the rest of your life?"

Funny how time had always been dogging them. Fate had conspired to give them seven nights in Paris, and they had only made it to five. Here in New York, they'd agreed to seven more, but in the end they'd needed eight.

He didn't want to sign on for another hitch. He didn't want to keep counting his time with her in single days and single nights. He didn't want to keep counting at all.

He wanted forever.

His throat burned as he answered, "With all my heart."

Just like that, the world around them narrowed to a pinpoint. It all went blurry except this moment, in this room. With this girl.

This girl who was staring up at him, nodding. This girl whose whole mouth bloomed with the most perfect, beautiful smile.

A happiness he'd never known spread like sunrise across his chest, his own lips lifting, the skies clearing in his mind at last, except—

Except—

He could have cursed himself. He still didn't have a ring.

God, his entire life with every resource at his disposal. He could've bought her a rock you could see from space, something glittering and expensive and ridiculous.

Something small. Smooth-edged, with a stone set flush to the band for when she spattered it with paint.

But right here, right now, he only had himself.

Himself and her and all the gifts she had brought to his life.

The rest of the world filtered back in, his vision returning to him. He twisted his head to the side, because right there, a bare foot away from him...

The paintings she'd done, the ones she'd made to work through her feelings, the ones that had brought her back to him—they were all of him. Except one. He remembered shooting the photograph she must have painted it from. They'd been kissing, lost in each other and in the press of flesh on flesh, and he had raised the camera. Pointed it at them and clicked the shutter.

And there they were. Their eyes closed, their lips pressed tight to each other's on the canvas, fine strands of lines sliced through the layers of pigment tying them one to the other.

He reached out. The raw edge of the canvas was exposed at the side, frayed strings peeling off from the fabric's coarse weave. He wrapped his hand around a loose thread. He pulled.

It came away so easily.

Sitting up, he took her hand in his. And he couldn't breathe. Outside of her and this room, he couldn't *see*.

Ever so slowly, he looped the canvas thread around her finger. The fourth one, on her left hand. He held the ends in his trembling hands and looked into eyes the color of his life and of art and of trust. The color of love.

"Kate. Will you—" He couldn't even get it out.

Spend your life with me. Marry *me.*

Because then her lips were on his, and it felt like the first and last kiss of his life.

"Of course," she said.

He tied the knot. He bound them together.

And all the empty places in his heart were full.

chapter THIRTY-ONE

The doorbell rang at five o'clock on the dot.

Looking up from the place settings she'd been rearranging for about the thirteenth time on the ridiculously large dining room table Rylan had insisted they needed, Kate met his eyes across the room.

The corner of his mouth flickered upward. "You ready for this?"

Her nerves fluttered. "Not like we have a lot of choice."

"It'll be fine." His hint of a smile edged higher into something real. Striding across the room to meet her, he took her hand and intertwined their fingers.

She took a deep breath. It *would* be fine. The place was even more spotless than his housekeeper usually left it. Everything had finally been unpacked, the additional purchases they'd made artfully arranged on the shelves and walls. All the food had been dropped off by the caterer hours ago, and what needed to be warmed up was in the oven, filling the house with scents of savory and sage. Making it smell like a home.

Just—she'd spent her last dozen Thanksgivings alone with

only her mom and a bunch of Chinese takeout. The idea of opening up their house to all these people . . .

And it was *their* house now. She hadn't given up her apartment, and she wouldn't until her lease was up. But more and more of her things had migrated over here. Slowly but surely, her studio on the third floor was coming together.

The doorbell rang again, and her heart raced. Rylan squeezed her hand. Nodding, she let him lead her to the door.

This whole thing had been her idea after all. "Orphan Thanksgiving," she'd heard it called. A bunch of people with nowhere else to go, choosing to spend the holiday together. Sharing fellowship and breaking bread. It was one hell of an eclectic crowd, though.

Her and Liam and a couple of the others from her program who couldn't afford to fly home this year. Chase and Sophie, whose parents were off skiing in the Alps and on safari in the Serengeti, respectively. Rylan, for whom this *was* home now, and Lexie and—

They threw open the door, and Kate did an actual double take.

A dark-haired, blue-eyed man with a glass-cutting jaw leaned against the railing of the porch.

"Evan," Rylan said. Of course.

Rylan's brother gave them each a smirk that was so familiar it almost hurt. Rylan welcomed him in, extending his arms, and Kate tilted her head to the side.

It was a hug, for sure. Maybe the briefest, most awkward hug she'd ever seen, but a hug all the same.

And it was subtle, because at first glance, the resemblance was so striking. But with the two of them standing close together, the differences stood out more sharply.

The longer hair, styled even more messily, and the studs on Evan's leather jacket and boots. The hint of ink peeking out from beneath his sleeve.

After barely a second, Evan pulled away, stepping past Rylan and into the house, and his gaze met hers. "You must be his bride-to-be?"

Kate's cheeks flushed warm, her fingers going instinctively to the new weight on her left hand. She twisted the ring around her knuckle, a simple sapphire and platinum band they had both picked out, and held it up for his inspection.

A crinkle appeared in his brow, but it smoothed over after a second. "Lovely," he said, and he extended his own hand. "Evan."

"Kate."

He grasped her palm and kissed the back of her knuckles, and in the background, Rylan growled.

"Down, boy," came another, sharper voice.

Somehow, Kate had missed Lexie coming in with Evan, but she looked to her with gratitude now. Lexie patted Rylan's shoulder before slipping around him, nudging Evan out of the way to give Kate a hug. That was new, but Kate didn't protest.

She glanced around her as she let her go. "No Dane after all?"

She'd only met Lexie's assistant once, while popping into the Bellamy offices to pick Rylan up for lunch, but that big man by Lexie's side had made an impression.

Lexie rolled her eyes, but there was something deeper there beneath the flippancy. Something...bitter. She waved a hand. "Family thing."

"Too bad."

"For him, maybe." Edging away, she held up a bottle, calling over her shoulder, "I raided Daddy's wine cellar."

Rylan nodded at her. He and Evan had remained near the

door, engaged in a quiet conversation she couldn't make out, but it made her frown all the same. Tension was just pouring off them.

"Best to leave them to it," Lexie counseled, heading off toward the kitchen and motioning for Kate to follow.

"You sure?"

"They can be as bad as Rylan and our father ever were." The corner of her mouth tugged to the side as she pulled out a wine opener. "Too much alike and yet not quite close enough to see eye to eye."

"Rylan only ever speaks well of him."

"Behind his back, sure. But some things were said to his face when Evan was headed off to school..." Trailing off, Lexie shrugged. "They'll figure it out."

Before Kate could worry too much about it, the doorbell chimed again, and whatever was going on between Rylan and his brother was moved to the backseat. In no time at all, the place was full, and Kate didn't have time to think about the tension in the air as she did her best to slip into some image of a hostess she'd only ever really seen in movies, pouring wine and making introductions. When Liam arrived, she held her breath. But Rylan just slung a casual arm around her waist and held his other hand out for Liam to shake, an easiness to him she would've been hard-pressed to imagine a few short weeks ago.

It looked good on him.

Finally, the timer on the oven went off, and the turkey and sides and fixings were transferred to serving platters and carried into the dining room. Rylan held out a chair for her near one end of the table and she sank down into it.

Then he took his own beside her, on the end.

And then it struck her—and maybe Lexie and Evan, too,

judging by the tight looks on their faces. He was sitting at the head of the table.

Where he had always belonged.

Evan was the first to recover. Shaking his head, he picked up a butter knife and clinked it against the side of his glass, and the whole table settled down. One by one, all eyes turned frontward, toward Rylan.

And he rose, tall and gorgeous and so assured, and Kate's heart pounded hard in her chest. This was her future right here. Her present and her forever. Her family, seated around her table in her home.

She had never felt so warm.

Rylan's gaze darted around the room for a moment as he took it in. Then it settled on Kate, and the smile that curved his lips was soft and true.

Glancing away, he nodded. "I wanted to thank you all for being here tonight." His throat bobbed and his voice dipped, losing some of the stiffness it had held. "As some of you know, I wasn't home for Thanksgiving last year."

Kate's chest gave a little pang at the thought of Rylan in Paris, still running after his world had fallen apart. Angry and alone.

He reached a hand out to her, and she took it. Staring right at her, he said, "So it means even more to me to be here this year. I'm . . . so grateful to be able to spend today with all of you." Looking up again, he cleared his throat. "And I'm grateful for a couple of other things, too."

He tightened his grip on her hand, and the seriousness to his mouth melted away.

Oh, hell.

"I'm grateful to announce the recipient of this year's coveted honors fellowship from Columbia University's Fine Arts Department is dining with us tonight."

Kate's whole body flashed hot, and she shook her head at him, but he wasn't about to be deterred.

"Congratulations to our very own Kate Reid."

Exhaling hard, she bowed her head in acknowledgment of the polite clapping. The less polite, more raucous applause from the end of the table where her grad school friends sat. Catching her eye, Liam raised a glass to her, and she lifted her own in reply.

After all her worries. After her fear that she would never find her vision or her voice. After she'd flouted the committee's theme...

She'd found her voice all right, and the day after she'd shown her paintings to Rylan, she'd loaded them right back into Liam's truck and driven them to campus. She'd marched into her appointment and explained that to her, sanctity meant reverence. It meant looking at something—at *someone*—and seeing so much more than what lay on the surface. It meant being willing to give up all reservations and all fear.

It meant love. It meant trust.

And her sacred space would always be in Rylan's arms.

Apparently, she'd been pretty convincing.

"And I have one other announcement to make," Rylan said. Running his thumb over her ring, he shot her a brilliant, shimmering smile. "Next June, we'd like to invite you all to share another meal with us."

Kate's stomach dipped when he tugged at her hand, urging her to stand. Rising, she let herself be pulled against his side.

And then she couldn't keep it in anymore; forget that half of them already knew. "We're getting married," she announced.

Dipping his head, Rylan kissed her hair, a firm, fiery press of lips as he said beneath his breath, "Tell them where."

Where else?

She gazed up into his eyes, and her heart was filled with so much love, she thought she'd burst.

"In Paris."

Where the story of their love had begun. Where a beautiful, lost man had come up to her, looking for so little both from her and from himself. Where they'd found more than either of them had ever dreamed.

And where the rest of their life together would start.

Lexie Bellamy knows just how to handle a
boardroom—what she doesn't know how to handle is her
distractingly sexy assistant Dane Huntley. The last thing
Dane wants is an extended business trip. But the chance
to spend uninterrupted time with his beautiful, fierce boss
is just too tempting to resist...

Don't miss Jeanette Grey's next
stunningly sexy novel

nine kinds of
NAUGHTY

Available Early 2017